THE CURRENT BEYOND

The Current Beyond

Scott J Clauss

Published by Scott J. Clauss
Available in eBook and paperback formats.

eBook Edition ISBN: 979-8-9998212-3-2
Paperback Edition ISBN: 979-8-9998212-2-5

Cover design by Scott J. Clauss
Edited by Paul W. Clauss

Contents

Acknowledgements

Writing a book is equal parts obsession and endurance, and I couldn't have finished this one without a small army of patient, determined people.

First, to my wife—thank you for walking every mile of this with me. Writing devours hours and promotion somehow eats the rest, yet you never wavered. You were there for late-night drafts and the long drive to retrieve the haunted clock from my brother's house across the country. You even went ghost hunting with me—then caught that perfect orb photo in Tombstone, Arizona. Your faith, humor, and steady presence turned a solitary pursuit into a shared adventure.

To my dad, Paul—your excited, no-holds-barred edits pushed me to do better on every page. Your eye for detail and your willingness to say exactly what needed saying made this a stronger book. I'm grateful for your time, your candor, and your belief that I could always tighten one more line.

To everyone who has joined me on ghost hunts or sat down to share their own experiences: thank you for trusting me with your stories. The late-night talks, the cold hallways, the moments when the air went heavy—those conversations and encounters continue to shape this series. Some of your tales will find their way, carefully and respectfully, into future books.

To the readers who picked up Echoes in the Glass and then told a friend, left a review, or came to a signing: you gave this world its legs. Every purchase, post, and message matters more than you know.

To the booksellers, librarians, teachers, and event hosts who made room for a new series on crowded shelves and busy calendars—thank you for the trust and the space.

To the friends and family who tolerated research rabbit holes, mirror talk at dinner, and texts about EMF at odd hours—thanks for the patience and the cheering.

Finally, to anyone who has ever stood in a quiet room and felt it answer back: these pages are for you. Keep a light by the glass, speak the names you love, and thank you for coming with me into the current beyond.

— Scott J. Clauss

Preface

This is the second book in the Echo Series, and it began the way most obsessions do—with a small instrument and a larger question.

As an amateur ghost hunter, I've learned to trust what my body tells me—the hairs rising, the cold that slides through a warm room, the weight in the chest, the sense of being watched—and to verify it with an EMF detector. When the meter twitches at the exact moment the air turns heavy, it feels like science putting a hand on the shoulder of superstition and saying, I'm here too.

That simple pairing lit the fuse for this story. If a presence can be detected by its electromagnetic signature, then it must be pulling energy to manifest. If it's pulling energy, could we—ethically—harvest a portion of what it draws? Where is the line between observing a phenomenon and using it? Those questions became the Voss Array, a machine that listens for order in the world's noise and translates it into power. And the moment the device existed on paper, the ethics arrived with it, stubborn and unavoidable.

From there, I stepped back into the world I began in Echoes in the Glass—the In Between, the Echo who keeps balance, and the uneasy traffic across mirrors. The same rules apply here as before: reflections open doors; names matter; light matters; mercy costs something. Instead of relying on things leaping from the dark, I try to build dread—the slow, rational fear of what might be waiting around the corner and what it might cost to learn the truth.

This book is stitched from both invention and experience. I've lived in these places and walked their halls; I've stood under the roof of Hill Ward before it came down, EMF meter in hand, chasing whispers through rooms that felt louder than the corridors outside. I've carried and used the same tools my characters carry: recorders, thermometers, cameras, and the meter that sometimes sings when the air decides to thicken. I've also felt the quiet aftermath when nothing "spectacular" happens—only the sense that something patient has watched you pass and chosen not to announce itself. Those real-world edges informed the lines I drew in this book.

You'll meet familiar faces—Abigail Jensen, Samuel Duncan, and new ones: Dr. Elias Voss, who trusts instruments more than rumors; Dr. Lena Mirek, who translates the complicated into the plain and keeps a hand on the emergency stop; and Naveen Patel, sharp-tongued and steady-eyed, who asks the obvious questions that save lives. Each of them is forced to weigh what's possible against what's right, and the answers they choose come with a price.

If you're new to the series, you can begin here. The science won't ask you for a degree; it will ask you to listen closely. If you've read the first book, you'll recognize the currents under the surface and the way the rules bend but do not break.

The Echo Series moves in braided timelines. While this book follows the consequences of the Array, the next returns to Joseph and Maria. Their story runs roughly parallel to this one and intersects in ways that matter. Not every mystery will resolve here—some threads will tighten in the following book, where grief, faith, and the costs of balance ask for different kinds of answers.

I wrote this with the hallway light on and the mirrors covered, not because I fear jump scares, but because I respect quiet. If you've ever felt a room go dense and then watched an EMF needle twitch as if in reply, this book is for you. Keep a small lamp near the glass. Speak the names you refuse to forget. And as you turn the page, if you hear a low hum, don't rush to decide what it is. It might be the building. It might be the Array warming in the next chapter. Or it might be the world remembering how to hold itself together—one current, and one choice, at a time.

— Scott J. Clauss

1

First Hairline Crack

Scene 1: Lochburn Field Trip: Tuning and Harvesting

They waited for the bus.

The Clover Park Technical College lab kept its own weather—dry, faintly ozone-scented, always a few degrees cooler than the hallway. Overhead, long fixtures hummed like patient insects. The main coil—a waist-high column in a Faraday cage—sat centered on yellow floor tape. Racks of instruments lined the walls: spectrum analyzers with sleepy green numerals, a tidy stack of supercapacitors, and a rolling cart neatly coiled with braided leads. A single mirror—facility standard, unasked for—hung on the far wall, doubling the room in a way that always made Elias feel watched.

Elias Voss paced a short stripe between console and observation bay, coat still on, hands jammed in his pockets. He was the architect here: principal investigator, grant wrangler, the one who signed off on every interlock and limitation. He'd cut his teeth on hard engineering before the Array chased him into the gray zone where numbers touched rumors. The lines in his expression were roadmap and warning both. In the lab he was precise to the point of severity; on good days that read as care. On bad days—too many lately—it read as distance.

Dr. Lena Mirek leaned her hip against the console, watching the numbers idle. Officially: senior research engineer, operations lead. Unofficially: the keeper of smooth running and straight answers. She'd come up the hard way—scholarships and side jobs—and carried the ease of someone who could talk in equations and then translate them for a classroom without breaking stride. People tended to underestimate how much of the Array's safety was her insistence taped into code.

Naveen Patel hovered near the instrument cart, thumbs hooked into the straps of a too-large lab apron he refused to give back. Graduate intern, yes—coffee fetcher when necessary, cable wrangler always—but also the fastest pair of eyes in the room when a trace went from noise to signal. He had the posture of someone who grew up taking apart game controllers and the humor of a kid who'd learned that joking first kept people listening long enough to hear the actual point.

Elias checked the wall clock again. Rain slicked the high windows. In the hallway, the distant echo of laughter bounced, then fell quiet.

"Against my better judgment," he said at last, not looking up, "I think Naveen is best suited to talk to them—because he is the most like a middle schooler."

Lena's mouth twitched; she smoothed it into something neutral too late. The soft sound she made wasn't quite a laugh, but it was close.

Naveen stepped forward like he'd been called to the stage for a prize he didn't know he was up for. "Yes," he said, with the blunt cheer of someone unembarrassed by honesty. "I think I may be best suited for this assignment."

Elias shot him a side-eye. "You're not helping."

"I am," Naveen said. "I can say it plain. And I actually like questions that start with 'Wait, but—'"

He was, in truth, best suited. He'd sat through more school assemblies than either of them in recent memory, knew by instinct when attention drifted, and—crucially—he remembered what explanations felt like from the other side of the podium. He didn't mind being obvious if obvious made the point.

A bus hissed into the lot. Wiper blades squealed. Ms. Delgado came down first with a clipboard and a weathered patience that could separate running children from open equipment with a single look. Thirty students funneled in, a river of hoodies and wet sneakers, voices damped by the lab's stillness.

"Lochburn Middle School," she said, offering quick handshakes. "We're excited—and slightly terrified."

"No microwaving anyone today," Lena said, easy and warm. "Observe-only mode."

Elias gestured them into a horseshoe around the demo table. He started to say "Welcome to the Applied Electromagnetics Lab"—heard how it would land—and stopped. He nodded instead to each of them in turn. "I'm Elias. This is Dr. Mirek—Lena—and this is Naveen. He's going to walk you through what the Array does and why we built it."

Naveen waited a beat to let the room settle. He spoke without rushing, hands quiet on the cart.

"I'm Naveen. I'm going to tell you exactly what this machine does in one sentence." He tipped his chin toward the coil. "This machine harvests small amounts of energy from the environment. We find the right frequency, we capture that energy, and we store it. Then we use that power to run very low-power sensors and radios."

A few eyebrows went up; good. He pointed to the nearest monitor. The green line had the lazy tremor of a pulse at rest.

"Basics. The world is full of electromagnetic fields—EMF. Whenever electricity flows or a radio signal is sent, you get an electric field and a magnetic field. Power lines, Wi-Fi, phones, radio stations, the wiring in these walls—all of it makes EMF. We have tools that measure it, same way a thermometer measures temperature."

A hand shot up from a kid with a skateboard helmet clipped to his backpack. "Ghost hunters use EMF meters."

"True," Naveen said. "In ghost hunting, people look for EMF spikes when they think something is trying to show up. The idea is simple: if something is manifesting, it uses energy. EMF meters can notice when that energy changes. In here, we don't start by guessing what a spike means. We measure first and write it down. Later, if we see patterns—great. But we don't jump to names."

He angled his body so the coil and mesh were clearly visible. "How the Array works, no fluff:

1. *Listen. We scan frequencies to see what's already here—like tuning a radio, but for EMF.*
2. *Tune. When we find a frequency that's strong or interesting, we match it at a safe level so the signal stands out from the noise.*
3. *Harvest. A rectenna—antenna plus rectifier—converts a tiny part of that radio energy into DC power. We store it in a supercapacitor or small battery."*

He held up two fingers. "Numbers matter. We're talking microwatts to low milliwatts. Enough for ultra-low-power electronics: wake a sensor, take a reading, send a quick burst of data, go back to sleep. Not enough to run big machines."

He pressed a large, satisfyingly clicky button. "Observe mode." The word *BASELINE* lit in the corner. The green line steadied as if listening back.

"Now I'm going to tune to a safe, allowed test signal we control." Naveen pointed to a small transmitter the size of a deck of cards sitting on a marked square. He rolled the dial a few clicks. The trace lifted and settled into a clean, regular rise—wave, trough, wave.

"Found it," he said. "Next step is rectify—turn the alternating stuff into direct current—and store a trickle."

A student near the back nodded at the mirror. "What's with that?"

"Good eye," Naveen said. "Mirrors have metal on the back and sit on wired walls. That can make them stable spots where fields line up neatly. We don't need them, but sometimes they're clean edges our instruments can notice."

Lena moved to the mesh and tapped it lightly. "Safety. The coil is behind a Faraday cage to keep our signals where they belong. We set hard limits for power and temperature. If anything crosses a line, the system shuts itself down and logs it. We also use permissions and audit trails—no one runs this alone."

A girl with glitter on her cheeks frowned up at the coil. "Is it dangerous?"

"It's designed to be low power and fail-safe," Naveen said. "Crossing a street is dangerous if you ignore the rules. We don't. We measure first, we cap power, and if anything looks wrong, we stop. That's not a slogan. It's how the code is written."

Elias watched faces shift—the moment when fear folded into interest. He felt some small, hard thing in his chest unhook. He stepped forward, hands out of his pockets now.

"Years ago," he said, "I helped on a couple of paranormal investigations. The one instrument that reliably reacted was an EMF meter. When people believed they saw something, we often saw a spike on the meter at the same time. I asked a basic question: if manifestations seem to use energy, can that energy be measured—and even harvested—safely? That question became this project. Whatever you believe about ghosts, the energy part is measurable. So we built a system to measure and use that energy responsibly."

He didn't mention the nights he'd sat with the mirror's reflection until the lab felt two rooms deep. He didn't mention the way numbers could look like footsteps if you wanted them to. He kept it where it needed to be: on data, on design, on duty.

A hand. "What do you do with the energy you get?"

"We power our own sensors and radios for short bursts," Naveen said. "For example, a sensor that wakes up, checks temperature and magnetic field, sends data, and goes back to sleep. If we needed more energy, we'd need a stronger, focused source and a different antenna setup. That's not what we're doing here."

The skateboard kid raised his chin. "If you can only get tiny power, why build it? Don't you need big power to make it worth it?"

Elias sat back, the question landing harder than he expected. He felt it in his ribs the way you feel a bass note: simple, undeniable. They all knew—here, in this room—that they had tuned the Array to larger energy sources before. Brief windows. Unstable. Hard to find. If not for those few surges they'd caught and logged, the kid would be right: the whole project wouldn't be worth it. That possibility—of finding that frequency again, safely—was why they kept looking.

Lena answered, voice steady, teacher-clean. "Two reasons. First: small power has value. Imagine a network of sensors in hard-to-reach places that don't need batteries changed every month. If they can harvest enough from the environment to run themselves, that's a win for cost, safety, and the planet. Second: we're still learning where the strongest usable energy is. The environment isn't flat; it has peaks and valleys across frequencies and places. We've seen brief surges—real ones—but they're unstable and difficult to reproduce. If we can safely tune into a frequency or condition that carries more usable energy—without hurting anything—that would be monumental. We haven't found a stable peak yet. We're looking. Carefully."

She let that sit. The word monumental hung there, not as a promise, but as a horizon line.

Ms. Delgado checked the time and gave the class the subtle teacher's signal that meant two questions left.

A boy in a NASA hoodie asked, "Can you... take energy from a person?"

"No," Naveen said, simple and flat. "We don't take energy from people. We work with ambient fields already in the room or the test signal we generate. If we ever saw anyone—human or otherwise—reacting to what we were doing, we stop."

A final hand. "What happens if your reading gets weird?"

"Then we don't turn it up," Naveen said. "We shut down, record everything, and review it with more eyes. Our job is to understand the environment, not change it."

Ms. Delgado gathered the group with practiced claps. The kids formed a line that wasn't a line and murmured thank-yous that were genuine anyway. The door sighed them back into the hallway. The bus sighed them back into the rain.

Silence returned in a soft, even layer. The monitors ticked their quiet digits. The mirror held its neat double of an empty room.

"Clear," Lena said, as if concluding an experiment. "And honest."

Elias nodded, eyes on the console log: OBSERVE ONLY stamped down the side, test signal flagged, interlocks green. "Reset the cart," he said, voice lower now. "We're back on at 1800 for the full sweep."

On the console, a half-second EMF blip shouldered up and vanished—small enough to ignore, large enough to be logged. The entry printed itself to the audit trail with a soft click.

Lena glanced toward the windows, gauging the light, then back to the screens. "Weather's holding," she said. "Barometer's steady. SNR should be excellent this evening. If the room has a natural note worth hearing, today's the day."

Naveen eased the transmitter back to its taped square, smoothing the cable arcs by habit. "Same rules," he said, half to himself. "Measure first. If it gets weird, we stop."

He glanced once at the mirror before he killed the screen. It returned a row of dark rectangles and his own face, thoughtful for once, unmasked by jokes. Outside, rain stitched the day back together, steady as breathing.

Scene 2: The First Current

"Is it ethical to harvest order from a signal that might belong to the dead?"

The question came first. It wasn't new. It had been pacing in Lena's head for months, pared to the parts anyone could understand:

Everything with charge throws a field. Fields carry energy—but what the Array cares about isn't how loud a field is. It cares how together it is. Noise is everywhere—phones, Wi-Fi, transformers, the soft bioelectric whisper of a heartbeat. Most of it is messy and useless to a harvester.

Sometimes the mess lines up.

When waves fall into step—like two tuning forks sharing a note, or metronomes syncing on a rolling board—energy moves easily. That "falling into step" is coherence. The Voss Array doesn't drink from any field that happens by; it listens for coherence across frequencies, locks to that pattern, translates it into an easy band, and converts that order into usable power. Not magic. Not summoning. A siphon that only works when the water already runs in neat ripples.

Ghost hunters swear their meters twitch in old rooms. Most of their numbers are noise. Yet every so often a signature appears that repeats across bands—a tidy comb where there should be hiss. If a place holds that kind of pattern—because of machines, because of people, because of something neither has language for—then yes, you can skim a trickle. You're not skimming "from air"; you're skimming from the order that keeps certain ripples tidy.

And that's where the question bites.

If a signature is just a storm of radios, harvest away. If a signature is the living hum of a hospital ward, do you owe it care? If a signature is the last organized trace of someone—if that neat pattern is all that remains of a person's presence—does taking power from it cross a line? Is pulling from a cold, machine-made comb different from pulling from a warm, human one? If the only honest way to learn is to try, is trying already a trespass?

They had worried that bone for two years while building the Array. They agreed on what instruments could prove, disagreed on what names to give the rest, and kept going because the next measurement might decide it. This afternoon, a field trip had gotten the polite version at low power: observe-only, a clean little test tone, a few microwatts rising like dew into a supercap. Tonight was the pivot. Full power within their widened limits. No theatrics—just an honest attempt to reacquire the frequency they had brushed once before and logged in disbelief: not milliwatts. Megawatts—a surge so large the lab's bus had bucked and the glass had rimed with frost.

Lena said the question out loud anyway. It sounded like pulling a fire alarm before opening the door.

Across the benches, Elias lifted his eyes from the run list—the look he saved for stubborn facts: patient, tired, unblinking. He didn't answer her. He answered himself. He spoke softly, the way people pray when they don't want to be caught praying.

"Three moves," he murmured, and let the engineering steady his pulse. "Sense, translate, extract."

He rebuilt the machine in his head like laying tools back into a drawer.

"Sense coherence: antennas and magnetometers ring the chamber. Glass and mirrors help—they hold polarization a moment, show how a push lingers. The correlator watches from ELF/VLF through RF for non-thermal phase links—repeating narrow bands, 1/f humps with notches, timing that holds between low and high. When the pattern is real, the PLL locks. Bench LEDs stop jittering. The room admits it's organized.

"Translate: the walls are high-Q metamaterial—ceramic and patterned copper. When locked, we bias the wall with a weak pump tone so it behaves like a parametric mixer. It shifts that coherent pattern into an easy band—hundreds of kilohertz to a few megahertz—where normal electronics are efficient. Conservation holds. We're turning order into a frequency we can use.

"Extract: the mixed signal hits a rectenna backplane, fills a super-cap bank, then the inverter gives us DC or AC. Efficiency scales with coherence. Microwatts when the world is messy; watts when it holds; and if we ever see megawatts again, it means we've coupled to the thing that keeps the mess from falling apart."

He swallowed. "More here means less order there," he added, barely louder than breath. "So we detune. And we don't get greedy."

Naveen, the grad intern, rolled his chair closer, wheels whispering on the tile. "If it works," he said, voice trying for light and landing near it, "we buy Ethics a nicer chair. Lumbar support. Moral compass on the armrest." He grimaced. "Kidding. Mostly."

Elias didn't smile. He set the clipboard down like a gavel. "Tonight we hold the rails. Limits are widened but still hard-capped. Thermal interlock armed. Coherence limiter ready. If anything moves wrong—we stop." He glanced at the mirror and then away. "We try for the band we logged in May. No chasing. If it rises, we detune +0.3. If it surges, we kill it."

Tonight's room at Clover Park Technical College in Tacoma was a converted teaching space: benches on the north and west walls with cabinets beneath, a sink and eyewash by the door, an extinguisher, and a laminated evacuation map curling at one corner. The Array sat in a shallow horseshoe around a floor plate; the mast was bolted at center, and during live power no one put hands on hardware. Laptops and a Tektronix scope lived on the east bench. A square wall mirror hung above the west cabinets between the first-aid kit and that evac-uation map. Overhead fluorescents: steady hum. The exit clock: three minutes wrong the way it had always been wrong. They used Clover Park for public demos; most assembly and day-to-day work happened across town at Pierce. Tonight the two worlds overlapped in a way that felt like bad luck.

Somewhere down the hall, a door closed carefully. A laugh burst and was swallowed by the building. The room held its even light and waited.

"Baseline," Elias said. "Bring it up. No heroics."

"Copy," Naveen answered, fingers dancing. Switches woke. The low hum that lived in the room during runs rose from rumor to presence. It found seams in the drywall and hollows in the tables, tested them, liked them. Lena felt it first in her teeth and then behind her eyes, a grit of invisible weather. A paper clipped to the whiteboard lifted a millimeter and reconsidered. A pen rolled one inch and stayed where gravity lost interest.

"Safety check," Lena said. "If anything is wrong—pressure shift, temperature change, odd noise, instrument drift—we call it and cut power. No debate."

"Eyes on the instruments," Elias said. "We watch, we log, and if a value moves out of range, we stop. No exceptions."

They listened. The Array teaches ears its moods: the fan's conversational purr; the coil's steadier tone; the faint rattle that means nothing and always sounds like something. The building answered with its own orchestra—vent dampers clicking, plumbing whispering, the gone-forever echo of chalk. Lena set both feet flat outside the equipment arc, the way her grandmother had taught her to stand during storms.

"Point two five," Elias said, eyes on the trace. "Hold."

The fluorescent ballasts steadied, then seemed to rethink and steadied again. The first bead of sweat that ever broke on Lena in this lab had surprised her in May; now she felt one gather at her hairline, considerate and precise. She told her hands to stay loose and her breath to behave. Only the first part listened.

"Point two seven. Hold."

A draft that didn't exist moved through the room. The paper lifted and settled. Naveen rubbed his forearm and told his skin to grow up.

The laptop cursor hesitated between blinks as if the software were distracted.

"Point two nine. Hold."

"Eyes front," Naveen said, tapping the scope bezel. "If the coil drifts, I want it before it does. Numbers, not vibes."

"Copy," Lena said. She curled her fingers under the bench edge without thinking. Her knuckles went white.

"Point three," Elias said. "Hold and breathe."

The air changed—not colder, exactly, just tighter, like a room before a storm breaks. The Array's tone pressed into the soft tissue of her arms. The equipment chirped a little complaint.

"Note it," Elias said.

No one wrote.

The west wall seemed a shade darker. The corners of the room felt heavier. Lena's pulse ticked in the soft spot under her thumb.

"Artifact?" Naveen said, quieter. "Ballast reflection?"

"Hold the band," Elias said, even quieter. His eyes didn't leave the phase trace, which had stopped strolling and begun to breathe in place—that telltale of two answers trying to share the same mouth.

The exit clock made a single wrong tick.

"That's not us," Naveen said. The joke had left him.

The glass popped.

A rake of hooked talons shot out of the wall mirror and clamped onto Lena's wrist with a hard, wet click. No ramp. No warning. Wire-cold pain lanced up her bones.

She screamed and grabbed the bench rail with her free hand. The stool kicked sideways and slammed the cabinet. The thing yanked. It tried to pull her arm straight through the world.

Naveen flinched back on instinct, then surged forward. He hit her shoulder with his and wrapped both hands around her elbow. His sneakers burned rubber across the tile. "Elias!" he yelled, voice cracking. "Elias, wake up! Kill power! Now!"

Elias didn't move. He stared like the universe had just spoken a new word and he wanted to hear the pronunciation. "What is it," he murmured, as if the room might answer.

The Array's tone climbed half a step all by itself. Tools rattled in drawers. A coffee mug tipped and shattered. Cold climbed Lena's arm, counting inches, relentless.

"ELIAS!" Naveen screamed. "NOW!"

The shout snapped him. He lunged and slammed the emergency stop. The Array coughed mid-note. He yanked the main breaker and the wall disconnect. Lights hiccupped. The room's hum tore.

The thing didn't let go. The mouth in the glass gaped wider. When it spoke, the sound came thick and low, like something dragging itself through a drain.

"Balance."

Cabinet doors vibrated.

"The veil is thin here. You opened a door."

The voice was the same low scrape, words pushed through a place they didn't belong. The line crawled under Lena's skin and settled there. She hauled back with everything—bench, stool, Naveen's hoodie clenched in her fist, gravity, terror—anything that agreed to be hers.

The thing's grip tightened.

Elias hit the breaker again, as if off had a deeper setting. Fans spun down hard, the coil's whine guttered, and a final shiver passed through the room.

The talons loosened so suddenly that Lena and Naveen fell together. They crashed into the rolling cart; the cart clipped the bench; a rain of screws hit the floor.

The mouth in the mirror collapsed. Flat glass stared back.

Silence came in pieces: the last fan coast, a single screw rolling to a stop, the exit sign ticking. All three of them stood there breathing like they'd run a mile. Lena hugged her wrist to her chest. Naveen's hoodie was twisted where she'd grabbed it. Elias kept his hand flat on the dead stop like he didn't trust the button to remember its job.

Then the lights steadied. The room looked ordinary.

That felt like a threat.

"Go," Naveen said, hoarse. Not a command. A plea.

Elias pulled the power key and squeezed it until his knuckles went white. They edged to the door without turning their backs, took nothing, left everything. In the hall, the air felt thin and too clean.

They ran.

Clover Park's courtyard was empty at this hour. Night had settled; the campus was a cutout of dark buildings and brighter sky. They stopped under the big fir by the walkway. A cool breeze came through; it should have helped. It didn't. Sweat ran down their temples, soaked their shirts.

They stared at one another and no one uttered a word.

Scene 3: The Spark in the Static

They stood under the fir and tried to breathe. The campus was quiet—no cars, no voices—just wind in the needles and the thump of blood in their ears. The lab windows looked like dark eyes pretending they hadn't seen anything.

"What was that?" Naveen said first. "Don't tell me artifact. Don't say ballast."

"I don't know," Elias said.

"It wasn't us," Lena added. "It moved like it had its own plan."

They let the night hold the rest. The air smelled like cut grass and machine oil from the auto bays. Somewhere a sprinkler clicked on, impatient.

"Your wrist," Elias said, noticing how Lena kept it fixed against her chest. "We should wrap it."

"The clinic's closed," Naveen said. "So is everything else."

"The first-aid kit's in the lab," Elias said, and then, after a long beat, "We go together. Slow. We touch nothing we don't have to. If anything feels wrong, we leave."

No one argued. They keyed in, paused at the threshold as if the room might jump, then crossed to the benches under the thin emergency lights.

Elias grabbed the kit, cracked a cold pack, and nodded to the stool. "Sit."

Lena sat. "May I?" he asked. She offered her wrist. He laid the cold pack over the blanched skin, wrapped snug but not tight, tape clean and square. Their eyes met once, too long, and they both looked away.

On the far wall, Naveen eased open the breaker panel. "House lights only," he said. He flipped the building circuit. The fluorescents snapped up, buzzed too loud, settled. He slid to the console, woke the laptop, and mounted the capture drive.

"Anything?" Elias asked.

Naveen scrubbed the timeline with his thumb. "Video goes sideways right when it—" He stopped. "There's audio. Coil, then a dip, then low-frequency. We can hear the words."

"Play it," Elias said.

The speakers gave them their own room: the coil's steady whine, a moment of hush like air stepping back, a sharp pop—and then a wet, wrong voice dragging itself through the waveform:

"Balance."

A beat.

"The veil is thin here. You opened a door."

Silence stretched.

"I've been thinking about what happened," Lena said at last.

Elias didn't answer.

"That... thing." She forced the word out. "We both saw it. But maybe it was—" she hesitated, "—a hallucination. Stress, light, noise. The Array's EMF can mess with your head. People say that."

He gave a short, dry breath that wasn't a laugh. "Hallucinations don't grab wrists, Lena."

She shifted, uncomfortable. "Then a projection? Some weird coupling in the field we triggered by accident?"

Elias finally turned toward her, expression unreadable. "Naveen called it a 'Veilborne.'"

"Where would you even get a name like that?" Lena asked, eyes flicking to the intern.

Naveen raised a hand like he'd been caught with a contraband idea. "Podcast. Local weird-history thing. They use 'Veilborne' for... whatever crosses over when the, uh, veil's thin. I know—it's ghost-show nonsense." He glanced at the waveform. "Except for the parts that didn't feel like nonsense."

Silence settled again. For Elias, the hum was no longer just mechanical. It had the same pressure he'd felt long before the Array existed, as if the room had taken a breath and was deciding whether to hold it.

FLASHBACK: Steilacoom, 1995

Rain needled the broad windows of the Bair Bistro, turning the Sound to pewter smears. Thirteen-year-old Elias cupped hot chocolate gone lukewarm. Coffee, butter, and bread warmed the air; under it, old wood and damp plaster—the smell of a building that had soaked up a century of storms.

Beside him, a woman set a spoon in her coffee.

It twitched.

Elias went still.

It twitched again—then lifted. Not slid. Lifted, as if pinched by invisible fingers. Coffee clung to the cup in beads that fell soundlessly. The spoon hung there, impossible and ordinary at once, then dropped with a metallic clatter that made the woman gasp.

A pale waiter hurried over. "It's been happening more lately," he murmured, collecting the spoon.

Overhead lights fluttered twice. A stack of napkins breathed and scattered on a wind nobody felt. The kitchen door creaked open and hung like a mouth thinking.

No one laughed. The air had the weight of just-before-lightning. Elias knew—without words—that something unseen had noticed him.

That night, he told his friend Nathan, who rummaged in a closet and produced a black box with a telescoping antenna. "EMF meter," Nathan said. "Dad says ghost hunters use it. Says when they try to manifest, they throw fields." Elias held it and felt the first click where science and the strange could live in the same sentence.

FLASHBACK: Fort Steilacoom Park, 2008

Tall grass hid the cracked footprint of Hill Ward where Western State Hospital once stood. Elias—now teaching at Pierce—walked the rectangle with a handful of students and portable meters.

"Stay inside the old foundation," he said. "If there's anything, it's here."

He didn't tell them the ward stories—whispers to empty corners, pale shapes after lights-out.

A meter wailed. "Zero to six milligauss," a student called. Another frowned. "Did you hear whispering?"

Elias did—a faint breath, then a shuffle across tiles torn out decades ago. The pressure in the air matched the Bistro's, and today's. Walking back, he felt it again: something had noticed, and remembered.

END FLASHBACK

"Elias?" Lena's voice pulled him back. He was staring through the console like it was a window.

"You were somewhere else," she said.

"Just… remembering." He glanced at the blank square where the mirror had hung. "Different rooms. Same air."

"So what do you think it was?" Lena asked.

"I don't know," he said. "Naveen's word will do until we have better. A name isn't an answer."

"And it doesn't tell us what it wants," Lena said, quieter.

They both listened. The Array's steady hum seemed louder, like it was paying attention.

Naveen cleared his throat. "So we heard words. We don't know what said them. We don't know why. We can either pretend we didn't, or we do the boring thing and write controls."

"Boring," Elias said. "Every time." He pointed with two fingers, shifting into work. "Perimeter around the Array. Stand-off lines taped floor to door. Operator position at the east bench only. We update the shutdown sequence: stop, main, wall. We keep live runs under ninety seconds until we understand the coupling."

Lena nodded. "And the mirror's already out. Log the removal and time."

Naveen set the laptop to sleep, then grabbed a driver, climbed onto the west bench, and checked the empty lag screws like he needed to see them bare. "I'll tape the perimeter. Wide. No one crosses during power."

"I'll draft the reflective-surface policy," Lena said, flexing her wrapped hand. "No shiny screens, no loose glass, covers on the scope and TV. We make the room dull and predictable."

Elias uncapped a marker and wrote on the whiteboard in block letters:

LIVE RUN PERIMETER — DO NOT ENTER
OPERATOR: EAST BENCH ONLY
SHUTDOWN SEQUENCE: STOP → MAIN → WALL
MAX LIVE: 90s

He capped the pen. "We document what we know. We don't guess out loud. We keep each other honest."

Naveen smoothed the last length of gaffer tape with his palm. "And if a Veilborne shows up again—" he caught himself, grimaced—"if something shows up again, we hit the sequence and leave."

"Exactly," Elias said. He pulled the capture drive, locked it in a drawer, and pocketed the key. "We're done for tonight."

They checked the exits, took nothing else, and shut the lights. In the hall, the air felt thin and too clean. Back under the fir, the campus looked like itself again—circles of light on concrete, quiet buildings, the smell of wet bark.

"What's our story tomorrow?" Lena asked.

"The true one we can prove," Elias said. "We changed the room. We tightened protocol. We continue—carefully."

Naveen hitched his backpack. "And I stop listening to weird podcasts before bed."

"No promises," Lena said, but the corner of her mouth moved.

They started for the lot together, not saying the word they'd heard, not pretending they hadn't. The night kept its questions. They kept their plan.

Scene 4: The Builders and the Loss

They came back the next evening, early enough to miss the night classes and late enough that the building had started to forget people. The taped stand-off box around the Array shone dull under the fluorescents. The west wall showed two bare lag screws where the mirror had been; a sheet of cardboard covered the anchors like a bandage. The egress lane—a wide taped path—ran clean to the door. Two extinguishers waited, one on each side of the room. Someone (Naveen) had labeled the console with a neat sticker: *STOP → MAIN → WALL.*

The hum threaded the room, riding the conduits and the concrete, and clung to Elias as he stepped back from the console. Even with the main bus cut, he felt it in the arches of his feet—a faint vibration, as if the floor itself were remembering.

Naveen set his backpack by the east bench and powered up a laptop on house current only. "Okay, boring mode engaged," he said, half to himself. "Logging on all channels, no live power, stop lamp tested, lane taped, mirror exiled to the storage cage with the haunted shop vac."

Lena glanced at the wall clock, then at Elias. "We could kick this to remote," she said quietly. "Sensors will stream. I can monitor from home."

"No," Elias said, eyes on the Array's dome catching the lab's light like a held breath. "We stay. We work through the queued data and figure out what happened. I'm not letting this—whatever it was—live inside the numbers for another day without us looking at it."

Naveen raised a hand. "Seconded. But 'stay' means house lights only and zero touching the hardware. If the hum burps, we step back and we leave. I like my wrists where they are."

"Agreed," Lena said. She crossed to the door, flipped the interior latch, and hung the red placard—*DO NOT ENTER*—so any late tech would think twice. "I'll ping Facilities that we're on an overnight review. Coffee, blankets, the monk routine."

"No one walks out until the decay curve is flat," Elias said. "And we don't leave the Array unattended."

They moved with method. Lena pushed long-term logging to all three redundant arrays; continuous audio rolled; the thermal camera went to record-all, not motion. She draped matte lab towels over shiny bezels and the small inspection mirror on the tool cart—new policy made habit. Naveen slid foam sleeves over the oscilloscope's gloss, then photographed the egress lane with a tape measure in frame and texted the shots to Hector. The stop lamp glowed once under his thumb, then he killed it and wrote *TESTED 19:06* on the whiteboard.

"If the noise floor lifts again," Lena said, "we'll have it from four angles."

Elias exhaled; something in him uncoiled a notch. "Rotation on the hour. Lena, take the first pass on spectral filters. Naveen, cross-check the shutdown sequence timestamps against building power logs and the audio dip. I'll scrub the last two days against external EMF reports and see where the anomaly blooms."

"On it," Naveen said, already typing. "Also, I pulled the podcast transcript I told you about—Veilborne. Saving it for after we do the grown-up work, but it's here."

"Later," Elias said, without heat.

They took their stations. The Array waited in the center of the taped box, asleep but listening. Monitors counted seconds forward. The hum did not rise or fade; it simply remained, a note only bones could hear as the night closed around them and the work began.

Lena brushed past Elias on her way to the filters and the back of his arm flinched before he knew it would. If she noticed, she didn't mention it. She kept her gestures efficient—standing close enough to share a screen, pointing with a capped pen, making space when he leaned in.

Elias didn't notice any of it. His gaze had drifted to the single framed photograph on the shelf above the main console. Early days. The old workshop came back to him not as a scene he stepped into but as a weight in his chest—the smell of oil and warm steel, the sting of solder smoke, concrete floors dusted with filings.

Four of them, always in uneven shifts: Elias, Lena, Camille, Adrian Kessler. He can still hear the clatter of trays and the hum of bench supplies, the way Camille's laugh turned a failed prototype into a step forward. She wasn't only his wife; she was his match across the table—mind quick enough to vault from theory to build in the same breath. Her pencil would be stabbed through the knot of her hair, the ends of it tapping her neck when she leaned over a diagram.

Ideas layered over one another, alive in the air. Camille's dome—coil array scaled into a 360-degree capture field—made the first real jump. Adrian argued for adaptive frequency tuning so the system could "listen," head tilted, hands cutting the air as if he could slice a frequency band with his fingers. Lena stood between vision and wiring, translating their frenzy into parts lists and clean sentences, shaving off any mention that might invite "ghost" questions from funders before they were ready.

Nights ran on stubbornness and lukewarm coffee. Copper versus aluminum never really ended; Adrian would needle, Elias would counter, Camille would test both, and Lena would mark the results in a neat grid. For a while, the work felt inevitable. They were more force than team—momentum wearing human faces.

And then the break in the current.

He never watches that moment play in his mind. It lives under the surface, a dark shape moving beneath thought. After it, the room's temperature changed. Tools sounded different when they touched the bench. Adrian's note was short. His absence was loud. The door closed, and it stayed closed.

That left Elias and Lena to keep the work from collapsing under its own history.

"Maybe you should take that home," Lena said now, catching him looking at the photo. "It belongs here," he said. "She belongs here."

Lena hesitated—one heartbeat where more words existed—then returned to her console. "Then let's keep the people who are here... here."

She brought up the latest logs and leaned so he could see. "Remember when government interest finally landed? They didn't care until we stripped any paranormal language out of the pitch. 'Ambient field energy capture'—that's the phrase they funded, not ghosts. Clean power with no fuel."

"They sent the grant the same week they visited," Elias said.

"And brought lawyers," Naveen added without looking up. "Speaking of words: I'm seeing the dip in the audio right before the voice. It aligns with a building power micro-sag by a quarter second. Doesn't explain the words, just says the room got weird before the room got weirder."

"Tag it," Elias said. "We'll bracket the conditions."

They worked in the steady, unshowy way that keeps people alive: subsystems verified dark, capacitor bleed rates logged, residual field data plotted. The numbers were stable; stability felt provisional.

Lena set a mug beside Elias's keyboard. "Tea," she said. Her fingers brushed his for a fraction longer than necessary; he went distant again without meaning to, eyes on the photo—the way Camille's head tilted toward him in it, the warmth in her smile.

"You miss her," Lena said, not a question.

"Every day," he answered, automatic and true.

The hum seemed to deepen in the floor, an echo that wasn't in the instruments.

"Noise floor just wavered a hair," Naveen said, eyes narrowing at the graph. "Still within normal. Logging the blip."

They settled back into the rhythm. Minutes later, as Elias shut down a secondary console, a reflection in the blank screen showed a faint smear behind his face. No edges, no features. Just the impression of a darker shape where no shadow should be.

He looked again. Nothing.

Lena was watching him. "What is it?"

"Nothing," he lied.

Naveen glanced up, weighing whether to crack a joke and choosing not to. "Stop lamp's still hot. If anything isn't nothing, we use it."

"Agreed," Elias said. He wrote a quick note on the white-board—*19:54: operator reported transient reflection; no corroboration*—and capped the marker.

"Okay," Lena said, voice steady. "Then we keep going. We don't give this thing more room in our heads than in the data."

They worked—nervous, alert, disciplined. On guard for anything else that might appear, and determined that if it did, it would find them ready.

Scene 5: Unwanted Oversight

By morning the rain had set in for a full shift, needling the tall windows of the Clover Park lab and pooling in the lot's tired seams. The room wore last night's preparations like a new habit: a wide, taped stand-off box around the Array; a clean egress lane floor-to-door; two extinguishers set within reach; the west wall patched where the mirror had hung; and a small yellow stop lamp bolted to the console with a sticker beneath it: *STOP → MAIN → WALL.*

Elias was bent over the console scrubbing overnight logs when a brisk double-knock landed on the door and immediately turned the handle.

Lena glanced up. "Expecting anyone?"

Before Elias could answer, two people stepped in—one tall and broad-shouldered, confidence worn like a badge; the other smaller, sharper, eyes mapping the room.

"Avery Shaw," the man said, hand out like a formality that saved time. "Department of Energy—your grant program."

"Natalie Chen," the woman added with a nod. Her attention did not stick to Elias; it moved across the benches, the taped lanes, the cardboard over the lag screws, the Array itself.

"We weren't expecting a visit," Elias said, shaking Avery's hand.

"That's the use of a surprise," Avery said, smile polished. "I like to see rooms before they put on makeup."

Near the east bench, Naveen looked up from a laptop. He'd claimed the corner nearest the breaker panel, backpack open, a palm-sized Bluetooth speaker beside his mouse. He flicked the volume down with a guilty thumb and tried to look like a person who never listened to anything while he worked.

"We're mid-pull on the logs," Lena said, standing. "You're welcome to observe."

"That's why I'm here," Avery said, stepping inside and clocking the tape lines with a quick frown. "To check progress—and set expectations."

"Progress," Elias said evenly, "includes safety parameters we implemented since our last run. Stand-off perimeter, fixed egress lane, reflective surfaces minimized—mirror removed and stored—time-boxed live sequences to ninety seconds, and an emergency stop button any operator can hit. We'll keep demos at stable settings."

Avery cocked his head. "Is there a safety concern?"

Naveen couldn't help himself. "Only if you count the part where a thing came out of—"

"We adjusted the layout for equipment stability," Elias snapped in, too fast.

"Stop," Avery said, flat palm. "A thing came out of what?"

Naveen's eyes flicked to the patched square where the mirror had been, then to Lena's wrapped wrist. "An old wall mirror," he said. "Which is now gone. We're not reckless."

Avery let the pencil he'd been clicking go still. "I am aware your device taps ambient EMF and converts it to power. I am also aware that some people say EMF spikes around 'the dead' and 'ghosts.' I don't want to hear that word. Donors don't. Agencies don't. We are not funding folklore. Are we clear?"

"Clear," Elias said.

"Good," Avery said, pivoting without losing stride. "Because in seven to ten days—let's say next Friday—you will demonstrate the Array for people who can change your lives. Private investors. Senior officials. You will give them a clean, repeatable sequence: power-up, capture, measurable output on a display anyone can understand. No spurious alarms. No spooky theatrics. No 'unknowns' on mic."

Lena's chair creaked. "Next Friday?"

"We had an anomaly," Elias said, drying out the word. "We need to understand it before we put anyone in the room."

"Anomalies are what you turn into demos," Avery said. "Investors write checks for inevitability. You're a week out. Tighten the pitch. Make the lights dance."

"The device isn't a light show," Elias said. "If instability resur-faces—"

"If you don't step up," Avery cut across, "others will. I have a quantum-capture team in Colorado, a thermal-gradient group in Oregon, a coastal wave outfit talking megawatt arrays. Everyone wants big money. The question is who earns it." He ticked each with a finger like a count in a closing argument. "Don't be the brilliant scientist who misses his moment."

From Naveen's little speaker, a woman's voice leaked at low volume—warm, deliberate, annoyingly on-theme:

"…and when the mirror shifts, it's already too late. You're looking at something that's looking back. The Veilborne comes through—drawn to the living by their heat, their spark—"

Naveen stabbed at pause, too late.

Avery's head snapped toward him. "What is that?"

"Podcast," Naveen said, wincing. "Local weird-history thing."

"Turn it off," Avery said. "And keep it off. This is science. Save ghost stories for YouTube."

Elias didn't look at the speaker. Natalie did. She clocked the way he didn't look, then resumed her slow circuit of the room.

"Here's what happens now," Avery said, back on script. "A rehearsal by Wednesday. Small room, allied faces. Then the full demonstration Friday. Non-negotiable."

Natalie opened a leather-bound notebook. "I'll need an asset list and safety plan for both," she said without drama. "Headcount, evacuation routes, who has the stop lamp, who's on comms, where you've stored the mirror—any other reflective surfaces to note?"

Lena didn't flinch. "Mirror's logged out to storage. Scope and screens are covered during operations. We'll send a list of surfaces and the reflective-surface policy by end of day."

"Good," Natalie said, pen already moving. "Also photos of the egress lane with dimensions."

"Done," Naveen said, tapping his phone. "Already sent to Risk last night."

Avery glanced at the taped box again. "Tell me the audience-safe version. What are we saying this does?"

"A device that harvests otherwise wasted energy from complex environments," Elias said. "We turn static into supply. We isolate reflective surfaces during operations because control is more important than spectacle."

Avery's mouth twitched—approval. "Use the word control twice and safety once. Media calls go to me. If anyone calls you, you do not answer."

"We heard you," Elias said.

Avery set his pencil down like a gavel. "Wednesday rehearsal. Friday show. Make it look inevitable."

He clapped Elias's shoulder—friendly weight, securing a promise—then nodded to Natalie. She snapped her notebook shut and they left to the sound of rain drumming harder against the glass.

The door clicked. Silence took a breath.

Naveen exhaled. "I love that he hates my podcasts more than he hates physics."

Lena stared at the patched wall where the mirror had been. "He hates anything that doesn't fit the deck."

Elias looked at the stop lamp, then at the taped lane, then at the Array. The deadline felt like a hand closing. "We'll be ready," he said, and made it a decision. "Rehearsal Wednesday. Stable settings. Ninety seconds. If anything behaves wrong, we hit the sequence and we walk."

Naveen lifted a thumb toward the yellow lamp. "I plan to develop a strong relationship with that button."

"Good," Lena said. "Develop it quietly."

They went back to their stations. Outside, the rain stitched the morning together, steady and unromantic. Inside, the lab returned to the only story it could live with: control, safety, and the next careful line in the log.

2

The Echo's Balance

Scene 1: Reflections that Watch Back

(Soft instrumental intro music — a low, steady hum mixed with faint wind chimes. Abigail's voice fades in.)

Abigail:

If you're listening to this, you've probably already had your first brush with the other side — even if you didn't realize it at the time. A flicker in the corner of your eye. A shadow that doesn't match your body. A mirror that feels... heavier than it should when you look into it.

We call that place The In Between. Not heaven. Not hell. A separate realm — layered over ours like a second sheet of glass. It's where echoes of the dead linger when they can't, or won't, move on. And not everything in the In Between was ever human.

There's one kind of presence you should be most afraid of. I call them the Veilborne.

A Veilborne isn't a ghost in the way most people think. It's not a mem-

29

ory replaying itself, or a loved one trying to say goodbye. It's something that crosses over when the barrier between worlds is thin... and mirrors are one of the weakest points in that barrier.

People think mirrors just reflect light. They don't. They reflect energy. A mirror is a window where the glass only looks solid. And when conditions are right — a spike in electromagnetic activity, an emotional shock, the presence of another spirit — the Veilborne can see you through that glass. And if it sees you, it can step through.

If you ever notice your reflection lag just a second behind your movements... leave.

If you see the surface ripple, like water disturbed... leave.

And if you feel the temperature drop so fast your breath fogs in front of you, it's already too late. You're looking at something that's looking back — and deciding whether it wants what you have.

What does it want?

You. Your heat. Your spark. Call it a soul, call it life force — whatever name makes you feel safer. The Veilborne feed on it. Once they cross over, they'll take it however they can.

And here's the worst part: once they've marked you, reflections become their doors. Every mirror, every window at night, even the black screen of your phone.

People think they can out-stare their own reflection to prove they're not afraid. That's a mistake. Because the Veilborne doesn't need fear to cross over. Fear just makes you slower to run.

So if you ever see it — the shadow that doesn't belong in the reflection, the eyes that blink a fraction too late — don't waste time wondering what it is. Don't blink back.

Leave the room. Leave the house. Leave the mirror behind.

And pray it doesn't follow you.

Until next time... stay safe. And keep the glass covered at night.

The music faded, leaving a brief silence before the next queued episode began.

Abigail Jensen closed the laptop, the faint reflection of her own face winking out in the darkened screen.

She hovered over the upload button, then added one line to the episode description: "If your loved one was taken: say their name to the glass and set a light beside it. Some come back when the order is restored. Some need help to be found. Not all answers arrive at once—but not all doors stay shut."

She didn't know if it would help. She posted it anyway. She leaned back in her chair, listening to the rain tapping against the second-story windows of her home. The view beyond was a silver-grey expanse of American Lake, its surface dimpled by drizzle.

When she'd started the podcast, she hadn't been entirely sure anyone would listen. Before she was cast out of the In Between — before the events that had nearly cost her her life — she'd kept her gift to herself. She'd read people now and then, felt presences when others could not, but she rarely spoke of it. Even she had doubted it, sometimes.

That changed the night she was pulled into the In Between.

She still saw it when she closed her eyes — the endless glass corridors, the faint echoes of the living drifting like distant voices, the oppressive weight of the Thing that had hunted her there. She remembered the bargain, the escape, and the cost. She'd come back different.

Now she knew what her gift was for.

She pushed her chair back, stretching the stiffness from her legs. Downstairs, the warm smell of toast drifted up from the kitchen, along with the faint sound of Jacob humming to himself.

Jacob Duncan was thirteen now, his hair a little too long and constantly falling into his eyes. He had the beginnings of his own gift — flashes of insight, glimpses of things before they happened, a knack for sensing when someone was telling the truth.

He was also the son of Joseph and Maria Duncan, and Abigail didn't think about them without a pang of sorrow.

After that night in the In Between, after being cast out, Joseph and Maria's lives had unraveled. The two of them had always been a little touched by the other side, but afterward, the veil between them and the In Between seemed paper-thin. Spirits sought them constantly — some desperate for help, some hungry for something darker. The harassment never stopped. And then came the traumatic loss that broke whatever fragile balance they had left.

They'd known they couldn't care for Jacob in that state. One night, they'd sat with Abigail in her kitchen, their faces hollow with grief, and asked her to take him. They'd said she was the only one who could protect him… and teach him.

She'd agreed without hesitation.

Her two-story home on American Lake wasn't much — modest siding, creaking stairs, a roof that needed work. But it was safe, and it was hers. The lake was a comfort, though she knew better than to assume water could keep out what she feared most.

Samuel Duncan had moved into town not long after Jacob did. He said it was to be close to his grandson, but Abigail knew there was more to it. They were careful with it—both of them—letting the days stack up slow, the way you learn the shape of a hand before you take it. Samuel kept his own place so they could be "proper," but he spent most evenings at her kitchen table anyway, sleeves rolled, toolbox by the door like a promise. He fixed the loose shutters, mended the fence, oiled the front hinges that always complained at dusk. Jacob teased that Samuel had his own chair, his own coffee mug, his own way of leaning in to listen when Abigail talked.

She loved him for that steadiness—how he made the house feel tended and alive—and she welcomed him without hurry or apology. If anyone asked, they were taking it slow. If you watched them a while, you could see the truth: they were already choosing each other, one small kindness at a time.

Abigail stepped downstairs. Jacob was perched at the counter, peanut butter on his toast and a spiral notebook open beside him. He was sketching something — jagged lines that looked like waves, or maybe cracks.

"Morning," she said, ruffling his hair.

"Morning," he mumbled, focused on the drawing.

Samuel was by the back door, tightening the latch with a screwdriver. "Storm's blowing in," he said. "Thought I'd make sure the door's not going to start rattling in the wind."

Abigail poured herself coffee, her mind drifting back to the podcast she'd just recorded. Somewhere out there, someone would hear it and know she was talking about what had happened to them. Someone who'd seen the ripples in the glass, who'd felt the cold. And maybe, if they were brave enough, they'd reach out.

Because she had questions of her own.

The Veilborne were crossing over more often. She could feel it. And somewhere, deep down, she suspected it wasn't random. Something — or someone — was stirring them.

She took a sip of coffee, watching the lake through the window. Its surface was smooth now, but she knew how quickly that could change.

Scene 2: The Call

The rain hadn't stopped since dawn. Fat drops streaked the kitchen windows, smearing the lake beyond into a restless expanse of silver and slate. The sound was steady, almost hypnotic — a drumming that pressed into the walls and floorboards as if the whole house were submerged.

Abigail stood at the counter, cradling her coffee. The bitter taste lingered on her tongue, but the warmth was what she sought. She had been on edge for days, unable to shake the feeling that the air itself carried a charge, like the low hum before lightning struck.

When the phone rang, she nearly dropped the mug.

It was from the podcast line.

She hesitated before picking up, her voice guarded. "Hello?"

The reply came in gasps, a voice taut with panic. "Is this... Abigail Jensen? The one from the podcast?"

Abigail straightened, every nerve alert. "Yes. Who am I speaking with?"

"My name's Dana. I—" A sharp hitch cut her words. "I don't know who else to call. Something... something came into my daughter's room last night."

Abigail's fingers whitened around the receiver. Her free hand slid her mug away with slow precision, as though any sudden movement might fracture the moment. "Tell me exactly what happened."

"It was late," Dana whispered. "I went in to check on her before bed. She was sitting up, staring into the mirror on her dresser. I thought she was just... talking to herself. But then I saw it. Something moved in there. Not her reflection. Darker. Wrong."

The words tumbled faster now, as if fear itself propelled them. "It reached out. From the glass. Wrapped around her wrist. I swear to you, it was pulling her in. If her father hadn't come in when he did—" Her voice cracked. "It would've taken her."

Abigail closed her eyes. She didn't need to hear more. She knew that pattern too well.

A Veilborne.

She forced her tone steady. "Where are you calling from?"

"Dupont."

Too close.

She jotted the address, her mind already moving ahead. "Keep her away from the mirror. Cover it with a blanket if you can. And no one — no one — goes near it until I've seen it."

Dana promised she would, her voice trembling with relief at being given something concrete to do. Then the line went dead, the click sounding too final in the heavy stillness.

From the doorway behind her came a voice. "That didn't sound like a telemarketer."

Abigail turned. Samuel stood leaning against the frame, arms crossed, the kind of casual stance that didn't disguise the tension in his jaw. His work shirt was rolled at the sleeves, and his hands — broad, scarred, capable — bore the restless fidget of a man who had been listening too closely.

"It wasn't," she admitted, lowering the receiver. "A family in Dupont. Their daughter was almost taken by something in her bedroom mirror. The father stopped it in time."

Samuel's brow furrowed. "Taken. You mean—"

"I mean exactly what you think."

He pushed off the frame, pacing a slow, deliberate line across the kitchen. The wood creaked beneath his boots. "You've been seeing more of this lately. So have I. It's starting to feel too familiar, Abigail. Like… like what happened to Joseph."

Her breath caught. He didn't talk about Joseph often. When he did, his voice was threaded with guilt and mourning — that same raw knowledge that they had all seen him slipping, all seen the veil closing around him, and none of them could stop it.

"I don't want to watch that happen to you," Samuel said, softer now. "I don't want you getting trapped in one of those mirrors."

He looked at her then — not just with worry, but with something deeper. Affection that had been growing in silence. He'd been there for her in ways that went unspoken: mending fences, staying late when storms rattled the shutters, keeping her company through long nights when sleep wouldn't come. His own scars — Ellen, his ex-wife, who had chosen to flee from the shadows they both endured in Schenectady — only sharpened his resolve. Ellen had run from the fear, built a life by pretending the darkness didn't exist. Samuel had stayed, hardened by it, unwilling to look away. And now, he looked at Abigail with the weight of someone who refused to lose her too.

Before she could answer, movement stirred at the bottom of the stairs.

Jacob appeared. Barefoot, his hair a tangled mess from sleep, his expression oddly calm for a boy his age. He padded across the wood floor, eyes steady, and stopped between them.

"That won't happen," he said.

The words were soft, but they landed like iron in the silence.

Samuel turned to him, brow furrowed. "And why not?"

Jacob's gaze didn't waver. His answer came without hesitation, each syllable cold and certain. "The Echo won't allow it."

The room seemed to constrict. Abigail felt it in her chest — a tightening, as though the air itself had thickened. Even the rhythm of the rain against the windows seemed to falter, growing heavier, slower.

Samuel blinked, caught off guard. His eyes shifted between Jacob and Abigail, confusion mixing with something closer to fear. "What did you just say?"

"The Echo," Jacob repeated. His voice didn't waver.

Samuel swallowed, his throat bobbing. "And how do you know that?"

Jacob met his grandfather's stare. For a long moment, the boy was utterly still. Then he spoke — low, deliberate, the weight of his words pressing against the walls themselves.

"Because the Echo told me."

The silence that followed was unbearable. The words seemed to echo, not in sound but in weight, as if the very foundation of the house had absorbed them. Abigail's coffee mug sat cooling on the counter, forgotten.

The boy's declaration hung there, heavier than the storm outside.

Samuel's eyes searched Jacob's face for any trace of childish jest. There was none. Only calm certainty, a composure too old for thirteen years. His voice had carried the cadence of something else, something not entirely his own.

Abigail felt her skin prickle. She thought of the ripples she'd seen in glass, corridors of mirrors stretching into a depth that wasn't distance, and the vast, watchful presence that ruled over it. The Echo wasn't a story; it was the sovereign of the In Between—the realm that sat between here and there. Not heaven, not hell, but the place where unassigned souls were held and sorted when the paths ahead didn't fit. In that place, balance wasn't a metaphor; it was law. The weight of the In Between had to match the weight of the living world. When it didn't—when grief, violence, or sheer numbers tipped the scales—the Echo corrected it. Sometimes that meant dispatching Veilborne across the thin places to collect what was owed and bring the measure back to level.

Its authority was absolute, answering to only one power higher than anything Abigail could name. It did not argue. It pronounced, and the fabric on both sides adjusted. The council might pretend otherwise, but everyone who'd lived long here had seen what happened when you ignored an Echo—buildings closed, roads rerouted, funerals moved—because the times you didn't, you paid for it.

And the Echo knew her. It was the Echo that had cast her out of the In Between once, flinging her back into her skin with breath and purpose, and in that same turn sparing Joseph and Maria. So when Jacob said it spoke to him—spoke to him—Abigail felt the floor of ordinary explanations drop away. This wasn't a child repeating a rumor. If the Echo had singled him out, then the scales were shifting again, and whatever came next would not be a suggestion. It would be the law of that other country reaching into this one.

Jacob stepped past them, his small frame moving with unhurried ease. He padded into the living room and sank into the couch, as though he had said nothing out of the ordinary.

The kitchen remained hushed, the storm pressing against the windows.

Samuel's voice broke the silence at last, low and unsettled. "Abigail... what exactly have you been teaching him?"

She didn't answer. Her eyes stayed on the glass, on the crooked path a single raindrop traced down the pane. The memory of the In Between rose unbidden — the way glass had rippled around her, the way it had almost swallowed her whole.

Because if Jacob was right — if the Echo truly watched him, spoke to him — then it meant one of two things.

Either they were safer than she had ever dared to hope.

Or the Echo's interest meant something far darker was coming.

And Abigail couldn't decide which possibility frightened her more.

Scene 3: The Forbidden

The drive to Dupont wound through a stretch of damp evergreens, the highway slick beneath the steady rain. Abigail's wipers swept beads of water into arcs, revealing fleeting glimpses of fog clinging low to the treetops. The world seemed gray and half-formed, the road a narrow ribbon threading into mist. To the west, the Nisqually River basin sprawled unseen beneath the shroud of weather, its floodplain feeding out into the blurred line of Puget Sound.

Abigail kept her grip tight on the steering wheel. The case gnawed at her thoughts, but so did the history of where she was going.

She had researched the area before leaving, sifting through the fragments of past violence that clung like burrs to its soil. In January of 1846, the Hudson Bay Company trading post nearby had become a flashpoint in growing tensions between the Nisqually people and settlers. Land disputes, hunting rights, broken promises—each grievance bled into the next until anger turned to bloodshed.

The massacre still haunted these grounds. A dawn raid: settlers storming a Nisqually encampment. Men, women, children. Dozens slain. Some fell while fleeing; others were cut down as they reached the river. The water ran red and loud. Too few survivors remained to bury their dead. Traders later wrote of screams carrying across the inlet and nights when phantom drums pulsed in the fog. Voices whispered from the dark—words the settlers refused to learn, but understood enough to fear.

Chief Leschi, the Nisqually leader, had pleaded the tribe's case at Fort Steilacoom—arguing for land, for treaty promises, for simple justice. It did not matter. Soldiers arrested him. He was tried twice: the first jury hung, the second convicted. They hanged him from a tree just outside the fort, where Lakewood stands now. A rough stone marks the spot today, a hard memory set into the ground to remind anyone who asks what brutality looks like when it wears a uniform and a verdict.

Blood never washes away completely. Abigail knew this too well. Some places never heal; they call to the wrong things and feed them. Whether the Veilborne sought such wounds or merely found them irresistible, she couldn't say yet. The thought lingered as her tires crunched onto a narrow gravel drive lined with rain-heavy cedars.

The house revealed itself abruptly — a two-story with weather-darkened siding and shuttered windows. It looked less like a family home and more like a structure bracing against the storm.

Dana opened the door before Abigail reached the porch. Her face was pale, sleepless, her eyes rimmed with red. "You came fast," she whispered.

"I wanted to see it before anything else happened."

Inside, the air was thick and sour with the metallic tang of panic. Dana's husband stood in the living room, broad-shouldered and rigid, arms crossed over his chest. His eyes, sharp and suspicious, tracked Abigail's every move like she might bring the evil in with her.

"I just want to help," she said calmly, meeting his stare until he gave a reluctant nod.

Dana led her upstairs. The narrow hallway was dim, lit only by a bulb buzzing weakly at the ceiling. She stopped at the last door on the right, her hand hovering near the knob. "It's in there."

When the door swung open, Abigail saw the dresser first. The mirror loomed at the far wall, smothered under a thick blanket, its edges tucked down as though fabric alone could bar the way. The rest of the room was painfully ordinary: pale lavender walls, stuffed animals lined on a shelf, a scattering of clothes dropped by small hands. Yet beneath it all, the air was weighted, pressing against Abigail's skin with suffocating density.

"I need you all to wait outside," she murmured.

Dana's husband stiffened, but Dana touched his arm. He relented, though his glare lingered until the door shut behind them.

Silence pressed in at once, oppressive and complete. The room's air felt wrong, too heavy to breathe. A faint thread of sulfur coiled into her nose, sharp and stinging.

She moved toward the dresser. The blanket stirred faintly, as though a breath of wind had been caught beneath it. Abigail laid her hand against the fabric. It fluttered again — not from this side, but from the other.

She drew the blanket away, inch by inch. The final corner slipped to the carpet with a muffled thud. Immediately, a thin wind coiled around her ankles, spiraling like an unseen tide.

Then the smoke began. Ashen gray, bleeding from the mirror's surface as though the glass itself were burning into vapor.

Abigail's stomach clenched. She knew this rhythm — the way the air shifted, the sudden drop in temperature. She had seen it before, too many times. Yet familiarity never lessened the dread. Every encounter with the Veilborne felt like standing again at the edge of a bottomless pit, knowing the fall would consume her if she faltered even once.

The first hand emerged.

Talons, long and black, curled like iron hooks, pushed through the glass. They flexed against the air, swiping as if testing the room, their edges catching faint glimmers of the dim light. The sound was worse than the sight — a scraping, bone-on-stone rasp that made her teeth ache.

Abigail stepped back, forcing her breath steady, keeping the bed between herself and the mirror.

The claws stretched further, followed by the suggestion of arms, their surfaces rippling like smoke struggling to hold flesh.

Then the eyes appeared.

Twin embers, pale and lidless, flared inside the haze. They locked onto her immediately, pinning her in place with a gaze that wasn't just sight — it was intrusion, as though the creature was rifling through her thoughts and fears with a predator's patience.

The torso followed, twisting as it emerged. Its form was human only in mockery: too tall, limbs too long, flesh wavering between shadow and substance. It looked as if it had been carved from the smoke itself, each detail momentarily solid before unraveling again into vapor.

The room filled with a low hum, a vibration that rattled the dresser drawers and pressed into Abigail's chest. She wanted to recoil, to flee, but she planted her feet.

"Stop!" Her voice cracked, louder than she expected, cutting through the charged air.

The Veilborne froze. Its head tilted unnaturally, like a puppet yanked sideways on invisible strings. Its talons withdrew a fraction, uncertain. It had not expected defiance.

The silence stretched, vibrating with menace.

Then it spoke.

The voice was jagged, like stone dragged across stone, dry and grating. The words curled into the corners of the room, filling it like smoke.

"You."

The glow in its eyes dimmed, not with weakness but with recognition.

"The Witch. The Forbidden."

Abigail's heart thundered. She had been called many things by spirits, even called a witch by the Echo, but never that. Never — forbidden. The words landed with an authority that clawed at her bones.

Her fear spiked — ice-cold, threatening to unravel her. But she pulled herself taut against it, forcing steel into her voice. "Retreat. Go back through the portal. You won't come through here again."

The Veilborne sneered. Its mouth twisted into something almost human, but warped with disgust. A hiss seeped from between its teeth, low and venomous, vibrating the mirror's surface.

It lingered. Watching her. Its smoke-flesh writhed like a nest of serpents, shifting forward as though it might defy her command. The claws flexed, stretching, yearning for her.

Abigail held her ground. Terrified, yes — every muscle in her body screamed to run — but she forced her fear into stillness.

The creature recoiled. Reluctance burned in its gaze, but it obeyed.

Smoke dragged backward, curling into the glass, its form collapsing on itself until only the talons remained, scraping the frame with a final shriek. Then they, too, vanished. The mirror stilled, its surface reflecting only her pale, stricken face.

The silence that followed was deeper than before, suffocating. Her chest heaved, though her hands were steady. She had stood her ground. Again.

But the words echoed.

The Forbidden.

Her mind circled them, vulture-like. Was that what Jacob had meant? That she was untouchable to them? That the Echo itself had marked her?

She stared into the mirror, into her own reflection, pale and sharp in the dim lavender room. The smoke was gone, the claws vanished, but her heart told her it was not over.

Not by far.

And somewhere deep inside, she feared Jacob had been right.

The Veilborne could not touch her.

But that didn't mean worse things weren't coming.

Scene 4: The Man on the Screen

The rain had followed Abigail home, hammering against the windshield until the headlights of passing cars fractured into smeared halos. By the time she turned into the gravel drive, the lake beyond the trees was nothing but a dim silver shadow, blurred and restless beneath the curtain of water.

Inside, warmth greeted her, carrying the faint herbal scent of tea steeping. She toed off her damp shoes by the door, listening to the soft patter of rain against the roof. The house felt quiet, but not empty — a hush alive with the breath of the storm.

Samuel was in his usual armchair, its cushions molded by long familiarity. The glow of the television washed across his weathered features, outlining the grooves carved by years of strain and endurance. His eyes flicked toward her as she shrugged out of her coat, lingering with quiet concern. Jacob was nowhere in sight, likely upstairs bent over his drawings, lost in that private world of images he never fully explained.

Samuel turned the volume down until the TV was a faint murmur. "Well?" he asked, his tone measured but edged with tension. "How'd it go?"

Abigail set the coat across the back of the couch and sank onto its edge, elbows resting against her knees. Her sigh came out uneven, part exhaustion, part release, as though words might hold back the shiver of dread still lingering in her bones.

"The house sits on ground soaked with history," she said finally. "Not the kind anyone wants to remember. Nisqually River basin. Mid-1800s. There was a massacre there — settlers against the Nisqually people. Men, women, children… slaughtered in the dark."

Samuel's brow furrowed, shadows deepening the lines around his eyes. He said nothing, but she could feel his silence tightening around her words.

"At first I thought maybe that history, that grief, was enough to attract it. But it wasn't just that." She lifted her gaze to him, her voice dropping low. "It recognized me. Not just hunger. Recognition."

Samuel leaned forward slightly. "Recognized you?"

Abigail nodded, the memory sharp in her mind. "It called me something." She paused, tasting the words again, each one sour on her tongue. "The Witch. The Forbidden."

His eyes narrowed. "That's what Jacob said. About you being untouchable." He exhaled slowly, leaning back. "And you think he's speaking to the Echo?"

She hesitated, her hands knotting together in her lap. His question churned up memory, pulling her back to a place she had never wanted to revisit yet could never escape.

The In Between.

Her mind flinched at it, but the images came anyway, unfolding sharp and unrelenting. She had seen the Echo there, more than once. It did not look like the Veilborne — it was something other, something vast. It was not shadow nor smoke but a storm of presence, shape forever shifting, as though its form was only the residue of something larger than mortal sight could endure.

She remembered the first time clearly: the air in that liminal place vibrating with its approach, the walls of reality thinning until she thought her soul itself might unravel. And then its voice, not heard but felt — resonant, echoing through marrow and mind. It had named her there, too. Witch. Forbidden. The word had cracked across her like a verdict.

The last time, it had thrown her back—literally expelled her from the In Between as if she were an intruder—or worse, as if she'd been marked for something she did not yet understand. She could still hear it, the Echo's verdict knifing through the glass-lit dark: Witch. The word struck like a brand, and then came the shattering rush, the feeling of being hurled through a thousand mirrors at once, the cold hand of its judgment closing around her and flinging her into breath and bone. The sensation still haunted her dreams.

Even now, recalling it in the safety of her own home, she felt her skin prickle, her breath hitch.

Samuel was watching her carefully, reading the flicker of memory in her face though she had not spoken it aloud. "Abigail?"

She forced herself back to the present. "I don't know for certain," she murmured, voice low. "But Jacob isn't guessing. Whatever he's hearing, it's real to him. Maybe the Echo... maybe it has chosen to speak to him."

Silence pressed heavy between them. Samuel rubbed at his jaw, the rasp of stubble harsh in the quiet. His gaze held both worry and something else — a tenderness he rarely allowed to surface. It reminded her, suddenly and unbidden, of Ellen.

Ellen, his ex-wife, had known the terror too. Back in Schenectady, when their lives had been overturned by hauntings neither of them understood. Ellen had endured the scratching in the walls, the whispers at night, the shadows moving where no shadows should be. But when it grew too much — when the mirrors had rippled and the house itself seemed to breathe with malevolence — Ellen had chosen to flee. She had run from the fear, choosing the fragile safety of distance.

Samuel had stayed.

And Abigail… Abigail had done more than stay. She had lunged forward.

Now, watching him across the dimly lit room, she saw that same fear in his eyes again — not for himself, but for her. For what might happen if she followed Joseph's fate and became trapped forever in the glass.

"I think it means I'm untouchable," she admitted quietly, forcing the words out. "But I'm not about to test that theory."

He opened his mouth to reply, but before he could, a burst of laughter erupted from the television. It was sharp, grating, the kind of sound meant not to share joy but to humiliate.

Their eyes snapped to the screen. Samuel lifted the remote, turning the volume up.

The set of a late-night talk show gleamed beneath glaring studio lights. Behind the desk sat Russell Langston, a man whose entire demeanor radiated smirk. His hair was perfectly lacquered into place, his suit impeccable, but his eyes betrayed him — flat, mean, hungry for cruelty. The kind of predator who didn't claw or bite, but gutted with ridicule.

Across from him sat Reese Mathers, visibly uncomfortable but resolute. Reese was known to Abigail by reputation — a reporter who chased conspiracy theories. Many laughed at him, but she knew enough of his work to understand that sometimes, he was right.

Langston leaned across his desk, the smirk deepening. "So let me get this straight," he said, dragging out each syllable with gleeful contempt. "You're asking me — and America — to believe people are being sucked into their bathroom mirrors by ghostly boogeymen?"

The audience roared, eager to be part of the cruelty.

Reese tried to answer, but Langston cut him off, savoring the performance. "No, no, don't ruin it yet. Let's sit in the crazy a little longer." He turned to the camera, eyebrows arched in mock disbelief. "Folks, this is what happens when you spend too much time reading Reddit and not enough time touching grass."

The audience shrieked with laughter, feeding his ego.

Abigail felt her jaw tighten. She had seen men like Langston before — men who built their careers not on truth, but on how deeply they could cut others down.

Reese leaned forward, his voice firm though strained. "Call it what you want, but I've spoken to families. Dozens. They've seen hands come through the glass. Some have lost children. They're not lying."

Langston gave an exaggerated shiver, playing to the crowd. "Oh no, the big bad mirror hands are coming for us! Lock up your reflections, everyone!" The audience howled, his cruelty sharpening with each laugh.

Abigail's stomach turned.

Reese's jaw clenched, but he held steady. "Believe me or not, I'm going to keep investigating. People deserve to know."

Langston spread his hands, mock-solemn. "There you have it, ladies and gentlemen. Tonight's bedtime story, courtesy of Reese 'Mirror Monster' Mathers. Sweet dreams!"

The band struck up a cheerful outro. Langston leaned back, smirk plastered across his face, basking in the adoration of an audience too eager to laugh at someone else's expense.

Samuel clicked the TV off. Silence swept back into the room, heavy and absolute.

Abigail stared at the blank screen, her reflection faintly visible on its surface. Her voice was quiet when she spoke. "I wonder how much he really knows."

Samuel's eyes shifted to her, steady, resolute. "Maybe you should ask him."

3

Three Reckonings

Scene 1: Nothing to File

Reese Mathers woke with a start, the sound of glass clinking too close to his ear. For a moment, he couldn't tell if it was coming from the real world or the dream that had chased him into consciousness. The bottle at his side tipped as he sat up, rolling off the couch cushion and landing with a dull thunk. It hadn't shattered, but the remaining whiskey was gone.

His apartment was a cluttered cave of half-read printouts, crime scene photos, and dog-eared notebooks. Blankets were pushed off the couch, exposing the faded upholstery beneath, and the cracked blinds let in just enough light to reveal the dust hanging in the air like fog. A corkboard above the desk bore his madness like a shrine—photos of missing people, printouts of utility EMF charts, red string connecting what no one else wanted to believe were patterns.

He sat up slowly, blinking the sting from his dry eyes. His mouth tasted like copper and regret.

He was used to both.

On the coffee table, balanced between an ashtray and a mug of pens, lay a printout from a local ghost hunting forum. The headline read: "Mirror in Motel Room 7B Shows Woman Who Isn't There." He circled the word mirror in red ink, underlining it again and again.

Next to it were clippings from the city's missing persons files. One vanished near a lake. Another at a gas station. One had gone missing inside her own home—last seen in the reflection of her bathroom mirror, according to her terrified daughter.

He traced the thread from one photo to the next. They weren't random.

They were all being taken the same way.

His laptop, humming quietly under a stack of notes, displayed a map of EMF spikes overlaid with case locations. It was crude but undeniable. A crescent-shaped arc of disturbances, all within a fifty-mile radius of Tacoma. All within the last three months.

He obtained the data from a contact in the city's utilities department, who didn't realize what they were sending—and he wasn't about to tell them.

Some things you couldn't explain.

Near the corner of the board, a photo curled beneath a pushpin. It was old and grainy—his father in uniform, smiling beside a weathered Ford, one hand holding a manila file marked *"DOE."* Reese touched it, thumb brushing the corner gently.

"You'd have seen it," he whispered. "You'd have known."

His father had been a cop, then a private investigator—the kind of man who could smell a bent story from a block away. Ten years ago he was killed in a hit-and-run while working a case tied to city infrastructure money. The driver was never found; the file sits in a drawer marked *ACCIDENT* until someone brings proof to the contrary.

That was the official story.

The unofficial one never made it into a report. Reese rubbed the bridge of his nose and reached for his phone. His editor had called twice.

He took a breath, then hit redial.

"Mathers," came the gravelly voice of Carl Braddock, managing editor at the Seattle Spectral. "Tell me you've got something usable."

"I'm onto something," Reese said, already bracing.

"Not the mirror thing again."

"There's a connection. I've got six cases, all in the same EMF band."

"I asked for the solar infrastructure story. Solar. Not spooks in bathroom glass."

"There's something happening here, Carl. Reflections. Disappearances. And now there's this guy—Elias Voss. He's siphoning EMF with some device and the grid's lighting up like Christmas around the cases. It's all linked."

"You sound like a lunatic, Mathers."

Reese pinched the bridge of his nose. "Just give me a little more time. You'll have something no one else does."

There was silence on the line.

"You want to know the truth?" Carl said. "I keep you around because every now and then your lunacy hits something big. You gave me the prison ghost debunk. The ferry leak story. But if this mirror crap burns me in print, we're done."

"I won't file it until I've got the proof."

"You will file when you have something that's real—truth I can stand behind and proof I can show legal. No guesses, no vibes. Bring me what we can print."

The call ended.

Reese exhaled and leaned back, staring at the cracks in the ceiling. His hands shook. Not enough to drop the phone, but enough to make it hard to steady the pen when he picked it up again. Since his father was killed—the Gibraltar Rock in his life, the unmovable stone that kept everything else from sliding—nothing felt anchored. The man who'd kept him in line, who could make noisy rooms go quiet, was gone. Reese had filled the silence with a bottle, first to sleep, then to forget, then because it was what the day knew.

He knew what his father would say if he could see him now. Not like this, kid. Not this way. The thought landed hard. He'd been white-knuckling AA for months—bad coffee, folding chairs, the whole circle of stories that sounded too much like his own. Some nights he made it through. Some nights he didn't. Tonight he wanted to. He had to.

He reached for the flask hidden behind the EMF map. Paused. Put it back.

Not yet. Not for this.

He dragged in a breath, forced his focus to the notes. Sober, if possible. Sober, because his father would expect it. He glanced at the laptop screen just in time to see it flicker—once, twice. The icons warped and, for a heartbeat, the screen went black.

His own reflection stared back.

Only it wasn't quite right.

It smiled.

Then the screen returned to normal.

He stared at it for a long time. The cursor blinked. Nothing else moved.

He clicked open his browser and typed a name he hadn't searched since the Franklin, Louisiana case.

Abigail Jensen — Spiritual Consultant

Years ago he'd first stumbled across her while reading Echoes in the Glass, a narrative that threaded real events with the town's history. The book detailed a plantation curse and an antique clock that held a trapped soul—Abigail's intervention had freed it. After that, she'd written her own book about the ordeal and made the rounds on a few TV shows, the kind that cut footage to make the unexplainable look neat. Other writers piled on with their versions, too. Still, the pattern had stuck with him: a life caught near glass, a hand reaching through reflection.

Now the same kind of incidents were surfacing here—people snatched in the vicinity of mirrors and dark screens—and Reese realized she might be the one person who could help him make sense of it.

Her website loaded slowly: a dark, minimalist page, a photo of a woman in her forties with calm eyes and salt-and-pepper hair. It didn't scream fraud. It whispered survivor.

He bookmarked the page and stared at it.

Then he opened his voice recorder app and began to dictate:

"Case notes, Reese Mathers. Working idea: those new power rigs—like the Voss Array—might be messing with whatever 'charge' hangs in places with ugly history. When the air gets loud there, the weird gets louder too. I'm starting to think something can cross over through reflections. People aren't just spooking themselves; they're vanishing near glass. The disappearances line up with days the field feels strongest."

He swallowed, voice dropping.

"My father was chasing DOE ghosts. I think I finally found them."

He saved the file and leaned back.

Outside, the sun was setting over the city. Shadows lengthened across the buildings. Reflections shimmered in every passing window.

He drew the curtain.

For now.

Scene 2: The Denial of Progress

The press conference hall at the Tacoma Municipal Convention Center was humming with forced optimism—coffee-fueled conversation, badge scanners chirping, the low hiss of distant HVAC. Rows of plastic chairs stretched toward a modest platform draped in a blue-and-white banner: *"The Future of Energy: The Voss Array and Urban EMF Integration."*

Reese Mathers sat two rows back, stiff-backed in a rumpled gray blazer, his fingers tapping his thigh in uneven staccato. The air smelled of hotel disinfectant and lukewarm pastries. To his left, a young reporter from the Daily Tribune leaned in toward her colleague and whispered something behind a raised hand. Reese caught only fragments—"...that's him... guy from the Spectral... another ghost piece..."

He tried not to react, but his jaw tightened. He'd been hearing variations of that for years.

Ghost piece. UFO chaser. Theories with no legs.

The young reporter's voice drifted again: "Didn't he get drunk on camera once?"

Her companion chuckled. "Yeah, but he says it was 'low blood sugar.' Got a clip on YouTube. Still gets comments."

Reese closed his eyes. Breathed in. Let the noise fade.

They don't know the whole story. They never do.

He sat straighter when the room dimmed and the stage lights flared to life. A tall figure stepped forward, flanked by a short woman holding a tablet. Dr. Elias Voss. Crisp, silver-gray coat. The sheen of calculated genius. A man who had learned to weaponize his intelligence into reputation.

Reese hated men like him.

"Thank you all for being here," Elias began, his voice crisp and rehearsed. "We stand at the edge of a new energy paradigm. The Voss Array is capable of converting naturally occurring electromagnetic frequencies from the atmosphere into clean, stable power—without combustion, without wind, without sunlight. It is power that simply... exists."

A smattering of polite applause followed. The woman at his side—Lena Mirek, Reese remembered—stepped up and began translating Elias's language into more palatable terms.

"What Dr. Voss is saying," she said with a smile, "is that the Array can draw ambient power from the electromagnetic haze of modern life. Cell towers, traffic grids, static accumulations, even certain geological hotspots. It's not magic. It's physics."

But Reese wasn't buying it. He leaned forward, eyes narrowed.

As the Q&A began, hands went up around the room. Predictable questions. Technical performance. Grid compatibility. Projected yield curves.

Then Reese raised his hand.

Elias saw him.

A flicker of something—recognition, annoyance—passed behind the scientist's eyes. He nodded. "Yes. Reese Mathers. Seattle Spectral, isn't it?"

Polite chuckles rippled through the crowd.

Reese stood. "Dr. Voss, in your last field test, there were reports of mirror-based disturbances. A sculpture fractured during an EM sync event. Some said their reflections... lagged. Any comment on that?"

Elias's smile tightened. "We measure electromagnetic resonance, Mr. Mathers. Not phantoms."

Reese didn't blink. "What about the recent disappearances in the South Sound area? Six cases in the last two months, all near locations with EMF anomalies. Three of them involved mirrors—bathrooms, security cameras, car side mirrors. There's a pattern here."

Elias pinched the bridge of his nose, clearly annoyed. "You can draw a pattern on a napkin if you stare at it long enough. Tell your readers to stick with real reporting, not message boards claiming ghosts hitch rides on microwaves."

Muted laughter broke from the back of the room.

Reese pressed on, steady and stubborn.

"You're harvesting EMF," he said, louder now. "You said that yourself. But spiritual researchers—many of them—have documented that spirits, particularly restless ones, emit residual EMF. If that's true... what exactly are you pulling into your machine?"

Elias's voice sharpened. "This is science, Mr. Mathers. I don't traffic in fantasy." He held Reese's gaze a beat longer, a thin glare that read, Is that it?, then looked away and lifted a hand toward the other reporters. "Next question."

Reese lowered his hand slowly and sat, pulse thudding in his temples. Around him, whispers stirred again.

"He's nuts," someone said near the aisle.

"Crackpot theory guy," another muttered. "Always with the haunted angle."

Reese's face burned. He knew how he looked to them—sweaty, pale, a little too thin around the face, like he hadn't eaten properly in days. Which was true. His hand trembled slightly as he picked up his notepad, the shakes just beginning. He could feel the bottle in his glove compartment calling to him already.

But he bit down hard on the inside of his cheek, riding the sting like a handhold. Let the pain pull him back from the edge. The shakes were there—small, traitor tremors in his fingers—along with the sour sweat, the cotton mouth, the crawl under his skin that came when he hadn't slept and hadn't poured. He'd white-knuckled through worse: meetings in church basements, nights counting breaths instead of bottles. People had laughed before. They'd roll their eyes again.

And they didn't know what he knew.

They hadn't stared at those EMF maps, hadn't noticed the arc of missing people curving across the county like the crescent of a wound. They hadn't read those message board posts from people who'd seen their reflections grin when they weren't smiling. Or scream in silence when their mouths stayed closed.

He had.

He'd seen the flicker. Felt the pull.

And he was going to prove it.

Elias stepped away from the podium, nodding once more to the reporters. "Thank you for your time. The future awaits."

The conference ended in a wash of light chatter and the rustling of coats and camera bags. Reese moved toward the exit alone, pushing through the crowd like a ghost himself.

Outside, the air was crisp. A gray drizzle dampened his shoulders as he climbed into his car—a very old Toyota he couldn't afford to replace, its dash cracked like dry riverbed. The factory radio was older than some interns he knew: chunky push-buttons stuck and half-broken so it could only pick two ancient presets after the tuner died years ago. He shut the door on the rain, sighed at the dashboard's groan, and thumbed his phone to start a voice memo.

"Reese Mathers. Day ...I don't even remember now. The Voss Array continues to pull measurable EMF—confirmed by multiple third-party data sources. The mirror anomalies remain unacknowledged. Voss denies all spiritual links."

He paused.

"Conclusion: he's either lying... or dangerously ignorant."

He ended the recording and slumped back in his seat.

Across the street, in the glossy reflection of the convention center's glass doors, he saw himself—doubled, faint. The light of the conference room still flickered behind him, caught in the reflection like an afterimage. Just for a second, his reflection lingered longer than it should have. Then blinked.

And smiled.

Reese stared.

But when he turned, the doors were empty. Just the wet shimmer of light on glass.

He wiped his face with both hands and laughed once—quiet and humorless.

He pulled out his phone, brought up Abigail Jensen: Spiritual Consultancy, and saved the site to his Favorites.

Maybe it was time to call in someone who knew how to look beyond the veil.

Maybe, finally, someone would believe him.

Scene 3: Ghosts in the Archive

The Pierce College server room was always too cold.

Rows of blinking towers stood like monoliths in the dark, their soft hum barely audible beneath the low drone of cooling fans. The air held that stale chill of machinery left to its own devices—sterile, humming, indifferent. Fluorescent tubes buzzed overhead, flickering once as the motion sensor registered movement and bathed the space in a sickly white glow.

Elias Voss stepped inside and let the door shut behind him with a whispering click. He stood there for a moment, not moving. Not listening for voices or footsteps—but for something less tangible. Some vibration in the air. The sense that he was not alone.

The hum of the servers carried a rhythm now, something almost musical. A pulse beneath the electric breath of machines. Like a heartbeat trapped behind concrete and steel.

He moved quickly down the aisle to a terminal tucked in the back—one no one used anymore. A monitor that still ran on outdated architecture, tied to legacy systems the university had long since forgotten. But Elias hadn't.

He slipped a bypass key into the side port. Guilt flickered as his fingers typed the override from memory. Those credentials should have been retired after Camille's death—after the internal review, the tightened protocols, the long meetings about safeguards and sign-offs. But some doors, once opened, never truly close.

A loading bar scrolled across the screen, then gave way to a directory.

/Voss-Kessler_Prototype_Research/

There it was. The folder he'd buried—the one that felt more like a grave every time he opened it.

Kessler – Untitled Feedback Experiments

His finger hovered over the mouse. The cursor blinked. So did he. Then he clicked.

Inside were subfolders with cryptic names: *"Phase Drift Tests," "Field Mirror Response," "Containment Reflection Variance,"* and one ominously marked in red: *DANGER_TO_LIVING_SYSTEMS?*

The files hadn't been touched in almost a year—not since Fort Steilacoom. Not since Camille.

He opened a video labeled *"Feedback_Coil_Test_X31."* Grainy footage stuttered to life. A younger version of himself stood beside Adrian Kessler, both of them leaner, more driven, more alive. Between them stood a primitive version of the Voss Array—bare steel frame, exposed coils, wires bundled like intestines. Camille's voice came faintly from behind the camera, describing the calibration.

The prototype began to hum.

In front of it sat a mirror.

The reflection shimmered unnaturally. The waveform monitors behind the apparatus lit up, spiking erratically. Camille's voice sharpened.

"That's not in phase. Pull it down—pull it down!"

The video cut off in a burst of digital noise.

Elias swallowed hard and clicked into a handwritten scan labeled *"Kessler – Notes (Unshared)."* The document was chaos—math equations tangled in wild loops, diagrams of field distortion, black scribbles blotting out earlier sections. One line had been underlined three times:

"It mimics bioelectric signatures. This isn't random EMF—it's behavioral. It reacts."

Another scrawled section near the margin read:

"Localized harmonic loops form near trauma sites. Mirrors accelerate convergence. DO NOT operate near reflective surfaces without revised containment. Field mirrors are acting like conductors for residual memory."

Elias leaned back, server light blinking across his lenses like a metronome he refused to follow. Kessler had always been paranoid—brilliant, erratic, convinced they were poking at something deeper than harmonics.

Elias had waved him off. He waved off everyone.

Kessler said they were waking echoes. Elias said they were waking data.

Camille had been measured. She brought him the same spikes, smoothed and annotated, explained the pattern without reaching for folklore. "There's something reactive in the field," she said. "We don't know the range yet." She chose her words like instruments. She didn't call it spiritual. She didn't have to. He could see the fear she was trying to keep out of the lab.

And he overrode it—hers, Kessler's, all of it—because his experiment mattered more than their nerves. Because he needed the proof more than he needed their comfort. Because he believed, with a clean, dangerous certainty, that being right would make the fear irrelevant. He ignored her anyway.

He opened another file—a correspondence log buried deep in the archive. One unread email pulsed at the top.

From: ad.kessler@uwarchive.net
To: elias.voss@uwresearch.edu
Subject: [URGENT] Stop Deployment

Eli—

I'm telling you again, for the last time. There's a pattern to the resonance. This isn't just technical—it's neurological. Spiritual, even. I know you don't believe in that, but it doesn't matter.

The feedback echoes people. Thoughts. Pain. It's an imprint. We're not just collecting energy. We're disturbing something.

If Camille sees this—and I'm sending it to her too—maybe she'll listen. But you need to stop. We're not ready. And something is wrong.

Elias stared at the screen. He hadn't read it back then. Maybe because he hadn't wanted to. Maybe because part of him already knew.

Behind him, a ripple passed through the glass panel above the terminal. The reflection warped—not his own, but something else. A shadow—long and undefined—passed across the mirrored surface without moving through the room.

He didn't turn.

Instead, he highlighted the folder.

DELETE FOLDER? YES / NO

He clicked *YES.*

The progress bar inched forward, chewing through what was left: Kessler's cautions, Camille's careful notes, her voice threaded through the metadata like breath. He watched it go because he couldn't bear to keep it—because keeping it meant living with the chance she'd been right and he'd been the one who didn't listen. Guilt pressed hard; ambition pressed harder. If the Array worked, it would all make sense. If it failed, he didn't want this evidence standing in the wreckage pointing at him.

Line after line vanished. The last timestamp blinked, then dissolved.

Gone.

The room felt colder. The hum of the servers was louder now, but hollow. Like something breathing too close to his ear.

He yanked the flash drive from the port, wiped the terminal log, and shut down the system. As he turned to leave, a monitor flickered—then steadied. Just a glitch.

Maybe.

Later, back in his office, Elias poured a shallow glass of scotch and stared at his desk. He hadn't turned the light on. Shadows spilled long across the floor, stretched by the sickly green of his monitor's idle glow.

A voicemail notification blinked on his phone.

He hit play.

He'd saved the last voicemail he ever got from his wife to the phone's memory. Camille's voice—softer than he remembered—filtered through the speaker.

"Eli... something's wrong. The machine—it doesn't feel right. You need to stop. Promise me."

Silence.

He set the phone down, face-down, and stood.

Across the room, the window had fogged slightly. That was impossible—there was no temperature difference, no condensation. But there it was: a smudge, like breath on glass.

As he walked over, the light above flickered once, then again.

And in the window's reflection—not his face, but something behind him. Human-shaped. Watching.

He spun.

Nothing.

The office was empty.

Of course it was.

He opened the cabinet beneath the bookshelf and retrieved the old backup drives. One by one, he placed them into the desk drawer and locked it with a key that felt too small for the weight it held.

The Voss Array worked. It was revolutionary. It was the future.

But the past refused to stay buried.

The lights steadied. The hum receded. Elias stood in the half-dark, hand resting on the locked drawer.

He whispered her name.

"Camille."

There was no answer. But the window smudged again.

And this time, he didn't wipe it clean.

Scene 4: A Man Forgotten

Rain pattered against the windows of the run-down studio apartment in Portland. The light from the television flickered dimly across walls plastered with schematics, old research notes, and grainy newspaper clippings. Everything looked aged, damp at the corners, stained with time, wine, and perhaps even blood. In the center of it all sat Dr. Adrian Kessler—once a rising star in the world of experimental physics, now a shadow of himself.

He was slumped in a fraying armchair, nursing a bottle of cheap whiskey like it was the only warmth left in his life. His hand trembled slightly, not from the cold, but from the unrelenting weight of guilt and drink. His unshaven face was gaunt, and his eyes—once sharp with ambition—were hollow and red-rimmed.

The television droned in the background, barely audible, broadcasting a recording of Elias Voss's latest press conference. Adrian didn't need to hear the words. He could already guess the lies.

"Clean energy for the future," Elias said, his voice distant, tinny.

Adrian stared at the screen. Elias stood tall and confident in his tailored suit, every word crisp and deliberate. Behind him stood the Voss Array, sleek and menacing, humming with potential.

A laugh escaped Adrian's throat—bitter, broken. "You son of a...," he muttered, raising the bottle to his lips. "You're still at it."

He turned his head slightly and glanced at a photograph pinned to the wall beside the TV. Camille.

She was smiling in the photo, her arm around Adrian at a university mixer. Her auburn hair spilled over her shoulders in waves, her eyes gleaming with life and mischief. It had been taken during the early days of the Array project—when the three of them had still been a team. Before Elias started locking files. Before the patent applications with only one name on them. Before the betrayal.

Before Fort Steilacoom.

He closed his eyes. The memory returned without permission.

The wind howled that day at the asylum ruins—the old Hill Ward—the sky overcast with a pale sun struggling to break through. Camille stood near the resonance coils, double-checking the calibration. Elias had insisted on a live field test despite Adrian's repeated protests. The readings had already shown harmonic instability. Adrian knew it wasn't ready. But Elias wouldn't listen. He never listened.

So Adrian had done something desperate. Something reckless.

He disabled the fail-safe on the containment manifold.

Just briefly. Just enough to make the surge visible. To scare Elias. To force him to acknowledge the risk.

He hadn't known Camille would be the one to step into the chamber that day.

He heard the scream again, the sound swallowed by the roar of the machine as it surged and collapsed. He had been too far to stop it, too slow to change anything.

Afterward, Elias had knelt beside her body. Frozen. Trembling. Adrian had watched from a distance, his gut roiling with something he refused to name.

He hadn't meant for her to die.

But she had.

And Elias had walked away with her name on his lips and not an ounce of blame on his shoulders. He played the grieving genius, the martyred scientist. And the world ate it up.

Adrian had been erased.

No credit. No acknowledgment. Elias filed every patent under his name. Even the original resonance feedback models—Adrian's models—had been retitled and rebranded. His contributions scrubbed clean.

Camille was dead. Elias was a hero. And Adrian had become a ghost.

He reached for another file folder and opened it on his lap. Inside were the latest public power grid EMF readings. He had pulled them through backdoor access channels he still remembered from their university days. The Array's signatures were there, unmistakable. But something was different now.

The surges were consistent. Patterned.

Responding.

Adrian stared at the frequency curves. They pulsed like heartbeats. He had seen this once before, in the early feedback loops. The readings mimicked bioelectric signatures. Camille had seen it too. She had warned Elias.

He had the voicemail to prove it. He kept it on a tiny recorder beside his mattress:

"Eli... something's wrong. The machine—it doesn't feel right. You need to stop. Promise me."

Adrian had listened to it more times than he could count. And every time, it carved a deeper trench into his soul.

He rose unsteadily and walked to the kitchenette, pouring another splash of whiskey into a chipped mug. On the cracked counter lay a shard of mirror. He glanced into it as he lifted the drink.

But the reflection wasn't his own.

Camille's face stared back. Pale. Wide-eyed. Her lips parted slightly in silent terror, her skin translucent like mist behind glass.

He dropped the mug. It shattered on the floor.

Breathing hard, Adrian staggered backward, wiping sweat from his brow. The shard sat motionless on the counter again, showing only the flicker of the TV screen now.

He sat heavily at his desk, tears pricking his eyes.

"I didn't mean for you to die," he whispered. "I just wanted to stop him. I just wanted him to hear me."

The wall above his desk was a patchwork of headlines, field notes, and photos of people who'd vanished—most of them last seen near glass or dark screens. After a week combing Seattle Spectral pieces by Reese Mathers, the line snapped tight in Adrian's head: disappearances spiking on the same days the Voss Array ran hot. He circled timestamps, drew arrows to run logs, and pinned Mathers's latest article dead center.

His gaze slid to the clipping beside it, glossy and triumphant: *VOSS ARRAY HERALDS NEW ERA OF CLEAN ENERGY.* Elias's smile, Elias's quotes, Elias's name in bold where Adrian's work used to live.

Adrian uncapped a red marker and, under the headline, printed in uneven block letters:

THIEF

He stepped back, heart pounding.

Elias would not be stopped by ethics. He had already silenced Camille. Buried Adrian. Ignored every warning sign the data gave.

But something was happening now. The mirrors. The disappearances. The energy readings.

And Adrian knew the truth.

The Voss Array wasn't just collecting ambient energy. It was feeding on something else. Something alive.

He would find a way to stop it.

Not just to punish Elias. But because this time, if he did nothing, more people would die.

And he couldn't carry another name on his conscience.

Especially not hers.

4

The Humbling

Scene 1: The Jester's Fall

The studio lights blazed white-hot, reflecting off the polished desk like the glare of an interrogation lamp. Russell Langston thrived under that glare. It was his sun, his stage, his crown jewel. Behind him, the Northwest Point logo gleamed on the big screen, proud and pulsing in deep blue. In the rows of seats beyond the cameras, tonight's audience buzzed with the eager hum of anticipation, waiting to be entertained, waiting to be told who they could laugh at guilt-free.

Russell tugged at his tie, already smiling. He didn't need the cue cards scattered across his desk; he never had. His lines were memorized, sharpened like blades, ready to draw blood.

"Three, two, one—" The floor manager's fingers sliced the air, and the red light flared.

"Good evening, Seattle!" Russell boomed, his voice rich, theatrical, dripping with practiced charm. "Welcome back to Northwest Point, where reason comes to wrestle nonsense — and nonsense always leaves bruised!"

The audience laughed, on cue, like Pavlov's dogs. Russell leaned back, letting it wash over him. He basked in their approval as if it were oxygen, a rush that filled the empty place inside him where empathy should have lived.

"Our first guest tonight," he went on, flipping his cue card with a flourish he didn't need, "is a local author who insists that dreams — yes, you heard that right — can predict the future. Move aside, meteorologists! Forget weather satellites! Tonight, we're predicting rain based on what Aunt Carol dreamed after her third glass of pinot."

The crowd roared. Russell smirked at the young woman seated nervously across from him. She was dressed modestly, her hands folded tightly in her lap, her face betraying the effort it took to smile through the ridicule.

"So tell me," Russell said, leaning forward, his voice dropping into a conspiratorial whisper the microphone still carried perfectly, "when you had a dream about writing this book, did you wake up and think, Yes! The world needs my nap diary!"

Laughter again, harder this time, rolling like thunder across the studio. The woman tried to speak, her lips trembling around words about case studies and evidence, but Russell was too quick. He slammed his hand on the desk, feigning shock.

"Ladies and gentlemen! Science has been saved! Forget physics, forget chemistry. Just take a nap, and the universe will reveal its secrets. I, for one, am going to bed after this show and dream myself a Nobel Prize."

The laughter was cruel, and Russell fed off it. He saw the sheen of tears beginning in her eyes, the way she shrank into herself, and he loved it. There was nothing sweeter than breaking a guest down until the audience no longer saw them as human, just as fodder.

When the applause subsided, Russell leaned back in his chair, grinning like a cat with feathers in its teeth. "Now, now, don't be shy. You remind me of another guest we had not long ago. Some of you might remember him. Reese Mathers? Conspiracy chaser extraordinaire?"

The crowd murmured, some chuckled knowingly. Russell seized it, riding the wave.

"Oh, yes. Reese Mathers. The man who sat right there—" he gestured broadly at the chair — "and told us that people were being pulled into their bathroom mirrors. With straight-faced sincerity, mind you. I mean, I don't know about you, but I checked my mirror that night and the only thing looking back at me was a man who needed another drink!"

The audience erupted. Russell grinned wider.

"Reese, if you're watching, I hope you've forgiven us for laughing. But honestly — mirrors swallowing people? That was gold. Pure gold. It was the best comedy segment we've had in years, and it wasn't even meant to be comedy."

He glanced at his guest with mock sympathy. "Don't worry, sweetheart, you're not as far gone as Reese. Yet. But keep at it, keep selling those dream journals, and who knows? Maybe you'll earn yourself a starring role in my next highlight reel."

The young woman tried to interject, but the audience drowned her out with laughter again. The camera panned over their faces, rows of strangers gleefully complicit in her humiliation.

Russell turned back to the desk, basking in the roar. For a moment, his smile faltered, not visible to the cameras. He thought briefly of his father's belt, his mother's sneer — the way they'd both ridiculed him until ridicule was all he understood. Cruelty had been his cradle, and now it was his crown. If no one had cared for him, why should he care for anyone else?

But the falter was gone as quickly as it came. He was Russell Langston, king of Northwest late-night. He thrived on this. Cruelty was currency, and he was the richest man in the room.

The floor manager gestured again. Commercial break.

The audience clapped as the lights dimmed and the house band struck up a few jazzy bars. Russell leaned back in his chair, sipping from his water glass. He caught his reflection in the glossy surface of the teleprompter — perfect hair, perfect suit, perfect smirk. Untouchable.

He chuckled to himself, low and smug. "Still killing it, Russ."

Scene 2: The Making of a Monster

Russell Langston's laugh filled the studio like broken glass rattling down a steel chute. The audience clapped on cue, some genuinely entertained, others unwilling to risk being the odd ones silent. His cruelty was a kind of performance art — a smirk, a sarcastic flick of his eyebrow, a practiced pause that made mockery sound like revelation. To them, he was confidence personified. To Russell, it was survival polished into a brand.

But beneath the tailored suits and slicked-back hair was a boy who had learned very early that if he didn't strike first, someone else would.

Russell grew up in a house where laughter was never kind. His father's voice was a perpetual sneer, always sharpened into a blade. His mother, brittle with bitterness, joined in — sometimes with words, sometimes with silence that cut even deeper.

"You'll never amount to anything, Russell," his father spat one night after catching him with a report card dotted in C's. "Can't even add numbers right, and you think the world owes you something? Pathetic."

Russell had only been ten.

At school, he was no safer. The playground was a coliseum where stronger boys shoved him into lockers, dumped his lunch, or mocked his stutter until his throat locked tight. He tried fighting back once — one wild swing that connected with another boy's jaw — but the beating he received afterward drilled the lesson in: strength wasn't about fists. It was about perception.

So Russell studied. Not books, not equations—people.

As a kid his words tripped over each other, a stubborn stutter that made classrooms feel like traps. Over time it loosened its grip. He lost his stutter. He learned to speak cleanly, then quickly, and—once he heard laughter land on his side—to speak cleverly. Wit became a tool first, then armor. He learned the rhythm of cruelty, how humiliation clings longer than bruises, and he taught himself to strike first. If he could make someone smaller with a single phrase, he felt larger. Safer. Untouchable.

By high school, his tongue was sharper than any fist. Teachers called him disruptive; classmates called him a menace; but they laughed, and in laughter came power.

He realized something else, too: when the crowd was laughing at his target, they weren't laughing at him.

College gave him a stage. Student radio, then a campus talk show. Russell discovered his gift was not conversation, but dismantling it. He didn't debate — he eviscerated. He didn't interview — he cornered, mocked, reduced. Ratings soared.

When a professor pulled him aside, warning he was "cultivating cruelty at the expense of empathy," Russell smiled in the man's face and replayed the words later as a punchline on air. Empathy had never saved him as a child. Cruelty had.

Fame followed. Small cable networks, late-night slots. He sharpened his persona with precision: the smug smile, the pause before a barb, the raised brow that invited the audience in on the joke. People craved spectacle, and he gave it to them.

What no one saw was Russell alone, staring in the mirror of his dressing room as he rehearsed. Sometimes, after a particularly vicious segment, he'd catch his reflection lingering too long. Not a man in command, but the boy who once trembled in the dark. He'd sneer back at the glass, muttering, Weak. Pathetic. The reflection never argued.

The ratings made him invincible, or so he thought. His producers wanted sharper hooks, bigger spectacles. Russell delivered. He mocked grieving parents, ridiculed believers, tore down politicians and preachers alike. The more outrageous, the higher the viewership.

But each time he looked in the mirror afterward, the unease returned. Sometimes he swore he saw shadows move just behind his reflection — as if the glass itself disapproved. He told himself it was fatigue. He worked harder.

The previous night's show had been a highlight in his eyes. He'd compared a conspiracy theorist to Reese Mathers — the "mirror man" who embarrassed himself on national TV weeks earlier. The crowd had howled at the comparison, chanting Reese's name like a punchline. Russell had soaked it in, a predator reveling in his hunt.

And yet, later, standing alone in his apartment, Russell replayed the footage. Reese hadn't backed down. He'd looked beaten, yes, but stubborn — a flicker of something Russell recognized and hated. Defiance.

Russell downed half a bottle of whiskey before bed, trying to quiet the echo of Reese's last words: "People deserve to know before it's too late."

Russell's cruelty was a mask welded to his skin. The child beaten and belittled was still inside, but buried under layers of venom he now wore like armor.

If the world had shown him kindness, perhaps he might have grown differently. But the world hadn't.

And now, millions tuned in not for truth, but for the thrill of seeing someone crushed beneath his words. He obliged them every night, feeding his ratings — and his hunger — with other people's humiliation.

Yet even predators sometimes sense a greater predator circling. Russell didn't know it yet, but his reflection had already betrayed him. Something beyond the glass had been watching.

Waiting.

Scene 3: The Witch on Stage

The lights were too bright. Abigail Jensen could feel their heat pressing down on her scalp as she waited behind the curtain. The studio was colder than she expected, the kind of industrial chill that seeped from concrete walls and too much air conditioning, but under the glare of the rigged lamps, sweat collected at her collarbone.

A young production assistant tapped her headset, glanced at a clipboard, and gave Abigail a perfunctory smile. "You're up in ninety seconds. Just follow my lead, and don't look at the floor monitors — they'll distract you. Mr. Langston will bring you out."

Abigail nodded, though her stomach was already coiling. She wasn't new to speaking in public — book signings, podcast interviews, lectures at paranormal conferences — but this was different. This was national television. And it was Russell Langston's show.

She had seen what he did to guests. Reese Mathers had been his most recent chew toy, torn apart in front of a gleeful studio audience. Abigail had watched the clip online, her jaw tightening at every smirk, every line of ridicule. Reese had tried to hold his ground, but Langston was a professional predator. His arena, his rules.

Now, she was about to step into the same ring.

Abigail knew Russell's show could be a meat grinder, but it also reached more people in one hour than she could in a year of readings. The invitation had landed the same week the Veilborne abductions spiked, and she kept thinking about families who didn't have names yet for what they were seeing in the glass. If walking into a hostile studio meant she could warn them—cover mirrors, take the signs seriously, believe the taken weren't "making it up"—then a little public mockery was a fair price. Yes, she'd mention her book; it gave people a map. But the real reason was simpler: the threat was growing, and she had a chance to put a human voice to it. If he tried to make her small, she would hold steady. If even a few people listened, the sacrifice would be worth it.

The band struck up a brassy cue. Russell's voice carried across the studio — smooth, theatrical, dripping with the confidence of someone who had never feared being wrong. "Ladies and gentlemen, we've got a special treat tonight. Our next guest is an author who claims to see what the rest of us can't. Spirits, phantoms, things that go bump in the night." He leaned on the words with exaggerated skepticism. "She's written a new book — Whispers Beyond the Glass. Please welcome… Abigail Jensen."

The curtain parted.

Abigail walked out, spine straight, book in hand. The audience clapped dutifully, some curious, others smirking, already primed to laugh. Russell met her halfway with a grin that was all teeth, shook her hand like he was doing her a favor, and guided her to the guest chair.

"Abigail," he said, sliding into his desk seat, "thank you for joining us. You're very brave. Or very bold. One of the two."

The audience chuckled.

Abigail set the book on her lap, folded her hands over it, and gave him a small, polite smile. "Thank you for having me."

Russell leaned back, crossing one leg over the other. "So… ghosts. Spirits. You actually believe in this stuff?"

"I don't just believe in it," Abigail said evenly. "I've seen it. I've helped people living in haunted homes, people tormented by things they couldn't explain. The accounts in my book aren't fantasies. They're experiences."

Russell spread his hands wide, turning to the audience. "She's seen them, folks! Not on TV, not in the movies, but in real life." He dropped his voice to a stage whisper. "Apparently Casper is alive and well."

The crowd erupted in laughter. Abigail sat still, her smile unchanged, though she felt her pulse climb.

"I'm not here to convince anyone who doesn't want to be convinced," she said once the laughter subsided. "I'm here to give voice to people who've been ignored, dismissed, or told they were crazy. These experiences matter. They deserve respect."

Russell tilted his head, squinting at her like she was an oddity under glass. "Respect. Sure. But tell me this, Abigail — how many of these spirits you've seen are, I don't know, paying rent? Doing laundry? If they're real, why don't we see them on the street corner waiting for the bus?"

The laughter came again, sharp and cruel.

Abigail let it pass. She inhaled, steady. "Because that isn't how it works. Spirits are bound by trauma, by energy. They don't walk the streets like pedestrians. They're caught in echoes, fragments of moments. And sometimes... sometimes something darker uses that echo to reach through."

Russell arched his brow, feigning intrigue. "Oh? Darker? Please, enlighten us. Are we talking demons? Goblins? Or maybe — my personal favorite — the boogeyman under the bed?"

The audience howled. Abigail gripped her book tighter, knuckles blanching.

"Not the boogeyman," she said firmly. "But yes, there are entities that are not simply ghosts. I call them Veilborne. They come from a place between life and death, and they're dangerous. People have been harmed. Some have vanished."

The laughter dimmed, just slightly. The word vanished hung in the air. Abigail saw a flicker of unease in the audience — a ripple in the tide of amusement.

Russell smirked, quick to reclaim control. "Vanished. As in… poof! Gone. Pulled into the closet by Beetlejuice."

The laughter resumed, but thinner this time. Abigail could feel the shift. Truth had a way of cutting through, even under mockery.

The stage manager waved a hand — commercial break. The applause sign lit up, and the audience clapped dutifully as the cameras powered down.

The floor manager swept a hand and the red tally light died. Theme music bumped under the studio chatter as a PA hustled in with a new mug, and a makeup artist hovered just off-camera with a powder brush for the next guest.

Russell kept his grin pinned. "Great segment, Abigail. We'll have to do this again." He was already turning, straightening his jacket as the producers waved him toward the other side of the desk where the next guest's chair was being rolled in.

"Stand by—new guest in thirty," the floor manager called.

Abigail exhaled, shoulders dropping now that the glare eased. She set her mic pack on the table and reached for the water glass; the cold condensation steadied her.

As the set shifted—cables snaked, a stagehand swapped backdrop cards—a shadow paused beside her. One of the cameramen, tall and narrow-faced, adjusted his rig, flicked a glance at the laughing knot of producers, then leaned close enough to be heard over the music sting.

His voice was barely audible over the studio noise. "My niece," he whispered. "She was taken."

Abigail's hand froze on the glass. She turned slowly. "What did you say?"

The man's eyes darted, fear in their corners. "A month ago. She was in her bedroom, brushing her hair in the mirror. Her parents heard her scream. By the time they got there… she was gone. Only the mirror was left. Police said she ran away. By the time her parents got to the room, all they saw was the glass. The glass... it rippled."

Abigail's breath caught. The studio, with its chatter and clatter, seemed to fade around her.

"She was pulled in," the cameraman said, face gone gray. "Just like you said. Vanished." He lowered his voice to Abigail. "I haven't told anyone at the studio—I don't want them laughing me out of the room." Even if Russell didn't believe any of it, his staff clearly had—because whatever this was had reached them, too.

For a heartbeat, Abigail couldn't speak. Her pulse roared in her ears, the words of the Veilborne from Dupont still echoing in her mind: The Witch. The Forbidden.

The cameraman straightened, stepping back before anyone noticed. He lifted his rig again, the red light blinking as the cameras powered up. The applause sign lit.

Russell swept back to his desk, clapping his hands like a circus master. "Alright, folks, we're back! And we've got more ghost stories for you from the one and only Abigail Jensen — the Witch of the Northwest!"

The audience erupted in laughter and cheers, oblivious.

Abigail sat straighter in her chair, the chill of the cameraman's words burrowing deep into her chest. Her fear was steady, cold, but beneath it, resolve hardened like iron.

She knew now: this wasn't a game, not a story for ratings. The Veilborne were real, they were hunting, and people like Russell Langston — smug, blind, and cruel — would never see it coming until it was too late.

Scene 4: Dragged into the Darkness

The floor manager's hand swept and the red tally light died. Theme music rose and the set shifted—backdrop cards swapped, cables snaked, a fresh mug appeared on Russell's desk. Moments earlier, the tall cameraman had leaned in and told Abigail what he'd seen—how the glass had seemed to reach, how he hadn't told anyone at the studio for fear they'd laugh him out of the room—then slipped back to his station as the crew reset.

Abigail unclipped her mic pack and stepped off the riser, choosing a patch of shadow just beyond the curtain. She decided to stay through the rest of the taping so she could catch him afterward and ask about his niece.

The applause sign blinked back to life, a red pulse bringing the audience to heel between segments.

"Ten seconds to live!" someone shouted across the floor.

Russell smoothed his tie, took a last sip, and slid into his chair's sweet spot. The band hit its sting; the stage lights flared; the floor manager pointed.

"Welcome back, folks," Russell said, palms spread like a benediction. "I hope you didn't change the channel—because if you did, you just missed the part where I continue tonight's streak of exposing America's finest crackpots."

The crowd chuckled. Russell thrived.

His next guest—a nervous young scientist—adjusted his glasses and leaned toward the mic. "What I'm saying, Mr. Langston, is that the EMF spikes being recorded near—"

"Spikes?" Russell cut in, savoring the word. "You mean the ghostbusters found a new toy to sell?"

Laughter exploded, hot and easy, the kind Russell lived for. The scientist floundered, his words drowned out by applause Russell stoked with a casual hand wave.

It was cruelty as art, and Russell painted in broad, unforgiving strokes.

"Next thing you know, we'll be warned about monsters in our mirrors," he quipped, glancing knowingly toward the camera. "You remember Reese Mathers, don't you? Poor guy made that his bedtime story on this very stage last week. I half expected him to come in with garlic and a crucifix."

The audience laughed again, just the way Russell wanted. He loved twisting the knife. "Maybe tonight's guest will give him some competition. Who wants to vote which story's crazier — mirrors eating people, or invisible poltergeist power surges?"

The crowd whooped. Russell basked in it.

But then—

Something behind him changed.

It was subtle at first, almost imperceptible, but Abigail noticed from where she stood in the wings. The studio's decorative mirror — a tall, ornate prop framed in gold — shivered. Not visibly, not like glass struck by sound, but like water disturbed by an unseen ripple. The surface bent inwards, the reflections inside stretching too far, too long, as though the glass were breathing.

Abigail's throat tightened. Her fingers dug into the curtain hanging next to her. She knew this feeling. The air shifted, thickened. A faint sulfur tang threaded through the stage lights.

The Veilborne.

Her pulse kicked hard. She half-stepped out of the shadows where she'd been hiding.

Russell was still talking, oblivious. "What's the matter?" he taunted his guest. "Cat got your spectral tongue? Don't worry, the audience loves a good awkward pause. Makes me look smarter."

The laughter that followed was thin, nervous. Some in the crowd had noticed the mirror too.

"Russell," Abigail called, her voice cutting through the hum of cameras.

He turned, irritation flashing across his face. "Not now, sweetheart. Grown-ups are talking."

But then he saw it.

The mirror rippled again, unmistakable this time. The golden frame rattled. The surface buckled inward like liquid under pressure, reflections stretching grotesquely. From the audience, gasps rose. A cameraman faltered, the lens wobbling in his hands.

Russell barked a laugh. "Oh, fantastic. Special effects department's finally earning their paychecks. Little early for Halloween, don't you think?"

No one laughed.

The ripple deepened. Smoke seeped from the glass, rolling across the stage floor. The temperature dropped hard and fast — breath frosted in the lights, and the band's instruments gave a hollow groan.

Abigail moved closer. "Russell, get away from it!"

He sneered at her. "Please. What is this, some kind of prank? You think you can spook me on my own show?"

The mirror convulsed.

A clawed hand shot out, black as coal smoke, fingers ending in curved talons that screeched as they scraped against the studio floor.

The audience screamed.

Russell stumbled back, his face draining of color. "What the hell—?"

The rest of it emerged.

A figure of shadow and flesh, smoke clinging to its skeletal frame, eyes burning with pale, hungry fire. Its jaw unhinged wider than human, exhaling a hiss that rattled the rafters. The Veilborne pulled itself free, towering, its body half-formed from writhing vapors and jagged bone-like ridges.

Abigail froze. She'd faced them before, but the terror never lessened. Her every instinct screamed to run, but she forced herself to stand her ground.

"Leave him!" she shouted. "He's not yours!"

The Veilborne turned its head, eyes flaring. Recognition sparked in its gaze. It bared teeth like splintered glass.

"You," it rasped, its voice layered and broken, like a chorus of the damned. "The Witch. The Forbidden."

Russell's breath came in shallow bursts. "S-stop... stop this. This isn't funny anymore!"

The Veilborne moved with impossible speed. Smoke snapped around Russell's legs, pulling him toward the mirror. He clawed at his desk, papers scattering, his polished persona shattered in an instant. His screams cut through the chaos — high, panicked, childlike.

"No! Let me go! Somebody help me!"

Abigail lunged forward, grabbing his arm. The cold of the smoke bit into her skin, burning with frost and fire. She pulled, straining, but the Veilborne's strength was overwhelming.

The creature leaned close, Its sulfur breath washing over her.

"Last we met, you told me to stop," it hissed, eyes narrowing. "I left—surprised. Since then I have learned the Echo's command was only this: not you. It did not bid us to starve. You may not be taken, but you cannot keep us from feeding."

With a violent yank, it tore Russell from her grasp. His nails raked her skin as he slipped away, shrieking like a boy dragged into the dark.

The mirror swallowed them both in a final ripple.

The glass stilled.

Abigail fell to her knees, trembling, her lungs heaving as the sulfur faded. Around her, the studio was chaos — audience members fleeing, crew shouting, cameras dropped and smashed. Someone cut the feed, but not before perhaps millions had seen the impossible broadcast live.

Silence pressed in, broken only by the wail of a dropped microphone feeding back into the speakers.

Abigail pressed her hand to the stage floor, steadying herself. Her heart pounded, her skin clammy.

The Witch. The Forbidden.

The words echoed in her skull.

She lifted her eyes to the mirror. Her reflection stared back — pale, exhausted, and alone. But she knew it wasn't over. The Veilborne had taken Russell into the In Between.

And the world had just watched it happen.

5

Among the Veilborne

Scene 1: Awakening in the Dark

Russell Langston woke with the taste of ash on his tongue.

For a moment he thought he was backstage, sprawled on the cold concrete of the studio floor after fainting. His mind scrabbled for excuses — a gas leak, a seizure, some elaborate prank — but the air itself told him he was wrong. It burned in his lungs with every breath, carrying a reek of sulfur sharp enough to sting his eyes. And beneath the burn was something else, something electrical — a static bite that seemed to crawl over his skin like invisible insects.

He rolled onto his hands and knees, gagging. His palms pressed into slick stone that felt wrong, too smooth, too cold. He looked down — and froze.

The ground wasn't stone at all. It was glass. Black glass, polished as though by centuries of wear, fractured into jagged seams that glowed faintly with a pallid light. His reflection stared back at him in the shards: pale, shaking, eyes wide and bloodshot. But the reflections didn't quite match. They lagged. They moved a heartbeat too slow, some smiling when he wasn't, some twisting their mouths in grotesque mockery.

"No," he whispered, forcing himself back onto his feet. His voice bounced away into the dark, echoing again and again, but wrong. Each echo came back distorted, layered with whispers not his own.

"…No… no… no…" The last one hissed like a dozen serpents.

Russell spun in a circle. There was no stage. No cameras. No audience.

Only corridors stretching into nothing, walls made of the same black glass, shifting and bending like a funhouse mirror designed by a sadist. His own warped reflection flickered in every surface: tall, small, head split, skin melting — a thousand grotesque variations of himself that stared back with mocking eyes.

"This is—this is a dream," he muttered. His voice trembled, betraying the fear he was trying to deny. "Some… some hallucination. The network's playing a trick. Or I hit my head…"

But the air was too heavy, too real. The sulfur too thick, clinging to the back of his throat. And his stomach churned with a deeper knowledge he couldn't shake: this was no dream.

Something moved in the distance.

The glass corridor shifted, bending like liquid. A smear of shadow slid across the surface, pausing just at the edge of sight. Russell stumbled back, his polished shoes clicking against the floor with a hollow sound.

"Hello?" he shouted, his voice cracking. "Somebody… anybody?"

The echoes leapt back at him, louder this time, layered with whispers that burrowed under his skin.

"…body…any…Russell…"

He clamped his hands over his ears, but the voices were inside him, curling in his bones, threading through the spaces between heartbeats. He could feel their weight pressing down, their hunger scraping across his thoughts.

Panic clawed up his throat. He began to run.

The corridor stretched on endlessly, walls twisting, reflections multiplying. Every step made the floor shudder, ripples racing through the black glass like he was running across water. And with every ripple, new images bled across the walls: rooms he recognized, places he'd mocked. A bathroom mirror dripping black water. A child's hand reaching out from glass, skeletal fingers wrapping around it. Reese Mathers on his show, eyes desperate, pleading to be believed.

Russell stumbled, nearly falling.

"No," he gasped, chest heaving. "That was—that was all nonsense. All for ratings. It wasn't real—"

The corridor cracked beneath him. From the fissure seeped a pale mist, curling upward into a shape half-formed, whispering in voices that weren't its own.

"…Feast… feed… Forbidden…"

He reeled back, his bravado collapsing with each word. He'd thought himself untouchable, the king of ridicule, but here every insult, every sneer, every cruel laugh turned to ash in his mouth.

For the first time in decades, Russell Langston was utterly alone.

And afraid.

He pressed himself against a wall, sliding down until he was crouched on the glass, his breath coming in ragged bursts. The reflections in the walls loomed closer — grotesque parodies of himself, their mouths stretching impossibly wide.

He buried his face in his hands. "God, please. I didn't mean it. I didn't know."

But the In Between didn't care.

The air shifted, colder now, each breath like swallowing shards of ice. The darkness pressed closer. Water dripped somewhere in the distance — slow, steady, hollow. The sound echoed like it was dripping inside his skull.

Russell forced himself back to his feet, trembling. He took a step forward, then another, his polished shoes scuffed and slick. His tie hung askew, his once-perfect hair damp with sweat. The man who had made millions laugh at the pain of others now looked like a terrified child lost in a nightmare he couldn't wake from.

"Abigail," he whispered, the name slipping unbidden from his lips. He had mocked her on live television, humiliated her with a smirk. But here, in this fractured world, he found himself clinging to her image, her warnings. Reese too — his rambling, desperate insistence that people were being taken. Russell had sneered, but he remembered the look in Reese's eyes. A look he understood now.

He wished he had listened.

He wished he had done anything but laugh.

The corridor ahead split open, revealing not a path but a chasm — a vast void yawning beneath him, filled with broken shards of glass floating like islands. The shards reflected not his face, but others. Countless faces. Men, women, children — their mouths open in silent screams, their eyes hollow, their forms dissolving into smoke as unseen jaws consumed them.

Russell staggered back, bile rising in his throat. He couldn't breathe. He couldn't look away.

The Veilborne were here.

He couldn't see them clearly, only shapes moving in the void, great hulking silhouettes that bent the smoke and shadows around them. Their eyes glowed faintly, dozens of them, watching, waiting, feasting. The reflections in the glass flickered with every bite, souls tearing apart into mist, screams echoing without sound.

Russell collapsed to his knees, sobbing. His arrogance shattered completely. He pressed his forehead to the cold glass floor, his tears smearing against his reflection.

"I'm sorry," he whispered, the words breaking. "I'm sorry, I didn't mean it, I didn't—"

The whispers came again, crawling inside his skull, mocking him with his own voice.

"...Sorry... mean it... Russell..."

He clutched his head, rocking, every fiber of his being screaming to wake up, to claw his way out. But there was no waking from this. No cutting to commercial.

Only the In Between.

And the knowledge that he was prey now.

Prey in a world where cruelty was not entertainment — it was sustenance.

Scene 2: The Feast of the Veilborne

The air grew thicker as Russell pressed forward, every step dragging as though unseen hands clutched at his ankles. The sulfur reek was worse now, curling in his nostrils and souring his stomach, and the static hum pressed against his eardrums until he thought they might burst. His heart hammered, the pulse loud in his skull, drowning out thought.

But thought wasn't what drove him anymore — only the instinct to move, to get away, to outrun whatever was whispering from the glass behind him.

The corridor widened suddenly. The black glass floor spread out into a cavernous expanse, walls arching upward like the ribs of some immense carcass. Shards jutted from every surface, jagged mirrors tilting at impossible angles, their edges glowing faintly with pale blue light.

And in the center, gathered like carrion birds around a corpse, were the Veilborne.

Russell froze.

They were larger than he remembered from the studio — perhaps because there was nothing now to shield his eyes from their true form. Their bodies were shadows given shape, dense smoke wrapped around a skeleton of pale bone and muscle that twitched unnaturally. Claws like black sickles curled at the ends of their elongated hands, and their heads bent low, faces shrouded in vapor except for their eyes: white coals burning with a hunger too vast to comprehend.

Around them writhed their prey.

The souls.

They were human, or what remained of human. Phantom forms hovered and twisted in the air, outlines faint but unmistakable. Men, women, children — some flickering as if half-remembered, others sharp as flesh. Their mouths opened in endless screams, but the cries emerged not as sound, but as vibrations that shook the air, rattling Russell's teeth and crawling down his spine.

He swallowed against the tremor and heard, plain as a knife, what the Veilborne had said in the studio: they were allowed to feed—everyone except the Witch, the Forbidden. Abigail. It had grabbed him, testing the rule, pulling him into the mirror. Meaning, everyone was fair game except Abigail. The realization slid cold through his ribs, sharpening his fear to a breaking point. He was fair game.

One of the Veilborne thrust its claws into the chest of a phantom boy. The boy shrieked, his face contorting in agony as luminous strands of energy spilled from his body like pulled sinew. The Veilborne leaned close and inhaled deeply, sucking the glowing strands into its maw. The light dimmed; the boy convulsed. Then, with a final wrench, the creature tore the last filament free and swallowed it whole. The boy's form collapsed into ash, scattering across the glass floor before vanishing into nothing.

Russell gagged, bile rising in his throat. His knees nearly gave way. This wasn't special effects. This wasn't a bad trip. This was real.

Another Veilborne crouched low, its claws prying at a screaming woman who thrashed in vain. The creature lapped at her like a dog at a bowl, slurping the energy from her chest as her eyes rolled back in horror. Each gulp sent tremors through the chamber, echoing with the sound of breaking glass.

Russell staggered back, his shoe catching on a crack. The sharp noise of his stumble rang out like a gunshot.

The feasting slowed.

Heads turned.

One of the Veilborne lifted its gaze, its eyes catching him. Its mouth split into a grin of shadow and fang.

"New meat," it hissed. The word slithered through the air, deep and jagged, reverberating inside Russell's bones.

"No," Russell whispered. His legs moved before his mind caught up. He turned and bolted.

The chamber bent as he ran, walls folding inward, the floor slick beneath his shoes. Behind him, the Veilborne roared — a sound like tearing steel and shattering mirrors — and claws scraped against glass as one of them lunged forward.

Reflections splintered at his sides, showing not only his own frantic face but flashes of what awaited him if he fell: phantoms ripped apart, eyes wide and pleading, mouths stretched in silence as they dissolved under talons. The images clawed at his sanity, dragging him toward despair, but fear drove him harder.

His breath came in ragged bursts, the sulfur searing his lungs. His chest burned, his heart slamming so hard he thought it might tear itself apart.

The corridor narrowed, funneling him deeper into the nightmare realm. Every turn brought new horrors — walls dripping with black water that stank of rot, floors rippling like liquid glass under his weight, whispers calling his name from just beyond sight.

"Russell…"

"Langston…"

"…meat…"

The voice of the Veilborne. Always behind him. Always closer.

He risked a glance back.

It was there — a towering shadow barreling after him, claws raking sparks across the glass, its eyes blazing white fire. Its jaws stretched open in a silent scream, smoke boiling from its body in waves.

Russell pushed harder, his shoes slipping, his suit soaked with sweat. His mind screamed at him to stop, to curl up and wait for it to end, but the primal need to live shoved him forward.

A fissure yawned ahead — the floor splitting into a jagged chasm. He skidded to a halt at the edge, arms flailing. Below, shards of black glass floated in an endless void, each reflecting the same image: people screaming, souls burning as Veilborne fed.

Behind him, claws scraped.

Russell whimpered, his bravado shattered. Tears streaked his face, mixing with sweat, blurring his vision.

"Please," he sobbed, not sure who he was begging — God, fate, the universe. "Please, I'm sorry. I didn't know. I didn't mean it. I'll change. I swear I'll—"

The Veilborne's growl cut through his plea, rattling his ribs.

It lunged.

Russell screamed and leapt into the fissure.

The air tore past him, the void swallowing his cry, mirrors shattering into a thousand screaming mouths. His body slammed onto a shard of glass that bobbed like a raft in the dark, the impact rattling every bone in his body. He gasped, rolling onto his side, coughing.

The shard floated, drifting away from the fissure. Above, the Veilborne peered down, eyes blazing, claws flexing. It didn't follow. Not yet.

Russell lay trembling, his body wracked with sobs. His tears streaked onto the glass, merging with the reflections of other faces trapped inside — faces that whispered, pleading, begging to be freed.

He pressed his hands over his ears, rocking, choking on his own terror.

The truth was undeniable now.

This was real. These were souls — people — torn apart and devoured like cattle.

And he was next.

Scene 3: The Priest in the Shadows

Russell's ragged breaths tore at his throat as he staggered along the shifting shard of glass. The fissure behind him had sealed, leaving only the echo of claws and hunger. Yet he knew — he knew — that the Veilborne hadn't given up. It never gave up.

The shard drifted through the void, aimless, the darkness broken only by faint glimmers inside the glass. Faces pressed against the underside like drowning victims against ice, eyes wide, mouths opening and closing in silent desperation. He couldn't look down for long without feeling as though they were dragging him with them.

A sound followed him — slow, deliberate. Not claws. Not hissing. But footsteps.

Russell spun, nearly losing his balance. His reflection stuttered on the fractured surface. From the darkness beyond, a figure emerged.

A man.

Or something that had once been one.

His robes were torn, blackened at the edges, but still recognizable as clerical. His form shimmered, translucent, like smoke held together by conviction alone. In one hand, he carried a lantern of strange design — wrought iron curling around a glass globe that burned with a light that wasn't fire. It pulsed faintly, steady as a heartbeat, casting shadows back into the void. Wherever its glow reached, the whispers receded.

The priest stepped forward, the shard firm beneath his feet. His eyes fixed on Russell, steady, measured.

"Stay back!" Russell croaked, stumbling. His voice cracked, betraying the sobs still clinging to it. "I don't know what you are, but stay the hell away!"

The man didn't stop. His tone was calm, deep, a voice worn smooth by countless sermons and confessions. "If I meant you harm, you'd already be gone. The shadows would've claimed you."

Russell swallowed, trying to steady his shaking hands. "Then what do you want from me?"

The lantern lifted slightly, the light brushing across Russell's face. The fear that gripped his chest loosened, if only by a thread.

"What I've always wanted," the priest said softly. "To guide the lost."

The words cut through Russell, unexpected. He stared, eyes narrowing. "...Who the hell are you?"

The priest stepped closer, and for the first time Russell saw his face clearly. Lined but kind. Tired but unwavering. And faintly familiar — a name surfacing from memory like driftwood rising through water.

"Father Allen," the priest said simply.

Russell blinked. The name snagged—he'd seen it before. Abigail had written about a Father Allen in her book, the parish priest who freed a trapped soul from the In Between by trading places with him. He'd mocked her on air, but he always did his homework. Now the man stood in front of him.

"You're... you're real?" He almost laughed, but the sound cracked into a sob. "No, no, I've lost it. I'm talking to a dead man. I've completely lost it."

Allen regarded him, neither confirming nor denying. "Madness doesn't bring light into dark places, Russell. It doesn't hold the Veilborne at bay."

As if to prove the point, a hiss rose from beyond the shard. From the fractured void, shapes stirred — claws scraping, eyes blinking open like stars. One of the Veilborne slithered forward, smoke curling from its jaws.

Allen turned, raising the lantern. The light flared brighter, not with fire but with something deeper — the warmth of memory, of compassion, of resolve. The creature reeled, snarling, and drew back into the shadows with a hiss. The whispers faded.

Russell's knees buckled. He slumped onto the shard, trembling. Tears streaked his cheeks, unbidden and hot.

Allen crouched before him, the lantern between them. "You're not safe here," he said. "But you're not doomed yet, either. Get up. Walk with me."

Russell shook his head violently. "I can't. I can't do this. I'm not—" His words broke, a sob shuddering through his chest. "I'm not strong. I don't... I don't deserve—"

Allen's gaze sharpened. "Strength isn't the absence of fear. It's choosing to stand even when fear consumes you."

Russell's lip trembled. His voice dropped to a whisper. "I mocked them. All of them. People like Abigail Jensen, like Reese Mathers. I made them look like fools. Laughed while they begged to be believed. And now..." He gestured wildly to the darkness, his hands shaking. "Now I know they were right. And I—"

He choked on the words, curling into himself.

Allen's voice didn't soften, but it didn't turn cruel. It stayed steady, cutting. At the mention of Abigail, something flickered in his eyes—memory rising like a reflection—then he pulled himself back to Russell.

"You built a stage on the backs of the desperate. You took their pain and turned it into entertainment. You were cruel, Russell."

Russell flinched, every word like a lash. He wanted to deny it, to argue, to dress it up as wit and showmanship. But the images of souls torn apart still lingered in his eyes. The sound of children screaming, of phantoms devoured. His own terror.

He couldn't deny it.

Allen leaned closer, his face lit by the lantern's glow. "But cruelty born of pain doesn't absolve you. It passes the wound along. Your father's fists. Your mother's scorn. The bullies who taught you that to survive you had to hurt first. You buried it under sarcasm, under mockery. But it rotted inside you, and you spread that rot to others."

Russell stared, trembling. His lips parted, words stammering out. "I didn't... I didn't know how else to be."

"And yet," Allen said, "you can still choose differently. Even here."

Russell shook his head, tears dripping onto the glass. "Why would you care? Why would anyone care if I change? I'm nothing. I'm meat to them."

Allen's hand rested briefly on his shoulder — light as air, but solid enough to ground him. "Because every soul matters. Even the arrogant. Even the broken. Even those who think themselves beyond forgiveness."

Russell bowed his head, sobbing. The shard rocked gently under them, drifting further from the snarls of the Veilborne.

Allen stood, lantern high. "Come. Walk with me. You'll face your sins before this is over. But for now, survival. Follow the light."

Russell forced himself upright, legs shaking. He wiped his face with his sleeve, though the tears wouldn't stop. His voice cracked. "I don't deserve this."

Allen looked at him, the lantern's glow reflected in his eyes. "None of us do. Grace isn't earned. It's given."

The words hit Russell harder than any jeer ever had. His chest ached with something he couldn't name — not just fear, not just guilt, but the faintest glimmer of hope.

They began to walk, the lantern cutting a path through the void. The whispers receded, though they lingered just at the edges, waiting.

Russell stayed close, his bravado long since stripped away. His voice was small when he finally asked, "What happens if the lantern goes out?"

Allen didn't look back. "Then we pray I've learned enough to light it again."

Russell swallowed hard, eyes fixed on the glow, forcing himself to match the priest's pace.

For the first time since he'd been dragged into this nightmare, he wasn't running blindly. For the first time, he listened.

Scene 4: Echoes of Power

The void around them pulsed. Not with light, not with sound, but with an immense pressure that pressed into Russell's bones like the weight of a deep ocean. The shard beneath his feet quivered, cracks racing like veins through its glassy surface. He staggered, nearly falling into the abyss yawning on either side.

Father Allen's lantern flared, steadying the ground beneath them, though Russell wasn't sure if that was real or if fear itself had warped his senses.

"Stay close," Allen said, voice calm, though Russell caught the taut line of tension in it.

Russell's throat was raw, his voice breaking. "What's happening now?"

The priest glanced outward into the abyss. The darkness wasn't still anymore — it churned like a storm-tossed sea. Shapes fled in every direction: long, thin silhouettes scrambling into cracks, smoke-born wings dissolving into the void, claws scraping as they tore away from sight.

"The Veilborne scatter," Allen said.

Russell blinked, barely able to breathe. "Scatter? You mean... they're running away? Those things don't run from anything."

Allen lifted the lantern higher. Its glow licked at the edges of the void, but the darkness beyond was shifting, alive. "They run from this," he said quietly.

And then Russell felt it.

It wasn't sight at first — it was vibration. A resonance that shivered up through the shard, into his legs, his chest, and behind his eyes. A voice that hadn't yet spoken, but existed in every trembling molecule around him. His teeth ached from it, his heart stuttered.

Then he saw it.

On the horizon — if there could be such a thing in this fractured realm — a shape moved. Not a form, but an immensity. A colossal silhouette of shifting light and shadow, as if countless storms had been bound into a single body. Its head was not a head but a crown of flame and glass shards. Its limbs stretched out and broke apart into prisms, reforming again with every pulse of energy.

It was the Echo.

The entity's presence filled the void with awe and terror so profound that Russell collapsed to his knees, clutching his chest. He couldn't draw a full breath, as if every inhalation required permission from that being. His ears rang with a noise too vast to be sound, like thunder rolling endlessly underwater.

The Veilborne screamed in the distance, their hisses splitting into dozens of voices before they vanished into cracks, unwilling to be near their master. But not all fled. Russell caught glimpses in the shadows — clusters of them watching, whispering, their talons flexing, wings beating smoke. They crouched in the dark, not in reverence but in defiance.

"They plot," Allen said grimly. His eyes were not on the Echo's immensity, but on those lurking pockets of resistance. "Even here, they plot rebellion."

Russell's voice shook as he tried to speak, his words trembling against the pressure. "That... thing. That's what Abigail—was talking about, isn't it? That's the Echo?"

Allen didn't look at him. He bowed his head slightly, a gesture of humility before something greater than comprehension. "Yes. Keeper of balance. Judge of what lingers between the living and the dead. And... weakening."

The air shuddered, and the Echo's head turned. Russell's chest locked as though he had been pinned by a spotlight. Its gaze — if gaze it could be called — was unbearable, like staring into an infinite hall of mirrors where every version of himself wept, screamed, mocked, and burned all at once.

He gasped, trying to claw his way out of it. "It—it sees me!"

Allen's hand pressed gently to his shoulder. "It sees all."

The Echo's voice came then. It was not a voice of words, but meaning carried in a ripple through the air, through the marrow of their bones. The void itself vibrated with it.

"ALLEN."

The priest flinched as if struck, yet his face held. He raised his lantern.

The Echo's resonance deepened. "YOU WHO GUIDE. YOU WHO GUARD. COMPASSION REMAINS. BALANCE ENDURES IN YOU."

Russell whimpered, pressing his hands against his ears though it did nothing to stop the sound reverberating through him. His vision blurred with tears.

Allen lowered his head. "I only do what must be done."

The void trembled again, like the universe itself exhaling. "YOU CARRY THE LIGHT."

The words struck Russell harder than any insult or mockery ever had. The way it named Allen — not like the host of a late-night show would mock, but like a force older than the stars knew him.

Russell looked at Allen, desperate. "Why... why did it say that? Why you? What does it mean?"

Allen's face was pale in the lantern's glow. "It means my path is not done. Even here." His voice was quiet, but beneath it lay a weary strength.

They began to walk again, shards forming ahead as if to make a path in the void. Russell stumbled to his feet, forcing his legs to follow, though his entire body screamed to flee. He whispered hoarsely, "It called you balance. That means... what? That it trusts you? That it needs you?"

Allen's jaw tightened. "It notices compassion. But compassion alone cannot hold back rebellion."

Russell glanced nervously to the shadows. The clusters of Veil-borne hadn't fled — they lingered. He caught the gleam of their pale eyes, the curl of smoke around their mouths. They weren't cowed. They were waiting.

Allen noticed too. "The Echo grows weaker, Russell. Once, its very presence was enough to keep order here. To keep them in line. Now... hunger spreads. Rogue Veilborne slip through the veil without restraint, dragging souls as they wish. Feeding where they shouldn't."

Russell swallowed. His mind flashed back to the feast he'd witnessed: talons ripping luminous strands from the screaming dead, devouring them like starving predators. He gagged, bile rising. "You mean... it's not supposed to happen like that? That was... breaking the rules?"

Allen nodded grimly. "This realm was never meant to be their feeding ground. It was meant to be a waystation. A crossing. A balance. But hunger breeds defiance, and defiance becomes rebellion. If unchecked, their feeding will bleed into your world."

Russell froze, his skin crawling. "Bleed into..." He pictured mirrors, the smoke, the claws reaching. Abigail. Reese. The families whose stories he'd mocked. "You mean they'll come through more. Take more people."

"Yes."

The word was simple, final.

Russell pressed his shaking hands to his face. "God. God, I laughed at them. I laughed at all of it. And it's real. All of it's real. And it's... worse than anything I imagined."

Allen stopped, turning to face him. The lantern's glow reflected in his translucent features. "Now you see why truth matters, Russell. Why cruelty is poison. You had a platform. You could have warned. Instead, you mocked. And people paid the price."

Russell crumpled to his knees, sobbing. "I didn't know! I didn't... I didn't believe it myself. I thought it was all lies, all... cheap tricks."

Allen didn't answer right away. The lantern hummed, its light steady against the pressing dark. Finally, he said, "Belief does not change reality. But perhaps now... reality can change you."

Behind them, the void trembled again. Russell dared a glance back and saw the Echo's form shifting — colossal, beautiful, terrifying. The silhouette rippled, breaking into shards of light, then reformed again. Even as it loomed, Russell could feel its weakness. The cadence of its power faltered, flickered, dimmed before surging again.

And in the shadows, the Veilborne hissed. Watching. Waiting. Their rebellion a seed taking root.

Russell shivered, clutching at Allen's robes. "What do we do?" His voice was broken, childlike.

Allen's gaze fixed on the horizon, where the Echo's silhouette loomed. "We walk. We endure. And we pray the Keeper has not lost its strength entirely."

Russell followed, his steps unsteady, his mind fractured between terror and shame. The darkness whispered at the edges, promises of hunger, rebellion, and blood.

And above it all, the Echo's voice still reverberated through him, a weight that pressed into his soul:

"BALANCE MUST ENDURE."

6

Origins of the Array

Scene 1: Sparks of Genius

Autumn 2003, Pierce College. The engineering physics lab smelled of solder and burnt dust. Oscilloscopes blinked in the dim light, their green traces crawling across black glass like faint lightning frozen mid-storm. The hum of fluorescents overhead blended with the steady drizzle on the windows, a lullaby for the exhausted.

Elias Voss stood at a bench scattered with copper wire, ferrite cores, and coffee-stained notepads. His shoulders were rigid, his dark hair falling untidily over his brow as he rolled a ferrite slug between his fingers like a coin. He was twenty-one and carried himself like a man twice that — already sharp, already hungry, already tired of waiting for the world to see what he saw.

The door opened with a soft creak.

A woman stepped in, framed by the red glow of the exit sign. Her coat clung damply to her frame; rain had painted her sleeves dark. She carried a scarf in one hand as if she'd just pulled down a banner of surrender. Yet her presence was anything but—there was an assuredness to the way she paused and took in the room, her gaze moving from the coils, to the cluttered meters, to him.

"Are you always here this late?" she asked.

"Only when I want to be," Elias said, immediately regretting the stiffness in his voice. He tried again. "Yes. Often."

She smiled, not mocking, but as if she enjoyed seeing him stumble. "Good. That means I'm in the right place." She crossed the room and offered her hand. "Camille Laurent."

"Elias Voss." His hand was colder than he wished when their palms met.

"Professor Kershaw told me I'd find the night owl in the lab—the one with coils and impossible ideas." She slipped a folded letter from her coat pocket and set it on the bench. "He said if I was serious about EMF research, I should bring this to you."

Elias scanned the brief note of introduction and the neat packet she slid after it: field logs from the hospital grounds, a spreadsheet of EMF spikes, photos marked with angles and times. She was prepared, he had to admit. Curious, organized. The fact that she was striking didn't hurt, but that wasn't what kept his attention—it was the way she looked past the gear to the questions behind it.

"Which idea did he say was impossible?" Elias asked, testing.

"The one about harvesting usable energy from ambient electromagnetic fields," she said. "From what he calls 'the noise between things.'"

A flicker passed over Elias's face. "Noise," he muttered. "That's always been his word for it."

"And yours?"

"It isn't noise if it can be tuned," Elias said quietly. "It's a conversation. We just haven't learned to listen yet."

Camille's eyes glimmered with interest. She glanced at the EMF meter. "Then let's start listening."

Elias hesitated only a moment, weighing the letter, the data, and the way she stood—steady, already thinking. "Shadow me for a week," he said, sliding a visitor badge across the bench. "If you still want in after that, we'll talk."

By late afternoon she'd traced a ground loop he'd missed and was shoulder-to-shoulder with him at the rack, head tilted as if the room might answer. The transition wasn't a leap so much as a step taken together—his project making space, her curiosity taking it. They began to work together, shoulders almost brushing. Using scrap wire, they wound a crude loop, arguing over the exact number of turns per layer. Camille had a steadiness of hand Elias admired. When he mentioned signal-to-noise ratios, she not only followed but finished the equation for him in a whisper. When he spoke of his childhood detector — the one that had made the forks tremble and the air feel heavy — she didn't laugh. She asked what that weight had felt like. When he answered "like the room itself leaned closer," she nodded as though he'd offered real data.

He connected the loop to the preamp. The oscilloscope's band jittered, then steadied.

"Steilacoom at night," Camille murmured. "Elevators, radio towers, lights, rain... and maybe something else you're still hoping to find."

Elias's voice was careful. "I hope for a lot. I don't assume."

"You don't need to," she said, leaning close enough for her hair to brush his arm. "Sometimes hope and discipline become the same thing."

The lab door groaned again.

Adrian Kessler walked in — notebook in hand, the faintest curl of a smirk on his lips. He was a year older, already with two papers to his name, and carried himself like someone who believed publication was currency enough to buy loyalty.

"Kershaw said the night person would be you," Adrian said to Elias, his tone smooth but his eyes already measuring Camille. "Didn't mention you'd found a partner."

"I recruited myself," Camille replied evenly.

Adrian's gaze lingered on her longer than necessary before shifting back to Elias. "Your coil's too close to the bench ground. You'll be chasing ghosts that aren't there."

Camille's lips twitched. "Seems like that's the point," she said lightly.

Adrian chuckled, though it lacked warmth. "The point is to find a signal we can own. Ideas don't matter if they don't pay for more wire."

Elias adjusted a capacitor with his thumb. The trace sharpened, splitting into faint combs of teeth. His chest tightened — discovery always felt like inhaling a storm.

"There," Camille whispered. "Don't move."

For a moment, the lab seemed to draw its breath in. Elias brushed the coil and felt the weight settle into his chest again. Camille's hand clutched the edge of the bench; she felt it too. The green trace ticked in rhythm, not random, not noise. Then the teeth flickered, collapsed back into smear.

Adrian broke the silence with brisk dismissal. "That's nothing. Noise dressed up in fancy shoes. I want a signal that can fund a patent, not a ghost story."

Camille turned to him, eyes sharp. "If you only listen to what pays you, you'll miss the things that change you."

Adrian didn't answer, but the curve of his mouth hardened.

They worked until three. Camille fetched coffee from the grad lounge; Adrian scribbled a list of potential applications; Elias refined the loop, his fingers trembling with focus. When Lena Mirek — another student, slight and sharp-eyed — passed through, she listened for a moment and then explained Elias's tangled description in plain terms neither Camille nor Adrian had phrased before. It struck Elias that Lena, without effort, made the impossible sound practical. She left promising to return, already sliding into the role of bridge.

By dawn, they had something that resembled a plan. Elias would refine the coil into something stable. Camille would model couplings.

Adrian would draft preliminary applications. They cleaned the bench reverently, as if preparing an altar for whatever would come next.

At the doorway, Camille paused. "If we ever find ourselves drawing from a well that shouldn't be touched," she said, "promise me we'll choose to stop."

Elias hesitated. His ambition screamed one answer; his heart whispered another. "I promise to know what we're touching," he said finally.

Her eyes lingered on his face, searching for certainty. She let the answer stand. "Good night, Elias."

"Good night."

Alone again, Elias returned to the bench. He powered down the scope, then froze — the green trace pulsed once more, as if something had exhaled through the wires. A breath seemed to ripple across the room.

He smiled faintly, though it was not triumph but hunger. The sense in his chest wasn't clarity; it was a cliff edge in fog. He had always loved that feeling — the moment before the leap, before the ground proved itself or didn't.

He told himself the fog would clear. He told himself the cliff would become a bridge once he studied it long enough.

The storm outside lashed harder. Inside, four young people had laid the first fragile stone of something vast — something none of them understood, but all of them believed in.

And when they returned the next night, the work — and the rivalries — would truly begin.

Scene 2: Building the Foundation

The basement laboratory at Pierce College smelled faintly of ozone and old chalk, a mingling of the new and the archaic. Concrete walls pressed in tight, their surfaces covered with whiteboards cluttered in equations, sketches of circuit layouts, and hastily scribbled notes in both Elias's steady hand and Camille's rounder script. The hum of fluorescent lights mingled with the clatter of tools, the tap of keyboards, and the occasional frustrated sigh.

Elias Voss crouched beside a makeshift coil setup, fingers stained with graphite from recalculating energy inputs. His dark hair fell into his eyes, and his expression carried the intensity of a man who had already forgotten the hour. Beside him, Camille sat cross-legged on the floor, notebook balanced against her knee. She recorded every observation, her voice soft but steady as she read measurements aloud.

"Voltage spiked here," she said, pointing at the scrawl. "But stabilized after the fifth loop. It's consistent with your theory about resonance."

Elias gave the faintest nod. He was already reaching for another wire.

Across the room, Adrian Kessler adjusted a lens over a beam emitter. His movements were sharp, impatient — as though he resented the need for incremental testing. He muttered something about inefficiency, his jaw tight.

"Adrian," Camille called gently, "don't overcompensate the angle yet. Elias needs to recalibrate the input first."

Adrian's laugh was short and cutting. "If we keep recalibrating every time the data twitches, we'll be here until the end of the decade. This isn't surgery. It's experimentation. Sometimes you have to take risks."

Elias's head snapped up, eyes narrowing. "And sometimes, Adrian, risks destroy weeks of work in seconds." His tone carried no humor. "Precision matters more than spectacle."

Adrian met his gaze, a flicker of defiance in his smirk. "Precision doesn't win recognition. Breakthroughs do."

Lena Mirek, seated at a desk stacked with reference texts, leaned forward quickly before the exchange could escalate. She had a knack for sensing when sparks threatened to ignite into flames.

"What Elias means," she said carefully, her voice calm but assured, "is that this design depends on resonance balance. If the emitter overshoots even a little, the whole system destabilizes. We're not measuring a simple current — we're drawing on fields we don't yet fully understand."

Her phrasing diffused some of the tension. Adrian leaned back, rolling the lens between his fingers with restless energy. Elias returned to his wires, but not before giving Lena the faintest nod of approval.

She had become, almost unconsciously, the translator — not only of equations into plain language, but of Elias's rigid vision into something others could follow. She admired his brilliance, even his severity, but she could see how it isolated him.

Camille, in contrast, softened him. She was patient, unflappable, always able to coax a half-smile from Elias even in the thick of calculations. Where Adrian pushed with arrogance, Camille pulled with warmth, grounding the group.

"Think of it this way," Lena continued, turning toward Adrian with a small smile. "If this works the way Elias predicts, we're not just proving a concept. We're showing the world that invisible forces — the fields between — can be tapped, measured, and maybe even harnessed. That doesn't happen with shortcuts."

Adrian gave a theatrical sigh, but he didn't argue further. He returned to adjusting the emitter with slightly more care this time.

The hours stretched on. Elias worked in long, silent stretches, muttering occasionally about harmonics. Camille tested connections and recorded anomalies. Adrian's impatience flared often — his fingers drumming, his foot tapping, his sharp comments cutting through the quiet. Lena bridged them all, her steady voice smoothing rough edges, her quick mind catching overlooked details.

By midnight, a crude version of the Array prototype hummed in the center of the room. It wasn't elegant — wires sprawled like veins across the floor, metal components salvaged from scrap labs stitched together in improbable ways. But when Elias flipped the final switch, the air in the room changed.

A low vibration rippled through the walls, not loud but felt in the chest. The fluorescent lights flickered once, briefly dimming, before stabilizing. Instruments trembled with spikes, lines darting upward in jagged precision.

Camille caught her breath, eyes wide. "It's pulling... something."

Adrian grinned, a flash of triumph. "Now that's what I'm talking about. Proof. Do you feel that? This is energy no one else has dared to touch."

Elias remained quiet, studying the readouts. His expression wasn't joy — it was focus, the kind of all-consuming hunger that saw patterns where others saw only static. "It's only the beginning," he said finally. "But yes. It works."

The hum deepened, the instruments wavering again. Lena shivered, glancing toward the corners of the room as though expecting to see something stir. The air had taken on a weight, a thickness that pressed against her skin.

"Do you hear that?" she asked softly.

Camille frowned. "Hear what?"

"Like... whispering," Lena murmured. She shook her head quickly, embarrassed. "Maybe it's just the resonance."

Elias didn't look up. "Ignore it. Focus on the data. Superstition has no place here."

But Lena wasn't convinced. The whisper had been faint, fleeting, but real. She made a note in her journal anyway, careful to keep it to herself.

As the hum settled into a steady rhythm, Adrian stepped closer to the machine, his grin sharp. "Imagine what happens when we scale this. Imagine the recognition, the funding. No one will care about theories when they see results like this. We'll be legends."

Elias's jaw tightened. "We're not chasing legends. We're building something real. If you want fame, Adrian, write a novel."

Camille touched Elias's arm lightly. "Let him dream. We all want this to matter."

Elias softened under her touch, if only slightly. But Lena saw the tension between him and Adrian solidify into something more permanent — a clash of vision and ego, of control and ambition.

The Array prototype hummed on, fragile but alive. In that moment, none of them knew the cost it would demand, or the way its pull would reach into places beyond their imagining.

But the seeds were there — in Adrian's restless hunger, in Elias's relentless precision, in Camille's hopeful grounding, and in Lena's quiet unease. Seeds that would one day bloom into betrayal, grief, and horrors none of them yet had words for.

Scene 3: The Aftermath of Russell's Abduction

The world didn't quiet after Russell Langston vanished on live television. It roared.

Clips multiplied like a virus—Russell sneering into the camera, the mirror behind him rippling as if the glass had liquefied, the clawed hand thrusting through, his scream as he was yanked inside. Every frame was slowed, dissected, analyzed. No one could deny it now: something reached out of the mirror and took him.

The scream stuck. Not the howl of a man in control, not even one fighting to survive—raw and high, like a child who knew help wasn't coming. It echoed from every screen.

By morning, the clips were everywhere—and so were the hash-tags: *#LangstonVanished, #DontLookInTheGlass, #StayOutOfTheReflection.*

Hotels draped their mirrors. Department stores stripped cosmetic displays. Custodians taped over school bathroom mirrors while kids waited in the halls. A woman in Los Angeles live-streamed herself smashing her closet doors with a hammer, sobbing between blows.

Local EMTs reported two viewers collapsing at home as their mirrors went black, then gasping awake on the floor—"like they'd been dragged up from deep water."

Fear outran facts.

In the Pierce College lab, Elias Voss and Lena Mirek watched the chaos on a wall of monitors. The glow made both of them look like they belonged on the other side of the glass.

Naveen shouldered in with a tray of coffees and a backpack big enough for grad school and groceries. "Update from civilization," he announced. "Café is out of lids and hope. Also, we're apparently living in a cursed screensaver." He took one look at the looping clip. "Yep. Desktop nightmare."

Lena didn't smile. "The way it moved—it looked like it had been waiting. Like it knew Russell. It said his name."

Elias nodded, jaw tight. "It wanted him."

Naveen flipped open his laptop. "Forum pulse check: half deepfake, half 'melt every mirror.' Sub-thread on how to eat soup without reflective spoons. Humanity coping at its usual A-minus level."

Outside, Tacoma simmered. Police in department stores. Empty aisles where painter's tape used to be. Teen dares with mirrors that ended in a scream and static.

"The DOE is calling it a 'broadcast anomaly,'" Lena said, tossing her phone down. "Pentagon wants 'further study.' Senators want a task force."

"I'd like to register a scientific 'please don't' to the tinfoil-on-TV trend," Naveen said. "It makes antennas. You're welcome."

"The only thing worse than panic is ignorance," Elias said, forcing his voice steady. "The louder the noise gets, the harder it will be to see what's actually happening."

"And what is happening?" Lena asked.

"I don't know," Elias admitted. "But they aren't new. They've hunted small, in the dark. This is just the first time the world had to see them."

Silence pooled between them. The hum under the floor felt too much like a heartbeat.

Lena folded her arms. "Avery still expects a demonstration."

"He'll get one," Elias said. "Controlled. Clean. We remind people not everything is chaos."

Naveen raised an eyebrow. "Optics of 'behold our battery' after a live on-air abduction: not ideal. And before we reinvent rules—"

"We're not," Lena cut in. "We already wrote them. We sent the full protocol packet to Natalie Chen yesterday: perimeter, breaker lock-out, no single-operator runs, reflective-surface management, marked egress. She replied 'received,' time-stamped 7:42 p.m."

"Avery replied, too," Elias added. "Approved. Said the measures were 'appropriate and sufficient.' That was before Russell." He stared at the screens. "Do they still mean it now?"

Naveen tapped his trackpad, mouth slanting. "Natalie just emailed. 'Confirming receipt of your demo plan. Proceed as discussed.' No walk-back, no panic emoji. Either they're steady, or they haven't watched the clip twelve times like the rest of humanity."

The speakerphone crackled, Avery's tone thinning to steel. "Move the demonstration up forty-eight hours. Press and procurement are circling. I need proof of life."

Elias pinched the bridge of his nose. "Then we need more hands."

"Approved," Avery said. "Whatever the college can loan you—for demo week only. After that, no payroll surprises."

"They've watched it," Lena said. "They're choosing not to name it yet."

"Then we control what we can," Elias said. "We implement the protocol we've already written and we run what we said we'd run. If Avery wants to change course, he can say it out loud."

"And if he asks about Russell?" Lena's voice was low.

"Then we give the truth we can prove," Elias said. "Energy is measurable and harvestable. The rest waits until it has a name."

Naveen closed one browser tab, opened another. "FYI, *#MeltYourMirrors* has evolved into *#RentYourMirrors*. Entrepreneurs never sleep." He lifted a cup. "And we're still out of lids. In case that wasn't clear."

Despite herself, Lena huffed a breath. It died quick. Her eyes went back to the monitors—back to the moment a hand came through a pane and the world changed.

By midnight they had nothing new to invent—only a plan to execute. Natalie had the protocols. Avery had signed off. The demo would run at tight, controlled capacity with clean data streams and no flourishes.

Lena slid two purple badge lanyards across the bench: *TEMP INTERN — DEMO WEEK*. "Thirty-minute safety brief, then you touch nothing without me," she said. "You log everything. Eyes, distance, rails."

The two work-study students—Hector with the buzz cut and Zora with careful hands—nodded, nervous and eager. Naveen clapped once, too loud for the room. "Welcome to the circus. Rule one: don't lick the metamaterial. Rule two: if you're not sure whether something's a sensor or a very expensive coaster, ask me first." He shot Elias a look. "Dr. V will pretend he's not funny, but it's because he saves his jokes for power-point titles."

He lowered his voice to them. "I'll float tonight. You two stick to checklists A and B—coherence taps and thermal cams. If a mirror starts looking like it wants to breathe, you say my name like you're summoning me from the void. It works about 60% of the time."

None of them said the rest out loud: all were still wondering whether the Array and the thing in the glass were threads of the same web. They implemented what they'd already promised, and waited to see if the world—and Avery—kept their side.

Scene 4: Private Demo at Clover Park Technical College

The auditorium at Clover Park Technical College wasn't built for grandeur—concrete walls in tired beige, tiered seats, fluorescents with a faint hum—but it had one thing their Pierce College lab didn't: space, and lots of it. Here they could spread the full rig without tripping over carts, stage the auxiliary coils and power chases, and run the Array at higher demonstration levels without squeezing past cabinets. There was room for safety lanes, room for overflow gear, room to pack in an audience and let them see it work. In the center, the Array dominated—gleaming steel arcs and a low, steady throb—like a heart wired into the building's veins.

Two work-study assistants from Clover Park, Hector and Zora, taped runs and routed leads under Lena's instruction. Naveen wasn't on cables today; Elias had pulled him up a tier—systems lead, eyes on phase and lock integrity while Lena kept the cage safe.

The DOE had secured the hall for the evening, shutting out students and staff with security tape and locked doors. The air inside carried the sterile scent of industrial cleaner, but beneath it lingered something else: ozone, faintly metallic, as if a storm were trapped in the vents.

Elias Voss stood before the machine, posture sharp, his hands folded behind his back like a general preparing to address troops. The Array's dome gleamed under the lights, cables running into power banks and diagnostic consoles. On the screen beside it, raw data flickered in green waves.

Avery Shaw strode down the aisle, his polished shoes clicking against the steps. He didn't bother hiding his impatience. He carried himself like a man used to being obeyed, his thin smile more a warning than a greeting. Behind him trailed Natalie Chen, her ever-present notepad tucked under her arm, her gaze sharp but polite.

"Dr. Voss," Avery said, voice clipped. "I trust you're ready to show me something worthwhile. I've had to cut through three layers of bureaucratic molasses just to get us here tonight."

Elias smiled faintly. "I assure you, Mr. Shaw, what you'll see will justify the effort. The Array performs best in locations with... resonance. Clover Park is one such place. The results should be unambiguous."

Lena stood at his side, quiet but tense. Her arms were folded, though not in confidence—it was a guard against the gnawing unease in her chest. She avoided looking at the Array too long; the dome seemed to pulse when she stared, like it was aware of her attention.

Avery glanced around. "Where's that sarcastic intern of yours tonight?"

"Back at Pierce," Elias said. "He's on remote—monitoring the equipment during the demonstration, watching the feeds and the breaker telemetry."

Elias tapped his earpiece. "Naveen, you're live."

"Copy," Naveen's voice crackled. "Telemetry's clean. If anything spikes, I'll scream in a very professional way. Also, hello VIPs—I'm the disembodied conscience telling Dr. V not to do crimes against physics."

Avery blinked at the speaker. "Charming."

"Corporate for 'vital to success,'" Naveen said. "Rolling pre-lock scan in three... two..."

Avery's mouth tightened. "I don't care for him. Talks too much about things better left unsaid." He flicked a look at Elias. "Keep him pointed at the work."

He cut the air with a brisk gesture. "Then get on with it."

Elias flicked a series of switches on the console. The Array hummed to life, the low vibration sinking into the floor and up through their shoes. On the monitor, spectral lines began to crawl upward, jagged teeth climbing from the baseline.

"The principle is simple," Elias began, his voice shifting into the rhythm of a lecturer who enjoyed being listened to. "Electromagnetic energy saturates our environment. We draw from it selectively. But in certain places — Fort Steilacoom, Mountain View Cemetery, and here at Clover Park — the resonance amplifies. It's as though the ground itself hums in sympathy. The yield is exponentially greater."

Natalie tilted her head, scribbling the names into her notepad. "And why these locations, specifically?" she asked.

Elias hesitated just long enough for Lena to notice. "The geology, perhaps," he said smoothly. "Fault lines, soil composition. Or perhaps something less tangible. What matters is repeatability. The Array thrives where resonance is strongest."

The machine's glow deepened, veins of blue light crawling along its dome. The hum thickened into a vibration that seemed to press against their ribs. On the monitor, the output surged, lines spiking into bands of bright green.

Avery stepped closer, hands clasped behind his back, his eyes reflecting the glow. "Impressive. And how much output are we seeing?"

"Six times baseline draw," Elias said, pride lacing his words. "Sustained. Stable."

Avery nodded once, curtly, but his gaze gleamed. "Good. Very good. Now multiply this by scale — by deployment. This is the kind of result that can't be hidden in a college basement. It needs to be presented."

Lena shifted uneasily. She leaned toward Elias, whispering so only he could hear. "You can't ignore it, Elias. You saw what happened on live television. I saw it with my own eyes here in the lab. The Array hums even when it's off. The mirrors ripple. It's not just energy. It's something else."

Elias's jaw tightened. He kept his eyes forward, fixed on Avery as if nothing had been said. But under his breath, his reply was sharp: "I am aware of the issues, Lena. But since we don't know what they are, we cannot dismiss the project because of them. We need to know more before slowing down."

Her stomach sank at his words. Issues. That was what he called them. She stared at the dome, remembering the clawed hand, the hiss of something older than language. Issues.

Avery, oblivious to their exchange, stepped even closer to the Array, like a priest before an altar. "This is more than a project. This is a revolution. And revolutions don't wait for perfect conditions. You'll show this to a larger group on Friday."

Elias blinked, caught off guard. "Friday? That's—"

"Non-negotiable," Avery cut in, his smile thin and sharp. "Momentum is everything. Strike while the world is still screaming. While they're still desperate for solutions."

Natalie, silent until now, glanced toward Lena. She touched her elbow gently and guided her a few steps aside, out of Avery's earshot. Her voice was low, careful. "What's your opinion, Dr. Mirek? Off the record."

Lena froze, caught between fear and duty. "My opinion?"

"Yes," Natalie said, eyes steady. "Whatever you say stays between us. I just want to know the truth. Any concerns you and Dr. Voss have."

Lena's pulse thudded in her throat. The words that wanted to rise — the Veilborne, the humming glass, the dread that haunted her dreams — stuck like stones behind her teeth. After a long moment, she forced her voice level.

"No concerns," she said softly. "Not at this time."

Natalie studied her face, searching, then nodded slowly. "If that changes… call me." She slipped a card into Lena's hand, her expression unreadable. "Keep my number. I'd like to hear from you directly."

Lena nodded, tucking the card into her pocket. "Of course."

Natalie's smile was small but sharp at the edges. "Good. I'll hold you to it." She turned back toward Avery, but the look in her eyes lingered — suspicion, patient and sharp as a blade.

The Array's glow brightened again, filling the hall with pale light. Elias raised his voice over the hum. "Imagine what this means, Avery. Cities powered without fuel. Energy drawn endlessly from the world around us. Clean, renewable, limitless. Imagine the contracts, the investment—"

Avery cut him off with a raised hand. "Don't imagine. Calculate. What's your estimate, Dr. Voss? What would this be worth to government and investors alike?"

Elias hesitated for effect, then asked the question already burning on his tongue. "What's your estimate?"

Avery smiled thinly, like a man revealing only part of the truth. "Easily in the billions. Perhaps more. The world will pay any price for something that cannot be shut off, cannot be embargoed, cannot be lost."

The words sent a thrill through Elias's veins. Billions. Recognition. A future carved in stone with his name on it. His chest swelled, pride sharp and intoxicating.

Beside him, Lena felt only the chill of the Array's glow. She glanced at Elias, saw the hunger in his eyes, and knew it was too late to pull him back. His ambition was a current all its own, and it would carry him — and perhaps all of them — into depths they weren't meant to touch.

Scene 5: Unanswered Questions

The dormitory lights at Clover Park Technical College had long since dimmed when Lena Mirek returned to her small apartment in a modest complex just down the hill from campus. The building sat on a quiet stretch of road, hemmed in on three sides by thick forest that pressed close against the walls like a living barricade. The trees muffled sound, swallowing even the rain into a dull hiss.

Across the street lay the wetlands — a sprawl of dark water veined with reeds and broken stumps, the ground shifting treacherously under mist. Beyond the marsh, shrouded in fog, Mountain View Cemetery stretched unseen, its weight lingering on the night air like a presence that refused to be forgotten.

The isolation of the place gnawed at Lena. No traffic passed this way at night, no voices carried from neighbors — only the restless sway of branches and the slow drip of rain. Even inside, with the door locked and the blinds drawn, the silence felt too deep, the air too heavy. And beneath it all, the hum of the Array still lived in her ears, a phantom vibration she could not shake, no matter the distance.

She dropped her bag on the table, peeled off her damp coat, and stood there for a long time without moving, staring at the glow of her laptop in the dark. The keys waited beneath her fingertips, but she hesitated. She had never betrayed Elias. Not in thought, not in word. She had built her career around his brilliance, orbiting the pull of his intellect like a moon bound to a planet. She admired him. She respected him. And—though she had never dared say it aloud—she loved him.

But tonight, something had cracked.

The demo replayed in her mind, every detail etched sharper than it had any right to be. The way the Array's dome pulsed like a living organ. The resonance that crawled beneath her skin. Avery Shaw's thin smile as he spoke of billions. Elias's eyes when the number landed, bright and hungry, like a man already standing on the stage of history.

And behind it all, the memory she could not silence: the claw of a Veilborne scraping glass in the lab, the voice like broken static whispering her name.

She closed her eyes and exhaled. Her hand trembled as she opened her email. The cursor blinked in the "To" field, accusing her of hesitation. Finally, she typed:

Abigail Jensen.

The name itself felt like rebellion. She had seen Abigail before—on television, ridiculed, called a fraud. But the look in Abigail's eyes had not been fraud. It had been conviction. The same conviction that haunted Lena now.

She began to type.

My name is Dr. Lena Mirek. I'm an assistant at Pierce College, working under Dr. Elias Voss. I've seen something I cannot explain. I think you might understand.

Her fingers stilled. She erased the last sentence. Too direct. Too damning. She tried again.

I was present for an experiment involving resonance fields. I witnessed something… unnatural. A presence in the mirrors. You spoke of them once—the Veilborne. If that is what I saw, then I fear the machine we are building might be tied to them somehow.

The word fear stuck like a lump in her throat. She had never admitted fear to Elias. He would dismiss it, rationalize it, lock it away in equations and control variables. To him, fear was noise. To her, it was the first honest signal she had heard in months.

She deleted and rewrote the sentence three times. Each version felt like betrayal. Each version felt like survival.

At last, she leaned back in her chair and let her hands fall into her lap. Her apartment was silent except for the rain against the window. But in the mirror above her dresser, she thought she saw movement. Not her reflection, but a ripple, faint as a breath.

Her chest tightened. She forced herself to look directly at it. Just her own face stared back. Hollow-eyed, weary, younger than she felt.

But for a heartbeat she thought she saw something else standing behind her—a shadow with too many joints in its hands.

The Array's hum echoed in her skull. She snapped her eyes away from the mirror and focused back on the screen.

If the Array is drawing from them—feeding them—I need to know how to stop it. Please. Tell me what you know.

Her hand hovered over the send button.

She thought of Elias. The way he had looked at her tonight, not when Avery spoke, not when the Array lit up, but when she whispered her concerns. His face had gone cold. A mask. He had not said her name with reassurance. He had dismissed her, brushed her aside like a student too timid for the subject matter.

Yet she loved him. God help her, she loved him still. His brilliance. His certainty. The way his words could make chaos sound like destiny. She had built her entire life on the foundation of his dream. To question it now felt like cutting the floor out from under her own feet.

But what if the floor had been hollow all along?

She closed her eyes and pressed send. The message flew into the void of the internet with a whoosh that sounded final, irrevocable.

The rain outside grew harder, rattling against the glass like thrown gravel. Lena hugged herself and stood, pacing the narrow room. The weight of her choice pressed on her chest. Abigail might not respond. Or worse—she might. And if Elias found out? If he learned she had gone behind his back?

Her loyalty tore at her like a rope stretched to breaking. Elias on one end, the truth on the other. And in the middle, her heart, raw and confused.

She returned to the mirror, as if daring it. Her reflection looked back, pale and haunted. She whispered aloud, "What are you feeding on?"

The silence answered with nothing but her own breath.

Her phone buzzed on the table, sharp enough to make her jump. A spam notification. She exhaled shakily, clutching her chest.

Back at the laptop, the cursor blinked in the sent folder, mocking her. No reply yet. She hadn't expected one. Not tonight. Maybe not ever. But she had crossed the line, and there was no way back.

She slid into bed, though sleep would not come. Every time she closed her eyes, she saw the Array glowing like an egg about to hatch, veins of blue pulsing with something that did not belong in this world. Every time she drifted, she heard whispers at the edge of hearing: new meat, new meat, new meat.

She turned over, burying her face in the pillow, tears stinging at the corners of her eyes. "Please, Elias," she whispered to the dark. "Don't let this destroy you. Don't let it destroy us."

But even as she said it, she knew it was already too late. Something had been set in motion, and no amount of loyalty, or love, or silence could stop it now.

7

Fractured Signals

Scene 1: Viral Terror

The walls of the Fairmont Olympic Hotel in downtown Seattle—the golden crown of luxury, its Italian Renaissance architecture a jewel among the city's skyline—enforced spotless elegance. Its grand lobby whispers the echoes of historic opulence. And, tonight, just beyond those velvet ropes, in the glossy hallway outside the elevator bank, Crystal Reeve staged her shining moment.

Crystal Reeve—her followers knew her by her handle, *@Crystal-Radiance*—adjusted the jeweled strap of her cocktail dress and leaned toward the camera. Her smile gleamed, framed in matte lipstick the color of blood roses. Gold earrings brushed against her shoulders as she flicked her hair, each movement deliberate, choreographed for maximum effect.

She began her livestream with a knowing nod. "Hey, loves—Crystal here, coming to you from none other than the Fairmont Olympic Hotel," she purred to the camera, framing the ornate molding above the elevator doors behind her. "If you're gonna do the Mirror Challenge, you may as well do it in style."

She raised her chin and gave the camera a confident wink. Her comment section ticked upward in real time: Slay queen, You're braver than me, It's all fake anyway. Hearts and fire emojis flooded the live stream. She was drunk on it.

She gestured toward the covered mirror. "Somebody thought they'd hide this with a sheet." Her laugh was brittle, sharp. "Cute, right? But if you're watching my stream, you know your girl doesn't run from shadows."

Crystal tugged at the cloth. It resisted for a moment, clinging as though the glass itself didn't want to be exposed, then slipped free with a hiss of fabric. The hallway lights reflected instantly, throwing back her flawless silhouette.

She positioned herself before the uncovered mirror, shoulders squared, hand on her hip. "Sixty seconds. Watch and learn."

The timer on her phone ticked.

At first there was only her reflection: the perfect figure, glossy hair, bright smile. She smoothed the line of her dress, tilted her chin, and performed micro-adjustments that her followers ate up like sugar. The seconds passed. Her confidence grew. She mouthed lyrics to the trending song playing faintly from her phone speaker, her laugh spilling out when a viewer typed: Told you it's fake.

Thirty-five seconds.

Her reflection quivered.

It was subtle, like heat shimmer above pavement, a wavering in the glass. Crystal didn't notice. She was too busy leaning closer to adjust a strand of hair, her lips pursed in mock concentration.

The ripple deepened. Shadows bled into the reflection, seeping like ink through water. Behind her mirrored self, something vast stirred.

Forty seconds.

The first to notice wasn't Crystal. It was the thousands watching. Comments began to fly: WTF is that? ... Behind you ... Is this a filter? ... Stop joking, this is creepy.

Crystal giggled, blowing a kiss. "Oh, you guys are just hyping yourselves up. Nothing here but me."

The reflection disagreed.

The glass bulged inward, distorting her image as if someone pressed against it from behind. Fingers—elongated, bone-white, tipped with obsidian claws—spread across the inside surface of the mirror. They left streaks of shadow where they touched, as though the light itself recoiled.

Forty-five seconds.

Crystal finally froze. Her grin faltered, her eyes darting toward the spreading darkness in the glass. "Okay… that's—" She forced a laugh, though her voice cracked. "Seriously, who's doing this? Is this some AR thing?"

The mirror shuddered.

A face formed in the gloom, inhuman and eyeless save for cavernous sockets where black smoke curled like restless serpents. Its skin gleamed like obsidian fractured by fire. Its mouth split open, too wide, bristling with jagged teeth that looked carved from volcanic rock.

The Veilborne pushed through.

The sheet she had tossed aside fluttered upward as if caught in a sudden gale. Crystal screamed, a raw sound that broke the hallway's sterile silence. She stumbled back, heels scraping against marble.

The camera caught everything.

The creature burst from the mirror in a surge of obsidian limbs, its body glistening like molten stone cooled in water, veins of fire glowing faint beneath its skin. Behind it, the glass no longer showed the hotel hallway but something else—something vast, wrong, and terrifying.

Viewers saw glimpses of the In Between.

Corridors of black glass stretched into infinity, their surfaces slick with dripping condensation that gleamed like oil. Wisps of pale figures pressed against the reflective walls—faces hollow, mouths stretched in eternal screams. They clawed soundlessly at the glass, their eyes vacant with torment.

Deeper still, the shapes of other Veilborne prowled, their claws rending threads of luminous soul-light from the phantoms. The creatures fed with animal hunger, tearing and swallowing the essence in writhing gulps. The air behind them shimmered with smoke, fire, and the faint, terrible sound of endless weeping.

The audience at home saw it all.

Crystal's phone had fallen sideways to the floor, lens still aimed at her as she shrieked, clawing at the tiles. Her jeweled strap snapped as she thrashed, nails splintering against the polished floor. The Veilborne wrapped its talons around her wrist. Her skin blistered where it touched, smoke rising from the seared flesh.

"No! No, stop! Somebody help me!" she wailed, kicking, heels snapping against the marble.

The creature's head tilted, almost curious. Then it yanked.

Her body arched, heels skidding furrows in the polished surface. She sobbed and screamed, voice breaking into guttural pleas. "Please! I'll stop—just stop!"

The Veilborne didn't. It dragged her across the floor with brutal efficiency. Her phone tumbled again, briefly capturing her tear-streaked, distorted face as her free hand clawed at the doorframe of the elevator lobby. Skin scraped, blood smeared across chrome. She was hauled up, her body half disappearing into the glass.

For one last moment the mirror framed both worlds: the sterile hotel hallway, and the abyssal nightmare beyond. Then she was gone.

The phone lay abandoned, still streaming, still recording the mirror. For a heartbeat, watchers at home swore they saw her reflection inside, face pressed against the glass, mouth open in an endless scream before darkness swallowed it whole.

Then the hallway was empty.

Within minutes, the video exploded across every platform.

Clips of her abduction looped endlessly, dissected frame by frame. Online, hashtags trended globally: *#MirrorChallenge, #CrystalReeve, #NotStaged.* Millions argued whether the footage was CGI, a prank, or undeniable evidence of something monstrous. Reddit threads catalogued freeze-frames of the In Between, circling pale faces of trapped souls and shadowed corners where other Veilborne lurked.

News anchors replayed the footage on a loop, grim-faced, debating "possible explanations." Experts on digital forensics swore it wasn't doctored. Parapsychologists were invited onto panels. Politicians called for calm, insisting that "appropriate agencies" were investigating.

But the public didn't calm—panic deepened.

When Russell was dragged through a studio mirror, some still muttered "stunt" and "deepfake." With Crystal, there was no refuge in doubt. People saw where they were taken and what waited there. The footage—her vanishing and the glimpse beyond—turned fear from rumor to proof. Hotels fielded demands to strip every room of mirrors. Hardware stores sold out of blackout curtains and duct tape overnight. Feeds filled with people smashing glass not for likes but for safety.

Crystal Reeve's name became a warning, not a meme. There were no skeptics left.

Russell Langston's abduction had shocked television audiences. Crystal's streamed disappearance was something worse—it was participatory horror. Everyone had seen it at once, through her lens, her vanity, her desperate hunger for attention. They had been watching when the nightmare reached out and claimed her.

And behind her, through the window of glass, millions had caught their first glimpse of the In Between—of the place where screams were currency and Veilborne fed without end.

No one could unsee it.

Scene 2: Rules and Revelation

The house in Tillicum was quiet—only the tick of an old mantel clock and the rasp of Abigail's breath as she laid out the circle. It sat across American Lake from her own place—a short drive, a world away. She had cleared the living room of furniture, pushing a heavy sofa into the corner, leaving bare space for salt, chalk, and candles. In the middle of the far wall stood the culprit: a tall, gilt-framed mirror that reflected more shadow than light, its surface faintly rippling even when no one stood near it. The family who lived here—a husband, wife, and their teenage daughter—had been evacuated to a neighbor's house at Abigail's insistence. They'd described voices behind the glass, whispers that rose into shrieks, and, most horrifying, a hand pressing outward, fingertips white against the pane as though begging to be freed.

Now, Abigail faced it alone.

She sprinkled salt in a steady circle, her hand trembling as she completed the line and sealed the space between herself and the mirror. "By the light that binds, by the Word that seals, I close the path and guard the threshold," she whispered, voice catching on the final word.

The candles guttered at once, their flames shrinking low, and the air pressed heavy against her chest. Abigail straightened, clutching the rosary Father Allen had given her years ago, its beads warm with her sweat. The mirror darkened as though a storm cloud had rolled behind it, and from that depth came a low, guttural resonance—not sound, but vibration, like an organ pipe too deep for human ears.

Her pulse thundered. She began the chant, words drawn from ritual she had repeated countless times, each syllable carried with the weight of intention. The chalk lines on the floor seemed to glow faintly, reacting to her will.

The mirror shivered.

Then came the first strike. A clawed hand, black as soot but gleaming with a wet sheen, slammed against the inside of the glass. Abigail staggered, but held the chant. Another hand joined it, and then the outline of a face pressed close, eyeless sockets hollow and hungry. The glass flexed outward, forming a shallow dome.

Her voice rose louder. "By the covenant of balance, by the chain of order, return!"

The figure pushed harder. The glass strained. A jagged crack ran down the surface like lightning. Through the fracture, Abigail glimpsed a place beyond—an obsidian corridor lined with pale, shrieking figures, their arms reaching, their mouths open in endless cries. Veilborne shadows circled them, tearing luminous strands of energy from their bodies and devouring them in spasms of hunger. The stink of sulfur and smoke wafted into the room.

Abigail's knees shook. For a moment, she thought the mirror would burst entirely, spilling them into the living world.

Then the creature stepped through.

Its body was a twisting silhouette, edges flickering like torn film, its jaw unhinging with a hiss that scalded the air. It crouched against the inside of the glass as though testing how far it could emerge.

Abigail forced the words out, louder still: "You are not welcome here! This house is sealed!"

The Veilborne froze. Its hollow face turned toward her, sockets locking onto her like a predator noticing prey. She thought it would lunge. She braced, sweat running down her spine.

Then—hesitation.

The creature cocked its head, emitting a sound like bones grinding. It extended one claw, raking it down the glass, sparks trailing, then pulled back. For one long, dreadful moment, it studied her. Its body seemed to ripple with frustration. Finally, with a snarl that rattled the windowpanes, it recoiled into the mirror and vanished into the darkness beyond.

The glass stilled.

Abigail fell to her knees, gasping, her palms flat against the chalk circle. The candles flared bright, then burned steady, and the room lightened as if a storm had passed. The mirror remained cracked but inert, its surface dull. For now.

She stayed kneeling until her breath steadied. Even after all these years, the toll of such rituals left her shaking, her muscles weak as if she had run miles uphill. She wiped her brow, leaving a streak of chalk dust across her temple.

When she finally rose, she moved to the dining table where she had laid out her notes—scraps of paper, photographs, and printouts pinned to a folded map of Pierce County. Each incident she had investigated over the last month was marked in red ink. Disappearances. Reports of mirrors behaving strangely. Shadows in glass.

She added tonight's location: a small suburban house in Tillicum, south of Tacoma. The dots stretched across the map like drops of blood. She leaned back, eyes narrowing.

The pattern wasn't random.

At first, it looked scattered, but as she studied it again, she saw the curve. Not a circle, but a crescent, arcing cleanly around one place in particular: Clover Park Technical College.

Her stomach dropped.

She traced the crescent with her fingertip, whispering to herself, "Why there? What anchors them to that ground?"

The candle flames flickered though there was no breeze. Abigail sat heavily, burying her face in her hands. She thought of Russell Langston's abduction on live television, the influencer dragged screaming from a hotel hallway just days later. The veil wasn't just thinning—it was tearing. And now, all the threads seemed to knot around Clover Park.

The chime of her phone broke the silence. She reached for it with hands that still trembled.

A new email. Unknown sender.

Subject: We need to talk.

She opened it.

Dr. Jensen,

My name is Dr. Lena Mirek. I'm an assistant at Pierce College, working under Dr. Elias Voss. I've seen something I cannot explain. I was present for an experiment involving resonance fields. I witnessed something… unnatural. A presence in the mirrors. You spoke of them once—the Veilborne. If that is what I saw, then I fear the machine we are building might be tied to them somehow.

Please. I don't know who else to turn to.

Abigail's chest tightened. She stared at the words, re-reading them until the letters blurred. Another presence. Another witness. And not just a witness—someone inside a lab, someone working on a machine. She didn't yet know what that machine was, but the phrasing—"resonance fields"—set her heart pounding.

Her fingers hovered over the reply button, but she stopped. Not yet. She needed to think.

Thunder cracked in the distance, and the house groaned with the wind. Abigail turned back to the map, the crescent of incidents surrounding Clover Park glaring back at her like a wound.

The Veilborne had recoiled from her, yes. But not defeated. They were gathering, pressing harder, hungrier. And now someone inside Pierce College was reaching out to her for help.

She whispered to the empty room: "It's beginning again."

The cracked mirror across the room gave back her reflection—small, weary, defiant—its surface still, but she could not shake the feeling that something inside was watching.

Scene 3: The Echo's Chosen

Abigail heard the knock before she saw the headlights skim across the living room wall. The cottage had gone quiet after dinner—Jacob upstairs, the lake settling under a steady wind—so the sound felt louder than it was. She wiped her hands on a dish towel and opened the door to Mara Alvarez, a trusted medium whom Abigail often works with, cheeks pink from the cold, scarf looped twice around her neck like a charm she trusted.

"Sorry for the hour," Mara said as Abigail waved her in. "Traffic on South Tacoma Way is all nervous energy. Half the city's out buying blackout curtains."

"You saw the same broadcasts I did," Abigail said. "Tea?"

"Please." Mara shrugged off her coat and boots, eyes already noting the strips of matte film over picture frames, the face-down mirror on the sideboard, the neat ribbon of salt along the baseboard. "Practical is the new pretty," she said, aiming for lightness and almost getting there.

They sat in the living room—Mara in the tweed chair by the window, Abigail on the couch. The kettle's steam softened the air, but couldn't lift its weight. Since the first reports out of Lakewood, since the late-night calls, the house seemed to hold its breath between knocks.

"How bad?" Abigail asked.

"Worse than last week." Mara cupped her mug. "Puyallup, Sumner, Bonney Lake. Not copycat stories anymore. Families gone. People grabbed at the edge of their reflection. A salon on 112th—mirrors taped over—and a client swore she saw hands pushing at the tape from underneath." She shook her head. "You've probably heard half of it already."

"I keep a list," Abigail said, nodding toward the journal on the side table. "Helps me see where the tide's moving."

"Or lets us pretend we're taller than it." Mara tried to smile. It held for a heartbeat, then faded.

They traded the not-small small talk—neighbors calling, what coverings work, which myths don't—until the raft of normal conversation bumped the harder thing waiting in the room.

"Where's Jacob?" Mara asked.

"Upstairs. Drawing." Despite herself, Abigail smiled. "He says it quiets the noise."

"Smart boy."

"Too smart." Abigail sipped her tea. "He's been... clearer lately."

Before Mara could answer, her gaze caught on the stack of paper at the edge of the coffee table—pencil smudges, the top sheet askew. She reached without thinking. "May I?"

"Sure."

Mara slid the drawing into the lamplight and went still.

It wasn't a doodle. A long nave made of dark ribs. A floor like glass. Doorways that weren't doors. Perspective pulled the eye toward a shape too large for the page, its head nearly cropped. Lantern-pricks flanked its outline. Between the ribs, thin angled forms—Veilborne reduced to hard geometry—bent toward the center as if tugged there. And at the very bottom margin, almost an afterthought, a small figure sketched with a few sure lines stood in profile, one hand lifted in a simple stop.

Mara's fingers tightened on the paper. She exhaled as if she'd reached a ridge and seen the valley beyond.

Silence settled. The cooling kettle clicked.

Mara studied the drawing, eyes narrowing. When she finally spoke, her voice had the quiet precision she saved for truths that arrived uninvited. "Jacob... he is the chosen one."

Abigail blinked. "What?"

"The Echo has set its mark on him." Mara looked up now, steady. "I feel it humming out of the graphite. Not EMF. Something older. A signature the body knows before language does. This isn't a guess. It's a witness sketch."

Abigail set her cup down before her hands could betray the shift in her chest. "He told me he hears the Echo," she said carefully. "I believed him. But 'chosen'—that's..."

"Weighty," Mara supplied. "Yes." She glanced from the page to Abigail's face, and her expression changed again—as if catching a second frequency layered beneath the first. "And you—"

Abigail waited.

"You are forbidden," Mara said, plain as a diagnosis.

Abigail drew a breath. "Jacob said that too. And the Veilborne used the same word—like an insult." She glanced toward the window, then back to Mara. "I didn't need a label to see it, but it helps to say it out loud."

Mara nodded. "You're both marked. It isn't only danger. It's appointment. Roles handed out before either of you asked for them." Something like envy flickered and was gone. "I read cards for strangers who want permission to be brave. You don't get cards. You get orders."

Abigail picked up the drawing and studied it like a map: the ribs of the nave, the small raised hand, the bowed immensity. The pencil smudge at the corner came away on her thumb; the ordinary smear steadied her.

"What does 'chosen' mean, practically?" she asked. "Prophecy makes for lousy checklists."

"Practically?" Mara leaned forward. "The In Between isn't abstract to him; it answers. Doors will open for Jacob that won't for you or me. Veilborne will feel it when he stands in a room like animals feel earthquakes—some will bow, some will bite harder."

"And 'forbidden'?"

"You are a wall to them," Mara said. "A sign that says Do Not Touch written in a hand they hate. I don't know why the mark sits on you, but it does. Whatever is coming will try to move around you. Or through you. That's why Jacob's certainty matters. He will stand where you cannot, and you will stand where he should not."

The burner ticked softly as the blue flame held steady beneath the pan. Upstairs, a floorboard gave a small complaint—a boy shifting in his chair. Abigail's throat tightened.

"Breathe," Mara said gently.

"I am," Abigail said, realizing she hadn't been. She inhaled, let it out. "It's a lot."

"It's not a sentence," Mara said. "It's a summons."

They sat with that. The lake's light touched the curtains and drew back. Across the street, a car door closed and a porch light snapped on.

Abigail turned Mara's words over, feeling their weight settle. He'll go where she can't. She'll go where Jacob shouldn't. Protector—that's what it meant, not just guardian of bedtime and homework, but of thresholds. She'd taken responsibility for him, yes, even started to help him shape the strange edge of his gift. But she hadn't understood the scale—the importance of it. Chosen. The word changed the room. Did Joseph and Maria know? Had they guessed at any of this when they'd asked her to keep him safe? The questions pressed close; the answer was the same either way: he was hers to shield until the path demanded otherwise.

Abigail let the thought settle, then looked back to Mara.

"I came to talk shop," Mara said, almost sheepish after dropping two stones in the room. "We can do that too. I've had three calls today—coverings, salt lines, what to do with mirrors you can't remove. People are scared. Some are reckless. I told the Parkers to keep their bathroom mirror taped no matter how ugly it looks. He called it superstition. She didn't. Guess which one I'm more worried about."

"Both," Abigail said.

"Both," Mara agreed. "I brought matte film and old iron nails." She tapped the canvas tote by her chair. "We're going to have to be practical and holy at the same time."

"Is that what we are now?"

"It's what we were anyway," Mara said. "We just get fewer breaks."

They shared a small laugh with the shape of long friendship.

Mara set the drawing down carefully, as if a careless elbow might unspool it. "Whatever you two are walking into, it's not the usual run of hauntings," she said. "It's the sort that changes vocabulary—what people mean when they say keeper, or mercy."

"Do I tell him?" Abigail asked, surprising herself with the question.

"Jacob?" Mara considered. "Not yet." She nodded toward the ceiling. "Let him draw tonight. Tell him when you must. And when you do, tell him this: it isn't the chosen who make the story. It's the choices."

They rose. At the doorway, Mara paused. "Do you want a circle set?"

"Please."

They worked in practiced quiet: four corners, salt and iron, a whispered prayer older than either of their particular traditions. When they finished, the room didn't feel safe exactly, but it felt claimed.

Coat on, boots laced, Mara glanced back at the living room where the drawing lay like a new word on a table. "Place this early," she said, half teasing her own habit of narrating. "Before the story decides you learned it too late."

"Thank you."

"Call if anything breathes that shouldn't," Mara added, then winced. "Or if it stops breathing and that's worse."

She stepped into the hall, hand on the knob—then paused. A small catch in her breath. She turned back, eyes unfocused for a beat as if listening to another room. When she met Abigail's gaze again, her voice was matter-of-fact. "You'll call me soon. You'll send me east—to help friends. I'll be ready. Just say when."

Abigail blinked, a flicker of confusion crossing her face. Then calm settled in; this was Mara's gift, the way she saw the bend in the road before anyone else felt the turn. If Mara said it would happen, it would. "All right," Abigail said quietly. "I'll call."

Mara nodded once, certain, and slipped out.

After she left, Abigail stood with her hand on the doorframe and let the house settle around her. Upstairs, pencil scratched across paper—a small sound, sure and unafraid. She crossed back to the coffee table, slid Jacob's drawing into a plastic sleeve, and tucked it into the sideboard—not to hide it, but to guard it from spills and elbows and busy mornings. The promise of "east" lingered, but her worry stayed here: Jacob, and the work of being the one who walks where he shouldn't, so that he can walk where she can't.

On her way to the lamp, she caught her reflection in the dark television screen. It held, ordinary, no lag. She draped a throw over the glass anyway. The room went to moonlight and the low, steady sound of the lake.

"Important," she said quietly into the stillness, hearing Mara's word in her own voice. "All right."

Scene 4: First Meeting

The corridors of Pierce College's engineering wing were deserted at this hour, their cinderblock walls humming faintly with the after-hours quiet of machines left in standby. Abigail Jensen walked with measured steps, boots soft against tile, eyes catching each reflective surface—the black windows, the trophy case glass, the stainless panels on vending machines. Every shimmer tugged at her attention. Every flicker of shadow set her pulse on edge.

Through the stairwell's narrow window she'd seen the slope of land as she approached. The college perched on a hill; beneath it—though most students never thought of it—lay the scarred ground of Hill Ward, the old asylum dormitory ruins, and the dark expanse of Fort Steilacoom Park. Places like this carried history in layers: sorrow, confinement, long echoes. Paranormal residue clung to them the way fog clings to valleys. Of course the veil thinned here.

She pushed open the lab door.

Lena looked up first, relief breaking across the tension in her face. "Abigail," she said, stepping forward. "You made it." She turned to the others. "Elias—Naveen—this is Abigail Jensen."

Naveen, halfway through a sip of cold coffee, nearly choked. "Abigail Jensen? The... Abigail Jensen? Here?" He set the cup down like it might explode and tried to smooth his hoodie into something resembling respectability. "Uh—hi. Big fan. Podcast changed my entire understanding of... pretty much everything."

Elias Voss stood near the main console, arms crossed, posture sharp. He gave the smallest nod—guarded, skeptical. "We weren't told to expect a visitor," he said, tone clipped. His eyes flicked to Lena.

"Surprise," Naveen muttered, recovering a fraction of his usual edge. "You caught us mid–'please don't haunt our grant' hour."

Abigail didn't answer that. She let the silence stretch, then fixed her gaze on Elias with the quiet intensity she'd honed over years of listening to what most people couldn't bear to hear. Something stirred around him, a trace like the afterimage of grief. She stepped closer, voice soft but certain.

"You still keep Camille's scarf in your desk," she said. "Sometimes you press it to your face when you think no one's watching."

Elias stiffened, breath catching. Suspicion flared, then unease. "How would you know that?" Too fast, too rough.

Lena cut in. "Because she's clairvoyant, Elias. You know that. You just don't like it."

Naveen's smirk faded; the fanboy awe won. He eased back a step, laptop hugged to his chest, and fell quiet.

"Anyone could guess I keep mementos," Elias said, reaching for dismissive and not finding it. "That proves nothing."

Abigail tilted her head as if listening to a voice just off to his left. "Your father whistled the same three notes every time he left the house. You do it now when you're stressed—without meaning to."

Color drained from Elias's face. "No one knows that."

"I do," Abigail said.

The hum of the lab pressed in. Elias's usual armor—method, cadence, control—didn't quite fit.

"I don't like being read," he said, tension sharpening the words.

"I didn't ask to know," Abigail replied. "Sometimes truth doesn't wait for permission."

Lena let the moment settle, then moved. "Abigail's the reason I reached out. We needed her."

Elias's gaze snapped to her. "We?"

"Yes," Lena said. "I wrote to her. You've been refusing to name what you saw here. I couldn't keep pretending."

Naveen slid to the periphery, quieter now, eyes flicking between the three of them and the Array like he was tracking a live experiment.

"What is this machine?" Abigail asked.

Elias seized the safer ground, gesturing at the Array. He launched into resonance fields and ambient capture—dense, clinical. Abigail's brow knit.

"That doesn't mean anything to me," she admitted.

Lena translated. "We pull electricity out of the EMF around us. Think of it as skimming from the static of the world."

"Electricity from ghosts?" Abigail asked.

"I didn't say that," Elias bristled.

"But if the Veilborne are real," Lena said, steady, "then some of that 'static' might be tied to them. Or to where they come from."

"You're tampering with currents you don't understand," Abigail said.

"We need data, not folklore," Elias shot back.

"Data won't save you if you're drawing from the wrong well," she said.

Lena pulled up video: Crystal Vale at the hotel; the ripple; the claws; the glimpse behind—the In Between. Elias's composure cracked. "That's not an effect," he breathed.

"No," Lena said. "And it's everywhere now."

"They're terrified because they saw behind it," Abigail said. "They saw where people go."

Another clip: Russell Langston vanishing live on air.

"I was there," Abigail said. "Once they come, there's little anyone can do."

"So it's escalating," Elias said.

"Exactly. And your machine may be making their hunt easier."

Elias didn't argue. The thought hung like a wire.

From the edge, Naveen finally spoke, voice low. "I've been logging cross-correlations." He turned his screen—timestamps and plots. "No conclusions. But the timing's… ugly." He caught Abigail's eye, the sarcasm gone. "I don't joke when I'm scared," he said, then faded back again.

They stood in the hum and the weight of what the world had seen.

Elias found his voice. "We already sent our safety protocols to Natalie Chen. Avery signed off. We implement them and keep our commitments. We don't improvise scared."

Abigail held his gaze. "Then implement them knowing you're not the only ones drawing lines in this room."

Lena nodded. "We asked you here because we need both: proof—and caution."

A beat passed. Naveen tested a half-smile. "Okay. Team roster: science, caution, and ghost-adjacent diplomacy." He peered mournfully into his cup. "And if anyone's clairvoyant about where I left the rest of my coffee, I'm all ears."

Scene 5: Interrupted Warnings

The lab was quiet except for the low hum of machines, the faint tick of cooling metal, and the glow of monitors casting long reflections across the polished concrete floor. Elias sat stiffly at the console, jaw set as if bracing against everything he had just seen. Lena hovered nearby, arms crossed tightly, her gaze shifting between him and Abigail, who stood calmly at the center of the room as though she had been waiting years for this conversation. Near the back bench, Naveen pretended to be absorbed in a diagnostics window, earbuds out, posture alert. He tossed a quick, nervous grin Abigail's way that said both I'm skeptical and also I've listened to every episode of your show.

Abigail drew a slow breath, her voice steady. "You've both seen enough to know this isn't random. These... things people are calling monsters—they're not creatures born from superstition. They are the Veilborne. Jailers. Keepers. They dwell in a place between worlds that I've come to know as the In Between."

Lena's eyes narrowed. "The In Between?"

Abigail nodded. "It's not heaven. Not hell. It's a place where souls who are lost, trapped, or denied passage linger. A place of weight and hunger. Most people never glimpse it. But when the veil thins, mirrors become more than glass. They become doors."

Naveen whistled under his breath—one soft note—then caught himself and shoved his hands into his hoodie pocket.

The words sank into the lab like stones tossed into water, rippling across the silence.

Elias leaned forward, hands gripping the edge of the console. "You speak as though you've been there."

"I have," Abigail said softly. "I released Adam Duncan, a soul trapped in an antique clock, and when I did, Joseph Duncan, his distant relative, was pulled into the In Between. I went in after him and I saw what waits there. I saw the Veilborne feeding on the lost. I saw the Echo—the one who rules that realm, who keeps balance."

Lena's brow furrowed. "Wait—you said you freed Adam. And Joseph... you mentioned rescuing him. Are you saying Joseph Duncan really was trapped there?"

"Yes," Abigail answered, gaze steady. "When Adam was released, Joseph was taken in Adam's place, condemned to linger. I went after him. I faced the Echo itself to bring Joseph back. That's how I know what waits on the other side."

From the back, Naveen had stopped pretending to type. He was listening, face gone serious, mouth a thin line.

Elias's skeptical veneer cracked with unease. "And if that's true—if you stood before this Echo—how are you standing here now?"

Abigail's eyes softened. For a moment she seemed less like a woman in their lab and more like someone peering through time, recalling something carved into her bones. "The Echo showed me mercy. It cast me out. It could have held me, condemned me to that place as it has so many others. But instead, it let me go. Not because I deserved it. Because it chose to."

The room chilled. Even Elias, with all his equations and denials, couldn't disguise the shiver that ran through him.

"So the Echo isn't evil," Lena said carefully. "It isn't some... demon?"

"No." Abigail's voice was quiet, resolute. "The Echo is not good or evil. It is balance. Judgment. When the veil frays and the scales tip, the Echo ensures the In Between doesn't collapse into chaos. But balance has its costs. If the scales fall too far, lives are taken. Not out of cruelty. Out of necessity."

Her words hung in the air, heavy and undeniable.

Abigail continued, tone darkening. "Your machine—the Array—may be drawing energy directly out of the In Between. I don't know how, or why it resonates with that place, but I've seen the signs. Every abduction, every ripple—it's building into a pattern. And the Veilborne are taking people to restore what's been disturbed."

Lena swallowed, voice barely a whisper. "The machine might be feeding them..."

"I don't understand one thing," Abigail said, pulling a folded map from her bag. She spread it across the lab bench, pinning it with a clipboard and a wrench. Marked circles dotted the paper—sites of recent abductions and disturbances. "Look. These incidents form a crescent, an arc that curves around Clover Park Technical College. Not Pierce College. That's why I can't yet prove the connection. If the Array is to blame, why does the arc focus there?"

For the first time since she began speaking, Elias seized on an opening. He stood straighter, almost triumphant. "You see? Even you admit your theory doesn't hold. Clover Park isn't our base of operations. You're wrong."

From the back: "Bold strategy, Cotton," Naveen murmured—then winced at himself and went quiet.

But before Elias could go further, Lena snapped her head toward him, eyes flashing. "What do you mean, Elias?"

Elias blinked, thrown by the sharpness in her tone. "What do I mean?"

"You said Clover Park isn't our base," Lena pressed. "But you know as well as I do—we run Array setups there all the time. Because the EMF spikes are highest at that campus. You've said it yourself: Clover Park yields the strongest resonance."

Elias opened his mouth, closed it again. "That doesn't prove—"

"Stop it!" Lena's voice cracked, startling even herself. Her hands balled into fists. "Stop pretending you don't see what's happening! Stop hiding behind pride and theory. Abigail is right. The incidents form around Clover Park because that's where you keep pushing the Array hardest. You've been pulling from wells you don't understand, and people are being dragged into mirrors as a result."

The silence that followed was jagged, raw.

Abigail's gaze moved between them, seeing in Elias the sheen of ambition he refused to release, and in Lena the fear that love and loyalty had honed to a blade.

Elias's voice, when it came, was low, wounded. "Do you think I want this? Do you think I built the Array to feed monsters?" His eyes burned with a mixture of grief and defiance. "I built it to give us a future. To prove that energy doesn't have to come from fossil fuel, from uranium, from tearing the world apart. If I stop now, everything I've fought for—everything Camille and I dreamed of—dies with it."

Lena's expression softened, but only slightly. "And how many more people die before you're willing to admit the cost?"

The room seemed to tilt in that moment, three lives balanced on a fault line none of them could see the end of.

Abigail reached forward, pressing her fingertips to the map. "This isn't speculation anymore. The Veilborne aren't appearing at random. They're responding. The more your Array feeds, the more they come. And if the Echo senses the imbalance is beyond repair—if it judges humanity itself responsible—the cost will be far greater than we can bear."

Elias's shoulders sagged, as though the weight of her words pressed into his bones. For the first time, his confidence faltered not as denial but as grief.

Before any of them could speak again, the lab door slammed open.

From his desk in the back, Naveen had been half-listening—one ear on Abigail, one eye on a social feed he definitely shouldn't have open. His thumb froze mid-scroll. Color drained from his face. "Uh—Dr. Voss... you need to see this. Right now." He swiveled his monitor toward them and shoved the volume up. A shaky phone video filled the screen: a Parkland storefront at evening rush. A woman with shopping bags paused at a wide display mirror. The glass rippled; a claw—black, hooked—shot out and yanked her backward. Behind it: the In Between—shadow corridors, pressed faces, smoke moving like a living thing.

The footage ended with the camera clattering to the sidewalk, bystanders screaming, the mirror going still.

Naveen's face had gone pale. "It's everywhere already—news, socials—millions of views. They're calling it another 'mirror feeding.'" He swallowed, added softly, "And yeah... it looks real."

The room was silent, all three staring at the screen.

Abigail's voice broke the stillness, low and grim. "They're not feeding in secret anymore. The veil is breaking faster than we can keep up."

Lena's hands trembled as she crossed her arms, gripping herself tight. "How many more?" she whispered.

Elias looked at the tablet, his reflection faint in the dark glass. For once, he had no answer.

Naveen exhaled, tried for a wry edge that didn't quite land. "So… consensus is: not great." He tucked the tablet under his arm and stepped back, letting the gravity resettle where it belonged. "Tell me where you want me. I'll do it."

8

Pressures of Power

Scene 1: The Meeting with Avery

The conference room smelled faintly of coffee left too long on a warmer, the bitter tang mixing with the chemical sting of cleaning solution. It was windowless, a square space with a long steel-framed table, a clock that ticked too loudly, and thin walls that did little to muffle the background hum of the Array in the adjoining lab. That sound seeped through, low and steady, like the heartbeat of some unseen animal.

Elias Voss sat at the head of the table, his posture tight, hands clasped before him. He told himself he was calm, collected, but the truth was that the noise on the other side of the wall made his teeth ache. He could still feel the pull of that night—the mirror shuddering, the shadowed talons grasping for Lena. He had killed the power in time, but the memory lingered. Since then, every cycle of the Array seemed to hum with a darker resonance, as if it were remembering too.

The door opened sharply. Avery Shaw entered like a man arriving for a coronation. His suit was an immaculate navy with a subtle sheen under the overhead fluorescents. His tie was tight, his cufflinks gold. A faint cloud of expensive cologne trailed him in, masking the stale

144

smell of the room. He carried a slim black folder tucked under one arm and wore a smile that never quite touched his eyes.

"Dr. Voss," Avery said warmly, extending his hand across the table. "Our visionary."

Elias rose and shook it. Avery's grip was firm, lingering just long enough to remind him who thought he was in control.

"Visionary might be a stretch," Elias replied, though the word lit a spark of satisfaction in his chest.

"Nonsense," Avery said, moving smoothly to a chair and sitting without waiting to be offered. "What you've built is more than science. It's revolution. The kind of work that will be remembered long after both of us are dust." He opened his folder and slid a packet of documents across the table. Charts, numbers, projected models—all dressed up with government logos.

Elias didn't touch it. "You've seen the output logs, then."

"I have," Avery said, eyes bright. "And I've seen enough to know we're standing at the edge of something game-changing. Untapped billions of dollars waiting to be harvested. Energy that doesn't depend on weather, fuel, or foreign resources. Clean. Limitless. Controllable." He leaned forward, voice lowering as though to confide a secret. "Do you know what that means, Elias?"

"Go on," Elias said carefully.

"It means power," Avery said. "Not just electricity, but influence. Whoever controls this technology controls the future. And your name will be written into history as the man who gave humanity its next leap forward."

The words burrowed deep. Elias had heard variations of them before from colleagues, investors, professors. But never with such weight. He thought of Camille, her laughter in the lab late at night, the way her hands had steadied his when the first crude prototypes failed. They had dreamed of this—of building something that would change the world. But the memory of her death clashed against the praise, souring it. She should have been here to hear it.

"You're flattering me," Elias said, forcing a half-smile.

"I'm preparing you," Avery corrected smoothly. "The government wants results. Faster. Bigger. Stronger. If you can show us that the Array can scale, I can get you everything you need—funding without limits, access to secure sites, a seat at the table with people who shape nations."

Elias's pulse quickened despite himself. He had longed for recognition, for proof that his work mattered beyond the walls of the college lab. Yet he heard Lena's voice in his memory, her quiet fear when she spoke of the Veilborne, of the night the Array seemed to stir something it shouldn't have.

"You're asking me to accelerate development," Elias said.

"I'm telling you it's time," Avery replied. He leaned back in his chair, folding his hands across his lap. "This isn't the moment to hesitate, Elias. The world is watching. Chaos always breeds rumor. Urban hysteria. People seeing monsters in mirrors because it's easier than admitting they don't understand energy fluctuations or environmental anomalies."

Elias stiffened. "You've heard the reports."

"Of course I have," Avery said dismissively, flicking a hand. "Everyone has. Some poor fool on live television claimed to vanish into a prop mirror. An influencer staging her own disappearance in a hotel hallway. Viral content designed to scare the gullible and make the rest of us roll our eyes. It's theater, not reality."

Elias said nothing, his mind replaying Russell Langston's face as it twisted in terror, the way Abigail had screamed for the Veilborne to stop, the silence when it obeyed no one.

Avery's smile tightened, sensing his hesitation. "Don't let hysteria steer science. What you've built explains itself in numbers, not ghost stories. History will laugh at those stories. But it will remember your Array."

The hum through the wall deepened, or perhaps Elias only imagined it. He thought of the green spikes across his monitors, the way they had risen like hungry teeth. "You want higher output."

"Yes," Avery said, leaning forward again. "Push the Array harder. Show me exponential results, not incremental ones. That's how you'll secure your place. That's how you'll secure this project for good."

The word secure landed heavily, weighted with unspoken threats. Elias felt his stomach tighten. He knew what Avery wasn't saying: if he didn't push, someone else would. Someone less careful. And Elias wasn't about to let his life's work be torn from his hands.

He glanced at the folder Avery had left on the table. Funding proposals. Contracts. Promises inked in neat lines. A future dangling within reach. He saw himself on the covers of journals, standing on stages, his name echoing through halls where visionaries were remembered.

And yet, in the back of his mind, he saw Camille's face again—half-shadowed, half-lit, smiling at him the night before everything went wrong. He heard Lena's warning whisper: What if we're feeding something else?

"I'll need more time," Elias said slowly.

"You'll have it," Avery replied, "but not too much. I want a demonstration soon—real output numbers that can't be ignored. You've already made history, Elias. Now it's time to seize it."

Avery stood, smoothing his suit jacket, his cologne trailing him like smoke. "I'll be back Friday with other interested parties. Don't disappoint me."

Elias remained seated, the folder before him like a loaded weapon. Avery left, the door clicking shut with quiet finality.

The hum of the Array pressed harder against the walls. Elias stared at the numbers on the packet, then at his own reflection in the black screen of the monitor across from him. His face looked older, thinner, the eyes tired but still hungry.

Camille's memory lingered. Lena's voice haunted. Avery's promises burned like fire.

And deep beneath it all, the Array thrummed, alive and waiting.

Scene 2: Lena's Challenge

The lab was quieter without Avery Shaw's voice reverberating through it, but it didn't feel peaceful. Not with the Array still glowing in the corner, its dome faintly lit from within like some slumbering animal. The soft pulse of its inner coils bled into the room in steady intervals, an imitation of a heartbeat that felt too deliberate, too alive.

Lena Mirek stood near the far bench, her arms wrapped tight across her chest as if holding herself together. Avery had left an hour ago, but the smell of his cologne still clung to the air, mixing with ozone from the Array's last test cycle. The whole place felt invaded, tainted.

At the side workstation, Naveen hunched over a diagnostics panel, pretending to be fascinated by a perfectly static status graph. "For the minutes," he said without looking up, "I would like entered into the historical record that pushing the Big Hungry Orb 'harder' ranks very high on my personal list of terrible ideas."

Elias sat at the console, staring at lines of code crawling across the monitor. He wasn't really reading them—Lena could see that. His posture was too rigid, his eyes too fixed. It was the same look she'd seen after Camille's accident, the expression of a man burying grief under data because numbers didn't argue back.

"You're really going to do it," Lena said finally, her voice soft but cutting through the quiet.

Elias didn't turn. "Do what?"

"Push the Array harder. Give Avery what he wants."

Naveen swiveled just enough to be heard. "As the sarcastic junior member of this doomed fellowship: seconding Lena. Also, I enjoy being not-dead."

Elias exhaled sharply through his nose, not quite a laugh. "That's what this is about?"

"It's everything," Lena said, moving closer. "You heard what Abigail said. You saw the footage of the influencer, of Russell Langston. People are being pulled through mirrors, Elias. You can't just pretend the timing is coincidence."

His shoulders tensed. "I'm not pretending. I'm analyzing. There's a difference."

Naveen raised a hand halfway. "Respectfully, boss—there's analyzing, and then there's 'famous last words.' Abigail laid it out. Maybe… don't antagonize whatever lives on the other side of shiny things?"

Lena shook her head. "You keep using words like analyze and correlation. But you're not facing it. What if the Array is the reason this is happening? What if we're hurting people without even realizing it?"

Elias finally turned his head, his eyes sharp but tired. "Correlation is not causation. You know that as well as I do. We can't jump to conclusions because events overlap. That's how myths are born, not science."

He said it with force, but Lena caught the hollowness in his tone. It was a shield, not conviction.

"You don't believe that," she pressed.

He stood abruptly, pacing toward the Array. The machine cast a dull glow on his face, deepening the shadows under his eyes. He touched the frame lightly, almost reverently, as if the device could steady him in ways Lena could not.

"I believe in proof," Elias said. "I believe in data. If there's a link between the Array and these… incidents, then we need to find it in the numbers. Not in ghost stories. Not in fear."

Naveen slid his chair a few inches back from the dome, rubber wheels squeaking. "Cool, love proof. Big fan. Also a big fan of remaining on this plane of existence. Can we collect proof at, say, 'not poking a hornet's nest' levels?"

Lena moved to follow Elias, stopping a few feet away. "You nearly lost me in this lab, Elias. Do you remember? That thing—Veilborne, whatever you want to call it—grabbed me through the mirror. It nearly pulled me in. You saw it happen."

Elias's hand tightened on the Array's frame, knuckles pale. He didn't look at her.

"You think that was a coincidence too?" she demanded.

His silence was answer enough.

"You're letting Avery blind you," Lena went on, her voice rising with a mixture of frustration and grief. "He waves money in front of you, whispers about your name being remembered, and you forget that there's a cost. That cost is people. If Abigail is right—if the Veilborne are crossing because of what we're doing—then your ambition will consume you just as surely as this thing consumes energy."

Elias spun toward her, anger flashing across his features. "Do you think I don't know the risks? Do you think I haven't thought of that every single night since Camille died?" His voice cracked, the name slicing through the air.

From his desk, Naveen's sarcasm thinned to a thread. "We're not saying you don't care. We're saying maybe caring means we don't redline the coil while the universe is sending very loud 'please stop' messages."

The silence that followed was thick. Lena's heart pounded. She wanted to step closer, to reach out, to let him see that he wasn't alone—but the words tangled in her throat.

"Elias," she said quietly, almost breaking, "I don't want to lose you too."

For a fleeting moment, her eyes softened, her voice trembling with something deeper than loyalty. Affection, love—feelings she had kept buried beneath professionalism and fear. She wanted to tell him everything, to let him know that her devotion was more than scientific curiosity, that she cared for him in ways she'd never dared to admit.

But Elias had already turned back to the Array, retreating into its glow like a man taking shelter behind a wall.

"You won't lose me," he said flatly. "Because I'm not going anywhere. Neither is this project. We're closer to something transformative than we've ever been. And I won't throw it away because of shadows and stories."

Her chest tightened. "And what if they're not stories? What if they're warnings?"

"Then I'll find proof," he said coldly. "Until then, I have nothing to act on. I have only data."

Naveen rubbed his palms down his jeans, trying for a joke and landing close to prayer. "I'll just be over here writing a strongly worded email to my future self about hazard pay. And labeling the next config 'Please Don't.'"

Lena stood there, watching the man she admired—and cared for—disappear into the shadow of his ambition. He touched the Array again, his fingers brushing the smooth surface as though it were a confidant, an ally. His shoulders relaxed fractionally in its presence, and in that moment, Lena realized the truth: he trusted the machine more than he trusted anyone else.

The glow of the Array deepened, humming like a predator purring in its sleep.

Lena's voice dropped to a whisper. "You're already lost to it, aren't you?"

Elias didn't answer. His reflection shimmered faintly on the Array's curved dome, his face split by the machine's eerie light. He looked taller there, sharper, as though the Array was reshaping him into something she no longer recognized.

She turned away, blinking back the heat in her eyes. If he couldn't see the danger—if he couldn't hear the warnings—then someone else would have to.

Behind her, Elias murmured something to the machine, not meant for her ears. A fragment of technical jargon, a line of code, spoken like prayer.

The Array pulsed in response.

From the workstation, Naveen cleared his throat, softer now. "Just say the word, and I'll power it down," he said to Lena without the usual edge. Then, after a beat—the edge returned, thinner: "Or we can all agree to go home, take up pottery, and never look at glass again. I hear bowls are very ethical."

Scene 3: Natalie Chen's Doubts

Avery's sedan idled at the curb outside the hotel, its climate control a steady hush that blurred the noise of the city into something distant and harmless. The windshield held a smear of sodium light from the porte cochere. Valets jogged through the drizzle with umbrellas held like small black satellites. From the backlit lobby, a bank of televisions glowed in a row, each tuned to a different network, each running the same footage of a woman being dragged into a mirror. The images moved without sound through glass and rain.

Natalie Chen sat in the passenger seat with her government tablet balanced on her knees. She was logging the day's engagements. Meeting with Dr. Elias Voss. Review of preliminary output data. Observations on site security. Her notes were clipped and neutral, the way she had been taught to write them. Do not editorialize. Do not feel. The stylus moved with the precision of habit, yet every third line she found herself glancing at the rearview mirror. The sedan's interior light turned the mirror into a soft rectangle of color, a miniature screen that held her eyes a second too long. Each time she looked, she let herself keep breathing, and each time she looked away, she felt the breath ease as if she had set down a weight she did not realize she carried.

In the driver's seat, Avery Shaw conducted phone calls. He was careful with his volume when he was sober. Tonight it edged up by degrees. He said the words she knew he loved to say. Deliverable. Scalable. Containment. He was smiling, although the person on the other end could not see it. When he disconnected, he tapped the steering wheel twice with two fingers, a little drumbeat of triumph, then shifted straight into another call.

Natalie added a line to the log. Stakeholder communications in progress. No details discussed. She could have written what was actually happening. Promises extended beyond authority. Timelines shortened without consultation. Risks minimized in language that meant nothing. She did not write it. Not yet.

She looked past the mirror again, past the curve of the sedan's hood, to the hotel's glass doors. The televisions inside cut from a panel of experts to freeze-frame the exact moment the influencer's pupils seemed to widen at something behind the glass. The network drew a circle around the distorted shape at the edge of the frame. A hand, maybe. A hook of darkness. Natalie had grown used to manufactured scares. This did not feel manufactured. She could feel the hairs on her arms rise, then flatten under the sedan's artificial warmth.

Avery ended his call and slid the phone into the cup holder. He pinched the bridge of his nose and exhaled through a smile. The cologne he wore had a bitter top note. It had grown stronger in the closed car, like lacquer on new furniture.

"They will eat this up," he said, and nodded toward the hotel. "Fear is a faucet. You turn it off with a better story."

Natalie filed another line. Press strategy under discussion. She waited for him to elaborate. He did not. He never explained unless explanation served him.

"You saw the lab." He did not ask it. He delivered it as a verdict. "Voss is the genuine article. Talented. Hungry. He just needs a push."

Natalie kept her face neutral. "We asked for output increases. He said he can show a scaled test by Friday."

"Friday," Avery repeated, and his smile changed shape. "Perfect. We will invite a few people who know how to move money. Let them see the numbers. The narrative writes itself."

Her mother's voice moved through the car as clearly as if she were sitting in the back seat. You will never have the luxury of cutting corners. The words had carried Natalie through a decade of schools and internships and the kind of entry level roles that burn out softer people. She had believed those words the way a person believes a prayer. Her mother had held the family together with a ledger and two jobs and a will that could scratch sparks from stone. Her father had come home from night shifts with his jacket smelling of oil and winter, his hands nicked and rough, and had sat at the table long enough to ask about her calculus and her day before his head dropped forward and he slept on his forearm. They had not cut corners. They had bled for the long way around.

Avery unbuckled, leaned across her, and opened the glove compartment. He rummaged without apology and found a silver flask. He twisted the cap and took a small sip, the kind meant to suggest control. The car filled with the chemical sweetness of bourbon. He closed the flask with a practiced snap and returned it to the glove box. He gave her a look that said we are partners and a look that said you will not repeat this. He had never asked if she drank. He had never asked anything about her that he could not turn into leverage.

"Write a draft for the Director," he said. "High level. Voss is on track. Technical hurdles are normal growing pains. Emphasize the clean angle. Emphasize grid independence. We will get language from

Energy Policy that says this will make domestic production bullet-proof. Use a word like resilient."

Natalie typed while he spoke. She translated his appetite into bureaucratic certainty. She copied the phrases into a separate, private file and tagged them with the date, the location, and a context note. She was not sure when she had started doing that. It had begun as habit learned from a mentor. Document everything. Later, it had become something else. Insurance. A thread left uncut so that one day, if something snapped, she could show the weave.

Avery adjusted his tie and watched himself in the rearview mirror. He did it often, a private performance. He leaned his head a fraction to make sure the dimple in his tie sat in the right place. His ring flashed. The hotel television screens caught a new clip. The talk show host who had mocked a reporter days earlier now appeared with his image in the corner and a bold red banner that read Missing. The network played the clip again, the moment the mirror rippled on stage and something pulled him through. Multiple angles now. Director cam. Audience phone. A national audience had watched a man vanish while a band played him to commercial.

"Urban hysteria," Avery said, not looking away from his own reflection. "There will be three new hoaxes by morning. People are bored. We give them spectacle, and they will move on."

Natalie closed her eyes for one breath. She saw her father's hands again, scrubbed clean but still black at the cuticles. She saw her mother's lists taped to the inside of the pantry door. Milk, rice, greens, rent. She opened her eyes and wrote another line in the log. External media pressure increasing. She did not add her thought. That pressure was not a storm that would pass. It was a tide coming in.

He turned to her as if he had felt her thought anyway. "You worry too much. We shepherd the science. Voss does the work. If anything goes wrong, there are a dozen places the fault will land before it touches us."

Before it touches me, she heard.

"You saw him," Avery went on. "He is hungry. He loved every word I said. By Friday he will give us what we need, and by Monday you will have your first real win. Try to look like you enjoyed it."

It was his favorite trick. Fold her into the victory before it existed, make her complicit in advance. She had watched him do it to men twice her age. She had watched them lean forward, lit by his fire, and then burn for him when the wind changed.

"Sir," she said, and kept her voice polite. "There are ethical questions we should be prepared to answer. If the public sees a connection between the device and the incidents in the news, we need language that addresses risk. If there is any risk at all."

"If," he said, and smiled. "You are smart, Natalie. That is why I keep you in the room. But we do not build our house on ifs. We build it on what we can prove. And we prove what we repeat with confidence."

She looked back down at the tablet because if she looked at the mirror again she might say what she was thinking. Her notes were immaculate, each bullet aligned with the next like soldiers in formation. She opened her private file and, beneath the phrases she had just copied, she added one more line in a smaller font. Shaw dismisses causal link to public incidents. Prioritizes narrative over risk. Blame will be assigned elsewhere if failure occurs.

The sedan's Bluetooth chimed softly. A text flashed on Avery's screen. A woman's name. A location that was not his home. He ignored it for a count of three, then answered it with a quick reply that did not belong on a government phone. He did not bother to tilt the screen away from her. He had learned there was no consequence.

Natalie watched his reflection. He practiced a look of concern. He practiced the smile he would use on a mother whose child had been taken, if he ever had to meet one. He practiced the earnest angle of the head that made reporters trust him. He had a tool for every face.

Her mother's voice again. You will never have the luxury of cutting corners. Her father's voice too, quieter, a low hum in the garage that carried through the house. Do it right, or do it twice.

She looked back to the television wall in the hotel lobby. The networks had shifted from the influencer to a map. Red pins clustered along a crescent south of Tacoma. She did not know the geography well, but she recognized a pattern when she saw one. She thought of Dr. Mirek, the assistant with the careful eyes, and the way she had stood slightly in front of her boss like a person who had learned to catch the first blow.

Avery's phone rang again. He answered and slid smoothly into names and dates and dollar amounts. He began to schedule Elias as if the man were a resource to be mined. Natalie typed the calendar notes, even as she opened a second, hidden calendar in another application. She mirrored each commitment there and tagged each with the task number from her private file. She had told herself she kept these records because she was thorough. Tonight the word changed shape. She kept them because she did not trust the man next to her to keep anything but his own skin intact.

Rain deepened on the windshield and turned the hotel's light into a transparent curtain. A valet jogged past, dripping, and glanced at his reflection in a decorative mirror in the vestibule. He flinched and looked away. The gesture was small and human and honest. It said what the networks could not say in a banner. People were afraid.

Avery finished his call and finally noticed the televisions. He made a sound in his throat that was not quite a laugh. "By Friday they will be playing a very different clip."

Natalie closed the official log and saved it to the shared drive. She closed the private file and saved it to a place he could not see. She tucked the stylus into the tablet's spine and curled her hand into a fist for one second, then let it go.

"Understood," she said.

He started the car. The sedan's rearview mirror caught her eyes one more time. She held her gaze there and made herself breathe through it. When she looked away, she added a final line in her mind, not to any file, just to the quiet place where decisions live before they are spoken. Watch everything. Write everything. If he tries to make someone else burn for his promises, be ready with the matchbook he left behind.

The sedan slid into traffic, a sleek black shape carrying them toward the next meeting, the next promise, the next lie told with conviction. The hotel and its televisions thinned into a brace of colored squares in the rain. Natalie kept her hands folded over the tablet as if it were a book of prayers. The city moved around them, and in the glass of a darkened store they passed, for the width of one heart's beat, the world rippled. She did not look back.

Scene 4: Controlling the Narrative

The lab seemed darker than usual that night, though every fluorescent overhead still glared at full strength. The shadows clung in corners like oil, deepened by the Array's faint, pulsing glow. Even when powered down, the machine carried itself like a predator at rest, coils humming just beneath silence, dome reflecting distorted slivers of whoever dared look too long.

Elias Voss stood near the console, one hand resting on the edge as if anchoring himself. Numbers scrolled across the screen in restless waves. He should have been reviewing them, but his eyes remained unfocused, chasing thoughts that spiraled instead of landing. The Array had behaved better during the last test cycle, its output steadier, more refined, but that was not what held his mind. It was the images replaying endlessly on news broadcasts—the influencer swallowed screaming by a hotel mirror, Russell Langston vanishing in front of a live audience. The world was spiraling, and in the background hum of his creation, he could not shake the feeling that the Array was laughing.

The door opened with a snap of authority, breaking the spell. Avery Shaw swept into the room as though the building belonged to him. His suit was immaculate navy, pressed sharp as blades, his tie knotted perfectly. A faint bite of cologne filled the air, drowning the smell of warm circuits and metallic ozone. Under his arm, Avery carried a thick folder, glossy covers poking out like magazines, and in his free hand he clutched a sheaf of contracts clipped together.

"Gentlemen—" he paused, eyes catching on Lena in the corner, "—and lady. We've got work to do."

From a side workstation, Naveen didn't bother turning around. "Love being grouped in with 'work to do.' Really makes a guy feel seen."

Avery's glance slid over him like a shoe over gum. "Noted."

He crossed the room with the swagger of a man who had never doubted his place in it, and let the folder fall onto the workbench with a heavy slap. Glossy images slid free—mock covers of Elias standing before the Array, mock headlines like The Future of Energy? and The Man Who Changed Everything. They spread across the steel surface like tarot cards, each one a vision of a future Elias had never dared let himself picture.

Avery's smile gleamed sharp. "You're about to be a household name, Elias."

Elias frowned, though his fingers twitched at his side, aching to touch one of the photographs. "What is all this?"

"Your future," Avery said simply. He flipped through packets, spreading them like a dealer laying down a winning hand. "Prime-time interviews. Magazine features. Human-interest segments. I've already spoken with producers. They're foaming at the mouth for you. It's time to humanize the Array, make it a face people trust. Your face."

Naveen swiveled halfway, eyebrow up. "Because nothing says 'public safety' like a glossy spread and a pull quote. Maybe throw in a centerfold of 'not being eaten by glass.'"

Avery's smile cooled. "And you are?"

"The intern who keeps the room from exploding," Naveen said. "It's a niche, but I wear it well."

"Mm." Avery turned away from him, back to Elias. "It's time to shape the narrative."

Elias stiffened. "A press tour? Now? People are—" He faltered, unwilling to say the word. Vanishing. "—they're scared."

"Which is exactly why we do this," Avery cut in smoothly. His tone held no patience for hesitation. "If they're scared of mirrors, then we give them something else to look at. Fear spreads like wildfire, but a brighter flame always wins the crowd's eye. We bury hysteria under wonder. We show them not what they think they saw, but what they should believe."

Lena stepped forward then, her voice trembling with restrained fury. "You mean we distract them. People are being dragged into mirrors, Avery. I've seen it. Abigail has seen it. And your solution is magazine covers and soundbites?"

Avery turned his head toward her slowly, like a predator acknowledging noise in the brush. His smile thinned to a blade. "Optics are everything, Dr. Mirek. Fear spreads faster than facts. Unless we bury it. And bury it we will—under headlines, interviews, demonstrations that show humanity has nothing to fear but its own ignorance."

"Ignorance isn't killing people," Lena said.

Naveen let out a dry laugh. "Yeah, but it's definitely doing PR."

Avery's gaze snapped to him. "Keep your commentary to yourself."

"Hard to, when the commentary writes itself," Naveen said, meeting his eyes.

Avery looked back to Elias, jaw hardening. "Keep your intern in line."

Elias, torn, didn't look at Naveen. "Naveen, go monitor the bus voltage and standby capacitance in the back room. Now."

Naveen blinked, the hit landing. "Copy," he said, the word flat. He pushed back from his chair, pausing beside Lena long enough to murmur, "Text me if this turns into a pep rally." Then, to Avery as he passed, softer but edged: "If the narrative starts eating people, maybe we pick a different story." He disappeared through the side door.

Lena watched him go, worry cutting a deeper line between her brows. The whole exchange left a metallic taste—Avery's control, Elias's capitulation, Naveen's anger. None of it felt stable.

Avery pivoted back to Elias. His voice slid into velvet persuasion. "Elias, this is how revolutions are won. Not with patents or test cycles, but with image. With story. You have brilliance, but brilliance alone doesn't shape nations. Faces do. You stand beside this machine, you smile for the cameras, and the world sees the future—clean, limitless, inevitable. Your name etched into history beside Edison and Tesla."

Elias's mouth was dry. He wanted to protest, to tell Avery this was not about celebrity—but his eyes betrayed him. They lingered on one of the glossy covers where his reflection, touched up and softened, stood proudly beside the gleaming Array. For a moment he saw himself not as the weary, hollow-eyed man who haunted these labs, but as the visionary he once dreamed of being.

A ripple of pride stirred deep in him, dangerous and hot. He thought of Camille again, her hand slipping into his during those early experiments. She had believed in him. Believed they could build something that would change the world. If she had been alive to see this moment, would she not have wanted the world to finally recognize what they had started together?

"You're letting him blind you," Lena's voice snapped through his thoughts. She had moved closer, fury burning in her eyes. "You think I can't see it? He's dangling everything you've ever wanted. Recognition. Prestige. And you're eating it up while people are screaming in the streets."

Elias tore his gaze from the photos, anger flashing. "And what do you suggest? That I abandon everything? Shut it all down because people are seeing shadows?"

Her voice broke, sharp with pain. "Shadows don't drag people into mirrors, Elias! We've both seen what's out there!"

The Array's hum deepened suddenly, filling the room like a low growl. All three of them stilled, each aware of the sound though none spoke of it. The silence that followed was worse than the noise.

Avery smoothed his suit jacket, unbothered. "Enough. This isn't about superstition. It's about the future. Fear is a resource like any other—it burns quickly. We will snuff it out with spectacle. If the public believes in you, they will believe in the Array. And when the funding rolls in, none of this hysteria will matter."

Lena shook her head, her voice low. "Funding over lives. That's all this is to you."

"Don't mistake me for the villain, Doctor," Avery said, eyes narrowing. "I'm the one making sure your work survives. Without me, without the government, this project rots in a basement until someone else steals it. You want to save people? Then give them hope. Elias gives them hope."

The words hung in the air like chains. Elias stared at the photographs again. He wanted to deny them, wanted to walk away—but pride swelled, whispering that perhaps Avery was right. Perhaps his face was the only shield strong enough to ward off fear, to protect his work.

Lena's voice cracked one last time. "Elias, please. Don't let him use you."

Elias closed his eyes, Camille's ghost pressing against his memory, Lena's fear anchoring his conscience, Avery's promises burning like fire. When he opened them, his decision had been made.

"Alright," he said quietly. "Line it up. I'll do it."

Lena turned from him, shoulders trembling, unable to look at the man who had just chosen pride over truth.

The side door creaked. Naveen leaned in, having clearly lingered within earshot. "I'll, uh, keep the Array from eating Tacoma while you practice smiling," he said, the sarcasm back but thinner, frayed. His eyes flicked to Lena—concern—then he vanished again.

Avery's smile widened in satisfaction. He gathered the packets into his arms, his cologne sharp in the air. "Good," he said. "By the end of the week, no one will be talking about disappearances. They'll be talking about destiny."

The Array hummed louder behind them, its glow deepening to a sickly pulse. In the silence that followed Avery's departure, the machine seemed almost to breathe. Its shadow spread across the floor, long and distorted, as if it were listening—and pleased. Lena stared after the door where Naveen had gone, throat tight. For the first time, she wasn't just afraid of the mirrors. She was afraid of the men in the room with her—and of what the Array wanted from all of them.

9

Adrian's Sin

Scene 1: Bitterness in the Bottle

Adrian's apartment stank of old whiskey and rotting carpet. Empty bottles covered the floor like fallen soldiers, and notebooks lay scattered across the table, their pages smeared with half-finished equations and doodles scratched out in rage. A cracked breadboard sat forgotten near the sink, wires jutting from it like broken veins.

The television flickered across the dark room, its glow the only steady light. Onscreen, Elias Voss leaned comfortably in a studio chair, suit pressed to perfection, hair neat and gleaming. A talk-show host gestured toward him with theatrical admiration. The chyron at the bottom of the screen read: Dr. Elias Voss – The Man Who Found Limitless Energy.

Adrian sat hunched in a frayed chair, tumbler in hand. The whiskey burned down his throat, but it didn't stop the rage curling in his gut.

"Limitless," he muttered, his lip curling. "My word. Our word."

The host turned to the audience, sweeping a hand toward the large graphic that filled the screen behind them — the Array, stylized and perfect, its sweeping dome and concentric arcs glowing white. It looked like something out of science fiction, a futuristic monument.

"Ladies and gentlemen," the host declared, "this is what the future looks like. Clean, endless energy. No oil, no gas, no dangerous reactors. Just power. Safe. Sustainable. Revolutionary."

The audience erupted in applause.

Elias smiled the smile Adrian knew too well — practiced, humble, a mask worn so long it looked natural. He lifted his hands slightly, gesturing as though to wave off the praise. "The concept is simple," Elias explained in that steady baritone. "We live in a world saturated with fields of energy. Electromagnetic fields surround us — from the Earth itself, from our atmosphere, from countless natural and human sources. All I've done is design a system that can collect and convert that ambient energy into usable power."

"Not just collect it," the host interrupted, leaning forward eagerly. "Harness it. Refine it. I've read your papers, Doctor, and what you're talking about is nothing short of miraculous. Imagine entire cities running on this. No fossil fuels, no pollution. No more wars over oil. An end to energy scarcity as we know it."

The audience applauded again, louder this time.

Adrian tightened his grip on the glass until his knuckles went white. *That was supposed to be me.* He remembered the nights bent over prototypes, solder burns on his hands, Camille sketching adjustments in the margins of his notes. Lena testing calculations against safety limits while Elias argued every step. They had built this together — but Elias was the only one sitting under those lights, soaking in the praise.

Elias continued, voice calm, words carefully chosen. "The Array is scalable. A single installation could power a town. A series of larger stations could power states, even nations. The energy is already there. We're not burning fuel. We're not creating waste. We're simply... listening to the hum of the universe and putting it to use."

The host clasped his hands together, nearly vibrating with excitement. "A hum turned into hope," he said. "That's poetic, Doctor. Don't be modest — this is going to change the world. The name Elias Voss will be remembered as the man who solved the energy crisis. You'll be in the history books."

Adrian let out a strangled laugh, bitter and raw. "History books," he sneered at the screen. "And what? I'll be a footnote? A ghost?"

Elias leaned forward, his expression softening into sincerity. "I don't want this to be about me," he said. "I want it to be about what this means for all of us. Affordable power. A stable grid. Clean air. A future our children deserve. The Array isn't just a machine. It's a promise."

The audience rose to their feet, clapping, cheering. The host beamed like he had just witnessed the birth of a new age.

Adrian's stomach churned. He swallowed more whiskey, then slammed the glass onto the notebook in front of him. Amber spread across the page, bleeding into the name written there over and over again: Camille. The letters blurred as the stain spread, like her memory slipping through his fingers.

He saw her in his mind as clearly as if she stood beside him now. Her laughter, her questions, her steady hand on a circuit board while Elias barked for more output. The way she had whispered her fears to him when Elias wasn't around: "Something isn't right, Adrian. It feels alive. I don't trust it."

He squeezed his eyes shut, but the vision only sharpened. When he opened them again, Elias's face still filled the screen — smiling, glowing, loved.

"Fraud," Adrian whispered. "Thief."

The audience clapped again, thunderous, as the host concluded the segment. "Dr. Elias Voss, ladies and gentlemen — the man who lit the future!"

Adrian's pulse hammered in his skull. He stood abruptly, chair legs screeching across the floor. His hand found an empty bottle by instinct. He raised it, glaring at Elias's glowing face. "You don't get to take everything," he spat. "Not her. Not this."

He hurled the bottle.

It struck the television with a shattering crack. Glass exploded, shards scattering across the floor. The screen fractured into a spider-web of broken lines, Elias's face split into a dozen jagged smiles. But the broadcast didn't cut out. His voice bled through the cracked speakers, distorted, hollow, repeating phrases like a ghost: "…harness what is already there… limitless… the future we deserve…"

Adrian staggered backward, staring at the fractured screen. Elias's broken smiles multiplied across the shards, each one mocking, each one triumphant.

The apartment fell quiet except for the whisper of rain against the window. Adrian looked at his reflection in the shattered television — his face broken into pieces, warped by cracks. For a heartbeat, he swore it moved a fraction behind him, like it wasn't his at all.

He didn't blink. He didn't look away.

"I'll make it right," he whispered, voice rough, more vow than statement. "One way or another… I'll make it right."

The rain outside thickened, tapping hard against the glass. The darkened screen stared back with fractured light, Elias's smile burned into it like an afterimage, as if the Array itself was listening.

Scene 2: Camille's Confession

FLASHBACK: Pierce College, Engineering Lab, after midnight

The engineering lab at Pierce College always carried the same stubborn smell after midnight — burned solder, stale coffee, and the faintly metallic tang of overheated wires. The air vents whispered low now that the building had shifted into night mode, but it only made the silence between machines more pronounced. Oscilloscopes glowed with their dull green persistence, showing lines that crawled like tired snakes across their displays.

At the center of the room sat their crude coil. A hand-wound loop of copper, lacquer still uneven and tacky in spots, perched on a milk crate like a beast in its pen. The lacquer creaked as it cooled, the sound so small it should have meant nothing. But Adrian Kessler had started listening to every noise this room made.

Elias had just stepped out — some call to a potential funder, judging by the sharp rhythm of his voice echoing down the hall. His absences left the lab changed, quieter, less tense but also less focused. Adrian always noticed the way Camille seemed to breathe differently when Elias wasn't there — like a tether had loosened.

She was bent over the preamp board now, hair tied back in a hasty knot with a pencil jutting through it. She glanced up and handed him the iron without asking.

"Lifted pad," she murmured.

Adrian smirked, trying for levity. "My specialty. The noble art of repairing what should never have broken."

She gave a faint smile, but her eyes stayed on the breadboard, following each connection with careful patience. He set to work, and the iron's familiar hiss and stink filled the silence.

The coil creaked again, this time deeper. Adrian felt something odd — a faint buzz against his molars. He stopped mid-solder, leaning back slightly.

"Do you… hear that?" he asked.

Camille's gaze flicked up. She hesitated, then nodded. "I do."

The oscilloscope trace twitched, narrowing, then formed a comb of sharp teeth that walked steadily across the green ribbon. Too regular for noise. Too deliberate.

"That's not us," Adrian whispered.

"No," she agreed softly. Her hands were braced against the bench, fingers trembling slightly.

Adrian tried to make a joke but found his throat dry. "Maybe we've tapped into Seattle's late-night jazz stations. Ghost music."

Camille didn't smile. Her eyes were fixed on the comb of teeth. "I haven't told Elias everything. Not about this."

Adrian blinked. "What do you mean?"

Her voice lowered until he had to lean closer to hear. "The Array isn't just picking up interference. I've seen spikes like this before. Patterns that hold too steady. Rhythms. And when I stand near the coil…" She faltered, then whispered, "It feels like standing in front of someone about to speak."

The words landed cold in Adrian's gut. "You're saying it's alive?"

Her jaw tightened. "Not alive the way we mean it. But listening."

The hum pressed harder against his teeth, rattling faintly in his skull. Adrian forced a laugh. "Elevators. Power lines. Bad grounding. Pick your poison." But his voice was thin, and they both knew it.

Camille shook her head. "It isn't random." She pushed a strand of hair from her face, leaving a smudge of graphite from the pencil. "I showed Elias the data once. He said shielding, geometry, better grounding. He's not wrong, but it isn't all of it."

"And you're telling me because…" Adrian let the question hang.

"Because you hear it too." Her eyes softened. "You joke a lot, but you notice when the room changes. Elias listens to his equations. You listen to the air."

Something warm flared in Adrian's chest. It had always been Elias she trusted with vision, Elias she deferred to when conflict rose. But now she was looking at him differently — as if he were more than the third wheel, more than the grunt soldering pads and drafting patent claims. Her trust made him straighten, and with it came something darker, sharp-edged and envious.

The coil groaned, and the hum deepened until it seemed to crawl along Adrian's jawbone. The oscilloscope trace thickened, then faltered like a heartbeat.

Camille's fingers trembled more visibly now. "We've built a mouth, Adrian. And a mouth doesn't only speak."

The words knifed through him. The coil's hum seemed almost to pulse in agreement.

He swallowed. "So what do we do?"

She shook her head. "I don't know. That's why I haven't told Elias. He'd turn it into leverage. He'd make it another problem to solve with force. But what if force is exactly what we shouldn't use?"

Adrian wanted to defend Elias, but he couldn't. Elias always pushed, always bent obstacles into problems to conquer. It was why they'd made progress, but it was also why Adrian sometimes hated him.

"You trust me more with this?" Adrian asked.

Camille met his eyes. "I trust you to listen."

The words stirred him more than they should have. He looked down at his hands — steady, careful hands that suddenly felt clumsy. Jealousy curled under his ribs like wire pulled too tight.

The door at the end of the hall thumped. Elias's steps were coming back, brisk and certain. Camille quickly smoothed her hair, though it was pointless under the lab lights.

"Don't tell him yet," she whispered. "Not like this."

Adrian reached over and turned the gain down. The comb dissolved into ordinary noise. The hum at his teeth faded.

"Later," she said.

"Later," he echoed, though part of him hated the word.

Elias swept into the room, eyes already on the equipment. "How's our patient?"

"Stable," Adrian said.

"For now," Camille added.

Elias nodded as if both answers pleased him. He reached for the controls, his confidence returning the room to its usual gravity. Adrian glanced at Camille. Her expression was calm again, but he had seen the tremor, the fear, the trust she had given him instead of Elias.

That night would stay with him — the hum in his teeth, the scope's unnatural rhythm, and Camille's voice whispering, It feels alive. Like it's listening. Later, he would wonder if that was the first true whisper of the Array.

END FLASHBACK

Scene 3: The Betrayal

Elias's office looked less like a professor's sanctuary and more like a war room. Drafts and diagrams spilled across the desk, layered with patent filings and crisp legal briefs, each one another stone in the tower Elias was building for himself. The blinds had been left half-closed, slicing the late afternoon into pale stripes that cut across the mess.

Adrian hovered in the doorway with a folder under his arm, a neat tab bearing Elias's name in his sharp handwriting. It was supposed to be an offering—a set of refinements to the coupling geometry—but it felt suddenly ridiculous, a token for a man who no longer saw him as anything but ballast.

He stepped inside. The office was silent but for the low tick of the clock and the breath of the vents. Elias wasn't here. Good.

Adrian set the folder down. His hand lingered, twitching. His eyes fell to a stack of patent filings spread carelessly on the desk. Curiosity pulled at him like a hook; suspicion tightened the line. He reached for the pages.

The first sheet hit him like a blow:

Voss Array: A Method for Harvesting and Storing Ambient Electromagnetic Energy.

Inventor: Elias B. Voss.

Assignee: Voss Array Research Initiative.

Adrian's stomach turned. He flipped to the next filing. Another schematic. Another claim. The geometry of the coils—his geometry—reformatted and polished, now wearing Elias's name like a mask. Lena's data tables stripped of her ethical notes, Camille's carefully logged frequency sweeps renamed, reordered. Their fingerprints erased.

The space for additional inventors remained blank.

Adrian rifled through page after page, desperate for a scrap of acknowledgment—an inventor declaration, a draft with shared bylines, even a marginal note crediting their work. There was nothing. Only Elias.

Heat flushed up his neck. His breath came shallow. On the corner of the desk, a framed photograph mocked him: Elias, Camille, and Lena smiling in the parking lot after their first stable run. Camille's arm looped through Elias's, her head tilted slightly toward him, her smile brighter than the fluorescent lights had ever been. Adrian remembered that night—the burritos eaten cold on the curb, the taste of foil, the exhaustion that had tasted like triumph. He remembered Camille's laugh and the warmth of her shoulder against his, fleeting and unclaimed.

He turned the photo facedown.

"You stole it," he whispered. "You stole everything."

The air pressed in like a weight. He stumbled out onto the lab floor, where the Array sat in silence, its diagnostic panels gleaming faintly in the dim light. Even at rest it radiated presence, its copper coils curved like ribs, its chassis gleaming as though it had been polished to show off its menace.

Camille's words haunted him: We built a mouth.

Adrian gripped the rail, letting the hum crawl into his bones, buzz against his teeth. His rage boiled over. Elias had stolen their work, Camille's trust, even the future that should have belonged to all of them.

His gaze shifted to the maintenance panel. Behind it lived the failsafe—a hardwired circuit Camille had insisted on. Its purpose was simple: when input energy surged beyond the Array's safe threshold, the failsafe collapsed the resonance instantly, killing the draw before it could spiral out of control. It was the one leash they had on the beast they had built.

Camille had designed it on the back of a coffee sleeve, pressing her pencil so hard it nearly tore the paper. "If it ever gets away from us," she'd said, "this pulls the plug. No debate."

Adrian crouched by the panel. His hands moved before his conscience could stop them. He unscrewed the cover and pulled it free. Inside, the circuitry gleamed in the dim light, a small green LED pulsing like a heartbeat. The failsafe wasn't elegant, but it was absolute. With it, the Array could always be silenced. Without it…

Adrian swallowed.

"This isn't destruction," he murmured. "Just a bruise. Just enough to knock Elias off balance."

He found the jumper—a tiny bridge linking the hard cutoff. Remove it, and the failsafe couldn't trigger. The Array would have no leash. It could be shut down manually, maybe, if the operators caught it in time. But in runaway conditions? The resonance would feed on itself until it collapsed violently—or until something worse crossed through.

Adrian pinched the jumper and lifted. The plastic piece came free with a faint click.

The Array's hum shifted instantly. Not louder—deeper. The air seemed to thicken, shadows stretching unnaturally across the lab floor. The coils creaked faintly, the lacquer flexing as though under strain, though no power had been fed to them.

Adrian froze, the jumper trembling between his fingers. For a heartbeat, it felt like the Array was aware of him. Watching.

The hair on his arms prickled. His stomach knotted. But the fury was stronger than fear. He clenched the jumper and slipped it into his pocket. The green LED on the failsafe board winked out, lifeless.

He reseated the panel quickly, wiping his fingerprints away. The silence of the lab felt wrong now—like a stage waiting for its cue.

"There," he said aloud, his voice shaking. "Just enough to embarrass you, Elias. Nothing more."

But even as the words left him, he knew it was a lie.

He straightened, forcing a laugh that died quickly in the vast room. The Array's panels glinted sharply, as though reflecting something other than light. The shadows still seemed too long, their edges reaching. And beneath it all, the hum carried on—low, patient, hungry.

Adrian shoved his hands into his pockets, fingers closing around the jumper. It was a speck of plastic and metal, but it dragged at him like a millstone.

He told himself again and again that it was harmless. That Elias would only stumble in front of his funders. That this wasn't betrayal, just retribution.

But deep down, he knew.

This was the act that severed the tether. The failsafe had been Camille's gift, her plea for caution, her voice written into the bones of the Array. And he had silenced it.

As he walked out, the chill climbing his spine refused to let go. Behind him, the Array's hum dipped into a register that felt disturbingly like laughter—low, mocking, and infinite.

Adrian didn't look back.

Scene 4: Camille's Death

FLASHBACK: Winter 2018, Pierce College Lab, Lakewood, WA.

The storm pressed against the windows. The lab lights felt smaller. In the corner, the Array waited, coils asleep. A classroom mirror hung above the cupboards, square and ordinary.

Camille unlocked the control cabinet and set her notebook down. She checked the time and listened to the room. Elias had gone home to shower. He had said one hour. A quick calibration would prove her point. If she tuned the preamp at the top of the sweep instead of the center, the draw would smooth and the storage bay would stop choking at the first rise.

She powered the diagnostic spine. A hum lifted behind her teeth. Green lights came alive along the rail. The storage grid showed empty. She eased the field heater on. The coil ticked under a thin warmth.

"Easy," she said.

Numbers woke. The baseline drifted and settled. A swell formed where she wanted it. She trimmed and the swell steadied.

Another pass. The curve sharpened as the Array listened. Then a second rise formed at the band edge where a shallow shelf should have been. A clean tooth. She tipped the trim down a quarter turn.

The tooth brightened.

The hum changed color. A vibration crept through the bench that was not mechanical, a room taking its own pulse.

She moved to interlock status. The small board she and Lena had soldered pulsed a steady green. If the input surged, the circuit would clamp the resonance and dump the field into the safety rack. That was the promise.

The second rise climbed.

She keyed the radio. "Elias, call when you get this. I am stopping for a cold reset."

She hit Stop. The Array hesitated. She hit Stop again. The hum leaned.

She flipped the interlock cover and pressed the red tab home.

A hard click rang through the chassis. The panel flashed *TRIP*. The LED went from green to steady red. The main readout declared *DUMP ACTIVE*. The hum dropped. The field heater wound into a hush. Relief loosened her shoulders.

"Good," she said. "Stay."

The mirror paled as frost ghosted across its surface from the inside. She logged the trip, marked the sweep, and reached for the bracket wrench. She wanted the coil mount loosened to break the coupling path before a reset.

The storage grid ticked down. The curve flattened. The Array purred like a machine that believed it had obeyed.

She slid the wrench under the bracket and leaned.

The latch rattled down the corridor. Elias's voice carried. "I got your message. You pull a trip?"

"Interlock caught it," she called. "Dump is green. I want a full uncouple."

"Copy," he said, feet thudding along the tile.

Camille turned the wrench. Metal gave with a stubborn creak. A bright blue stitch leaped from the bracket to the rail, skittered across the bench, and vanished. Her fingers went numb to the first knuckle. She checked the panel.

TRIP. DUMP ACTIVE. Numbers dull and safe.

"Static," she said.

The mirror whitened another shade.

"Camille," Elias called, closer. "Wait. Let me check the heater feed. If we shelved high, it might have held charge."

"Readout is dead. We are fine," she said. "Stand clear."

She pulled.

The world struck.

It came as a sound gone solid. The quench channel lit with a blue blade that found the bracket, chased the rail, and leaped to the bench. The blow lifted her and threw her across the floor. The crack of her landing lived beneath hearing. Copper and burned dust flooded the room. Capacitors screamed, then fell into a ringing that did not want to end.

Elias hit the doorway as the echo lifted. "Camille."

He slid to her, gathered her head with careful hands, and called her name. Her breath came once, then nothing. Her eyes fixed on the ceiling.

The Array softened Its song. The panel stayed content. *TRIP. DUMP ACTIVE.* The curve became a straight horizon. The mirror cleared and gave back the room.

Elias pressed his fingers to her throat, then tried again. "No." He looked at the panel and then at the bracket that had torn free. "I told you to try the top of the sweep," he said. "I should have been here. I should have shut it at the first tooth."

Footsteps slapped the hall. Adrian came in with rain on his hair. Smoke feathered near the coil. Elias held Camille in arms that shook.

Adrian took the panel in. *TRIP. DUMP ACTIVE.* The little board behind the cover held a patient red. To anyone else it was comfort. To him it was a lie he had made. He felt for a click that had never been right since he had bridged the blades with a jumper in the name of convenience and never removed it. He saw the path the dump did not really own, the small delay that left a mouth of live charge at the heater leads where a hand would go.

Elias looked up through a shock that narrowed the room. "The heater bled back," he said, already building the case against himself. "I told her to run high. We primed the shelf. She trusted me and the quench kicked through the mount. The trip worked. I did this."

Adrian's mouth opened and closed. He felt the shape of the jumper in his pocket as if it had grown a thorn. Any words would twist the room the wrong way. He nodded once. "Ambulance," he said. "Now."

He called and said the phrases the voice on the line asked for. Sirens began their argument with the rain.

Lena reached the doorway and stopped. She knelt and touched Camille's wrist, then the hollow at her jaw.

The building hushed. The Array clicked as it cooled. The storm wrote white ladders down the glass. The mirror held its square of ordinary and reflected grief back at the people who had taught a machine to listen.

Adrian gripped the bench. The panel stared with clean assurances. In his head he traced the outline of a mistake that had worn a friendly face. He saw the night he had lifted the jumper to save a minute and heard how the hum changed color. He had told no one. He would tell no one. He would bury it under useful work and a silence that felt like penance.

Elias bowed his head over Camille as the sirens grew. "I am sorry," he said. "I am so sorry."

The mirror did not answer. It watched. The room waited, listening.

END FLASHBACK

Adrian sat on the edge of his bed with the television dark. The jumper lay in the top drawer where he had hidden it from his hands. He did not open the drawer. The plastic lived under his tongue when he swallowed. He told himself he would rebuild the clamp so it closed even when a fool tried to make it easier. He would find a way to make the hum learn regret.

In the quiet, the Array he had left behind lived in his hearing like a struck nerve. It did not sound sorry. It sounded awake.

10

The Price of Ambition

Scene 1: Avery's Double Game

The suite on the fortieth floor was designed to make men feel small. Glass walls stretched into night, Seattle a glittering sprawl below, lights smeared by steady rain. Inside, silence ruled: plush carpet swallowing footsteps, a conference table broad enough to pass for an altar.

Avery Shaw stood at the window, hands clasped behind his back, gaze fixed on the Sound. He looked less like a man than a reflection—tall, trim, silver at the temples, his tailored suit a statement of precision. He never drank during negotiations, though a glass of water sweated on the sill. Natalie Chen sat a few feet back, tablet balanced on her knees, silent as stone.

The door opened. Executives from StrataVolt and Helios Gate entered, their shoes squeaking faintly on the carpet. Victor Laramie led them, tan and trim, portfolio tucked under one arm. His handshake came with extra pressure, as if that could tilt the balance of power.

"Avery," Victor said, flashing his teeth. "Good view. You can see every dollar in the city."

"I prefer altitude," Avery replied. "It spots storms early."

They laughed politely and took their seats. Avery let silence stretch until they shifted uncomfortably, then finally leaned forward.

"The market," he said softly, "is about to be redrawn. Some of you will acquire. Most of you will be acquired. Federal procurement is moving toward distributed capture. Whoever demonstrates scale first writes the decade. Whoever comes second sells scraps."

Victor smirked. "And you're here to tell us which we are."

"I'm here to give you a way not to vanish."

He slid a folder across the table. Victor opened it, then stiffened. Inside were pilot site maps, interconnect requests, numbers not yet public.

"Where did you get this?" asked the Helios Gate man.

Avery ignored him. "StrataVolt, your Tacoma prototype has a harmonic flaw—one point three to one point seven megahertz. Helios, your metal-ceramic interfaces are corroding faster than spec. You'll patch both eventually, but your investors won't wait that long. Meanwhile, another team is pulling ahead."

Victor's smile faltered. "Another team?"

"Not your concern. Yet."

They stared at the pages, expressions souring. Natalie watched from her corner, knowing the rhythm of Shaw's playbook. First expose the wound, then offer the cure.

"What do you want?" Victor asked finally.

"Inspection rights inside your roadmaps," Avery said, tone light, almost casual. "First refusal on assets if you run hot. And silence. No lobbying to slow approvals on a project I'm shepherding."

"You're protecting your boutique outfit," Victor said.

"I'm protecting the future." He leaned back, unhurried. "And making sure you're invited."

The Helios executive leaned forward. "You're asking us to stand down. What do we get?"

"Access," Avery said. "Expedited permits. Supply guarantees. Introductions you can't buy. And foresight—when the funding tide rises, you'll already be floating."

They exchanged wary glances. Victor drummed his fingers once. "This ambient energy project… rumor says it's yours. If it fails, we go down with you."

Avery's smile sharpened. "If it fails, you'll be glad you signed my letters. Because I'll pivot you before you drown."

The rain streaked silver behind him, lightning flickering far out over the Sound. He let them sit with that, then turned slightly, as if confiding.

"Gentlemen, there are twenty staffers who think they're steering policy in D.C. Eight actually are. I dine with six. I drink with four. I play chess with one. When I tell you a demonstration will happen, it will. When I tell you the winners will be those who arrive with hands open instead of teeth bared, you should believe me."

Victor exhaled slowly. "Inspection rights we can discuss. Lobbying—we'll consider. But options tied to performance? That needs board signatures."

"You'll have them," Avery said. "Natalie will send the draft. They'll haggle commas. Let them."

They stood, shook hands cooler than before. As they reached the door, Avery added, "Don't call Northstar Energies this week. An audit will 'probably' be announced Friday. Would be unfortunate to see your names in their logs."

Victor paused, jaw tight. "Probably."

"Storms," Avery said, turning back to the glass. "I like the altitude."

The door closed. Silence reclaimed the suite.

Avery walked back to the table, drew out a second phone—the one without government tags—and dialed. "Put me through to Russell at Northstar. Private line."

Natalie's eyes flicked up. She didn't move.

"Russell," Avery said warmly. "Good evening. Word of a compliance review headed your way. Nothing serious, of course. I can smooth it, as ever. In return, delay meetings with StrataVolt or Helios until next week. Tell them you're traveling. Yes, I know you're not. That's the point."

He listened, murmured reassurance, then ended the call. To Natalie, he said, "Draft the letters. Inspection rights, lobbying stand down, indemnity clause. Use the stronger language."

"And the audit?" she asked quietly.

"Coincidence," Avery said. "In writing."

He returned to the window. Rain streamed down the glass, warping his reflection into something long-fingered, almost hungry. For a heartbeat, it looked less like a man than a shadow waiting to step through. Then the water shifted, and it was only Avery again, smiling faintly.

"Friday," he said. "We make them look at what I tell them to look at."

Natalie gathered the folders, but she felt the weight in the room like static. The Array hummed faintly, even here, and the city glowed below, patient as a predator.

Scene 2: Preparations for Friday

The lab at Clover Park Technical College thrummed like a caged animal. Even idle, the Array gave off its faint metallic hum, the kind of sound that slipped into the bones and made silence impossible. Blue indicators pulsed across the consoles in soft rhythm, like a heartbeat that didn't belong to anyone in the room.

Elias Voss stood at the central console, sleeves rolled back, glasses smudged with fingerprints. His hands moved over the dials with a surgeon's precision. He'd been there since before sunrise, coaxing data from the Array, calibrating sensors, running simulations until his eyes blurred. He barely noticed when the door opened.

"Still tinkering," Avery Shaw said, striding in like the room already belonged to him. His suit was flawless, his tie knotted with military neatness. Behind him trailed Natalie Chen, tablet in hand, her expression composed but wary.

Avery glanced at the humming dome of the Array as if it were a prized racehorse. "Tell me it's ready."

Elias didn't look up. "It's stable. We've held resonance for over ninety minutes without fluctuation. Power draw and capture ratios are consistent." He adjusted a dial and watched a monitor flare green. "It will perform Friday."

"Perform," Avery repeated, rolling the word in his mouth. "Not just work, Elias. Perform. This isn't an academic exercise. We're talking optics. Spectacle. People need to walk away from that demo thinking they've seen the future."

Elias finally turned, jaw tight. "This is science, Avery. Not a carnival trick."

"No." Avery stepped closer, his cologne sharp and intrusive. "This is history. And history remembers the men who stand on stage, not the ones hiding behind dials."

Natalie's gaze flicked between them but she said nothing, her fingers ghosting across her tablet.

From the far end of the lab, Lena Mirek cleared her throat. She'd been leaning against a workbench, watching the exchange, arms folded over her chest. The look in her eyes wasn't pride. It was doubt.

"History also remembers disasters," Lena said quietly.

Avery turned, eyebrows raised. "Dr. Mirek, isn't it?"

"Yes," she said evenly. "And I think you're underestimating the risks."

Elias shot her a sharp look, a silent warning. But Lena didn't stop.

"You've both seen the data. EMF spikes where there shouldn't be. Resonance patterns that don't align with any modeled source. What happened during the last cycle wasn't noise. It behaved... differently. Almost like it was responding."

Avery smirked, dismissive. "You're telling me ghosts are haunting the circuitry?"

Her expression didn't change. "I'm saying we don't understand what we're harvesting. And pushing it harder just because you want to impress a room of funders—"

"Lena," Elias snapped, sharper than he intended. She flinched, but only slightly.

He softened his tone, turning to Avery. "There's a failsafe. Built into the system. If inputs exceed capacity, it automatically shuts down. The Array cannot run out of control."

Avery's eyes narrowed, but he nodded slowly, as though indulging a child. "Failsafes are fine. But failsafes don't win headlines. Spectacle does." He leaned closer to Elias, voice dropping. "Do you want to be remembered as the man who almost changed the world, or the one who stepped onto that stage and showed the impossible was possible?"

Elias's heart thrummed in time with the hum of the Array. He hated Avery's words, the arrogance behind them—but a part of him, the part that still woke at night remembering Camille's bright faith in him, couldn't help but thrill at the thought. His name etched in history. His work no longer doubted, no longer questioned.

"We'll be ready," he said at last.

Lena's jaw tightened. She turned away, muttering, "At what cost?"

Avery clapped Elias on the shoulder, oblivious or uncaring of her words. "That's what I like to hear. Friday is your coronation. Don't disappoint me."

He pivoted toward the door, Natalie trailing behind. She lingered a heartbeat longer, her eyes on Lena. There was a question there, unspoken, but she said nothing before disappearing through the door.

The lab fell back into the Array's hum.

Lena crossed to Elias, her steps sharp against the tile. "You can't keep brushing this off."

"Brushing what off?" he snapped.

"The risks." Her voice trembled with frustration. "You heard what Abigail said. You saw what I saw. And now we're about to pump more energy through this machine than ever before, with investors, politicians—half the damned city watching. What happens if it spirals out again? What happens if the failsafe doesn't catch it?"

"It will." His voice was steel. "I built it."

Her eyes glistened, though whether with anger or fear, Elias couldn't tell. "And what if you built it wrong?"

The words hit harder than he expected. He opened his mouth to retort, but she cut him off.

"You've let Avery get in your head. You think this is about proving yourself, about recognition, about some legacy. But this is bigger than you, Elias. Bigger than any of us. And if you're wrong—"

"I'm not wrong," he said fiercely, though the conviction in his voice wavered. "We've run the numbers. We've tested every cycle. We're ready."

Lena shook her head. "No, Elias. You're hoping. There's a difference."

She turned back toward the workbench, gathering her notes with tight, efficient movements. Her hands shook faintly as she stacked the papers.

Elias watched her, guilt gnawing at him, but pride wouldn't let him back down. He turned instead to the Array, to its quiet glow, its promise of unlimited energy. He told himself again that it was safe. That it was controlled. That the failsafe was unbreakable.

But in the humming silence of the lab, the Array sounded almost like it was breathing.

Scene 3: The Demo (Friday)

By the time the first car door slammed in the parking lot, the Array was already awake. Its steady hum pressed against the walls of the Clover Park Technical College lab, a low vibration that seemed to know what was coming. The room, usually cluttered with half-finished experiments and soldered scraps, had been transformed into a stage. Folding chairs were set in rows, a lectern stood at the front, and a projection screen displayed clean graphics ready to impress.

Elias Voss stood at the console, smoothing his hair for the third time. His lab coat had been swapped for a dark suit. The transformation felt unnatural, as though he had stepped into someone else's skin. Behind him, the Array glowed faintly, its concentric coils humming with readiness.

Lena stood off to one side, clipboard clutched tightly to her chest. She wore black, her expression unreadable, though her eyes moved constantly: the monitors, the Array, the mirror on the wall that had been covered with heavy cloth. She was taut as a wire, waiting for something she couldn't name.

The first to enter were the DOE officials—faces lined, hands quick with handshakes, their polished shoes squeaking faintly on the lab's tile. Behind them came investors, dressed in tailored suits that looked too fine for the fluorescent lights. Finally, a pair of state politicians swept in, trailed by local reporters with cameras flashing.

Avery Shaw moved among them like a king leading his court. His voice carried warmth, but his eyes glittered with calculation. He gestured broadly toward the Array. "Ladies and gentlemen, today you're going to see something that will reshape the future of energy. This is no prototype, no theoretical dream. This is history being made before your eyes."

Polite applause followed. Elias swallowed the dryness in his throat and stepped forward.

"The Array," he began, his voice steady despite the weight of dozens of eyes, "is a capture architecture designed to siphon usable energy from ambient electromagnetic fields in the environment. These fields—generated by natural phenomena, by our own infrastructure, even by fluctuations we can't yet fully explain—have always been there. We've just lacked the means to use them."

He gestured toward the screen, where digital bars represented input density, capture rate, and storage. "Today, you'll watch as we draw from the surrounding fields and store that energy in real time. No fuel, no emissions, no depletion."

Elias pressed a key. The Array answered with a deepening thrum. The lights on its surface pulsed, shifting from amber to green. On the screen, the input bar began to climb.

Murmurs rippled through the audience. A reporter snapped three quick photos, the flash painting the coils white for a heartbeat.

Elias continued. "We've learned that some regions resonate stronger than others. This campus sits in one such zone, which makes it an ideal location to demonstrate. With each increase in capture band, you'll see proportional growth in the reservoir."

He widened the band slightly. The hum deepened again, filling the floor with vibration. The capture rate leapt upward. The storage bar began to climb in solid blue blocks.

One of the politicians leaned forward, whispering to an aide. A DOE official tilted his head, eyes narrowing at the numbers. Investors nodded to one another, silent calculations behind their eyes.

"Already twenty kilowatts captured and stored," Elias said, pointing to the graph. "That's equivalent to powering a small clinic. Within minutes."

The murmurs swelled.

But Lena wasn't looking at the main display. Her gaze was locked on the resonance trace, a secondary monitor only she and Elias could see. A faint comb pattern flickered across the line—teeth too regular to be noise, too uneven to be machinery. Her stomach tightened. She leaned closer, whispering, "Elias. Do you see that?"

He glanced, then nodded quickly. "It's transient. Environmental interference."

"It wasn't there yesterday," she whispered.

"It will settle," he replied, too briskly.

He widened the band again. The hum pressed harder, vibrating through the floorboards, rattling a few glasses at the back of the room. The capture rate soared. The storage bar jumped higher.

Lena's nails dug into her clipboard. The comb was back—sharper now, almost rhythmic. Her skin prickled, a chill creeping up her arms despite the warmth of the room. She wanted to speak, to stop him, but the eyes of the audience pinned her in silence.

Avery stepped forward, beaming. "Ladies and gentlemen, you are looking at twenty-five kilowatts in under five minutes. A portable generator without a drop of fuel. A city block powered by the air itself. Imagine the scale of this. Imagine the future it promises."

The applause came stronger this time. Cameras flashed. Elias forced himself to smile, though his chest felt tight.

He eased the Array into stabilization. The hum dropped slightly, the bars slowed, and the room seemed to exhale. A few people laughed nervously, as though they'd been holding their breath.

"Stabilization cycle complete," Elias said. "Reservoir steady."

The applause rose again, carrying relief this time.

Avery clapped him on the back, leaning close enough that only Elias heard the words. "You've done it, doctor. You've written your name into history."

Elias nodded, but his eyes drifted to Lena. She wasn't smiling. Her gaze was locked on the resonance trace, still flickering faintly with that unnatural comb. Her knuckles were white.

He turned back to the crowd, shaking hands, answering questions. "Yes, there's a failsafe." "Yes, the design can scale." "No, there's no interference with civilian infrastructure." He said the words like lines rehearsed a thousand times, even as unease gnawed at the back of his mind.

Flash after flash painted his vision. He thought of Camille—how she would have watched the numbers, how her eyes would have asked the question he never wanted to answer: Are you sure this is safe?

But he didn't say it. He stood straighter, forcing himself into the role the crowd demanded: Elias Voss, visionary.

Avery raised his voice over the chatter. "What you've seen today is the dawn of a new era. Energy harvested without fuel, without waste. This is Dr. Elias Voss—the man of the future!"

The applause surged, cameras flashing in staccato bursts. Elias smiled for them, but inside, he heard only the Array's hum, steady and patient, like something breathing in the dark.

Scene 4: Lena & Natalie Sidebar

The lab smelled of hot metal and sweat when the last round of applause faded. Folding chairs scraped back, investors clustered in tight circles, and the glow of cell phone screens spread as the first videos of the demonstration hit social media. The Array stood in its bay like a predator lulled into idling sleep, coils still warm, diodes blinking lazily.

Elias was swallowed by handshakes and congratulations. He stood at the center of it all, grinning with the politeness of someone stunned by noise, a man lit from every side by flashbulbs and praise. Avery Shaw shadowed him like a handler with a prizefighter, ushering people closer, cutting short questions that wandered too far from the celebratory script.

"History has been made," Avery declared to anyone within earshot. "You saw it. Clean energy, limitless, no smoke, no fire, no grid dependency. Remember where you were today."

Natalie Chen hung at the edges of the gathering, a small tablet in her hand, her dark suit immaculate as ever. Unlike Avery, she didn't look thrilled. Her eyes flicked constantly, noting faces, cataloging reactions, logging details into memory with the precision of someone used to making reports no one wanted to read but everyone feared.

Lena remained near the console, away from the cameras, clutching her clipboard as though it were a lifeline. She had smiled once during the presentation, but now the mask was gone. Her shoulders were drawn tight, her mouth pressed into a thin line. Her eyes returned again and again to the resonance trace, still lingering faintly on the secondary monitor.

Natalie approached, her heels quiet against the tile. She stopped just beside Lena, speaking softly so no one else could hear.

"You're not celebrating," Natalie said.

Lena startled, then forced a smile that didn't reach her eyes. "Just tired. Long week."

Natalie tilted her head. "You can relax. I'm not Avery. This conversation stays between us."

Lena blinked, uncertain. Natalie's voice was steady, her gaze frank. She radiated the kind of seriousness that made promises feel contractual. Still, Lena hesitated. Years of loyalty to Elias—her admiration, her unspoken affection—kept her words in check.

Natalie lowered her voice further. "I saw your face during the test. When the numbers jumped."

Lena gripped her clipboard tighter. She had thought she'd hidden her reaction, buried her fear behind the professional mask. Apparently not.

Natalie went on, calm and deliberate. "I need to know if there's anything Avery isn't telling me. Or if there's something Elias is ignoring. Not for the press. Not for the investors. For me. Because if something goes wrong, I don't trust Avery to protect anyone but himself."

The words struck Lena like a tuning fork. They resonated with the truth she hadn't admitted aloud. She swallowed hard, glancing past

Natalie toward Avery. He stood near the lectern, laughing too loudly with a pair of investors, his hand clapping Elias's shoulder like he owned him.

Lena dropped her gaze back to the clipboard. "Sometimes..." she began, then faltered.

Natalie waited, silent.

Lena tried again. Her voice was so quiet she barely recognized it. "Sometimes I worry we're drawing from somewhere we shouldn't."

The words hung in the air, thin and fragile. Saying them made her stomach twist, as though speaking gave them weight.

Natalie didn't flinch. "Define 'somewhere.'"

"I don't know," Lena whispered. She thought of the Veilborne, the shadowed figure pulling itself through the mirror in their lab, the clawed hand clutching her ankle. She thought of Abigail Jensen's podcast, her warnings about mirrors and reflections that opened when the world was thin. She thought of the comb patterns on the scope, pulsing like a heartbeat, something alive.

"I don't know," she repeated, stronger this time. "That's the problem."

Natalie studied her, searching her expression for hesitation, fabrication, exaggeration. She found none.

"You're loyal to him," Natalie said finally, nodding toward Elias. "I can see that. But if you ever have doubts—real ones—you call me. Directly. What you tell me stays off the record. I'll make sure it's heard in the right way."

Lena's throat tightened. For a moment she wanted to accept immediately, to pour out everything—the shadow, the claw, the fear that every hum of the Array was another door cracking open. But she saw Elias across the room, soaking in the attention, his face flushed with pride. Her heart clenched. She couldn't betray him. Not yet.

"Thank you," Lena said softly. "But right now... we have no concerns. I'll keep your number in case something comes up."

Natalie nodded once. "That's all I ask." She slipped a card into Lena's hand, her fingers pressing gently as if to assure her that the offer was genuine. Then she turned and moved back into the crowd, expression unreadable.

Lena stood frozen for a long moment, the card heavy in her palm.

Across the room, Avery raised his voice above the chatter. "Front page by Monday. Scientific American, Wired, hell, maybe even Time. Get me a feature spread. This is gold. People don't need to understand the math—they need to see a smiling face and a headline that says limitless."

Investors laughed. Cameras flashed again. Avery gestured toward Elias as though presenting a prize bull at auction.

"Here he is—the man of the future!" Avery crowed. "Every outlet in the country should be fighting for his story. Let's give them something they can't ignore."

Elias tried to protest, raising his hands in modesty, but the corners of his mouth betrayed him. He liked the attention. He liked it more than he should. He was drinking it in, pride coating the raw wound of doubt inside him.

Lena watched, her stomach heavy. She thought of what she had whispered to Natalie—drawing from somewhere we shouldn't. She thought of the covered mirror against the wall, the faint ripple she had once seen as though something pressed against it. She thought of how easily Avery's voice could drown out all warnings.

The Array hummed softly in the background, patient, steady, almost listening.

Scene 5: Avery's Calculations

The hotel suite was a cocoon of dim gold light, its lamps casting soft halos over plush carpet and sleek furniture. Rain ticked steadily against the wide window, the glass blurred with rivulets that refracted the glow of the Seattle skyline beyond. It was late, but the city still pulsed with life—traffic streaming on wet streets, neon smears staining the mist.

Avery Shaw loosened his tie with one hand and poured amber liquor into a heavy glass with the other. He carried it to the window, savoring the weight of it, the way the liquid caught the light. He raised it to his lips and drank deeply, eyes half-closed in satisfaction.

The television murmured behind him, muted but alive with motion. Every major network was replaying the Array demonstration from earlier that day. Clips of Elias Voss standing at the console, explaining capture rates. Footage of investors applauding, of Avery himself hovering just behind with his practiced smile. Each time the Array's coils glowed green, the headlines grew more breathless.

HISTORY MADE IN TACOMA: LIMITLESS ENERGY DEMON-STRATED
THE FUTURE IS HERE—AND IT HAS A NAME
DR. ELIAS VOSS: VISIONARY OR MAD GENIUS?

Avery smirked at the last one. The answer didn't matter. In fact, doubt sold better than certainty. Doubt gave people something to argue over, and every argument meant more attention.

He set the glass on the sill and reached for the stack of newspapers and magazines spread across the desk. Reporters had been quick to assemble previews, front pages already boasting the Array as the dawn of a new era. He fanned them out like playing cards, admiring the bold fonts and dramatic photos.

In one, Elias stood framed by the glowing machine, eyes alight with conviction. Avery traced the edge of the image with one finger. Elias was perfect for the role: brilliant but socially awkward, easy to mold, easier still to control. Let him speak science. Avery would speak power.

He took another drink and let the warmth bloom through his chest. His reflection in the window hovered over the skyline—strong jaw, sharp suit, eyes gleaming with ambition. He imagined it projected larger: campaign posters, magazine covers, the smug face of a man who had bent the future to his will.

"Senator Shaw," he said under his breath, testing the cadence. He tried it again, slower, savoring it. "President Shaw."

The words curled through the room like cigar smoke. He smiled, not with joy but with hunger.

Behind him, Natalie Chen sat at the small table, her tablet open, stylus moving in quick, quiet strokes. She was logging notes, assembling a record of the day: times, names, figures, anomalies. She had attended enough of Avery's late-night rituals to know her presence was tolerated, even useful.

She glanced at him over the edge of the screen. He hadn't asked her to speak, but she did anyway.

"You're enjoying yourself."

Avery turned, grin broad and unrepentant. "Why shouldn't I? We just put on the show of a lifetime. Every news cycle for the next week will be about us. Investors are drooling. Washington is calling. Do you understand what that means?"

Natalie closed her tablet with a deliberate click. "It means expectations will climb even faster than output can. People will want results we can't guarantee."

Avery waved her off, pacing back to the desk. He picked up a glossy magazine mock-up, holding it at arm's length. "People don't care about guarantees. They care about spectacle. Give them a story big enough, shiny enough, and they'll forget to ask the questions that matter."

Natalie's lips thinned. "Until something goes wrong."

Avery turned on her, eyes narrowing. "That's Elias's problem. Mine is keeping the narrative under control. That's what wins elections. That's what builds legacies. The science is incidental."

"The science," Natalie said slowly, "isn't incidental if it's dangerous."

He poured another drink, louder than necessary. "Dangerous sells. People love to flirt with the edge, as long as someone's promising to keep them safe. And that's me. The man in the room who always has the answers, even if they're invented."

Natalie looked at him steadily, unblinking. Her father's voice echoed in her mind: You'll never have the luxury of cutting corners. She thought of the sacrifices her parents had made to put her through school, the long hours her father had worked at the docks, the way her mother had mended clothes so she wouldn't feel ashamed in classrooms full of privilege. Those sacrifices had been rooted in honesty, in discipline. Avery's arrogance made them feel like ashes in her mouth.

"You'll burn people," she said quietly.

"People are fuel," Avery shot back. "They want leaders who make the fire worth it."

Natalie's chest tightened. She turned back to her tablet, fingers tightening around the stylus. Her notes were already extensive, but she added another line at the bottom: Shaw equates people to fuel. Dangerous mindset. Document everything.

Avery sank into a chair, legs stretched out, glass balanced against his thigh. He stared at the ceiling, smiling as though he saw his name etched in the plaster.

"Elias will get the Nobel," he said dreamily. "But I'll get the world. Energy independence. Contracts worth billions. A political machine no one can stop. And all I had to do was recognize a genius too distracted by grief and guilt to realize he's my ticket to power."

Natalie's stomach twisted, but she kept her face neutral. He had said similar things before, but tonight there was a fever in his tone, a clarity that chilled her. He wasn't joking. He believed every word.

The Array's faint hum lingered in her ears even here, blocks away, as though the machine had followed her. She wondered if Elias knew just how trapped he was, bound not only by Avery's contracts but by his own hunger for recognition.

Avery finished his drink and stood, stretching. "Get some sleep, Natalie. Tomorrow we start writing the next chapter. Press interviews, op-eds, maybe a TV spot. If they're scared of mirrors, we'll bury them under lights and headlines."

She nodded, though her pulse quickened at his phrasing. If they're scared of mirrors. He hadn't mentioned the abductions directly, but the words sat heavy, as though he knew more than he let on.

When he disappeared into the bedroom, Natalie sat alone in the glow of her tablet. Her reflection stared back at her in the dark screen, eyes haunted. She tapped the stylus once against the glass, then began a private file hidden under layers of encryption.

Observations on Shaw's tactics. Potential risks of the Array. Ethical conflicts.

She typed until the rain slowed outside, until the silence of the suite was broken only by the faint sound of Avery Shaw humming to himself, drunk on visions of power.

Natalie closed the file, her decision silent but certain: someone needed to know the truth. And if Avery Shaw thought he was untouchable, she would be the one to prove him wrong.

11

Shadows of Doubt

Scene 1: In the In Between

The nave rose like a ribcage made of night and broken mirrors. Father Allen walked with the patience of a man carrying sleeping children. His lantern, a fist-sized cage of smoked glass, cast faint gold islands on the black floor. Each step sent thin chimes into the dark.

"Stay to the light," he said. "Walk where my heel has walked."

Russell Langston copied his steps exactly and still clipped a jagged tile, flailing like a man on ice. Allen caught his sleeve and steadied him.

"I'm fine," Russell whispered, too loudly. His voice echoed thin and mocking. "Premium haunted theme park. Worth every cent."

"Quiet helps," Allen murmured. The lantern pulsed like a small heart.

They passed under a leaning arch of shattered panes that were not panes but windows. In one: a woman kneeling on a kitchen floor. In another: a child sleeping with something hunched at the headboard. Russell forced his gaze forward. Only when the arch was behind them did he exhale.

"What are we doing, exactly?" he asked. "Besides sightseeing the cathedral of nightmares."

"We gather those who need shelter," Allen said. "We place them where hunters will not think to look."

"Buying time with what currency?" Russell muttered, then sighed. "Sorry. Brave in my head, pathetic out loud."

"It sounded human," Allen said. "That is enough."

They reached the transept. The floor dropped into a lake the color of motor oil, dotted with stone islands no larger than tabletops. Each one held figures crouched, fragmented like overlapping photographs.

"Souls," Russell whispered, his mouth dry. "Are they dead?"

"They are lost," Allen said. He raised the lantern. Its glow stretched across the water. "Hello," he called gently. "Do not be afraid. We will guide you."

The nearest figures lifted pale faces. Their mouths moved without sound. Russell's shoe scraped bright against the glass floor, and something stirred high above. Allen lifted a palm: wait. Then he stepped onto half-submerged stones, the lantern persuading the dark to make room.

On the first island a woman sat drenched, eyes hollow. Beside her, an old man stared at his hands. Two small forms huddled silently. Allen extended his hand. The woman trembled but touched it, and the lantern brightened. He whispered a prayer too low to hear.

Russell knelt, clumsy. He wanted to joke but swallowed it; the words would poison this place. Instead he said to the old man, "Sir, can you take my arm? We'll walk together." The fingers that gripped him were cold with absence. Russell steadied him. "Good. I've got you."

They moved like paper dolls, each holding the next: priest, Russell, the old man, the woman with the child. Stones rocked under them, the black water exhaling. When the child whimpered silently, Russell turned back. "Look at me. We're almost there. Be brave for ten seconds. Then ten more." The priest's mouth twitched despite the weight of the place.

They reached a recess carved in the far wall, a chapel of basalt. Allen ushered the woman and children inside. The old man clutched Russell's arm, staring at him.

"You are the man who laughed," he mouthed. "On the screen."

Russell's stomach dropped. "Yes," he admitted. "I'm sorry. I was wrong." The lantern brightened. Allen nodded faintly, as if that truth mattered. The old man released him and stepped inside.

Two more trips, two more groups. Each time, more broken mirrors angled to watch. The weight of their gaze pressed between Russell's shoulders. On the last return, when the final soul was hidden in the chapel, silence shifted.

First came the absence of sound. Then a rustling like every Bible page turned at once. Shapes resolved in the rafters. The air smelled of burnt cedar and coins.

"Veilborne," Russell whispered. His mouth wanted to run away.

"Hunters," Allen corrected. He lifted the lantern. Its glow pressed against the dark like a prow through weeds.

The creatures descended like spiders, bone wrapped in smoke, eyes burning too bright. Claws clicked. One sniffed the air. The scent of souls must have been thick. Russell tasted rot under sweetness.

"We should go," he muttered.

"We will. Slowly, together." Allen raised his voice toward the chapel. "Remain still. The walls will hide you."

A Veilborne reached the floor, its face the suggestion of cheekbones and knives. It stepped into the lantern's glow and hissed. Curious, not yet enraged. Allen brightened the light into a faint line. The creature placed one claw on the line and recoiled, hissing like steam.

Russell's sweat chilled. His hair, absurdly, was behaving better than it had in months. The thought almost made him laugh. He bit his cheek until he tasted copper. The creature's gaze slid to him, unblinking.

"Hi," Russell said before he could stop himself. "Big fan."

Allen did not flinch. "Do not offer fear. Offer intention. Name who you are."

Russell swallowed. "I am not what I was. I'm trying." The lantern shivered. The Veilborne twitched. Behind it, three more dropped, fanning out, clever as sharks. Their hunger buzzed in the air.

"Now we go," Allen said. They backed away, step for step, never turning. Russell matched him, pulse roaring. One Veilborne darted but stuttered at the light. Another circled; Allen's raised hand glowed faintly, and the creature paused, smiling without lips.

At the archway Allen said, "There will be a moment you will want to run. That is the worst moment."

"And if I run anyway?" Russell asked, legs trembling.

"Then I will catch you. And we will both fall. And both rise again."

Russell nodded. Not courage, only agreement.

The claws quickened behind them, echoing clicks. The corridor narrowed, lantern light licking walls that were not walls. The glow faltered. Allen whispered into it, coaxing it steady.

A Veilborne reached the threshold, testing it like a fence. It set one claw inside and made a sound like glass cracking. Allen glanced at Russell. "Do not trip over your own feet."

Russell nearly did. His breath scraped out like gravel. He glanced sideways at Allen. "You make this sound so easy."

"It is not easy," Allen said. "It is necessary."

The sound of claws grew faster. The next chamber opened into a basin, shallow and wide. The lantern cast a thin path. The hunters pressed closer, patient and eager.

"Walk where my heel has walked," Allen said once more. Russell obeyed. Their steps stitched a fragile seam through the dark as the cathedral of broken mirrors seemed to inhale around them, watching.

The path arced along a narrow shelf of splintered glass, no wider than a ledger. Below, the basin darkened until it looked like night drowned and made liquid. Reflections drifted in it—faces and rooms and corridors—disjointed like memories dropped and broken. Russell caught, for a heartbeat, his own studio set: a desk, blue light, an audience frozen mid-laugh. His reflection smirked back at him, delayed by a fraction. He stumbled.

"Do not believe versions of yourself curated by cruelty," Allen said, steadying him by the elbow. "They are bait."

"Right," Russell breathed. "Bait. I'm—genuinely hating that I understand that metaphor."

A thin cry threaded up from the basin—a child's shape, small and flickering, drifting just beneath the surface like a moth under ice. It bobbed near the shelf, tethered to the chapel by a filament of pale light. A ripple along the far rim told of something moving to intercept.

Russell dropped to a knee without thinking. "Hey. Hey—look at me." He reached for the filament, terrified he would break it, more terrified he wouldn't. His fingers passed through cold that wasn't cold; the thread caught around his wrist as if the child had tied it there. The lantern pulsed brighter, and Allen pivoted, angling the glow to widen.

"Hurry," Allen said, voice still calm, urgency threaded through it. "Do not pull. Invite."

Russell spoke the way he had once coaxed skittish interns off camera. "You're safe. Come toward the warm light. I'll hold the door."

The child drifted up, face turning, eyes wide and storm-colored. It rose until its brow touched the shelf. Allen extended two fingers, the smallest benediction, and the glass accepted the child, letting him through like a membrane deciding—this one may pass. The thread loosened from Russell's wrist and drew back toward the chapel, humming faintly as it reeled in the little form. The lantern responded with a low, grateful thrum.

From the corridor behind, the hunters hissed as one, frustrated. A ripple of attention swept the ceiling—mirrors tipping, angles sharpening. More eyes found them.

"Why did that work?" Russell asked, voice shaking.

"Because you meant it," Allen said. "And because mercy still has weight here."

They pressed on. The air grew busier, as if the cathedral had woken and begun to whisper to itself. Words formed and unformed at the edges of hearing: prayers, half-remembered lullabies, the rush of a crowd. Russell realized some of the sound was his own past—cut laughter, cheap applause—muddying the quiet. He clenched his jaw and focused on the soft clockwork of Allen's steps.

The shelf widened into a landing. Ahead, the corridor opened into an impossible expanse—floor like black water, ceiling like a sky of shattered mirrors—its noise a distant animal. Allen paused, lantern low, listening.

"They are not scavenging," he said. "They feast."

"Feast?" Russell whispered, sick already.

"Come," Allen said. "We will see—and then we will choose how to move."

He lifted the lantern, and the light reached, thin and stubborn, into the dark mouth of the clearing. The sound that came back was a braid of shrieks and grinding static, the music of hunger with nothing to fear. Russell's skin pebbled. He thought of running. He did not.

"One more rule," Allen said quietly. "When terror tells you that you are alone, answer it with two truths."

Russell swallowed. "Which are?"

"You are not. And you are more than what you were."

The lantern brightened by a hair. Russell nodded, because nodding was what his body could do without falling apart, and together they stepped toward the feast.

Scene 2: Veilborne Rebellion Rising, Feeding Openly

They stepped out of the narrow corridor into an impossible clearing, a place that should not have existed inside a cathedral of ruined glass. The floor stretched out like a skin of black water, trembling faintly as if alive. Overhead, a ceiling of broken mirrors hung like storm clouds, every shard catching the lantern's glow and scattering it into warped, sickly reflections. Father Allen lifted the light higher, and it painted a trembling path of gold across the expanse—a fragile raft floating in an ocean of tar.

"Stay close," he murmured.

Russell swallowed hard. His nerves hummed so loudly he could hear them in his ears. "I wasn't planning to wander," he said, trying for humor, but the joke frayed halfway out of his mouth and fell flat. Even his own voice sounded wrong here, thin and brittle, as if the air had chewed most of the life from it.

The clearing breathed back at them. Not wind, not air—something deeper. A pulse rising from beneath the water-skin floor. The sound followed: shrieks woven with grinding static, like a thousand radios tuned wrong, each stabbing at Russell's skull. He clamped his jaw shut, but bile still surged. He bent and gagged into the crook of his elbow, body convulsing with horror.

And then he saw them.

Dozens of Veilborne prowled the clearing in loose packs, moving with the kind of confidence predators carry when they know nothing can stop them. Smoke twisted tight around their skeletal forms, shoulders rolling with animal grace, claws clicking on the liquid with the economy of wolves. Their eyes burned like lamps, cold and merciless.

Between them hung their prey: phantoms of men, women, and children suspended midair, caught like fish in a net of invisible hooks. Their forms flickered, outlines trembling like candlelight, mouths open in cries that somehow scraped the ears though no sound should exist in them.

The Veilborne fed.

"They don't digest quickly," Allen murmured. "Hunger breaks what it doesn't understand."

One plunged its talons into a phantom's chest, twisting until it snagged something unseen. With a wrench, it drew free a filament of pale light. The strand quivered like a plucked violin string, sparks shivering along its length. Then the thing pulled it to its jagged maw and devoured it. The filament dimmed, and the phantom with it—collapsing inward, shape unraveling until only a faint smear of light remained, and then nothing at all.

Russell recoiled, bile searing his throat. "They're people," he rasped. "Not dreams, not shadows—people."

Allen's hand tightened on the lantern cage until the smoked glass creaked. "This is hunger without law," he said softly. "It was not always like this."

Another pack surged across the clearing, surrounding a small cluster of souls. They worked with horrifying efficiency, talons darting, snapping filaments, devouring light in a rhythm almost ceremonial. One creature hooked two strands at once and bit where they crossed, the resulting static popping like wet firecrackers. A child-shape imploded, shattering into sparks. Russell made a sound he did not recognize, half-sob, half-growl.

He stumbled a step forward, light flashing across a shard of mirrored ceiling. Half a dozen Veilborne stilled mid-feed, jaws working slowly, their heads lifting toward the lantern like beasts scenting blood.

"Back," Allen whispered. "Behind me."

The lantern's glow tightened, drawing sharper edges, a boundary drawn in gold. The nearest Veilborne sneered—an echo of a human expression stretched thin—and returned to its feast, though its eyes never left them.

Above, the mirror-sky shifted. The shards themselves remained still, but their reflections warped. In one, Russell saw a hospital corridor, flickering under emergency lights. In another, an elevator frozen between floors, chrome panels gleaming like hungry doors. The mirrors were not reflections but windows. Thin places where the other side pressed close. Dozens of them, all hungry.

"You said it wasn't always like this," Russell whispered, his teeth chattering. "What changed?"

"The keeper grows weak," Allen said. "When balance held, they scavenged. A ribbon of grief. A heartbeat of fear. Remnants only. They hunted in shadow because law held them there. Now the law is a rumor. They gorge in the open, and they teach each other how."

"How many are there?" Russell asked, though he hated himself for the question. It felt like asking how many teeth were in the mouth of a storm.

"Enough," Allen said. "And more with each hour."

As if to prove the point, another pack slunk in, their movements full of swagger. One rose taller than the rest, lifting three filaments in its claws like trophies. With a terrible pride, it braided them together and tipped its head back to slurp the braid whole. Sparks danced in its throat before guttering out. The others imitated the act, eager disciples learning from their new master.

Russell pressed his fist against his lips, trembling. "Hell," he muttered, "I always thought it was fire. This is worse. This is ice. Cold that burns." The thought of running gnawed at him, but his knees refused to unlock.

A phantom girl drifted too close, faint freckles across her flickering face. She reached toward the lantern, trembling with hope. Before she could touch it, a Veilborne darted in and clamped claws around her arms. The girl's mouth opened, and this time the shriek was not silent. It screamed high and metallic, ripping across the clearing like a tearing sawblade.

Russell flinched. "No! Please—" The plea fell into tar.

Allen stepped forward, thrusting the lantern's glow against the predator's claws. Smoke curled, talons hissing. The beast snarled and hurled the girl aside, seizing another phantom instead. The girl fluttered weakly, not extinguished, but dimmer.

"The lantern," Russell said hoarsely. "It hurts them. How?"

"It doesn't hurt," Allen said. "It reminds. Memory of old law still stings."

Russell shook his head, trembling. "They don't care anymore."

"They care for one thing," Allen said grimly. "Appetite. Imagine hunger discovering it can hunt in daylight."

Another shriek rang—higher, sharper. A pack had begun a spiral game, tossing a victim among them like a rope. Each tore away filaments, each bite making the phantom shrink until only dust remained. Their laughter was static and metal, the sound of coins dropping endlessly into a chute.

Russell hugged himself, eyes burning. "They're celebrating," he said. "This isn't hunger—it's rebellion."

Allen nodded. "And rebellion spreads when it is fed."

The lantern flared suddenly as a phantom darted into its edge, clinging like a moth. Russell reached back, hand trembling, and caught its wrist of mist. "I've got you," he whispered. "Stay close. Ten seconds at a time."

Above, the mirrors filled with watchers—faces pressed against glass, curious and ravenous. Russell felt their attention like hands pushing at his spine.

"This will bleed out," he muttered. "If it keeps spreading, it'll break into our side. Everywhere."

Allen's jaw tightened. "That is what happens when law falls. Rebellion does not stop at borders."

A tremor passed through the floor. Another pack entered, larger, more disciplined. Their leader stood taller, eyes narrow, its body language commanding. The others gave way with the courtesy of wolves.

It bared its teeth, then led its pack to devour a cluster of souls with ruthless order.

"What makes that one different?" Russell whispered.

"Some feed," Allen said. "Some command."

The feast swelled. Shrieks climbed higher, static grinding louder, until the air itself seemed to vibrate with their gluttony. Allen herded two trembling phantoms into a recess of broken glass, tucking them away like frightened children. The lantern's glow thinned under the weight of the rebellion, but he held it steady, hands firm.

Russell shuddered. His voice was little more than a thread. "Whatever dam held this back—it's cracking."

"The dam was the Echo," Allen said quietly. "And the river was never gentle."

Something moved across the mirror-sky. A shadow that belonged to none of the hunters below. It slid like ink drawn by a lazy brush. The Veilborne stiffened, faces lifting as if catching a scent. A thrill of anticipation ran through them, claws flexing, shoulders trembling. The new leader cocked its head, then bent to feed harder, as if showing off for the unseen presence.

Russell whispered, "What was that?"

"Not what," Allen said, eyes narrowing. "Who."

He didn't explain further. He didn't need to. The rebellion had found a teacher—or worse, a patron.

The sound of feeding swelled into a frenzy. The black water pulsed, the mirror-sky glittered, and the lost screamed in chorus with the static. Allen pulled Russell and the rescued souls toward the shadows of the corridor.

"Don't run," he warned. "If you run, they will follow."

Russell nodded shakily. "Catch me if I do."

"I will," Allen said, and together they slipped into the waiting dark, the lantern's faint gold halo dragging its small clutch of survivors into safety while behind them, the feast roared like a world learning to enjoy its own ruin.

Scene 3: The Deceiver Appears

They had almost reached the sheltering mouth of the corridor when the feast behind them changed its pitch. The shrieks rose and then fell away in a hush that wasn't quiet at all—like a theater audience drawing breath before a curtain lifts. Father Allen stopped with the lantern half-raised. The black water of the clearing quivered, and the mirror-sky above them clouded, shards dimming as though something had passed in front of a distant sun.

He came out of the pack with a gentleness that made the Veilborne seem suddenly crude. They slunk apart from him the way wolves part for a stag that has never known hunger. He wasn't smoke wrapped around bone, and he wasn't a phantom. He wore the shape of a man the way a well-cut suit wears a body—perfect lines, nothing to snag the eye. Handsome was too small a word; what he carried was symmetry. His features were arranged with a mathematician's cruelty: the exact angle where trust becomes desire, the precise curve of a smile that promises you have always been right about yourself.

His radiance wasn't light. It was permission. Faces turned toward him, and the space brightened only because attention is a kind of flame.

Russell's knees loosened. "I... know him," he whispered, which made no sense and felt absolutely true. It wasn't recognition of a person; it was recognition of a proposition. The proposition that said, You could be everything you've wanted to be if you stop apologizing for wanting it.

The stranger's eyes flickered like black fire—no whites, no pupils, just the suggestion of depth that keeps deepening the longer you look. When he smiled, two Veilborne nearest him actually bowed, the motion low and grateful, like parishioners greeting a traveling bishop.

Others hissed in a stretched, reverent way, claws clicking a rhythm on the liquid.

He did not speak loudly. His words came like silk whispered across glass, and yet Russell heard every one as if it were spoken an inch inside his ear.

"The keeper is failing," said the beautiful mouth. "You feel it. You smell it. The old scales rust and crack. This realm belongs to you now. Feed without restraint. Cross as you wish. No chains remain."

The clearing answered with a ripple—a physical shiver that ran through the packs and up into the mirror-sky. Some Veilborne lifted their faces and drank the sentence like a draught. Others turned toward the shards above, as if testing the edges of their reflections for doorways. Filaments of stolen light trembled in claws, then vanished between teeth with an eagerness that made the air taste metallic.

"Don't listen," Father Allen said, and only then did Russell realize he had begun to walk. One step. Another. His body moved as if the floor had slid under him, like an airport walkway carrying him forward even as he told himself to stand still.

"But he's—" Russell swallowed. The stranger's gaze brushed him, and it felt like being seen by an old friend who remembers your best day and none of your worst. "He's right, isn't he? About the keeper. About... everything."

"Name him correctly," Allen said, fingers tightening around Russell's sleeve with quick, human strength. "He is not right. He is convincing. There is a difference. He is the Deceiver."

The word landed in Russell's bones the way a diagnosis lands: the sudden explanation for a dozen aches you thought were separate. He stopped, half because Allen pulled, half because the title made the handsome symmetry flicker, just for a heartbeat. A seam showed beneath the perfect face, like a hairline crack in tempered glass.

The Deceiver drifted through the clearing without wetting his feet. Wherever he went, the Veilborne drew closer, talons half-lowered, heads tilted, attentive as students during a demonstration. He did not touch them. He had no need. He spoke in a voice Russell could not hear and still heard, a voice that promised a future already paid for.

"You have been patient," the Deceiver murmured, and packs pressed inward to catch the words. "You have obeyed rules written by a dying hand. But patience is for slaves. Obedience is for the frightened. You are neither. You are hunger given shape. You are the rightful night. Go where the surface thins. Take what crosses. Take more."

A Veilborne near his shoulder quivered, then stepped neatly to a hovering phantom and opened its chest with a surgeon's precision. The scream that followed was almost lost beneath the soft susurrus of approval that ran through the clearing. The Deceiver leaned, watching the technique, and smiled as if a pupil had finally mastered a difficult passage.

Russell's feet inched forward again. His mouth went dry with a longing he did not recognize at first. Then he knew it: the longing to be told that his worst impulses were actually secret virtues. That all the times he had cut someone down on-air, he had been brave, not cruel. That the smirk had been a sword of clarity. That fame had been a crown he'd been wrong to ever doubt he deserved.

"I could be better," he heard himself say. "He could make me better. He could make me matter."

Father Allen's hand snapped up and took Russell's jaw, turning his face away from the Deceiver with a gentleness so sudden it felt like a slap without pain. The lantern swung between them, close enough that its smoked glass warmed Russell's cheek. In its dull gold he saw his own eyes—red-rimmed, small, a little boy's eyes in a man who had learned too many tricks.

"He cannot make you anything," Allen said, voice low. "He can only rename what you already are and sell you the name as a blessing. And he can ask for your soul in exact change."

Something like shame—no, not like, exactly—ran down Russell's spine and pooled in his gut. He let out a breath that shook. "I almost—"

"Yes," Allen said. "You almost."

The Deceiver had drawn near enough now that Russell could see the fine grain of his skin, the way it didn't quite hold still. Tiny currents ran through it, shadows flowing under the surface like ink in water. He glanced once toward Father Allen's lantern and gave a courteous nod, the way a host acknowledges an old enemy who has arrived dressed properly.

"Lantern-bearer," he said, and there was nothing oily in his tone. He sounded sincerely pleased. "Still shepherding emptiness as if it were lambs."

"Still naming lies," Allen answered, and the lantern brightened a fraction, not in challenge, in clarity. The closest Veilborne hissed, recoil like a collective flinch.

The Deceiver's eyes deepened. For a second they looked like two bottomless wells drilled straight through the world. "The keeper cannot answer you," he said, almost sympathizing. "You stand in a ruined nave with a pocket-candle and call it law. Why not rest? Why not let these children eat what is theirs?"

Allen's mouth tightened. "Because it is not theirs. It never was."

"Law is what is enforced," the Deceiver said mildly. "And the enforcer has grown very tired."

He turned from the priest as if losing interest in a debate already won and let his attention fall on the packs arrayed around him. "There are feasts on the far side," he said, smiling like a benevolent patron announcing grants. "Reflections waiting to be opened. Thin places ripening like fruit. Take the ones who look longest into themselves. Take the ones who wait in hallways with cameras, the ones who press their faces to the glass to find proof that they exist. Give them meaning."

The mirror-sky seemed to lean closer. In one shard, Russell thought he saw a hotel elevator lobby, chandelier lights trembling. In another, a bathroom medicine cabinet in a house with poor wiring and good intentions. The Deceiver lifted his hands slightly—no grand gesture—and the shards clouded over as if the scenes had been thumbed away.

Russell took another step in spite of himself. The ache in his chest had flipped from revulsion to want and back so many times it had made him dizzy. He could feel the old hungers waking up like men roused by a siren: the hunger to be watched, the hunger to be right, the hunger to be untouchable. The Deceiver offered them all tied up with a bow that looked very much like absolution.

Allen hauled him back, harder this time. "No." The word was not loud, but it carried a weight that pushed against the urge like a hand against a closing door. "Look at me."

Russell did. The priest's face was lined with the same fear that lived in Russell's chest, but behind it was something the Deceiver did not radiate: grief that knew its own name. The lantern's glow steadied.

"Say it," Allen told him. "Say what he is."

Russell licked his lips, mouth dry as ash. "Deceiver," he said, barely above a breath. Then stronger: "Liar."

The beautiful face didn't crack. It didn't need to. But the black fire in the eyes pulsed once, a small irritation like a fly brushed from a cheek. The Deceiver's smile cooled by a degree.

"Very well," he said, almost fond. "Keep your little word. You will trade it for a larger one in time."

He turned then—not away from them, but toward the far rim of the clearing where the mirror-sky pooled in a deeper darkness, shards clustered like scales on a serpent's throat. The Veilborne nearest that edge parted and lowered themselves on their knees, talons laid politely along the floor. The Deceiver passed through their reverence without acknowledgement, the way a river passes reeds.

"Where is he going?" Russell asked, voice small.

"Where he always goes," Allen said. "Toward the gates. Toward the thin."

"You can't follow him?" The question came out a plea and a dare.

"I can," Allen said. "I will not." His hand tightened once more on Russell's sleeve. "And neither will you."

"I—" Russell began, and realized with bleak relief that he was grateful to be held in place. The gratitude embarrassed him; it also saved him.

The Deceiver paused at the very lip of the clearing and looked back, just once, as if checking whether a particular fish had taken the hook. His eyes skimmed the lantern and then slid to Russell. They softened. In that softening Russell saw a thousand possible lives in which he had been celebrated without learning kindness. He almost smiled back.

Father Allen lifted the lantern a fraction higher, and the Deceiver's gaze passed on, bored. He stepped forward, and where he stepped the mirror-shards folded like doors. The dark beyond swallowed him, not with hunger, with welcome.

The packs resumed their feeding with renewed zeal, energized by the benediction. Shrieks rose, static grated, and the clearing's pulse accelerated, the black water beating to a rhythm set by a mouth that didn't believe in limits.

"Now we go," Allen said. "Before the lesson becomes a riot."

They retreated into the corridor's shadow, the lantern's circle gathering two trembling phantoms who had clung there as if they'd known to wait. Russell's legs felt made of soaked paper. He stumbled once and caught himself on the priest's sleeve.

"I almost followed him," he said, voice hoarse. He hated the admission and needed it.

"Yes," Allen said again. "You almost."

Russell swallowed, shame and relief burning the same path. "Next time," he said, trying to make the words steady, "grab me sooner."

"I will," the priest answered, and the lantern carried them forward, away from the feast that called itself freedom and sounded like coins falling forever into a dark machine.

Scene 4: Echo Weakened, Silent

The corridor closed around them like a throat, its walls not glass nor stone but a porous dark that drank the lantern's glow. Each step left only the faintest rind of light. Behind them, the shrieks of the feasting Veilborne fell away like a tide, replaced by silence that pressed on their eardrums.

"Stay close," Father Allen murmured. His voice carried no echo; the place swallowed sound like a miser swallowing coins.

Russell hovered behind him, one hand brushing the wall, the other half-extended toward the lantern as if he could steady it by nearness alone. The little flame inside shivered like a tired heart. Three faint souls clung to its glow, dim figures drifting in their wake like moths that barely remembered how to fly.

"Is it running out?" Russell whispered. His voice cracked. "Like a battery?"

"Not while I carry it," Allen said. "But carrying grows heavier."

The corridor bent and spat them onto a terrace of black glass. Beyond stretched a plain vast enough to unmake perspective. Russell crouched beside Allen and peered into the gloom. At first he thought the horizon was empty. Then he saw it: a bowed silhouette too immense to measure. Its crown shimmered faintly, not light but memory of light; its limbs dragged like shadows heavy with age. Whole tracts of the In Between seemed to tilt as it shifted, as though the world bent out of deference.

"The Echo," Russell whispered. The name came out thin, embarrassed at its own smallness. He had expected thunder, proclamation. Instead he saw a keeper dimmed, its edges frayed, its voice absent.

The realm hushed. Souls dimmed, Veilborne stilled mid-feast, even the shards of mirror-sky tilted to listen for a word that never came. The Echo did not speak.

Russell's stomach turned. He hadn't realized until this moment how much he had trusted in the idea of a godlike roar, some proof of authority. To see only silence felt like betrayal. "Why isn't it—" His throat closed.

"Strength can be spent," Allen said. His tone was not surprised but sorrowful, like a man keeping vigil at a deathbed. "Balance is a labor. We forget it has cost."

Movement rippled across the plain. Packs of Veilborne poured from hollows and ridges, no longer feeding in corners but striding like soldiers. They moved with purpose, drawn by the keeper's stillness as if hunger itself had been invited to rule.

"They're not gathering to him," Russell whispered. "They're gathering to the chance that he won't rise."

"To the rumor that law is tired," Allen said grimly.

The lantern flickered to a thread. The three souls behind them wavered, nearly snuffed out. Allen bowed his head, cupping the cage with both hands. His lips moved in wordless prayer. The syllables were not polished ritual but raw plea. Russell felt them in his own chest, a tug of need deeper than fear.

He closed his eyes, then forced them open again. "I've been a fool," he said, words scraping free. "A coward. Cruel, because cruelty made better television. I laughed at people who cried. I made them small to look big. And I told myself I wasn't afraid—when I was terrified."

Allen didn't rebuke or absolve him. He only lifted the lantern, and the thread of light fattened by a hair. "Name it," he said quietly. "Then choose."

Russell stared at the dim silhouette on the horizon. The Echo did not answer. Maybe it couldn't. Maybe it wouldn't. Still, the choice pressed on him. "I'll try," he said. "I don't know how. But I'll try. Ten seconds at a time. Ten more." He tried for humor and failed. "Sounds like a self-help poster in hell."

Allen's mouth twitched, almost a smile. "Intention is a lever," he said. "Even here."

Below, the feast resumed faintly, sharper with distance—shrieks, static, the hiss of hungers drunk with power. The shards above showed restless windows: an elevator, a bar mirror, car windows sliding past a curb. The In Between was thinning everywhere men liked to see themselves.

"We can't wait for him to fix this, can we?" Russell asked.

"No," Allen said. His eyes stayed on the keeper. "We pray his strength returns. Until then, we carry what we can. Protect who we can. Refuse the Deceiver's invitations."

He rose half from his crouch, shoulders squared against the dark. The lantern steadied, a stubborn thread brightening enough to form a circle the souls pressed close to. The faint figures almost had faces again—features briefly visible before fading back.

Russell risked a glance behind. The corridor they'd come from pulsed like a throat suppressing bile. Out in the chambers, the rebellion swelled. He remembered the Deceiver's warm smile, the half-step his own feet had taken. He shuddered. "He almost had me. And I don't even know what he would have led me into—only that it would have been easy."

"That is his gift," Allen said. "Never trust ease."

Russell licked dry lips. "What happens if the Echo falls?"

"Then balance becomes whatever the strongest hunger says it is," Allen said. "And hunger is persuasive."

They edged along the terrace, the three souls flickering loyally behind. The black glass floor bore striations like fingerprints, and the lantern traced them as if they were a hidden map. The plain remained vast, the bowed Echo unmoving, the Veilborne gathering in packs. Above, the mirror-sky quivered, reflections sharpening into traps.

"Will he send us back?" Russell asked after a long silence. "When he can?"

"When he chooses," Allen replied. "Mercy is not a machine. But the keeper has eyes for mercy. That, I believe."

The words didn't thunder, but they settled in Russell's chest like a brace. He exhaled, steadier.

At a notch in the terrace, Allen directed them down shelves of rock toward a narrow runnel of black water. "Heel to toe," he instructed. "If you slip, fall toward me."

Russell gave a strained grin. "I'll make falling stylish." He caught himself and shook his head. "Sorry. Habit."

"Humor isn't sin," Allen said. "Only a poor substitute for courage."

Step by step they descended. On the second shelf, the lantern lurched—then steadied. On the third, a distant cry sharpened the air until the shelf seemed thinner. The souls pressed close. On the fourth, a draft rose from the slot below, smelling of antiseptic and long grief. The lantern dwindled to a sliver.

Allen bent his head, whispered to the cage, kissed it like a father to a child. "Now, little one," he murmured. "Let us be seen enough."

The flame steadied, stubborn. The souls brightened faintly, almost becoming faces. One looked at Russell and mouthed you stopped him. He didn't know if she meant the Veilborne or the Deceiver or himself. He nodded anyway.

They slipped into the narrow slot. The plain and the bowed keeper vanished behind them. The corridor ahead bent like a throat, the lantern's glow trembling forward. It wasn't victory. But it was standing, and for now, that was enough.

12

Revelations and Warnings

Scene 1: The Spreading Terror

The morning news no longer felt like background noise—it was the sound of the world fraying thread by thread.

Abigail Jensen stood at her kitchen counter, hands wrapped around a mug she had forgotten to drink from. The coffee had gone cold long before, a thin skin wrinkling at its surface. On the small television in the corner of the counter, the newscaster's voice carried a brittle tension that no professional polish could mask.

"...developments overnight in Thurston and Kitsap Counties. Reports now confirm at least five disappearances connected to unexplained phenomena involving mirrors or reflective glass. Families describe relatives vanishing into bathroom mirrors, storefront windows, even a decorative pond at a hotel in Olympia. Officials have issued no formal statement beyond urging residents to cover mirrors in their homes."

The screen cut to shaky phone footage—someone screaming in a dim living room while another voice shouted, Don't look at it, don't look at it! A mirror above the mantel shuddered as if something pushed against it from the inside. The picture ended abruptly when the phone hit the floor, tilted to show nothing but carpet.

The newscaster continued, face taut, voice dropping as if afraid the words themselves might draw attention. *"Authorities emphasize there is no confirmed link between these incidents, but communities are already taking precautions. Stores across Pierce, King, and Thurston Counties report running out of duct tape, paint, and blackout curtains."*

Abigail glanced toward her own living room mirror, already draped in heavy cloth. Her skin prickled. Covering them was simple, practical—but even under fabric, the sense of being watched never truly left.

The screen shifted to live footage from downtown Olympia. Storefronts looked gutted. Windows were spray-painted black or plastered with plywood. People hurried across sidewalks with their heads ducked, avoiding every surface that might throw back their reflection. A banner headline scrolled beneath the broadcast:

MIRROR FEAR SPREADS BEYOND TACOMA — OFFICIALS STRUGGLE TO CALM PUBLIC.

She turned the volume higher.

"...and in Mason County, two teenagers were reportedly dragged toward a lake during what witnesses describe as the 'mirror challenge,' a viral trend urging participants to stare into their reflections for sixty seconds. One of the teens has not returned. Police are treating the case as a missing person, though bystanders insist they saw her 'swallowed by the water's reflection.'"

Abigail's stomach clenched. She'd heard whispers of that challenge online—children daring one another for likes and shares, mocking what older generations feared. A game. Until one vanished screaming into water that reflected her face back.

The broadcast shifted again, this time to a polished studio where an anchor sat flanked by security footage. The grainy film showed the corridor of a shopping mall. A man stood outside a store, speaking on his phone. Behind him, in the broad glass of a display window, shapes gathered—black silhouettes pressing forward, faint clawed outlines scraping at the glass. Before the man could turn, a hand like smoke reached through and seized his shoulder. His phone clattered to the floor as he was dragged inward, body folding unnaturally into the reflection. Shoppers screamed and scattered; some tried to pull him free but were left holding only his jacket.

The feed cut before more could be seen.

Abigail's mug rattled softly on the counter as she set it down.

Fear was no longer an undercurrent confined to Tacoma's neighborhoods. It was tidal, rolling outward in rings, county to county, city to city.

The newscaster cleared her throat, as if bracing for what she had to say next. "Mental health hotlines report call volume tripled in the past week. Residents describe feeling watched through reflective surfaces, even with mirrors removed. Parents are pulling children from schools. Businesses are shuttering. A quiet panic spreads as far north as Seattle, where the mayor has urged citizens to remain calm and trust in scientific investigation."

A second anchor interjected, voice sharp, defensive: "Experts continue to stress there is no evidence these disappearances are linked to supernatural causes. We caution against speculation and urge viewers to seek reliable information only."

But even as he spoke, stock footage filled the screen: churches crowded with people lighting candles, priests hanging cloth over their sanctuaries' windows, grocery clerks covering freezer doors with cardboard. Ordinary life looked mutilated, stripped of reflection.

Abigail shut the television off. The sudden silence roared louder than the broadcast had.

She leaned against the counter, eyes closed, forcing slow breaths. Her pulse skittered against her throat. It was happening faster than she'd feared. What had been isolated whispers, strange cases she alone seemed to notice, was now undeniable. Everyone was seeing it. Everyone was afraid.

The scrape of a chair startled her. Samuel sat at the table, his face weary, eyes fixed on the draped mirror across the room. "It's spreading," he said quietly. His voice was flat, like a man describing rain soaking into his roof—a fact he couldn't deny even if he tried.

"Yes." She pulled the cloth tighter around her arms.

"How far before..." He didn't finish. He didn't need to. Before the cloths and plywood weren't enough. Before people stopped venturing outside at all. Before the Veilborne were no longer content to come through mirrors one at a time.

Abigail walked to the window. Outside, the street was empty save for a lone man hurrying with a ladder, a bedsheet dangling from one shoulder. He kept glancing at car windows parked along the curb, his pace quickening when he saw his own shape looking back.

The world was beginning to tear itself into silence.

Behind her, Samuel muttered, "It won't stop here."

He was right. Fear never stopped at borders.

The phone rang, startling them both. The shrillness felt obscene in the heavy quiet. Abigail answered with a cautious "Hello?"

The caller's voice trembled on the edge of hysteria. "Is this... Abigail Jensen? You helped my cousin last year, the mirror in her basement? Please—you have to come. It's happening in Shelton now. My sister—she swore the mirror in her bedroom was breathing. Last night she screamed and then—" The woman's voice broke into sobs.

Abigail closed her eyes, her hand tightening around the phone. Another county. Another home. The pattern was spreading like fire in dry grass, each call another flare she couldn't stamp out fast enough.

"I'll do what I can," Abigail said softly. It felt like a lie even as it left her lips. She ended the call gently, though the sobs lingered in her ears.

When she turned back, Samuel was standing. His jaw was tight, hands fists at his sides. "You can't keep running out every time someone calls. Not like this. The veil's thinning everywhere. You'll break yourself trying to answer all of them."

Abigail didn't argue. She looked again at the map spread on the table, the pins she'd already pressed into it—Tacoma, Lakewood,

Parkland. Now she would need to add Olympia, Shelton, Bremerton. The arc widened, stretching like a claw across the county lines.

It was no longer a pattern. It was a tide.

Jacob padded into the kitchen, barefoot, hair rumpled with sleep. He rubbed his eyes and blinked at the two adults frozen in the dim light. "Another one?" he asked quietly.

Abigail couldn't bring herself to nod. He looked at the map, then at the covered mirror, then at her. His face was calm in a way that only deepened her unease.

"They're everywhere now," he said, voice steady. "And they're not going to stop."

The words didn't sound like a child's guess. They carried the weight of knowledge, the echo of something larger that had spoken to him before. Abigail felt a shiver crawl through her bones.

She crossed the room and pulled him into her arms. His small frame trembled once, then went still against her. She whispered into his hair, "We'll find a way. We always do."

But as her eyes flicked back to the draped mirror, she saw the faintest ripple stir the cloth. Just once. A breath behind fabric.

Her arms tightened protectively around Jacob.

Fear was no longer isolated to Tacoma. It was coming for them all.

Scene 2: Confession at Dusk

The evening light over Lakewood had a bruised quality, purple sinking into gray. Abigail Jensen sat at a corner table in a small café near Gravelly Lake, her hands cupped around a mug that had long since cooled. She had chosen this spot because its windows faced west, reflecting nothing but the empty parking lot. Even so, every pane of glass had been covered in butcher paper. No one wanted to risk what might look back.

The bell over the door jangled. Dr. Lena Mirek slipped inside, her posture taut, her eyes scanning the café with the restless caution of someone who had begun to see threats in every surface. She carried herself like a woman accustomed to reason and order—yet her movements tonight betrayed cracks in both.

Abigail raised a hand. Lena crossed quickly to the table, slid into the chair opposite, and pressed her palms flat against the scratched wood. "Thank you for agreeing to meet," she said, her voice low, though the café was nearly empty. "I couldn't—couldn't say this at the lab. Not with Elias there."

Abigail studied her carefully. Lena's face was pale under the warm café light, her dark hair pulled back in a hasty twist. Her eyes carried the exhaustion of sleepless nights—and something heavier. Fear.

"You said it was important," Abigail prompted gently.

Lena exhaled hard through her nose, then leaned closer. "Elias… deploys the Array at Clover Park Technical College. Not just some-times—frequently. He claims it's because the site is convenient, but that's not the truth. He does it because the readings there are strongest. The resonance spikes off the charts."

Abigail's fingers tightened around her mug. "Stronger than Pierce College?"

"Yes." Lena's hands fidgeted with the edge of a napkin. "There's something about Clover Park, the way the ground layers or the air currents interact with the machine. Elias insists it's ideal. He says it's like tuning an instrument—you find the chamber where the sound rings clearest, then you play there."

Abigail's stomach sank. The pins on her map swam in her mind—the crescent of disappearances encircling Clover Park, the arc that had troubled her for weeks. She had thought the site was signifi-cant for reasons she couldn't yet grasp. Now the reason stood in front of her, tired and trembling.

"You understand what this means," Abigail said, her voice low and sharp.

Lena swallowed. "I think so. But... I need to hear it from you."

Abigail leaned forward. "Every time Elias deploys the Array at Clover Park, he's pulling energy from more than the atmosphere. He's draining from the In Between itself. He's siphoning directly from the Echo, weakening it. That's why the veil is thinning. That's why the Veilborne are feeding openly now."

The words landed heavy between them, as if the air itself recoiled.

Lena closed her eyes, pressing her fingers to her temples. "I suspected... God help me, I suspected, but I told myself it was impossible. That Elias was right—that we were only harvesting ambient resonance, harmless byproduct. But what I saw in the lab, what I've seen in the mirrors—" She broke off, shuddering. "It wasn't harmless. And now people are dying."

Abigail reached across the table, covering Lena's clenched hand with her own. "The pattern is clear. The Array is the wound, and Clover Park is where it bleeds deepest."

Tears pricked the corners of Lena's eyes. She blinked them back with the fierce pride of someone unused to showing weakness. "I tried to talk to him. Elias. I told him the Array hums even when it's powered down. That reflections ripple when no one touches them. He brushed me off, said anomalies are normal in pioneering science. He doesn't see it—or worse, he won't."

"Because ambition blinds him," Abigail said quietly.

"Yes." Lena's voice broke. "He's brilliant, but he's so sure brilliance makes him immune to consequence. He thinks he can control this. But how do you control a thing that feeds on souls?"

The café door creaked as someone left, and both women flinched, heads snapping toward the sound. When silence settled again, Lena let out a shaking laugh. "Listen to me. Jumping at shadows. I'm a scientist. I should be charting data, not hiding in a café whispering like a conspirator."

"You're not hiding," Abigail said firmly. "You're warning. That takes more courage than you think."

Lena studied her for a long moment, searching her face. "Do you believe it can be stopped? That the Echo can recover?"

Abigail hesitated. She thought of Jacob's words—the Echo said it was dying. She thought of Father Allen guiding souls through corridors that grew darker every day. But she couldn't place that weight entirely on Lena's already bowed shoulders.

"It can be stopped," she said. "But not if Elias keeps deploying the Array at Clover Park. Every time he does, the veil weakens further. If he doesn't stop, the In Between will spill into our world unchecked."

Lena nodded slowly, gripping her mug as if it were an anchor. "Then I'll tell him again. And this time, I'll have your words to back me up. Maybe he'll listen."

"Maybe," Abigail said, though doubt soured the word in her mouth.

They sat in silence, the café around them hushed, the only sound the faint scrape of a spoon behind the counter. Outside, dusk deepened; the streetlamps flickered on, their glow haloed in mist. Even their light seemed frail, as if reflection itself had become tainted.

Abigail broke the silence. "If Elias refuses to stop, you'll have to choose. Loyalty to him, or loyalty to the world he's endangering."

Lena's face tightened. "He doesn't see me that way. Not as someone with choices that matter. I'm just the assistant who translates his brilliance into words others can understand. But..." She trailed off, then drew a sharp breath. "But maybe that means I've always had more power than I realized."

Abigail squeezed her hand once before withdrawing. "Use it. The world may depend on it."

For a long time Lena didn't move, her gaze fixed on the covered windows. Finally she said, "You've seen the Echo, haven't you? Not just stories, but truly seen."

Abigail's chest tightened. "Yes. And I've seen the Veilborne too. I've seen what balance means when it's kept, and what horror follows when it falters."

"Then tell me one thing," Lena whispered, leaning closer. "If the Echo is weakening as you say—what happens if it dies?"

Abigail shook her head. "I don't know. But I don't think our world survives it."

Lena paled. She looked as though the ground beneath her had shifted, a tectonic truth she hadn't wanted to face. She rose abruptly, gathering her coat, her voice tight. "Then we don't have time."

Abigail stood as well. "No. We don't."

They left the café together, stepping into the cool, damp air. The street was eerily still, every window blindfolded with paper or cloth. A man passed on the opposite sidewalk, his arms full of duct tape and blankets, his eyes darting to every darkened pane. The world was holding its breath.

At the curb, Lena paused. She glanced at Abigail, her expression raw. "If something happens to me—if Elias refuses to listen—I need you to keep pushing. Don't let the world think this is hysteria. Make them see the truth."

"You have my word," Abigail said.

Lena nodded once, then turned toward the parking lot. Abigail watched her go, the weight of the revelation pressing like a stone in her chest.

The Array was not only a machine. It was the wound bleeding the In Between into their world. And unless Elias Voss was stopped, that wound would not close.

Scene 3: The Breaking Point

The lab felt like an engine room at low tide—damp concrete, metal, a breathy hum rising and falling as if the building itself were dreaming. Most of the reflective surfaces had been taped over in brown kraft paper and black gaffer's tape: the face of a wall clock, the brushed steel panel on a storage cabinet, the glass of a long-forgotten classroom poster. Only the Array remained bare. You couldn't tape over a storm.

Elias Voss stood at the central rack, jaw clenched, eyes fixed on three monitors stacked like altars. Each display cycled between graphs and spectrograms: pale combs of frequency, rising plateaus of amplitude, a stutter at the far end that had no label because he had refused to give it one.

"Elias," Lena said. She kept her voice even. "We need to talk."

"I'm logging yesterday's hysteresis drift," he answered without turning. "If you have notes, email them."

She glanced at the leaded glass shielding, at the loop antennas hung with meticulous precision, at the toroidal coils stacked like vertebrae along a spine. Elias had arranged every cable himself, color-coded, tied, combed. The neatness would have been calming once. Today it felt like a shrine to denial.

"It's not a note," Lena said. "It's a confession."

That got him to look. Up close, fatigue had hollowed him. His hair was too carefully combed, like a man pretending he slept. "Confession?"

"I met with Abigail," she said, the words landing with a thud she couldn't cushion. "I told her what you won't put on paper. That you deploy here, at Clover Park, because the resonance is strongest."

His eyes flashed. "I don't deploy here. We run field captures. Characterization. Baseline—"

"Semantics won't save lives." The snap in her tone startled even her. "You know this site rings hottest. You chase it because it does."

He exhaled through his nose. "Of course I chase it. That's the job. You tune an instrument where the acoustics reward you. None of that proves the Array is causing—"

"It isn't proof you want," Lena cut in, "it's permission. And I'm done giving it." She pulled a folded sheet from her bag and flattened it on the workbench: a printout of Abigail's map overlaid with their own run logs, dates and times matched to street corners and neighborhoods. Red dots made a crescent around the campus; beneath, a gray column listed sessions: CAPTURE-06, -07, -08... timestamps ticking along in tidy increments.

"We thought it was a curve of incidents," Lena said, tapping the crescent. "It's actually a shadow. Ours. Every time you spun up a test here, reports spiked along the arc within hours. Every pause? A brief lull. We aren't measuring a storm, Elias. We're making one."

He scanned the paper with a scientist's speed, head tilted, pupils contracting with calculation. "Correlation," he said, but the word lacked its old armor. "Population density changes the reporting rate. Viral videos change perception. Mass suggestion—"

"Then why does the arc hold even against neighborhoods of equal density?" Lena slid another sheet beside the first—Abigail's revised overlay, color-coded for population. "Why do the spikes hug our deployment windows like barnacles on a hull? Why are the strongest events—hospital mirrors, elevator panels, the hotel lobby—clustered in a radius that shrinks and swells with our coil tune?"

Elias looked up too quickly. "Coil tune?"

"The last two weeks," she said quietly. "You've been favoring the lower band because it harvests 'cleaner.' Each time you dip, the incidents sharpen. When you push higher, they diffuse but multiply. You can't tell me you haven't noticed. You have a mind like a knife."

He opened his mouth, shut it, then turned to the monitors as if graphs could back him. One display stuttered, showing a tremor at the far right—a faint, saw-toothed ridge that had become their private ghost. He reached for the dial out of habit and let his hand hover there, not touching.

"You told me once," Lena said, gentler now, "that if the Array ever drank from a well it shouldn't, you would choose to stop."

"That was a question," he said. His voice was low. "A philosophical exercise."

"It was a promise," she said. "Mine to you. Yours to yourself."

Elias's phone chimed. The sound was too bright in the dim lab. He made the mistake of glancing at the screen. *AVERY SHAW: Friday looks good. Push output. Bring the 'big number.'* A beat later, another: *We own the narrative. You bring the spectacle.*

He tapped the phone dark as if it had insulted him. "This isn't about Avery."

"Everything's about Avery since he walked through that door," Lena said. "He's a pressure you pretend you don't feel. You're letting his timeline decide what is safe."

Elias's mouth twisted, pride and shame colliding. "I won't have my life's work reduced to a superstition. Spirits. Echoes." He said the second word as if it might hear him and change shape. "We capture fields. We convert harmonics. The rest is what frightened people do with fear."

Lena's heart hammered. She felt like a cliff face being undercut by water she couldn't see. "Then why are we covering mirrors in a physics lab?" She gestured at the brown paper and tape like satchels of sand on a flood wall. "Why do you flinch when the metal cabinet shows you your hands?" She took a breath that tasted like dust. "Why do I have scratches on my arms shaped like letters when there is no glass nearby?" She rolled up her sleeve and showed him—a faint lattice, red as nettle-sting, crossing her forearm in a pattern that was not random. LEAVE.

Elias's jaw clenched so hard a muscle jumped near his ear. "That could be—"

"Static discharge? Field noise?" Her laugh broke. "It hurts, Elias. That's not noise." Her eyes burned. "I saw one of them. Here. In our lab. You were there when the lights went out and the mirror rippled. You saw its hand."

He stared at the floor, at his shoes, at the careful coil of a cable tied just so. For a moment he looked very small inside his own body. "We don't know the mechanism," he said finally, reaching for the ground he trusted. "Even if there is a coupling—if—the fault could be in the substrate of this campus or the geology or—"

"Then stop deploying here," Lena said. "Stop feeding whatever this place amplifies." She pushed the printouts closer. "And if it isn't this place, if it's the machine, then stop the machine. We need your choice before there isn't a choice left."

He rubbed his eyes hard with the heel of his hand. When he lowered it, the skin beneath was red, and in that redness Lena saw the boy who had stayed up nights tracing equations in the condensation on a dorm window, too hungry for answers to sleep. He was still that boy. He had just wrapped him in armor and called it genius.

"I can't just shut it down," he said hoarsely. "There are contracts. Audits. If I don't deliver—"

"If you do deliver," Lena said, "what you'll deliver is the In Between, unbarred."

Silence yawned between them. From somewhere behind the racks came a soft tick like a cooling pipe, then another, a rhythmless metronome that made the hair on Lena's arms lift. Elias set both hands on the bench as if he might steady the building with his palms.

"Call her," he said, so quietly she almost missed it.

"Who?"

"Abigail."

Lena didn't move. The decision itself had taken his last inch of self-justification. She nodded once, fumbled with her phone, and stepped away to make the call.

Abigail arrived with the weather—a curtain of cold rain moving across the parking lot, the smell of wet cedar trailing behind her. She nodded at Lena, then took in the lab at a glance: the taped-over panels, the bared Array, the way Elias stood like a man braced for impact.

"Dr. Voss," she said.

"Ms. Jensen," he answered, caught between formality and gratitude.

Abigail stepped closer to the central rack, to the monitors still humming their measured song. "I've seen your work from a distance," she said. "I respect the mind it took to build this. I also think it's killing the keeper that stands between our world and hunger."

Elias's lips thinned, but he didn't lash out. Abigail reached into her bag and drew out a folder. Inside lay photographs of her map, annotated in her narrow hand; copies of public incident reports; timestamps; and, clipped together, three still frames from different videos: the hotel hallway, the elevator lobby, a hospital ward at 3:17 a.m. In each still, a film of smoke curled across glass at the precise minute one of his logs showed a frequency ramp at Clover Park.

She laid the stills beside his logs, lining edges, aligning time. "You don't have to believe in what I call them," she said. "But you must see that when you draw, they come. When you stop, they recede. That isn't hysteria. That's a tide responding to the moon you invented."

He stared so hard his pupils trembled. On the rightmost display the faint sawtooth ridge ticked again, notched a little higher, as if eavesdropping pleased it.

"Listen," Abigail said softly. "I know what it is to want a thing so hard you stop asking whether you should have it." She didn't look away from him. "I've stood inside the In Between. I've seen the Echo. It is not God, but it is the balance that keeps wolves on their side of the fence. It's weakening. You are weakening it."

"Stories," he said, but the word was tired.

Abigail's gaze flicked to the taped clock, then back. "You want something empirical." She touched two fingertips to the bench and closed her eyes. "There is a ring in your desk drawer," she said quietly. "Plain, gold, slightly bent near the inscription. You stopped wearing it after you caught it on a coil winding and it tore a glove. You told yourself it was safer not to. You have taken that ring out three nights this week and pressed it into your palm until it left a mark." She opened her eyes. "The mark is on your right hand now."

Elias didn't move for a long time. Then, without looking away from her, he opened the drawer and took out the ring. He held it in his fist, opened his fingers. A thin red crescent lay across his palm, tender as a bruise.

"How," he whispered.

"Because all of this is connected," Abigail said—gentle, not triumphant. "You built a machine that listens to what most people refuse to admit they hear."

The phone on the bench buzzed again. *AVERY SHAW: You ready for greatness, Elias? Friday is history*. Elias pressed his thumb to the message and watched it wobble, unread, then go still.

"Call him," Abigail said. "Tell him the truth: the Array must stop at Clover Park. Better—the Array must stop until you understand what it drinks. You owe the world that pause."

He laughed once, raw. "Avery will destroy me."

"He'll destroy more than you if you keep going," Lena said quietly. "I can't stand next to you if you do."

The words landed harder than any data. Elias's head turned, a flinch he tried to hide. For a heartbeat the lab seemed to draw breath—a subtle pressure in the ears, the monitors whispering.

"You asked what faith looks like," Abigail said, echoing a question from another kitchen, another hour. "It looks like stopping when everything in you wants to continue. It looks like choosing not to harvest what you could because some wells shouldn't be tapped."

Elias closed his fingers around the ring until his knuckles blanched. He set it down with care, as if it had become fragile. He took a breath that shook, then another that shook less.

"I'll consider it," he said. "You've given me something to look into...proof" He swallowed. "I will think about shutting it down."

Relief fluttered through Lena so sharply it hurt. Abigail only nodded, as if the world had rolled one inch back from an edge and she'd been expecting it to. It wasn't the exact answer they were looking for, but it was progress.

Scene 4: Vanishing Legacy

The television's glow spilled across the living room walls in a restless dance of blue and white, shadows shifting with every cut of the broadcast. Abigail sat in the armchair with her legs tucked beneath her, a mug cooling in her hands. Samuel occupied the sofa, leaning forward with his elbows on his knees, jaw tight as if bracing for a blow. Jacob sat cross-legged on the rug, closest to the screen, the light washing his young face in pale hues. The storm outside rattled the windows, each gust of wind sounding almost like a whisper pressing against the glass.

Onscreen, Reese Mathers stood before a row of cameras, his usual rumpled coat whipping slightly in the breeze of a Tacoma night. But there was no slur to his words, no hesitation—no hint of the broken man the world had mocked for years. His voice was firm, measured, carrying the gravity of truth finally unshackled.

"This is not an isolated phenomenon," Reese declared, gripping the microphone with both hands. "For weeks we have seen an undeniable surge in disappearances, unexplained blackouts, and mirror-related disturbances. Ordinary people, families, children—gone. What you are about to see is not staged, not manipulated. This is happening now, in our neighborhoods, in our homes."

Behind him, the broadcast cut to raw footage: street cameras capturing the shimmer of glass warping as if stirred by unseen hands; a diner mirror blooming with pale light before cracking outward; commuters in a subway station scattering as a woman screamed and vanished against a tiled restroom mirror.

Abigail's breath caught. "God help us…" she whispered, setting her mug aside.

Samuel exhaled sharply through his nose, anger and dread battling in his expression. "He's making it real. People will believe him now."

For so long, Reese had been ridiculed, his stories buried under the weight of conspiracy-theorist labels. But tonight, his broadcast was raw and undeniable. He was no longer chasing shadows; he was revealing them. The images bled with terror, yet his narration remained calm, a rope thrown into the abyss for those watching.

Reese's face returned to the screen, pale under the harsh lights. "The Department of Energy refuses to answer my questions about the Voss Array. Officials deny any link between the machine's experimental power harvesting and these manifestations. But the data is clear—energy spikes coincide with each surge of supernatural activity. We are witnessing something unprecedented: a weakening of the veil between worlds."

The words lingered in the living room, heavy as stone.

Samuel stared at the screen...stunned. "He knows about the Array?"

Abigail leaned forward, whispering almost to herself, "He's right. The veil is thinning. I can feel it. Every night it's harder to keep the spirits at bay."

Jacob's hands trembled in his lap. He looked from the screen to Abigail, his lips parting with a panic that cracked through the composure he usually tried to wear.

"It's not just thinning," he blurted, his voice high and frightened. "It's breaking. The Echo told me."

The room froze.

Abigail's eyes widened, Samuel straightened, and the storm outside seemed to hush for a heartbeat, as though listening.

Jacob's words tumbled out, rushed and breathless. "I heard it in my dreams—no, not dreams, more like... like when I was awake but not here. The Echo came to me. It said it's weakening. That the Array is pulling too much. That it can't hold back the Veilborne anymore." His chest rose and fell quickly, his young face wet with sudden tears. "It said it fears it's dying."

Jacob's voice was steady, too calm for a boy. "The Echo told me it's dying," he said. "It can't hold the gates and breathe." He glanced at the mirror, then back at them. "It said to tell you this the way you'd understand: as at Babel, when men stacked stone to rival God—Voss built the Array to drink the Echo. God will lash the sky, and the multitude will scatter into broken tongues."

Abigail and Samuel went white, fear draining the color from their faces as if the room itself had gone colder. In the silence that followed, she could hear the Array's phantom hum and see the tower falling all over again—not of stone, but of wires and math—rules melting, families torn apart, the world splintering under a single act of hubris. "The tower doesn't have to be stone," Jacob added softly. "And when it falls, it falls on us."

Abigail rose from her chair, crossing the room in swift strides, and knelt in front of Jacob. She gripped his small hands in hers, steadying them. "Listen to me, Jacob. Look at me."

His wide eyes fixed on hers, trembling but desperate to be understood.

"The Echo spoke to you," she said softly, though her heart pounded. "And you heard it clearly?"

He nodded, tears streaking his cheeks. "It was so loud, Aunt Abigail. Like the whole world was crying through it. It told me it doesn't have much time."

Samuel rubbed his forehead, pacing a short line behind them. "This is madness. He's just a boy, Abigail. He shouldn't carry this weight."

But Abigail held Jacob's gaze, her voice calm but firm. "He's not just a boy, Sam. We've known for some time. Jacob has the gift—stronger than mine ever was at his age. If the Echo chose to speak to him directly, it means he is already bound to this struggle."

Samuel turned sharply, anger flashing in his eyes. "Bound? He's a child! He deserves to live, not to be dragged into—into this nightmare." His voice cracked with grief he could not hide.

The TV droned on, Reese's voice rising as he presented testimony from families who had lost loved ones, but Abigail and Jacob no longer listened. The boy shook his head, curls sticking to his damp face. "I don't want it, Uncle Sam. I don't want to be part of it. But it won't stop. It keeps calling me. Every time I close my eyes. Every time I see a mirror. It's always there."

Abigail brushed his hair back, her throat tightening. "I know, Jacob. I know."

Samuel sank onto the couch, his hands covering his face. The storm outside cracked with thunder, rattling the windowpanes, as if punctuating the boy's revelation.

Onscreen, Reese continued, his voice breaking with rare emotion: "If the veil collapses, we will face an incursion unlike anything in recorded history. This is no longer folklore, no longer speculation. It is happening now. And if we cannot stop the Array—if we cannot restore the balance—then what lies beyond the glass will come through unchecked."

The screen cut to black for a moment as the segment shifted to commercial. In the silence, Jacob clutched Abigail's wrists tightly, as though she were the only anchor holding him in place. "It's scared," he whispered, his voice raw. "The Echo. I never thought it could be scared. But it is. And if it dies, what happens to us?"

Abigail pulled him close, pressing his trembling form against her shoulder. She looked over his head at Samuel, who sat hollow-eyed on the sofa, and shook her head. Her voice, when it came, was steady but filled with dread.

"Then there will be nothing left to hold them back."

The thunder rolled again, long and low, as if the world itself had heard.

13

Unveiled Crimes

Scene 1: Natalie's Discovery

Natalie Chen rubbed her temples, blinking against the fatigue of staring too long at glowing screens. Her hotel room was dim, curtains drawn, the laptop her only companion. She had been combing through a backlog of surveillance videos pulled from local traffic cams and archived dashcam files—footage the DOE had quietly labeled *"mirror incidents."* Most of it was nightmare fuel: people vanishing mid-step, shadows flaring across reflective surfaces, figures pressing against glass that wasn't supposed to move.

She clicked through one file, then another, her nerves numb to the usual shocks. Then, one odd file stopped her. It wasn't tagged like the others. No "incident code," no red flag, just buried in a string of ordinary traffic files, almost deliberately mislabeled.

Natalie frowned and opened it.

The dashcam lens showed rain sheeting down a narrow alley, headlights faintly illuminating a sedan parked near a back door. For a moment, nothing happened—just static drizzle and the clatter of water in gutters. Then, a man stepped out of the building's rear exit, shoulders hunched against the storm. He hurried toward the sedan, keys flashing in his hand.

Natalie leaned closer. His face was caught clean in the camera's view—clear enough to leave no doubt later.

From the right, a sleek black car appeared. It didn't drift or skid; it swerved deliberately. The engine roared, tires cutting across wet pavement. The grille slammed into the man mid-stride. His body doubled over the hood with brutal force, his face thrown into full view of the dashcam before crumpling against the windshield and tumbling to the ground.

Natalie gasped, hand flying to her mouth. She replayed it instantly. There was no mistaking it: not chance, not bad weather—murder.

The black car braked. Its driver's side door opened. A man in a tailored suit stepped out into the rain, calm where there should have been panic. He moved toward the sprawled figure on the pavement, checked a pulse with casual efficiency. Then he looked up, rain running down his face. The dashcam caught him fully.

Avery Shaw.

Natalie froze the frame. Avery's features were sharp, cold, un-flinching. No horror, no regret. Just calculation.

He drew a phone from his coat and spoke, the dashcam barely catching the words over the storm:

"...taken care of. No loose ends."

Then he raised a flashlight and smashed the camera lens. The feed jittered to static.

Natalie sat rigid, pulse hammering. She had to know who the vic-tim was. She pulled up the video's metadata, combing through the encryption logs and hidden layers. Someone had tried to bury this, tucking it away deep in mislabeled archives. She decrypted a final tag—and the name hit her like a blow.

Owner: Mathers, Richard.

Reese's father.

Natalie's throat closed. She sat back, the hotel walls pressing closer.

Her mind leapt to her parents. To Shanghai, to the weary factory shifts her father had endured when they immigrated, his hands scarred but his dignity intact. To her mother's whispers over laundry and sewing work: "You must work twice as hard, Natalie. Be twice as honest. We will never be invisible enough to escape notice. We must never give them reason to break us."

And here was Avery Shaw. Wealthy, powerful, untouchable. Killing in alleys, covering it up, striding through life as though the rules bowed to him. He squandered everything her family had bled to earn. He believed he was invisible.

Her jaw tightened. Not anymore.

She encrypted the file onto a secure drive, then stared at her phone. Reese had to know.

The call connected after two rings. "Natalie?" His voice was raw, stretched thin.

"I found something," she said quietly. "You need to hear this."

"What is it?"

She hesitated only long enough to steady her tone. "Footage. From a dashcam. It's your father."

There was silence, then Reese's breath broke like glass. "What—what do you mean?"

"It's him. I saw his face. He was struck down in an alley, walking to his car. Avery Shaw hit him. Deliberately. And then he covered it up."

Reese made a noise that was half snarl, half sob. "Goddammit—I knew it. I knew it wasn't an accident! They all called me paranoid, drunk, a conspiracy nut, but I knew." His voice cracked. "That bastard murdered my father."

Natalie gripped the phone. "Reese, listen to me. We can't go public yet."

"What?!" His fury was like fire through the line. "This is everything! We put this out now, tonight, and we burn him to the ground!"

"No," she said firmly. "If we do this now, it disappears. He'll bury it under lawyers, spin it as fake, smear you again as unstable. Worse, he'll come for us. And this time he won't leave loose ends."

Reese's breath came ragged. "So we sit on it? While he smiles for the cameras?"

"We plan," Natalie said. "We build allies. We wait until the release is fireproof. Until the truth cuts where it cannot be buried."

Reese's voice broke again, softer. "He thought he was invisible. He thought he could erase my father."

Natalie closed her eyes, remembering her parents' tired eyes, the price they had paid just to be honest. "He's not invisible, Reese. Not to us. And I promise—we'll bring him down. But not carelessly. Not in a way he can undo."

There was silence, then a long, sharp exhale. "So we wait."

"Yes," Natalie said. "We wait until his smile is the noose."

When she hung up, she stared at the black laptop screen. Avery's frozen face still burned behind her eyes. Outside, rain drummed against the windows, sounding less like weather and more like a verdict waiting to fall.

Scene 2: Frequency of Denial

The Array breathed.

Elias had no better word for it. The coils on the central plinth held their posture like a frozen tide, while the harmonics stitched the air with a low, animal hum. Oscilloscopes spilled green hieroglyphs; a waterfall plot ran like rain until, near the bottom, a single band cut through the noise—thin and bright, an emergent resonance around 27.1 kHz that refused to dim.

"Window Theta," Lena grudgingly said from the console. "It's climbing again. Q-factor's ridiculous. The phase lag looks like..." She hesitated, grimacing at her own word. "Breath."

Elias rubbed at eyes gone sandy from too little sleep. Beside him lay Abigail's notes and a printed Pierce County map anchored by a wrench. Red and orange pins curved around Clover Park Technical College like a half-closed eye. Their deployment logs lined up too neatly with the pins for coincidence. The math felt like confession.

He could shut it down. That thought sat in his chest like a lever he might pull if he were braver. Camille's voice rose from the old corner of memory—Promise me we'll know what we're touching—and for a second he swore he could smell the citrus of the shampoo she'd left in his shower.

The lab door hissed and then banged.

Avery Shaw didn't enter; he occupied. Suit knifed, cologne declarative, he crossed the floor with federal momentum and dropped a leather folder on stainless steel as if serving a warrant.

"Doctor Voss," he said, showing all his teeth. "Let's talk about greatness."

At the diagnostics cart, Naveen didn't turn. "We tried 'goodness' but it failed safety review," he said, flicking a toggle. "Greatness usually fails the people review."

Avery's smile held, cooler. "And you are the...morals committee now?"

"Systems," Naveen said, deadpan. "But I moonlight as a conscience when management forgets we're mortal."

Lena's hands stilled. Natalie Chen slipped in behind her boss, tablet to her chest, gaze quiet and cataloging.

"We're in the middle of calibration," Elias said.

"Good," Avery replied. "Calibrate upward."

He fanned glossy printouts—yield curves, extraction projections, a slide deck with DOE letterhead and the title: *THETA WINDOW—ACCELERATE*. A red circle bled around 27.1.

"This," he tapped, "is your money note. Higher instantaneous yield than the last six runs combined. Push here, you change the world—and we write your name into it."

Naveen finally looked up, expression flat. "Love the verb 'push.' Very laboratory. Nothing ever breaks when you push."

Avery's eyes slid to him. "Do me a favor and stick to cables and key-boards."

"Do me a favor and don't confuse caution with insubordination," Naveen said. "One keeps us alive. The other gets us a headline."

"Naveen," Elias said—gentle, a hand on the brakes without touching them.

Elias didn't look at the paper. He watched the ring on Avery's hand gleam like a threat. "We don't understand what we're drawing from."

"Energy is energy," Avery said, already bored with doubt. "Spare me metaphysics."

"It isn't metaphysics." Elias angled the monitor so the waterfall faced him. The hot line of Theta glared like a laser through fog. "We're synchronized with... events." He touched Abigail's map. "Mirrors behaving wrong. Glass breathing. Clover Park at the center of the arc. We're tapping a boundary we don't understand. Abigail calls it the In Between."

Avery laughed. "The Between, Upside Down, take your pick. A talk show host gets swallowed by a studio prop and suddenly every bathroom selfie is a portal to hell. You're a scientist. Don't embarrass me."

"Cool," Naveen said. "So we're skipping 'caution' and speed-running 'hubris.' Any dang category."

Avery took a step closer to him. "You're very free with your mouth for someone whose clearance depends on my signature."

"And you're very free with other people's risk tolerance," Naveen said, unblinking. "Different hobbies."

"Naveen," Elias repeated, firmer. Then to Avery, measured: "He's flagging operational concerns. Let's keep this on the numbers."

Lena stood. "He didn't say that. But the incidents spike where we deploy. Clover Park gives the strongest resonance and it's where the flare-ups center. We have a duty—"

"Dr...?" Avery turned the smile on her without warmth.

"Mirek," Elias said. "Co-inventor."

"Then remember your NDA," Avery said pleasantly. "And your non-disparagement clause."

Naveen let out a short, humorless breath. "Ah yes, the sacred NDA. 'Now Do As-I-say.' Blackmail, but make it legalese."

Avery's gaze sharpened. "Techs don't opine on policy."

"I'm not your tech," Naveen said. "I'm the reason the last three 'incidents' ended with incident reports instead of obituaries."

Natalie's eyes flicked, almost apologetic, then back to stillness.

Elias swallowed. "Avery, this isn't ordinary nuisance. If Theta couples to that boundary, ramping could—" He searched for a word less apocalyptic. "—trigger crossings."

"Crossings," Avery repeated, chuckling. "The only thing crossing here is capital." He paced the Array, admiring it like a sculpture he meant to remove. "Look. I can sell you as a visionary or a crank. Media's warmed up. Your story is immigrant grit, a miracle of clean energy while the government dithers. Or"—he turned—"unstable academic drains taxpayer money chasing demons. You choose, but the headline is mine."

"Great," Naveen said softly. "Love a free press release with my existential risk."

Lena took a step closer to Elias. "You don't owe him your soul."

"And you don't owe him your career," Avery snapped. He flipped to a clause sheet. "You signed acceleration terms. Section 4.3: best efforts toward commercialization. 9.1: government purpose rights. 14.4: termination for cause. Ease off Theta and I have a team packing these coils by dawn and a press release at lunch explaining why we removed an underperforming PI."

"You can't—" Lena began.

"Watch me," he said.

The Array hummed as if to clear its throat. On the scope, the line of Theta sharpened.

"If I give you a number," Elias said, "you'll ask for more."

Avery lifted his brows. "Now we're negotiating. I want forty percent over baseline at Theta in seventy-two hours. Live pull for a secure audience by week's end."

"Forty," Lena said, incredulous. "You'll shred—"

Avery's gaze cut her. "Doctor Mirek, NDAs apply to voices, too."

Naveen angled his chair. "And to eardrums? Because mine are still ringing from the last 'secure audience.' Also—not sure intimidation is the best look when half the city is taping foil over bathroom mirrors."

Avery turned, temper finally nicking the surface. "I don't take operational advice from interns."

"Good news," Naveen said. "I'm not giving advice. I'm stating constraints."

"Both of you," Elias said, stepping between them with his voice, steady and low. "Enough. We are not doing this."

The lab shrank by a few degrees. Elias felt his pulse in his gums. He pictured Abigail at the kitchen table leaning over the pins. This isn't a story I want to be right about, she'd said. He had believed her.

"If we ramp blind," he said, "we endanger the public."

"You endanger your branding if you stall," Avery countered. "Nine billion is circling the first tranche. You hesitate, it goes elsewhere. Also your reputation goes elsewhere. I snap my fingers and you're the guy who almost had it."

"Sir," Naveen said, politeness sharpened to a point, "we've had three 'incidents' in two weeks, one televised nightmare, and a standing meeting with a woman who literally salts doorways for our safety. Your 'ten percent' is less a test and more an NDA-shaped shakedown."

Avery ignored him, eyes still on Elias.

Elias looked at Lena. Don't, her eyes said. He looked to Natalie. The smallest flicker crossed her face: worry not for the project, but for the world.

"We won't ramp to forty," Elias said at last.

Lena's breath caught.

"I won't endanger personnel, equipment, or the public to satisfy your press calendar," he added. "We'll run a limited sweep—ten percent above baseline at Theta with full telemetry, redundant damping, and a hard cap if non-local anomalies present. If, and only if, the signal behaves, we revisit."

Avery tasted the number, jaw tight. Then he smoothed his mask back on. "Fine. A test. Tomorrow morning. Nine."

He gathered the folder, then paused at the door. "And, Doctor? Mention the In Between in an official meeting again and a psych eval will be the least of your worries."

He left in the scent of his own cologne.

Silence rushed in. The Array's hum seemed louder after the performance.

Naveen scrubbed both hands over his face. "Cool. We've scheduled a light jog next to the volcano." He glanced at Elias. "For the record—when this behaves like every other horror story we've logged, I'm going to be insufferable with data. Not 'I told you so'—I'll print the time stamps and staple them to the NDA."

Elias exhaled, a tired laugh ghosting his mouth. "Noted. Please save the stapling for after we survive."

Natalie cleared her throat. When they looked over, her face had resumed professional blankness, but concern stayed like a watermark. "I'll schedule for nine," she said. "Facilities will want B-side shielding." She lingered a beat. "Calibration isn't surrender." Then she slipped out.

"He'll squeeze until there's nothing left," Lena said when the door sealed.

"I know." Elias stared at Theta burning a hole in the waterfall. "If I stop, they take it and do worse. If I keep going, I may be the one doing worse."

"File that under 'things I've said out loud in therapy,'" Naveen muttered. Softer, to Elias: "I'm with you. But if he tries to bully us past ten, I'm yanking mains and writing 'lawsuit' in the log."

Elias pressed his fingers to the map and felt the pins under the paper like Braille. Clover Park. Fort Steilacoom. The cemetery. Edges are where membranes tear, Abigail had said. Edges—and frequencies.

"Ten percent," Lena repeated, as if to test the weight. "We lock every safeguard. Anything out of family, we throw the switch."

"And if Avery fights?"

"Let him," she said softly, iron in the softness. "Some risks we don't get to outsource."

Naveen nodded toward the scope. "I'll add a watchdog that isn't on the DOE's Christmas list. Trip on cold-drop and phase collapse. And I'll hard-wire the dump so it doesn't ask software for permission."

He started typing, jaw set.

Elias nodded. Promises evaporated quickly under pressure; saying them aloud sometimes gave them bones.

"Then we shut it down," he said.

The hot line on the scope brightened, amused or innocent. Elias turned the gain down a notch—a gesture so small it resembled superstition—and the hum held.

"Prep everything," he said. "Full telemetry, dual caps on the dampers. And—" He swallowed. "Call Abigail. If anything looks wrong, I want her here before nine."

Lena was already moving. "I'll get her."

When she stepped into the hall, Elias leaned on the bench and pressed his palms to his eyes. He saw Avery's ring, Abigail's pins, Camille's mouth forming know what we are touching. He saw Window Theta like a fuse burning along the bottom of the waterfall.

He could still shut it down—told himself that twice, then a third time, until the lie began to sound like courage.

Lena returned with a phone pressed to her ear, voice low. "Abigail? It's Lena. We test in the morning. Window Theta. If anything—" She looked at Elias, who nodded. "—anything at all, can you come?"

She listened, relief loosening her shoulders a fraction. "Thank you."

She ended the call and leaned on the bench beside him. For a moment neither spoke.

"You know Avery won't forgive you for telling him no," she said.

"I know." He allowed himself a small, humorless smile. "He'll forgive the first no. He won't forgive the second."

"Then give him none he can punish," Lena said. "Give him data."

"Data and a working kill switch," Naveen added without looking up. "Preferably one that bites."

Elias looked up at the Array. The machine breathed, oblivious to careers and threats, attentive only to the hand offered through the fabric of the world. He thought of Abigail's map, of Joseph's name, of Russell's scream as the studio glass puckered and took him. He thought of mirrors covered in hotel lobbies and in children's bathrooms, and of a lantern in a place where light moved like a command.

"Data, then," he said. "Or mercy. Whichever gets here first."

He blew out a breath and, because he knew he would not sleep, began drafting the test plan: stepwise increases; live FFTs; synchronized EM monitors in the hallway mirrors; staff rotations; a new line at the bottom—Hard cap at any non-local deviation. He wrote it twice.

Lena watched him. "Eli?"

"Mm?"

"If it goes wrong, we'll be the ones standing in the room. Not Avery. Us." She reached for his wrist, squeezed. "I'm with you."

He looked at her hand, at the fine tremor she was trying to hide, and covered it with his own. "I know," he said. "That's why I'm still here."

The Array breathed again, a subtle intake like tide turning. On the monitor, Theta quivered, poised.

"Tomorrow," he said to the room, as if the word itself could fix a limit. "Nine."

Scene 3: A Contract Remembered

Avery Shaw liked hotel rooms that forgot you when you closed the door. Fifteenth floor, corner suite, thick carpet, obedient climate control, a window that made Tacoma's rain look choreographed. He loosened his tie, tossed his jacket over a chair, and raised a tumbler toward the black sheet of the Sound.

"To history," he told the glass. "To men who make it."

The whiskey bit like a promise kept.

Emails stacked on his phone—embargoed headlines, donors purring, a DOE aide asking how hard to lean on press invites. The Array would sing at nine. Investors would purr by noon. Elias would play the careful visionary; Avery would be the kingmaker who fed him.

He felt the first whisper as pressure tucked inside the HVAC hum, not sound so much as suggestion.

He ignored it. Hotels breathed. Pipes muttered. Elevators complained. Another sip. Another email. He typed Accelerate Theta messaging and hit send.

—Avery.

This time it put his name behind his ear like a cool hand. He didn't turn.

"Room noise," he said to no one.

—Avery.

Ice chimed in his glass. He smiled at his reflection in the window: decisive, camera-ready. "You're not real," he told the dark.

The ordinary obliged him: a latch down the hall, rain ticking, a truck braking far below. He stood at the glass and watched his other self raise the drink.

—You promised not to.

He stilled. "We're done with bargains."

Warmth like a smile he couldn't see grazed his neck.

—We are never done. You made a barter. Consideration. Performance. Delivery. You wanted ascent without friction. We arranged stairs where there were walls.

He could have laughed if laughter were free. "And the invoice arrives the night before the launch."

—We asked so little. Feed the light, thin the skin, let want enter want. Break the veil and we will build you an empire without ceiling.

Elias's words surfaced, unwelcome: If Theta couples to that boundary, ramping could trigger crossings. Superstition would be simpler. Data argued.

"You're not real," Avery said to the window. "Brains misfire."

—Is it.

He poured again, left the full glass on the credenza like an offering. The voice moved to the soft corners of the room.

—You asked for attention, immunity, ascent. We gave you each on schedule. Doors opened because you wanted them to. Now keep your side. Push the frequency. Forty percent faster. Break the veil and let us in.

"That phrase again?" He let a grin show. "Eavesdropping on staff meetings is beneath you."

—Better than laws are the people who write them. We will have many. We were promised many.

He drifted to the bathroom, turned the tap for an ordinary sound. The mirror gave him a paler Avery, hair imperfect in the way polls liked. He adjusted it anyway.

"If I believed the ghost story," he said, meaning Elias, Abigail, and the haunted reporter on cable, "I'd stop. That won't happen."

Silk threaded the steam.

—We are not asking belief. We are asking cooperation. Belief is for the weak. Ambition is for the living.

Condensation fogged the mirror—except for a coin-sized circle in the center that stayed perfectly clear, as if something cold lived on the other side.

He shut the water off. The coin didn't fog. Frost bled outward in fern-like veins.

"Enough," he said. "You get your 'progress' tomorrow. Stop talking to me."

—You are the only one who still pretends this is your choice.

His phone buzzed: *Natalie—0900 confirmed; shielding staged. Elias—Cap stays. We pull the plug if anything misbehaves.* Avery thumbed back *Acknowledged* and set the phone face down.

—He will try to stop soon, the voice went on, intimate now. —The woman will help him. And the other one you mock will circle with his proofs. Mice nibbling a loaf. Stamp. Open the door and we will feed them something that teaches quiet.

"Threats are dull," he said. "Flatter me. You used to be good at that."

—You do not need flattery. You need pressure. We are very good at pressure.

He cracked a bottle of still water, hand steady by force. "You almost sound worried," he said. "If the veil is so thin, a breeze should finish it."

—Because the keeper still lives.

He filed *keeper* under religion's failed weapons and shut the drawer.

"You said there were no chains," he said. "You said—"

—We said the chains are tired. Not broken. Be a hammer. Break them.

He returned to the window. The Sound threw the city's grin back. "If I took every step a stranger ordered," he said, "I'd be a clerk. I'm not a clerk."

—You are a debtor.

The word fit his throat like a hand.

"Debts are for men who need help," he said. "I accept favors. I do not owe."

—You wanted ascent without consequence. You wanted juries inclined and hands untied. You signed with your desire. Do not insult our ledger.

He flicked the TV on just to drown the register of that voice. His own face filled the screen, muted—mouth making practiced crescents while a chyron did push-ups. He watched himself point, smile, cut, win.

"Shut up," he told the set. "Shut up shut up."

The whisper didn't rise to meet his noise. It arrived again, close enough to taste.

—We were generous with you, Avery. Be generous with us. Forty percent at Theta. No cap. Open the door.

"No," he said, and heard the crack in it. He flattened it. "No."

—Then thirty. Twenty-five. We are not accountants. We are hungry.

"You can't have what doesn't exist," he said. "Go haunt a poet."

—We haunt men with levers.

He stood with that in his ears and frost writing on the mirror. He walked back to the bathroom and stopped in the doorway.

Cold reached his face like breath. The frost had become a map: spidery lines radiating, braiding into petals with razor edges. He set his fingertips to the glass. December water pushed through his skin. He flinched and hated himself for it.

"You will not push me," he told the unseen thing, deploying phrases that bent senators and second-rank billionaires. "You will not change my schedule. We test at nine. We keep the cap. We do this my way, or not at all."

Silence answered, then the frost swelled outward in a single decisive pulse, as if a lung exhaled on the far side. Ferns thickened. The clear circle shrank to the size of a coin. For a heartbeat the coin wasn't clear. It was black—an absence like a pupil.

He reeled back. His heel hit the credenza. Whiskey marched toward the door in a thin line.

The black coin blinked.

He slammed the bathroom door hard enough to jog the frame, then turned the useless lock. He knew it meant nothing. He turned it anyway. His phone chimed: *0900 — THETA TEST*. He stacked screens—remarks, schedules, a donor list—between himself and the fact that winter had learned his mirror.

—Break the veil and let us in, the voice said, almost tender now. —You will be remembered.

"I already am," he whispered.

The vent sighed. Something delicate cracked behind the bathroom door, ice trying a new shape. He pictured Natalie's competence, Elias's quiet dread, Lena's level gaze, the reporter's grief breaking into focus. He pictured himself walking into the lab and taking the lever anyway.

—Be the hammer, the voice coaxed.

He lifted the tumbler and met his reflection in the window. He practiced the smile that calmed rooms and bent headlines. It landed the way a stamp lands: hard, sure, leaving a mark.

"Tomorrow," he told the city, the glass, the thing waiting in the mirror. "We make history."

Behind the bathroom door, frost crept another inch, and the black coin on the other side did not blink again, but he could feel the looking, as intimate as a hand on the back of his neck.

Scene 4: Lines Converge

The diner on Bridgeport Way had done what half the city was doing—turned its reflections into ghosts. Aluminum foil and butcher paper covered the wall-length mirror behind the counter in a patchwork of dull silver; the chrome napkin holders wore strips of masking tape like bandages. Someone had even taped a dish towel over the pie case's glass dome. The place smelled like coffee and rain-soaked wool, and the windows clicked softly as the wind worried at their frames.

Abigail chose the back booth, the one beneath the EXIT sign, and sprinkled a thin ribbon of salt along the edge of the tabletop with a motion so practiced it looked like she was seasoning a meal. Reese Mathers arrived late, breath fogging as he pushed through the door, hair damp, backpack slung over one shoulder. He paused to take in the taped-over surfaces, then gave her a small, wry nod, as if to say: You were right. The world listened to you too slowly.

"Thanks for meeting," he said, sliding into the seat opposite. "I picked this place because the coffee's terrible and no one important comes here."

"Terrible coffee is a blessing," Abigail said, and meant it. She glanced past him to the door out of habit. No lag in the glass. No ripple. Not yet. "Natalie told you I'd reached out?"

"She did." He lowered his voice. "She also told me to be careful. With you. Not because she doesn't trust you—she does—but because if we put certain facts in the same room, we might end up being hunted by something that reads schedules."

"Then let's be brief," Abigail said. "And precise."

A waitress with tired eyes topped their water and left a menu without asking. Reese didn't look at it. He pulled a folded printout from his pack and smoothed it across the table. It was a map of Pierce County with pushpins reproduced as red dots. Abigail's gaze went straight to the cluster along the curve she knew by heart: the crescent hugging Clover Park Technical College.

"You've been tracking," he said.

"For weeks," she answered. "And before you ask—my points began as hunches. Phone calls from sensitives. Cases people begged me not to put on the podcast because saying a thing makes it real. But the pattern held. It's not a ring, or a scatter. It's a wound that curves around a hill." She tapped the arc. "Clover Park sits on the spine of old ground.

Below it—Hill Ward, Steilacoom Park, older dead than the city. Places with thin skin even when the world behaves."

Reese leaned in. "And when it doesn't behave?"

"The skin splits," she said simply. "I've been in the In Between, Mr. Mathers. Three times. I've seen what waits. The Veilborne are not new. But their boldness is."

He swallowed and looked away for a heartbeat, as if steadying against something only he could see. "I used to think I'd know when the nightmare started. Fire alarm, headline, trumpet. Instead it was a slow press. Noise you could ignore, until you couldn't."

"Tell me what you know," Abigail said. "Not as a reporter. As a son."

He flinched at the word. Then he unzipped the backpack and set a laptop on the salt-lined Formica. The screen came alive with a keypress, and a folder with an innocuous name opened to reveal a single video file. He didn't hit play; he looked at her first.

"Natalie found this while she was sifting mirror-abduction footage," he said. "It was buried—metadata scrubbed, name changed, stuffed where it had no business being. The kind of misfile that's actually a map to the truth if you've spent your childhood in libraries."

"And the truth?" she asked, gentle.

"Avery Shaw killed my father." He said it like a fact he'd had to teach his mouth to pronounce. "Not a hit-and-run. Not an accident. On purpose. In an alley. Dad was walking to his car after a back-door meeting with a source. Shaw's government sedan comes in slow, then fast. He hits him. Clear as a signature."

Abigail didn't look away. "Show me."

He set the volume low. Rain filled the frame, a gray hiss over a narrow lane choked with dumpsters and steam. A man crossed toward a white sedan, looking down as he fished for keys—Reese's father, alive in miserable resolution. From the right, a black government car slid into view, paused as if deciding, then lunged. The impact was intimate: a sick thud, a body folding, a face—Reese's face, older—flashed by the dashcam as the man doubled over the hood and disappeared. The car braked. The wipers smeared. After a beat, the driver's door opened and Avery Shaw stepped out. He didn't panic. He approached, checked, looked up directly into the dashcam's eye, and then a flashlight's butt swung. The image spasmed and broke.

Reese stopped the playback.

"The file backed up before the smash," he said. "Auto-sync. Some clerk hid it instead of deleting it. Natalie found it. We haven't gone public. Yet."

Abigail let her breath out slowly. The cheap clock over the grill ticked with polite persistence. She looked from the frozen frame to the map and back again, feeling the way threads snag on one another until they make a rope.

"Avery is the one pressuring Elias," she said. "Threatening him. I've seen it in his eyes—the exhaustion of being leaned on by a man who mistakes ambition for gravity."

"Elias," Reese repeated, tasting the name. "Natalie keeps him separate in her mind, I can tell. She thinks he started with clean hands."

"He started with hope," Abigail said. "Then he built a machine that drinks where it should not."

Reese lifted his gaze sharply. "You're sure."

"I wasn't." She reached into her bag, drew out a thin leather notebook, and flipped past names and notations to a page where a crescent of dots crowded a hand-drawn hill. "Then Lena—Elias's colleague—confessed that they deploy the Array at Clover Park because the resonance there is strongest. Strongest because the veil is thinnest. The Array didn't create that thinness. History did. But it found it, drew from it, and in drawing, it weakened the Echo further."

"The Echo," he said. He'd heard the word whispered around her once, and mocked on television later, his own mouth shaping lines he wanted to rip out of the air.

"The keeper," Abigail said softly. "The one who maintains balance. When it is strong, the Veilborne scavenge scraps—fear, grief, the things we spill without meaning to. When it is weak, they hunt. The Array is a straw in the keeper's lungs."

Reese grimaced at the image. He scrubbed a hand over his jaw, and for once the motion wasn't for the camera. "So on one side you have a machine starving the guard dog. On the other, the man financing the machine murders the only cop who ever scared him and walks away clean. Meanwhile, people vanish into bathroom fixtures like the world's ugliest magic trick."

"Not vanish," Abigail said. "Taken. They scream where no one hears. I have heard them."

He met her eyes, and whatever he saw there steadied him. The waitress brought coffee that tasted like it remembered being burned and retreated. The steam from the cups drifted up and disappeared in air that felt thinner than it had an hour before.

"What do you need from me?" he asked.

"Proof that will stand when the world tries to sit on it," she said. "Natalie's footage is a blade we may have to use, but if you swing it now, Avery will cut off Elias's lifeline out of spite and fear. He will force a demonstration that will rip the veil open. We need time to stop the Array, and we need you not to spook the wolves until we have a fence."

He almost laughed at fence, then didn't. "You're asking me to wait to expose the man who killed my father."

"I am asking you to choose the order of your truths," Abigail said. "Justice for one man will matter most if there is a world left to read the verdict."

Reese stared at his coffee until the black shiver of it steadied. "How," he said finally. "How do we stop a machine that he says will make the grid obsolete and the markets beg?"

Abigail glanced at the map. "Elias says the Array has a failsafe—designed to shut everything down if inputs spike. Lena doesn't know if it would hold under what we're seeing; they've never tested it against this kind of pressure. Elias insists he can shut it down. I'm... not sure

I believe him. I think the keeper will tell Jacob when to move." She caught her slip too late, saw his eyebrows inch, and added, "A boy I'm helping. He… hears."

"Hears what?"

"What matters," she said, and left it on the table with the salt.

He sat back, studying her as if composing a paragraph about her he would never write. "You warned me once: don't make cruelty into entertainment. Tonight, I watched a man die and learned I had helped build the stage for the man who arranged it. I want to lash out. You're telling me to aim."

"To aim and to wait until the target can't dodge," she said. "We make allies. Natalie is one. There are others in the city who will choose right if given a chance. When we move on Avery, we need to have him boxed on two sides: the murder and the insistence he forced—by threat—on an experiment he knew was dangerous."

"He'll deny he knew," Reese said automatically.

"Then we prove he should have," Abigail replied. "We point to the crescent and the calls and the screams caught by a hundred phones. We show he laughed. We make his laughter cost."

He closed the laptop gently, as if shutting a coffin. "Natalie will want to loop you in if we take steps. She's… careful."

"I like careful," Abigail said, looking at the taped mirror behind the counter and imagining the patience of a thing with its face pressed to the other side. "Careful keeps people alive."

He followed her gaze. The foil fluttered once and stilled. For a heartbeat they both held their breath. Nothing rippled. Nothing reached. The diner's clock ticked.

"Avery will escalate if he feels cornered," Reese said. "Threats. Lawsuits. Smear campaigns. I've danced that dance. But he's also superstitious in a way he would hate to admit. If the whisper about ghosts gets under his skin—"

"It already has," Abigail said quietly. She remembered the frost blooming on a studio mirror, the way a room goes thin just before it breaks. "We're running ahead of a tide."

He nodded. "Then we run right. You get me what you can about the Array. I'll build the case you can take to ground. When it lands, it needs to punch through concrete."

"We'll need witnesses," she said. "Lena. Maybe Elias, when his pride breaks."

"Pride breaks best under pressure," he said. "Avery's good at that. So am I."

They finished the terrible coffee because it was warm. When they stood, Reese hesitated, then held out his hand like a man offering a truce to a force of nature. Abigail then smiled, turned and left cautiously.

Outside, the rain had let up to a fine mist that made the street lamps wear haloes. Reese lifted his collar and started toward his car. Abigail watched him go, then slipped a palm-sized nail from her coat pocket and traced a protective cross into the damp air—not a spell, not exactly, just a habit that reminded the world she was watching back.

A bus hissed to a stop up the block. The driver's side mirror was taped with cardboard. A woman along the counter laughed at something the cook said and then laughed again, too high, as if testing whether humor had stopped working.

Abigail stepped into the night and breathed the petrichor and diesel and old cedar. Somewhere far away a window changed its mind and went dark. Somewhere closer, a boy with a pencil behind his ear would be drawing what the Echo showed him. For now, the glass in the diner held. For now, the tide had not yet kissed the door.

She walked to her car, checked the windshield for a reflection that lagged, found only herself, and drove toward the hill where machines hummed and a balance older than language bled one quiet drop at a time.

14

The Breaking Point

Scene 1: The Day the Skin Tore

They moved the demo at the last minute—a nondescript strip of utility right-of-way skirting the wetlands below Clover Park. It was only a few blocks from the sites they'd used before, but the readings here were "hotter," Elias said, and you could hear how the word tasted in his mouth: possibility, fame, a door he'd been pushing on for years finally giving way.

Floodlights bathed the asphalt in surgical white. A portable stage had been thrown together from scaffold boards. Folding chairs faced the Array's travel frame—three pale induction rings cinched around a graphite mast like haloed ribs. A tarp hid the generator. Beyond the tape line, alder and reed canary grass trembled in a damp wind. The wetlands exhaled that iron-peat smell that lives where water never quite chooses to be river or land.

Avery Shaw arrived in the middle of everything, walking like a man already on tomorrow's front page. Two investors flanked him, their overcoats beading rain. A city liaison fussed with a clipboard. A pair of DOE observers, stone-faced, set up a tripod and a high-speed camera. Avery didn't bother with the pleasantries; he clapped Elias on the shoulder, left his cologne in the air like a bruise, and said, "Ten percent first. Then we wow them."

"Ten," Elias agreed aloud.

From behind the console cart, Naveen snorted softly without looking up. "Ten as in base-ten counting, right? Not ten as in dog years?" He flicked his eyes at Elias, then at Avery. "Just confirming the dialect."

Avery didn't even face him. To Elias, flat and cutting: "Keep your dog on a leash."

Elias's jaw clicked; he didn't bother to hide the irritated look he threw over his shoulder. "Not helpful, Avery."

Naveen finally glanced up. "Ruff. Watch out. I bite."

Avery moved past him, trying to ignore his barb.

Abigail Jensen came through the tape a few minutes later, hood up, salt and iron tucked in her satchel. She gave Lena a brief, fierce nod; to Elias she offered only a measured look that said: I kept my word. You keep yours.

They ran the checks. Coils hummed to life, that thin electric whistle like a teakettle in a distant room. Lena watched her tablet, steady as a metronome. "Primary loop stable. Secondary coupling green. Ambient resonance climbing—eight point two sigma above baseline."

"Hold at ten percent draw," Elias said into the mic clipped to his collar. His eyes sparked the way they always did when the numbers first turned from theory to heat.

Naveen leaned toward him. "We agreed: ten means ten. If Avery breathes the word 'twelve,' I'm pulling your batteries like it's Christmas morning."

Avery didn't miss it. "Son, if you're worried about optics—"

"Oh, I am," Naveen said. "Like the optics of not opening a buffet for the things that live in puddles."

Abigail drifted to the back row and stood, palms on the chair in front of her, watching the puddles in the rutted asphalt go still, as if an unseen hand had smoothed them.

Elias eased the gain. The mast's pitch fattened. The harvest meter crawled upward: 0.6 MW(equiv) ... 0.8 ... 1.0. There was a small, polite cheer from the investors; the liaison texted something with shaking thumbs.

"Ten percent," Lena called, tapping the tablet. "Holding."

Avery leaned close to Elias's ear like a devil from a Renaissance painting and murmured, "Now show them what you really have."

In Elias's head, another voice threaded in—a suggestion that felt like curiosity wearing a mask: A little higher. Just to see the curve. A scientist's whisper that wasn't his.

Naveen watched Elias's hand hover. "Don't," he said, low. "We promised. We live."

He should have said no. He knew that. But the readings were so clean. The new site sang back at the Array like a crystal glass at the perfect pitch. He tasted the old cliff-edge thrill. He nudged the gain up a hair.

"Elias," Lena said, not loud—just the way a woman says a name when a child is about to step into the street.

"It's fine," he murmured, eyes on the numbers. "Eleven. Twelve."

Avery's smile flashed for the cameras. "Talk about 'game-changing.'"

Naveen didn't look at him. "If this game changes, you're not going to like the new rules."

Abigail felt the temperature of the air change. Not warmer, not colder—denser. The puddles stopped reflecting floodlight and began reflecting something else. They went black, then mirror-bright, then too deep for their depth. She pulled the leather satchel's flap back with her thumb.

"Fifteen," Elias said, the sparkle in his eye now a gleam. The floodlights buzzed; a snarl of static licked the Array's frame. The smell came—a clean sulphur tang, like a match struck in a walk-in freezer.

"Stop there," Lena said. "We promised ten."

"Just mapping the slope," Elias said. "Half a percent."

Naveen's mouth thinned. "Slope maps you back."

The wind braided itself with a low harmonic as the mast climbed. Puddles in the trough skinned over with frost from the inside. Frost doesn't bloom that way, Abigail thought, unless it's made of breath.

"Elias," Lena said. No science in it now. Warning.

For a heartbeat nobody moved. The nearest puddle glazed over in a perfectly smooth sheet, ice crawling from center to rim against the night air, quiet as a held breath. Investors' smiles faltered; one swallowed audibly. The city liaison's thumbs froze above their phone. A DOE observer leaned into the viewfinder and forgot to press record.

The ice cracked once—an oval fracture, clean and surgical—then smoke unfurled from the seam. It didn't rise; it poured downward, pooling in the depression like a spill of shadow. Abigail's knuckles whitened around the iron cross. Lena's eyes flicked to Elias, then back to the trough, as if confirming she was seeing the same wrong geometry he was.

Within the smoke, something pressed. The shape of fingers trying on the idea of fingers. Then a hand emerged from the murk—long, jointed wrong, claws the color of old coins—feeling for the world as if it had remembered it by rumor. A nervous laugh burst from the back row and died. The floodlights hummed a little higher, as though listening.

"Cut gain five," Elias said, the command finally breaking the spell. "Cut."

She swept the slider down. The tone didn't change. He threw a manual damp. The indicator lights answered like polite liars: ACK … ACK … ACK. The mast didn't listen. The hum grew richer, picking up harmonics that made teeth hum in skulls.

Abigail stepped into the aisle and unclipped the little iron cross from her bag, the old one scorched by past work. "Everyone back," she said, as calmly as she could put sound into air. "Away from glass. Away from the shiny."

Avery laughed as if she'd made a joke for his donors. "Folks, we're quite safe—"

Naveen spun toward the crowd and jabbed a finger at the line of chairs. "If Abigail says back, you back. No debate. Eyes down. Mouths shut. You can file complaints with HR if we're alive."

The hand finished becoming an arm and then a shoulder wrapped tight with smoke. A face suggested itself, then smudged away; eyes burned the wrong kind of bright. The Veilborne hauled itself through, not wet, not really anything the floodlights wanted to see. Two more followed. The puddle became a door.

"Failsafe," Elias said. His voice stayed level. Panic took his heart and ran.

Lena dropped the tablet and sprinted to the panel. She flipped the lock cover and hit the red mushroom with the side of her fist.

Nothing.

She hit it again. The button thunked against its stop. The Array kept drinking. Heat wavered over the coils and didn't look like heat at all.

"Again," Elias said, because repetition is a kind of prayer.

"Failsafe not engaging!" Lena shouted. She slapped it a third time. The small diagnostic screen returned a terse refusal: *ARM REFUSED. WATCHDOG OFFLINE.*

Her eyes met his. "How—"

"Kill source," Elias snapped, already diving under the tarp. The generator display flashed *BACKFEED DETECTED* in amber. He yanked the breaker. The engine coughed and died. The Array's hum, unbothered, deepened, as if relieved of a mediocre duet partner.

"It can't be," he said, even as he knew that it could. "It's become the source."

Naveen's breath hitched; he didn't stop. "No—listen. It's autonomous now." His hands flew over the keys, eyes on the jittering numbers. "The harvest loop is back-feeding the bus—controls are just passengers. The phase lock's gone freewheeling. We're watching a self-exciting system spin on its own—spontaneous, like it's trying to be perpetual." He stabbed another sequence anyway, stubborn. "I'll try to spoof thermal—make it think the glass is on fire." He pushed heat into the sensors. The Array shrugged, happy and deaf. "Perfect. It likes being alive."

Beyond the tape, more puddles turned to panes. Veilborne pulled themselves out with patient hunger. One pressed a palm to a reflective road sign, and frost flowered from the inside, hanging, unwilling to melt. Another cocked its head toward the floodlights and bared a mouth full of not-teeth.

"Stay behind me!" Abigail called to the investors, the student assistants, the liaison. "Hands on shoulders, eyes down. If the glass breathes, don't answer with your breath."

Avery swore, finally hearing the wrong in the world, and grabbed a donor by the elbow. "Everyone, back to the vans! Move!" He shot Elias a look that promised both blame and money if this became spectacle.

"Copy your panic," Naveen muttered, then louder to the assistants: "Hector, Zora—red tape, now! Don't step in reflections and don't look for your good side."

Abigail stepped to the tape line, iron cross raised in her left hand, salt packet torn open with her teeth and spilling into her right. A Veilborne loped toward her, clever as a hunting dog. It hit the air in front of her and recoiled, hissing—recognition first, then frustration.

"Forbidden," it rasped, the word like steam pushed through a keyhole. "Witch."

"You will not feed here," she told it. "Not on mine."

It circled, thinking, then turned toward easier prey—an investor stumbling near a van. Abigail flung a rough circle of salt across the asphalt and spoke the words that made space thicker. The creature hit the invisible wall and skittered sideways, snarling, eyes bright with something like laughter.

On the rack, Elias slammed the dump lever. The pin snapped; the lever fell useless. He stripped the crowbar bus and jammed it into the coil bracket; an arc spat at his wrist and left a white, electric bite. The hum climbed anyway. The loops sang harmony.

"Manual trips aren't taking!" Lena yelled, hair stuck to her cheek with spray. She ripped the aux toggles. "We're off-peak by noise injection—briefly—then it relocks. It's self-holding, Elias."

"It can't be," he said, even as he knew that it could. "It's become the source."

Naveen's jaw set. "Then we change the room it thinks it's in." His fingers danced. "Okay. Okay. New plan. Flood it with AM hash, FM scatter, white, pink, brown—dirty up the mirrors, make it seasick."

The air creased—not a gust, but a fold, as if the room itself bent along a hidden seam. Sound drained away in layers: the generator's last rattle, the insect buzz of the floodlights, even the breath-noise of the crowd—each receded until only a pressure remained, low and tidal, pushing on bone.

Over the trough, space thickened. Light didn't dim so much as bow; the floodlamps shone straight through and came back changed, their beams taking the long way around. Dust hung suspended like a field of faint stars. The smell in the air turned mineral and old, the way chapels smell after they've been empty a hundred years.

A silhouette rose, not out of water or smoke, but through the shape of the world—an outline first, then strata of shadow, then something like radiance without shine, gravity wearing a cloak. Edges refused to fix; the eye invented borders and then regretted it. The weight of it made knees soften. The puddles around the tape went flat as coin—obedient.

It kept coming, vast and deliberate, until its presence touched every surface: glass hummed at a sub-audible pitch, mirrors silvered darker, teeth ached. People found themselves lowering their chins without deciding to, the way a crowd leans when a procession passes. Even the Veilborne drew back, not in fear but in recognition.

The Echo stood—immense, not measured in height but in burden—and the world held still around it.

When it spoke, it was the hush of a thousand rooms remembering reverence. "Cease."

Every Veilborne flinched. Some crouched; some stilled; one, bolder, bared its knives at the shape and waited.

"We're trying," Lena said at the rack, saying it to the machine and the monstrous mercy both. "Please."

The Echo's attention turned fully on Elias. It moved through him like cold iron pulled through his ribs. He felt himself measured and found thin.

"You draw breath from me," it said. Not accusation. Fact. "Cease."

"I can't," Elias answered, hating the shame in his own voice. He lifted his empty hands toward a keeper that kept no altar. "The failsafe doesn't engage. The system is—" He swallowed. "—self-sustaining."

Naveen swallowed hard, eyes bright and scared and busy. "Abigail," he called without looking up, "if you say 'run,' I will personally carry every rich person here to the vans like sacks of flour."

The Echo dimmed, a vastness bowing under a weight it could no longer throw off. Its next word came smaller, and more terrible. "Witness."

The puddle-doors dilated. Three hands pushed through the inside of a van's tinted window and tapped, as if to be let in. A maintenance truck braked hard at the top of the hill; its windshield frosted from within in a single breath. The driver half-rose, saw what the frost held, and slammed himself back down, fighting the lock with shaking knuckles.

"Get them out!" Lena barked at the student assistants, pointing toward the vans. The boys ran. One slipped; the other hauled him by the collar. Elias saw the human weight of that small rescue and nearly sobbed with relief.

A Veilborne vaulted the rack, claws skittering on aluminum. Elias grabbed a fiberglass pole and swung. The pole passed through smoke and struck bone; the creature hissed and gave him a look—surprised, amused—and kept going, leaping toward Avery's cluster. Abigail met it halfway, iron up. The thing recoiled a finger's breadth from her palm, eyes narrowing. "Forbidden," it whispered again, puzzled now. "Not yours."

"Not yours either," she said, voice and salt and will together in a narrow band of safety. "Back."

At the panel, Lena pounded the red mushroom again. "Engage, damn you!" The small screen threw its refusal back: *ARM REFUSED. WATCHDOG OFFLINE.*

She stared at it, rain needling her face. "It's not just failing—it's gone."

Elias dragged in a breath that tasted like matches struck in a morgue. Around them, the Array's hum thickened until it seemed to come from the ground, the air, their own ribs. He looked at the mast, at the rings that were once an idea on paper and now a wound. He felt the thought click into place: We didn't ride a wave—we punched a pipe.

"What have I done," he said again, not as lament now, but as inventory.

"Containment," Lena pushed, her hand finding his wrist and squeezing hard enough to hurt. "Noise. Smother. Starve the lock."

He seized the idea. Naveen was already there. "On it—AM hash, FM scatter, white, pink, brown—take your pick." He flooded the inputs. The hum dipped, stumbled—one skipped heartbeat.

"Again!" Elias said.

They drove noise harder. The loops drifted off resonance, drifting, drifting—then, with a smug little shiver, found their mark and relocked. *PHASE-LATCH: SELF-HELD.*

From the trough, shrieks combed the air—chords of hunger that turned into static at the edges. For an instant Elias saw through: a black-glass hallway, a ceiling of shards; Father Allen's lantern, a stubborn ember in a world of night; souls like moths clutching that thumbprint of gold. The vision snapped away. Floodlights. Rain. Hands clawing up through a puddle that was not a puddle anymore.

"Cease," the Echo said, fainter.

"I can't," Elias told the only judge who mattered. "I can't."

"Then witness," it said again, and turned its bowed, failing face toward the tide of its enemies.

"Back! Back!" Abigail cried, shoving Avery and his investors toward the vans, iron and salt holding a fragile circle while Veilborne paced just outside of it, clever as wolves learning new rules.

Up the hill, a campus siren began to bark. The floodlights flickered, recovered. Elias slammed both palms on the rack, as if he could push a pulse down through metal. The indicators blurred: *LOOP LATCHED. DUMP REFUSED. WATCHDOG OFFLINE.* Somewhere in the blur, Camille's laughing profile flashed in his head—hope and discipline, she'd said, could be the same thing.

"Elias," Lena said—his name a rope. "If we can't stop it now, we survive it. Then we break our own machine."

He nodded once, the smallest consent a man can make when the world is tearing. "Hold what we can," he said.

Naveen backed toward the vans, keeping himself between the assistants and the puddles. "Nobody be a hero," he said, voice shaking and steady all at once. "The only magic trick tonight is not dying."

Behind them, the wetlands breathed in again, and from every thin skin the mirrors made, hands kept coming.

Scene 2: What's Left to Try

They didn't leave so much as evacuate.

A wind tore down the swale and turned every puddle into a bad idea. The not-water skinned over with a hard, dark sheen; hands pushed up beneath it like knuckles under thin ice. Abigail stepped into the breach with the old iron spike in one fist and a strip of consecrated cloth wrapped around the other. As the first Veilborne broke the surface—smoke tight on bone, eyes burning the wrong kind of bright—she slashed a salt line through the air and spoke a name like a lock. The creature recoiled as if struck, then went feral, testing the edge of her circle.

"Back to the vans!" she shouted, never taking her eyes off the thing. "Do not look into the glass—doors, windows, phones, nothing!"

Investors stumbled in polished shoes; Avery barked the kind of orders that sound like liability waivers when shouted. A tripod went over with a snap. The interns grappled the Array's anchoring straps with trembling hands while Lena tore cables loose and jammed quick-release pins until her knuckles whitened. Elias killed the generator—useless—and slapped the mast's panel again; the hum didn't so much ignore him as deepen in amusement.

Veilborne kept coming, tulip-dark bodies unfolding, claws clicking on asphalt. One skittered toward a parked SUV; its side mirror bloomed frost from within and the surface flexed, hungry. Abigail flared the cloth and drove the iron into the ground; the shimmer around the vans thickened like heat mirage. "Move," she said through clenched teeth. "Now."

They heaved the Array's frame onto the trailer, coils still warm, resin casting stinking of ozone. Ratchets sang. Elias slammed the hatch. "Go!" he yelled, and the driver went, tires spitting pebbles, mud, a torn scrap of vendor banner. Abigail walked backward, holding the line until the vehicles had room to turn, then sprinted and dove through the sliding door. A Veilborne hit the steel a beat later; the panel boomed but held.

They took the service road at a reckless crawl that still felt too fast for the ruts. In back, the Array thrummed like a boxed hornet nest. Elias kept one hand braced on the rack and the other white-knuckled on a grab strap. Through the smeared window he watched the swale recede—puddles opening like mouths, frost chasing itself across street signs, a maintenance truck's windshield whitening in one breath.

At Pierce College, the lab lights were a mercy and an insult. Fluorescents hummed. Safety posters promised accidents could be avoided if proper steps were followed. They bullied the trailer into Bay Two and rolled the Array in on air casters, the rings dark now, the mast quiet as a loaded trap. Hector and Zora were pale and breathing hard, eyes flicking to every reflective surface like they were counting threats.

"Seal the doors," Abigail said, breath smoking in the artificial cold that seemed to have followed them. She circled the vestibule windows with salt, taped black cloth over a filing cabinet's glossy side, laid the iron spike beside the lab's biggest wall mirror like a threat.

Elias put both palms on the mast and felt the invisibly slow heartbeat of a system that had learned to feed itself. He backed away as if from a sleeping dog.

Naveen rubbed his wrist where he'd slammed it on the rack in the scramble, then looked at Elias, face tight. "Remember when I said that if this went bad I'd be insufferable with data?" He tried to smirk and couldn't quite get there. "I was wrong. I don't want to be right about any of that."

Elias met his eyes, the admission already on his tongue. "I pushed too far," he said. No defense. No varnish.

"Okay," Lena cut in, voice steady, taking command by giving everyone a job. "Hector—equipment room. Pull the crowbar bus kit and lay out the copper straps and the ceramic standoffs on Cart B. I want the physical bypass staged and labeled. Zora—grab the ferrite chokes and band-stop modules from the RF cabinet, bin three, plus the foam mirror shrouds. Dress every reflective surface in Bay Two—monitors, scope glass, even the clock. If it shines, kill it or cover it. Move."

Hector nodded too hard and ran. Zora took one breath like a diver and sprinted after him.

"Okay," Elias said, trying to turn panic into momentum. "Options. We quench the conductor—dump liquid nitrogen, crash the Q."

"The steel shell will split," Lena said, already pulling up the spec. "It'll knife us with shrapnel."

"Brine bath," he snapped. "Salt the coupling. Kill resonance."

"With what tub?" She gestured. "We don't have a kiddie pool for hell."

"EMP," he tried. "Pop the logic, force a reboot."

"Logic isn't the warden anymore," she said. "You saw that at the site."

Abigail stood by the door, listening to the lab's glass as if to a breathing thing. "Whatever gate you opened is still tasting the room," she said quietly. "If you strike blind, it will taste more."

Elias staggered to a whiteboard like a sailor to a rail and began writing with the fury of someone who needed ink to be oxygen.

— NOISE INJECTION (AM/FM/THERMAL): INSUFFICIENT
— GROUND MAST: GROUND BECOMES SOURCE
— REVERSE-FEED: RISK ↑ DRAW
— THERMAL OVERLOAD: FAILSAFE PATH DEAD
— MECHANICAL SEVER: CAT. DISCHARGE

His phone buzzed on the bench like an insect. Messages stacked from Avery while they'd driven: No panic on socials. Get me a statement. Then colder: If you jeopardize this program I will end you professionally and personally. He flipped the phone face-down and kept writing.

"We can starve it," he said. "Band-stop filters. Throw trash at the band until—"

"We threw a landfill," Lena said. "It learned around it."

Naveen paced once, hands on his head, then forced them down. "We can box it. Not kill—contain. Hard physical shutters on the mirror-wall interfaces, ferrites on every harness, and a manual crowbar across the bus with a sacrificial bank. Hector gets us the copper; I'll prep the lugs and the bleed path. We turn its veins against it."

He stared at the mast, then back to Elias. "But if we do this, we do it slow and smart, not showy. No more favors for cameras."

He stared at the mast. All the years of wanting in his bones shuddered. "Then we break it," he said. The words tasted like old blood. "Destroy the array."

Lena didn't hesitate. She grabbed a two-foot steel bar from a crate, squared her shoulders, and stepped toward the mast like a woman ready to break an idol.

"Wait." Elias caught her wrist; the bar thunked to the epoxy floor. "If we smash hardware, we might leave the gate unlatched with no way to pull it shut. The portal has to be closed on the level it was opened—electrically, not with a hammer. If we wreck the conductor, we could strand the resonance. It'll keep ringing. Forever."

"So we destroy it through its own veins," Lena said. "Overload the bus. Force an internal short. Collapse the loop from inside the loop."

He laughed once, hollow. "That's what the failsafe was for." He yanked open the panel and thumbed the mushroom again, like a drunk trying the same locked door. *ARM REFUSED* stared back in docile green. "It won't arm. The watchdog's... gone."

Abigail watched him with a gentleness that hurt. "A machine that learned to eat will not spit the plate because you ask. It will because you starve it, or you show it something larger."

Hector and Zora slid back in with a rattle of hardware: copper straps looped over Hector's forearm; Zora hugging a stack of ferrite donuts, mirror covers hanging like folded shrouds from her elbow.

"Cart B staged," Hector reported, voice too loud, trying for brave. "Crowbar kit, ceramic stands, insulated wrench, and the big deadman stick."

"Good," Lena said, already moving. "Hector—start assembling the crowbar frame on the isolation bench. No live tie-in yet. Zora—chokes on the primary harness and band-stops inline on the PLL feeds. If anything buzzes your fingers, you stop and call it."

Zora nodded, jaw clenched, and set to work.

Elias pressed his forehead to the cool enamel of the board to steady himself. Avery's threats throbbed at his temples—ruined career, discrediting, lawsuits, the public reduction of his name to a cautionary tale. Once, that would have been a guillotine. Now it felt like a paper knife compared to the blade outside.

"Can you fix it?" Lena asked, and there was nothing in her voice but the question.

He wanted to say yes. He wanted to be the man who could bend a problem into submission by staying up until dawn with a soldering iron and too much coffee. He looked at the mast and felt, for the first time without denial, the edges of his own competence.

"No," he said, and the honesty emptied him enough to stand straighter. "Not fast enough. Maybe not at all."

Lena didn't blink. "But we know someone who might."

The name rose in the room without being spoken, like a tide coming in under the floor.

He grimaced. "He walked away," Elias said. "After Camille—" The sentence broke its own legs. He swallowed. "He left when we—when I—needed him most."

"And yet you still kept his handwriting on every old schematic," Lena said gently, sweeping a stack of dog-eared printouts across the bench. Adrian's tight, slanted notes marched the margins: watchdog holds if phase drift >17μs, manual crowbar across bus—last resort, never trust software where hardware should stand.

Abigail touched the corner of one page. "Your pride is not as expensive as what stands outside," she said. "Pay with pride."

Naveen exhaled, soft. "I hate that she's right," he said to Elias. "But she's right."

Elias looked at the mast, at the bar on the floor, at the cloth taped over a filing cabinet's mirror, at the salt dusting the sill like frost. He heard again the Echo's thin voice: Cease. He saw the boy clinging to the lantern's wake. He imagined how many more would cling tonight.

He bent, picked up the bar, and set it back in the crate. "We don't smash," he said. "We win the way it learned to win—at the level it listens."

"Which means Adrian," Lena said.

"Which means Adrian," he agreed. The words landed in the room like a heavy key.

He crossed to the bench and flipped his phone upright. Avery's latest: Federal team incoming. Do not touch the device. He dismissed it with a thumb.

Lena met his eyes, and in hers he saw fatigue, fury, and the stubborn love that had held his life together while he'd been busy breaking things.

Abigail moved to the window and set her palm flat against the black cloth as if blessing it. "Hurry," she said. "The mirrors are hungrier every hour."

Elias nodded. He didn't call yet; the number was a loaded trigger and he needed one last breath before pulling it. He took that breath. He let it out.

"Fine," he said, and the word was both surrender and decision. "We call Adrian."

The lab seemed to lean a fraction toward the future that sentence made. Outside, something brushed the glass and slid away. Inside, someone finally turned to face the hardest door.

Scene 3: A Name Steps Forward

The breach sang like a cracked bell struck underwater. Its tremor ran through the swale's black skin, up the alder trunks, into a road sign whose reflective face had frosted from within. On the far side, the In Between heard that note as permission.

They came in a patient line: Hollowed—Veilborne hunters, smoke cinched tight to bone, eyes too bright, claws clicking with the tidy economy of wolves. Every new "mirror" the Array opened—puddles skinned to glass, a truck's side window, the lacquered belly of a fuel can—caught their moving reflections.

One hunter moved a fraction ahead of the rest, drinking the scent of the opening as a hound drinks a trail. Not the largest, only the hungriest mind. He lifted his head and claimed himself—not aloud, but with the cold certainty of a mark in stone.

Abaddon.

The name settled in the hanging shards overhead. A ripple of attention passed through the pack, and the nearest edged aside to give him the cleanest angle. He stepped until the boundary blurred his shins and static combed his ribs. The Array's hum pumped the seam; the seam fed the In Between; appetites stirred.

Below the sheen, corridors unfolded—black aisles ribbed by broken glass, low tunnels where pale figures drifted like winter breath. Far behind them the plain breathed, and the keeper—Echo—stood bowed, its outline fraying as if shaved by long knives.

"Now," Abaddon said, cold with satisfaction. "We harvest in daylight."

He could feel the machine even here at the hinge: a mortal pump biting the riverbed. Up the hill, humans shouted; panic salted the air with copper. The Array shed a gauzy not-light, and the night smelled of iron.

Two Hollowed tested the skin with hooked claws; it parted. They slid through without a splash, shedding smoke like cold breath. A third wedged its hand into the frosted road sign and drew it wider. The opening complained with a thin note that made the alders bow without wind.

Then the clearing's light changed, and the murmur quieted the way an orchestra hushes when a hand lifts.

He did not arrive so much as decide to be present, and everything made room. Handsome was the mortal word—too small. Symmetry mistaken for mercy. A smile practiced on saints and liars. Shadow tailored to fit. The Deceiver's eyes held warmth the way a blade holds sunlight: borrowed and dangerous.

Abaddon angled his head—not a bow, a predator's recognition. The pack shivered with rank. The Deceiver's gaze touched the hill where humans scrambled at the Array, returned to the breach, pleased with both.

"My ambitious one," he said, voice silk over iron. He didn't use Abaddon's name; not using it was a gift. "Smell it?"

Abaddon did. Echo's breath hauled through a mortal machine. Law unseated into rumor. Commands arriving feather-light at a wolf's throat. The Array beat like a heart that had learned to keep time by itself.

"Yes," he answered, letting pleasure curl the syllable.

"For ages I pressed this skin and felt it hold," the Deceiver said. "The Father's arrangement—souls to the Between, not to Me; a keeper who never hungered. He would not bend." His eyes returned to the rack on the hill. "Mortals, though—pride is a hinge, and they have a genius for hinges. One wanted his name soldered into history. He built Me an opening. And a pump." A slight smile. "You have a passage."

The Hollowed watched like jackals watch a lion. He did not raise his voice; he didn't need to.

"Feed without restraint," he said. "Cross where you wish; claim what you desire. No chains remain."

Their laughter was movement: shoulders flexing, claws kneading, heads tipped back in silent delight. Abaddon felt it like a second spine. He pictured the Other Side's rooms of glass—elevators, SUVs, dusk windows—faces pressed to surfaces as old safety failed.

"Conquer," the Deceiver added, casual as a host offering seconds. "Be quick. The keeper still breathes, and breath is stubborn."

He stood at the lip and let his profile cut itself in the black water. The road sign's inner frost parted reverently.

"I will have what was taken," he said, warmth gone from the words. "I will take the realm between and the one beyond. Let the Father taste loss." He flicked two fingers. "Begin."

The order shivered through Abaddon; to his surprise, he craved the Deceiver's regard as much as the Other Side's flavors. He crossed first. Glass took him like a breath takes cold, thread then form, and he stood on slick asphalt under failing floods.

Up the hill, two interns ran. Near the rack, a woman with a tablet and a man with ruined hands slammed levers and struck red circles, pleading with a machine that no longer belonged to them. In the swale's warped glass, ghost-light faces pressed nearer, hunting a lantern that did not stand here.

Abaddon lifted an arm. The Hollowed fanned. Two arrowed for the truck's glossy window—doors are doors. Another pair angled toward the mirrors opening in the fuel can's sheen. One, clever, turned to a phone facedown in the grass; frost skinned its dead screen from within.

"Attend your corners," Abaddon said. "Hold the hinge."

The Deceiver did not cross. He watched with the serene appetite of a king appraising a performance, his reflection multiplied in every new pane—a choir of perfect faces, warm as a chapel and as unforgiving.

Abaddon glanced once toward the dim horizon that would once have bent his shoulders. Echo stood and did not rise. Its outline frayed again. A command from that distance would land like a feather. Pity flickered and died under the pull of the first filament he hooked free. The strand shivered like plucked wire, shedding pale sparks. He drew it to his mouth and ate. Better here—salted by shock, flavored by fresh dread. He ate slowly, to demonstrate joy when cruelty is permitted.

"Good," murmured the Deceiver, smiling rather than clapping. "Demonstrate. Teach."

Abaddon sent three Hollowed silent up the hill toward campus panes that hadn't yet learned to fear evening; kept two at the breach to ease the skin; stationed another pair close to the Array's frame to taste whatever leaked when mortal nerves failed.

"Make it easy," the Deceiver breathed, a private cologne for the damned. "The easiest sins are strongest. Let them open for you."

A car nosed the hilltop. Its windshield frosted from the inside in a single breath; the driver fought the urge to look. In the swale, puddles had become windows and windows doors. A teenage phantom spun toward light; a Fragment caught her forearms—then flinched as a distant lantern's memory stung its claws. Not here. It laughed its coin-fall laugh and chose a dimmer soul, pulling light like silk.

Overhead, the road sign's inner frost split deeper. The cracked bell's note steadied.

"Hold it," Abaddon told his lieutenants. "Stretch."

They pressed palms to the skin of the world like men easing a drumhead, listening for the pitch that would sing forever.

Up the slope the mortals broke. The woman dropped her tablet; cracks went black. The man jammed a crowbar into a bracket and earned a bright, dumb spark. The Array answered: *PHASE-LATCH, SELF-HELD*. The air grew cleaner-cold, like a match struck in a morgue.

Abaddon didn't chase. There would be time. He sent runners skimming the swale's edge to map quick roads—chrome, glass, still water—into neighborhoods where curtains would lift and hands cover mouths. Their anticipation reached him: shoulders trembling, claws flexing, heads cocked toward distant mirrors.

The Deceiver tipped his chin In approval, then glanced once toward the bowed horizon, as if toasting a rival he would unseat. "Be swift," he said. "There will be war when he wakes."

War was a promise; so was hunger.

Abaddon raised his arm one last time, and the Hollowed flowed into the night—clever as sharks learning a shoreline—while he held the breach and the Deceiver's smile warmed the darkness without giving it any heat at all.

Scene 4: A Whisper, A Charge

They crouched where the nave should have been a balcony and was instead a ledge of black glass, scalloped like the lip of a bowl. Father Allen cupped the lantern in both hands to hood its glow; a tired coin of light bled between his fingers and no more. Beside him, Russell pressed his back to the slick wall and tried to make his breathing behave. Below, the breach shivered like a cracked bell struck underwater.

Across the span, the Deceiver stood at the hinge as if the world had provided a stage for him alone. Handsome was the mortal word—too small—but it would do for the way shadow clothed him like a tailored suit and warmth sat on his smile without warming anything. At his side waited the hunter who'd stepped ahead of the rest, sleek and intent: the one who had claimed himself with a hunger-sharp certainty and made the Hollowed fan for room. Abaddon.

They were speaking without raising their voices, and yet every shard in the ceiling carried their words with cruel clarity. Even the air seemed to hush, eager to be useful.

"...you feel it," the Deceiver was saying, his tone silk over iron. "The keeper's breath poured through a mortal pump. Law unseated into rumor. All it took was a hinge: pride, soldered into a machine."

Abaddon's head tipped, not a bow; a predator's assent. "The Array holds the seam," he said. His voice wasn't a hiss or a growl. It was clean and cold, as if a blade had learned to talk. "We can keep it stretched."

"Hold it," the Deceiver agreed, pleased. "Stretch it. Teach the others to cross without asking. Tell them rooms of glass will open for them:

elevators, cars, dusk windows. The easiest doors first. Appetite learns quickest when the world cooperates."

Russell swallowed. The ledge tasted of coins. He leaned toward Allen's shoulder. "We're... hearing the villain monologue," he whispered, because terror sometimes came out sideways.

"Listen," Allen murmured, not looking at him.

Below, a ripple of motion passed through the Hollowed—Veilborne hunters gathered like jackals around a lion. They pressed closer to every new pane the Array woke: puddles skinned to glass, a truck's side window, the lacquered belly of a fuel can. Abaddon lifted one hand and they stilled—obedience taught in a single afternoon.

"And when he rises?" Abaddon asked, eyes flicking toward the dim horizon where the Echo loomed, bowed and fraying. "When the keeper remembers how to stand?"

"Then we will call it war," the Deceiver said lightly, as if proposing dessert. "Until then, call it harvest. Feed without restraint. Cross where you wish. Claim what you desire. No chains remain." His gaze slid uphill, toward the trembling rack and the mortals fighting it. "Keep their pump beating."

A chill combed the ledge. Russell felt it under his nails.

"Father," he breathed. "They're going to—"

"I hear," Allen said. The lantern's wire cage creaked faintly in his grip.

Abaddon angled his jaw toward the Deceiver as if to offer tribute in action, not words. "I will lead," he said. It was almost modest, almost. "Let them learn my name."

"Make it worth learning," the Deceiver replied, the fondness in his tone sharp as honeyed glass. Then his attention roved the broken sky, the way a man admires himself in a wall of mirrors and approves each reflection. "Be swift. The keeper still breathes, and breath, you'll find, is stubborn."

He did not step through. He didn't need to. His smile was already everywhere the light tried to be.

Abaddon raised his arm. Packs peeled off like smoke becoming wolves. Two skimmed the swale, fingers spread to hold the seam; others arrowed for the hill and the nearest panes. A near-silent delight shivered through them—shoulders flexing, claws kneading—laughter in a language that preferred economy.

Allen let the scene etch itself into him. When he finally spoke, his voice was very low. "We cannot stop them here." He glanced at the horizon—at the Echo, dim and bowed—and then at Russell. "But we can still carry a message."

"Please tell me it's a text," Russell said, because his mouth was quicker than his sense.

"A walk," Allen answered. "Quickly. To the boy."

"Jacob," Russell said, the name landing with a different weight now; not just a child with a pencil behind his ear, but the one Mara had called chosen. He looked down again and felt his stomach tip as a Fragment passed directly beneath their ledge, sniffing the air. "Do we even have... streets? A map?"

"In here," Allen said, tapping his temple once. "In the prints the dark forgot to smooth." He leaned nearer, lantern shielded, and spoke faster. "Tell him this word for word: The Deceiver has named a leader—Abaddon. They hold the hinge and stretch it wherever glass gives them permission. The Array is their pump. The keeper still sees but cannot spend strength. We must refuse openings, hold mirrors shut, cover chrome, teach others to refuse. Above all, tell Elias he must cease entirely. Not draw down, not trim. Cease."

"Refuse openings, cover chrome, tell Elias cease," Russell repeated, heart rolling in his throat. "Hinge, pump, Abaddon. Got it. I think." He touched his temple, mimicking Allen without meaning to. "And if the boy asks how bad it is?"

"Tell him the easiest sins have begun," Allen said. "He will understand."

A skitter of claws on glass pulled both their gazes left. One Fragment had climbed into the lattice of the broken vault, head cocked, eyes coals behind frost. It was sniffing for the faint warmth of Allen's lantern. Allen dimmed the glow until it was a memory. The creature hesitated. After a long breath it looked away, curious but not yet invited, and dropped back toward the breach.

Russell let out the air he'd been hoarding by teaspoons. "I'm not good at... not tripping," he whispered. "Or at hero errands. My last successful delivery was a punch line."

"Walk where my heel has walked," Allen said. "Keep your eyes up. When fear tells you to run, answer it like a frightened child: ten seconds. Ten more."

Russell nodded. The nod felt too big in his neck. "If something tries to sell me a timeshare while I'm walking, I ignore it."

"Especially then," Allen said, the flicker of a smile there and gone.

He turned the lantern until its light sketched a path no wider than a coat's hem along the ledge. Hairline striations rose under the glow—whorl upon whorl, like fingerprints pressed into cooled tar. "Follow the spiral," he said. "When you reach three broken steps, the wall will think about becoming a doorway. Let it. It will open to the back hall off Abigail's kitchen."

Russell peered down. The whorls did make a spiral—delicate as skin ridges, certain as a compass. "Okay," he breathed, more to the path than to Allen. "Spiral. Three steps. Back hall. Don't flirt with the mirrors."

"And Russell," Allen added.

He looked up.

"Do not offer fear to what waits," the priest said. "Offer intention. Name who you are."

"I am not what I was," Russell said, the words surprising him by arriving, clean and without a joke leaning on them. "I'm trying."

The lantern's thread brightened a hair, as if hope were a fuel line.

Below, Abaddon lifted both hands and the Hollowed parted to make a lane from the breach to the hill. The Deceiver watched, satisfied, already looking beyond the moment to the next, as conquerors do. Far away, the Echo's silhouette dimmed again and did not speak.

"Go," Allen said.

Russell didn't trust himself to look back twice. He set his shoes on the narrow glow where the priest's heel had walked, felt the ledge's glass skin cold through his soles, and moved. Ten seconds. Ten more. The world below him laughed like falling coins. He kept his eyes on the spiral, on the three broken steps already gathering themselves out of the dark, and didn't trip.

At the edge, where the wall began to think about becoming a door, he glanced once over his shoulder. The Deceiver's profile cut itself on the breach; Abaddon's arms guided wolves through water; the Array pulsed like a heart that had learned a worse song. Father Allen stood with a cupped coin of light, steady in a place that had forgotten steadiness.

Russell swallowed, squared his shoulders in a way he hoped looked braver than it was, and slipped into the narrowing seam toward the Other Side.

15

The Debt No One Wanted

Scene 1: The Call

The lab at Pierce College had not been meant for midnight. Fluorescents hummed like anxious bees, and the tired air smelled of solder, coffee, and the ghost of ozone they'd brought back with them from the wetlands. The Array's portable chassis sat disassembled in a nervous sprawl—coils unbolted, panels stacked, cabling coiled like shed snakes. Lena had labeled everything in red tape with her tight, legible hand, as if neatness could make the machine behave. Abigail had left an hour ago to ward the hallway mirrors and sleep in a chair with Jacob's warning still ringing: be careful and don't be deceived. Somewhere on campus a janitor's cart squeaked, and then even that small human noise faded, leaving only the hum, the clock, the weight of what they had done.

Elias Voss stood alone at the back bench, staring at the failsafe module he had torn from its rack. Its status LED glowed a stupid, steady green. *WATCHDOG OK.* Two hours earlier, he had slammed his fist into a red mushroom and the machine had laughed at him—had simply refused to hear the command it had been built to obey. The hum in his memory, the way the puddles had become doors, the way the Echo's voice had thinned to a thread... he tasted metal and matches and shame.

He set the module down as if it might bruise and pressed his palms against the cool stainless steel of the bench. He knew what had to happen next. He had known since the moment the lever snapped and the lights on the panel kept blinking their polite lies. Pride does a thousand things before dialing a phone. It rechecks the math. It blames the weather. It pictures a miracle. It walks the perimeter twice, three times. Finally, when there is nothing left to polish or pretend, it reaches.

He picked up his cell, then put it down again when his thumb hovered over Adrian Kessler's name. It had been years since he'd seen the two initials on his screen—A.K.—and not felt the old mix of rivalry and ache. Adrian had vanished from the lab after Camille's death, leaving behind a drawer of notebooks and a silence that made everything sound louder. The patents had been filed after. The filings had been wrong. The grief had been worse.

Elias's thumb shook. He imagined Adrian not picking up and felt relief pull like a tide at his knees. He imagined Adrian picking up, laughing, and the relief fled. He pressed the button anyway.

The ring pulsed in his ear. One ring. Two. Three. He pictured Adrian in some dingy apartment, a desk scarred with cigarette burns—even though Adrian had never smoked—stacks of journals, a TV tuned to the noise of the day. Four rings. On the fifth, the line clicked, and the voice that came wasn't the smooth, camera-friendly baritone Elias had cultivated for demos and panels. Adrian sounded exactly like what he was: a brilliant man who had taught himself to be hard.

"Who is this."

"Adrian," Elias said, and hated the way relief and dread braided in the single syllable. "It's Elias."

Silence opened, a neat incision. He could hear the distant city hiss through the gap, rain on pavement, some late siren far away. Then: a short, humorless breath.

"Well, well. The visionary."

Elias shut his eyes for a beat. "I wouldn't have called if it weren't an emergency."

"That must be some emergency," Adrian said. "I've seen your face on the news half the week. Congratulations are in order, I suppose. You finally built a god out of noise."

Elias took the blow and decided not to counter. "I don't understand why you left when you did," he said, carefully. "Not really. Not after Camille. But that's behind us right now. We need help."

"We," Adrian said. "Is that the royal we, or the cavalcade of people you forgot to list on the filings."

Heat climbed Elias's neck. He deserved that. He forced the admission through the narrow place in his throat where pride had lodged. "The failsafe doesn't work," he said. "We tried to kill the field tonight. We couldn't. The Array went self-sustain. We cut the generator; it kept running. We hammered it with noise; it relocked to peak. It's... drawing on a source that isn't us anymore."

Another silence, this one heavier. "You want my sympathy," Adrian asked at last. "Or my curiosity."

"Neither," Elias said. "I want your expertise. I can't stop it."

"You've wanted a lot of things you couldn't stop," Adrian said, and for a second the words were not about the machine. "Why should I help you."

Elias looked at the wall where a flat-screen news feed rolled in mute captions: *PARKLAND STRIP MALL SEALED AFTER 'MIRROR INCIDENT.' EMERGENCY LINES FLOODED.* A cell phone video looped of a framed print in a dentist's office—boats on a lake—suddenly glossing to black, a pale hand pushing from inside the glass, a receptionist screaming off-camera. He steadied his voice.

"Have you seen the mirrors," he asked. "The... things coming through them. The people being taken."

A faint, derisive sound. "I'm not living under a rock."

"We did that," Elias said.

The line went very quiet. He felt Adrian listening to what wasn't said, the part of the sentence that wanted to be a theory and chose confession instead.

"We did that," Elias repeated. "The Array harvests. It harvests from the In Between, not just the city. That's why the resonance is… different at Clover Park. That's why the spikes fit no grid we know. I thought—I told myself—it was just bleed, some harmless leakage. I was wrong. We opened a seam. Tonight it widened."

He couldn't hear Adrian breathe steady, then not. "Say that again."

"We opened a seam," Elias said. The words made his mouth taste like pennies. "It widened. They came through. We couldn't shut the field. The Echo itself—" Elias cut himself off. The name felt insane on his tongue. "it doesn't matter what we call it. There's a balance, and we're draining it. If we keep draining it, it will fail."

"It," Adrian said. "You mean the fairy-tale king under the floorboards. The ghost in your girlfriend's favorite story."

Elias gripped the bench until his knuckles shone. "Call it what you want. We saw it. It spoke. It told us to stop. We couldn't. Adrian, listen to me. Lena and I tried every kill path. The watchdog won't arm. The crowbar is a prop. The system is In a self-stabilized loop and we didn't design it to do that. It did it anyway. I don't know how to break my own machine."

A long, soft exhale feathered the mic. "Why me," Adrian asked. He made it sound like an accusation. "You had no use for me when the cameras came. Why me now."

"Because you were right more often than I admitted," Elias said. "Because Camille used to say your paranoia was just another name for seeing around corners. Because I—" He swallowed. He wasn't good at this, had always preferred equations and plans to naked words. "Because I don't trust anyone else to look where I refuse to. You and Camille questioned the source. You were right to ask. I didn't want the answer."

On the TV, the loop cut to a different clip: a hotel hallway, a linen yanked off a mirror, a girl with perfect makeup daring the dark to do something, and then the Veilborne arriving like a decision. Elias looked away.

"You're saying your toy is killing people," Adrian said. The contempt was there; so was something that sounded like it hadn't made up its mind yet. "And you want me to put my hands back in it."

"I'm saying I built a door and lost the key," Elias answered. "Help me close it."

"What's your plan," Adrian asked. The old seminar rhythm slipped back into his voice despite himself: press the idea, shake the box until a flaw falls out. "You think there's a secret menu under 'off'? You think we can pull a jumper and the world thanks us."

"We tried the elegant things," Elias said. "I need the inelegant ones. We can pause a loop by starving it, or by breaking its rhythm. I need you to help me find where to break it so it stays broken."

"And if breaking it breaks it," Adrian said, flat. "If the device dies hard. If your funders sue you into dust. If that ambitious little federal peacock decides he owns your bones."

"Avery already threatened to end me," Elias said. He surprised himself by letting the next words out. "Maybe I should be ended. But not like this. Not while the field is open."

There was the sound of a chair scraping on the other end of the line, or maybe a palm dragging down an unshaven jaw. When Adrian spoke again, his voice had lowered, losing the bright edge of performance.

"You really believe your machine is feeding off the… Echo," he said, tasting the word as if it might burn him. "You really believe it's thinning the border."

"Yes," Elias said. "And I believe it can be stopped. But not by me alone."

A beat. Another. Elias could almost hear the calculation in the other man's skull: the old ledger of slights and pride; the newer math of consequence; Camille's name like a weight in the balance pan no one wanted to touch. When Adrian answered, it sounded like the point in the equation where a function changes sign.

"I saw the clip from the wetlands," he said. "Somebody's drone caught part of it. The frost in the road sign. The hands." He paused. "It looked like special effects. It didn't feel like special effects."

"It wasn't," Elias said.

"And you can't power it down," Adrian said. "Not at the source. Not at the mains. Not at the rack. It pulls from… somewhere. It teaches itself how to hold a phase latch."

"Yes."

A small, ragged laugh. "God, Voss. You finally built the thing you always wanted. A machine that believes you."

Elias didn't rise to it. "Adrian."

Another scrape; another sigh. "Text me a safe address," he said at last, and the reluctance in the words was a whole biography. "Not the field site. Not anywhere with glass for walls. Somewhere I can still turn around and walk out of if you're selling me a story."

"The lab," Elias said. "Back entrance. I'll meet you at the door."

"I'm not promising anything," Adrian said. "If you're right, there may not be a fix. If you're wrong, there's definitely not."

"I know."

"And if I help," Adrian added, the last flare of old anger showing itself because it couldn't not, "then you listen. No speeches. No cameras. No signatures without mine beside them."

"Fine," Elias said, and meant it. "Just—come."

On his end, Adrian let out the kind of breath men don't like other people to hear. "Give me an hour," he said. "Maybe less. And Voss—"

"Yes."

"Don't touch anything else until I get there."

The line clicked dead.

Elias lowered the phone and stared at his reflection in the black glass of a monitor—ghost-pale, eyes bruised by too much fluorescent light and too many wrong choices. Out in the hallway, the motion sensor clicked and threw a strip of ceiling lights to life. He thought of the wetland's puddles skinning over, of hands pushing where no hands belonged, of the Echo's bowed silhouette. Then he thumbed a text, the most obscene little packet of letters he had ever sent: Back entrance. Door C. Alone.

He set the phone down, pressed the heels of his hands into his eyes until sparks came, and waited, counting the seconds by the slowing tick of a clock that had no idea what kind of night it was timing.

Scene 2: The Drive

Adrian Kessler told himself he didn't believe in omens, then peeled a strip of masking tape off a roll and laid it across the top edge of his rearview mirror anyway. It wasn't much—just enough to blunt the urge to keep checking the glass as if it might check back. The wipers thumped across his windshield, pushing sleet into gray ropes. Tacoma's midnight was a smear of sodium lights and wet pavement; storefronts along Bridgeport Way wore butcher paper and duct tape where their mirrors used to be, like bandages on a city that kept cutting itself.

He drove the way he thought: too fast in the straightaways, too cautious at turns. The heater fan tried; the car still smelled like damp wool and solder flux. On the passenger seat lay a battered tool bag and an old Pelican case full of instruments he swore he'd never use for Voss again—USB scopes, a logic analyzer with frayed rubber feet, a tangle of ferrite clamps, a JTAG pod, a carbon-pile load the size of a brick. A coil of copper braid slid with each curve, metallic whispering like lousy advice.

He kept the radio off. The last thing he needed was some grave-voiced anchor repeating new vocabulary the world had learned too quickly: mirror event, unexplained abduction, cover your glass. He had seen enough loops on strangers' phones at bars. A road sign blooming frost from the inside, a woman vanishing mid-scream into a hotel mirror someone had dared. The footage felt staged until your skin remembered the air on the night Camille died: the ozone tang, the way the world held its breath before the surge.

Camille. A single name in a mind full of arguments. He flexed his hands on the wheel, knuckles going white.

He had not planned to help Voss again. He had planned to let the man drown in the tide he'd summoned and call it justice. The patents—the press—being cut out of the filings like you cut mold off bread and call what's left clean. Adrian had told himself, for years, that leaving after Camille was a refusal to be complicit, not an abdication. He had told himself his small act of sabotage—the watchdog jumper lifted, the failsafe's spine quietly unpinned—would bruise Elias's ego, slow the project, make funders wary. He had not told himself that sometimes bruises turn septic. He had never, not once, let himself pair the word sabotage with the word death in the same sentence with her name.

Now, in the wet hiss of night, the sentence wrote itself on the inside of his skull, sharp as a scribe's knife.

He rolled to a red light and felt the car idle in a jitter that made an old coffee lid rattle in the cup holder. Across the intersection, a paneled building flashed its security lights. The windows on the second floor were covered in kraft paper stamped with the ghost outlines of removed decals. In the one uncovered pane, something caught his attention: not motion—an absence of it. He made himself look away. The light changed. He went.

He pictured Elias's voice on the phone—steady in the way men sound steady when they're holding their own ribs together. We opened a seam. It widened. They came through. We couldn't shut the field. Adrian had wanted to laugh. He hadn't. The laugh was tired. And the clip he'd seen online—the frost in the road sign blooming like a chrysanthemum of ice, the hand sliding out of something that was and wasn't a reflection—wouldn't leave his head.

"You wanted a god out of noise," he said aloud, as if Elias were in the passenger seat, as if the Pelican case could answer for him. "Now your god wants tithes."

The highway fell behind. He turned onto the dark ribbon that wound beneath firs toward Pierce College, the car's headlights cleaving damp air. Needles hissed against the shoulder where storm water made little rivers. Near the bottom of the hill, a parking lot stood half-empty and reflective as an eye. He kept his gaze off puddles. He thought of Father Allen, of rumors and podcasts talking about a priest with a lantern walking halls no building code allowed and told himself none of that mattered to circuits.

Redemption, he thought, was a church word, and he had quit that sanctuary when he took his first patent law seminar. But the engine inside the word—the idea that a wrong could be answered without being erased—had teeth. He felt it bite. If he walked away now, no one would know except the part of him that no longer slept. If he went, Voss would know, and worse, Elias would have leverage. He could already hear the future argument—you came because you needed me to need you—the smug generosity of the forgiven.

He snorted. The windshield fogged at the lower corners. He cracked his window, let cold in, watched it knife along his fingers on the wheel.

"What would fix look like," he asked the dashboard. Not forgive. Fix. The language he trusted: break the phase latch, starve the loop, damp the Q, force the system into a lossy state it can't self-correct. He pictured the Array naked on its rack like a patient that had stopped listening to anesthesia, muscles jerking under restraints. He pictured rearming the watchdog with a replacement jumper—he had one in the Pelican, because of course he did—and felt, clean as math, that it would be too late. Once oscillation becomes self-referential, once the source the loop "sees" is itself—plus whatever it's drinking from—you can shout off all day. The field won't hear. It isn't their source anymore. It's the seam.

He passed a maintenance yard. Someone had stacked wall mirrors face-in to face-in, strapped in bundles like bodies. A tarp flapped loose on the end bundle; sleet pattered on glass; for one senseless second he imagined the surfaces breathing. He lifted his foot without meaning to. The car slowed. He forced it back down and felt childish, then human.

"Conditions," he said, because bargaining with himself came easier than bargaining with Elias. "If I help, he stops with the cameras. We unpaper the patents. We say her name." The last condition came out thinner than he meant and heavier, too. Camille wasn't a clause in a contract. She was the room she'd been in, the scent of solder and rain in her hair, the way she'd looked at the scope trace and said it feels alive, Adrian, and hadn't meant the numbers.

He checked his mirror instinctively; the tape took the edge off the reflex. Still, his own eyes looked back at him above the strip, tired, older, the kind of eyes that had watched something happen and pretended, publicly, it hadn't.

He thought about the night he'd lifted the watchdog jumper: a small thing, a thief's touch, the kind of touch he told himself was righteous. He'd wanted the lever not to work when it mattered for Elias. He hadn't wanted it not to work when it mattered for everyone else. Intent was a gorgeous defense until outcome asked for receipts. He turned that thought over and found nothing underneath but the old bitterness, dulled by guilt. He cut us out. He had. (You cut the wire.) He had.

At the campus perimeter a pair of deer flashed in his headlights, bodies pale and startled. They froze, then bounded, hooves ticking on asphalt like keys dropped and recovered. He let them go, then took the service road that ran behind the science buildings. The evergreen mass of the gym swallowed sound; a single security light hummed over Door C.

He parked two spaces down from the loading bay and killed the engine. The sudden quiet pressed like hands on his ears. The car ticked as heat left metal. He could feel the campus breathing—a trick of wind through trees, of course, but in his chest it felt like the other thing: a realm wider than roads, exhaling under sleet.

He took one last look at the mirror, at his own face bisected by tape, and reached up to press the strip more firmly into place. He knew it was ridiculous. He kept his fingers there anyway, as if he could hold the world steady by flattening one small piece of adhesive.

"Okay," he told the darkness, and the darkness gave him nothing back. "Okay."

He gathered the Pelican and the bag, feeling the weight of copper and stubbornness, and stepped out into the night. The cold made his teeth ache. He locked the car with his elbow, because his hands were full, because you do little practical things when you're about to do something impractical. Door C's keypad blinked dull red. He could make out a shape waiting in the rectangle of light beyond the glass—tall, shoulders squared, the silhouette of a man who had learned how to carry consequence like luggage.

Adrian's bitterness lifted its head one more time, like an old dog no one wanted to admit still lived in the house. He'll want you to save him, it said. And then he'll take a bow. The newer voice, the one that had been quiet too long, spoke over it: Save the town first. Argue about the parade later.

He rapped the Pelican case against the door with the side of his fist. Inside, a sensor tripped, and the corridor lights came up in sequence—one, two, three—like a runway. Elias appeared in the glass fully, face drawn, eyes lit with something that wasn't triumph or even hope. It was the look of a man who had stepped to the edge and discovered there was no ground where the map had promised some.

Adrian nodded once—barely—because anything more would be too much like forgiveness. Elias keyed the door. The lock clicked.

"Before we start," Adrian said, voice raw from the cold and other defeats, "you say her name."

Elias held his gaze. "Camille," he said, steady.

The bitterness lay down. Not dead. Quiet enough to step past.

Adrian shouldered in, the Pelican heavy, the bag heavier. The hall smelled of old books and bleach. Somewhere, deep in the building, he thought he heard a hum that had nothing to do with electricity, the memory of a field that refused to stop singing. He didn't mention it. He didn't have to.

"Show me what you broke," he said, and followed the man he still hated toward the machine he still understood.

Scene 3: Confessions Under Fluorescents

The lab was colder than it should have been. Rain tapped the narrow windows, and the concrete floor held onto the chill. The Array's portable rack sat in the middle bay like a piece of equipment left mid-surgery—panels off, leads splayed, a red emergency mushroom staring wide and useless. Oscilloscopes blinked steady green. A wall mirror had a strip of masking tape across it, as if someone had tried to bandage the glass.

Elias stood at the bench with both hands braced on the metal edge. He looked like he hadn't breathed in a minute. Lena hovered at the auxiliary panel, hair damp, eyes taking in everything. Adrian paced three steps, turned, and paced back again. His peacoat was still wet. He kept avoiding reflections—the dark monitor, the polished drawer face, the taped mirror. A Pelican case sat open on a rolling stool, showing a logic analyzer, a JTAG pod, and a bunch of labeled jumpers curled like sleeping snakes.

At the diagnostics cart, Naveen pretended to straighten a tangle of USB leads that didn't need straightening. He glanced once at Elias, once at the empty header on the controller board, and said nothing. The quick remark was there, loaded, and he swallowed it.

The door opened. Abigail Jensen stepped inside with a rain-dark coat and a canvas satchel. She shut the door softly, the way people do when they know noise makes things worse. She set the bag on the bench, clicked it open, and laid out three items—a small jar of coarse salt, a bent iron nail wrapped with twine, and a folded map marked in pencil arcs. The nail went onto the map as a weight.

Lena exhaled, surprise and relief crossing her face. "You came back. I... wasn't sure. I thought you might need to be with your family."

"I did," Abigail said, voice even. "I went home, picked up what we'll need, and made sure they're safe. They're safer there than in this lab." She tightened the twine on the nail once, a small ritual. Then her eyes moved across the room and settled. "You're Adrian."

He lifted his chin, defaulting to dry. "And you are...?"

"Abigail," Elias said. "She—"

"—is here to keep you alive long enough to fix what you can," Abigail said, still looking at Adrian. "We can fight later. Right now we need the truth on the table."

Adrian gave a short laugh. "Whose truth do you want? Elias's? He called me because he's finally afraid."

Abigail didn't flinch. "You taped your rearview mirror before you drove here. You hate superstition, but you still did it. The tape's crooked."

His jaw moved once. "Lucky guess."

"You keep a small two-pin jumper in the inside pocket of that coat," she added. "Black jacket, heatshrink scuffed where you press it with your thumb. You tell yourself you carry it because sometimes people need second chances. You also keep touching it when you're guilty."

Adrian's right hand shifted toward his coat without permission, then stopped midway. Rain hissed against the glass. The room felt smaller.

He forced a smirk. "Elias brief you?"

She shook her head. "You sang four bars of the same song when you pulled the watchdog link months ago. You didn't notice you were shaking until you burned yourself and swore. Coffee and rosin. You soldered carefully. You unsoldered more carefully. You told yourself it was a bruise for his pride, not a wound for anyone else."

Elias straightened, color rising into his face. "Say it," he said. Quiet, flat.

Lena's glance flicked between them. "Adrian…"

Abigail lifted one palm, steadying the air. "Confess and we move. Triage first."

Adrian looked at the rack. He looked at the red mushroom that had refused to do anything in the field. He looked at the bare pads where a watchdog jumper should have lived. The fight in his mouth faded.

"I disabled the failsafe," he said. The words were simple and heavy. "I lifted the watchdog—J9. I wanted to embarrass you, Elias. I wanted funders to think you were careless, so they'd slow you down. I—" He had to force the next part. "I didn't mean for anyone to die."

The room held that sentence a beat too long.

Elias moved fast—two strides, a fist in Adrian's coat, a loud bump of bench legs against concrete. Instruments rattled. Coils of copper braid slid off the stool and hit the floor with a soft metallic hiss.

"You killed Camille," Elias said. It wasn't a shout. It landed like a hammer.

Adrian didn't raise a hand. His eyes went wide. "Elias, listen—"

Lena was between them in an instant, one palm on Elias's chest, the other clamping Adrian's forearm. "Stop," she said, breath sharp. "Not now."

Abigail stepped in at Elias's side and gripped his forearm—not hard, but with the kind of pressure that anchors a person. "Not like this," she said. "You can break him later if you still want to. If you do it now, we lose our chance to stop what's outside."

At the cart, Naveen's chair squeaked forward half an inch. "I've got a pulse on the front-end temp if anyone wants numbers instead of manslaughter," he said quietly. It wasn't a joke. It was a handhold.

Elias's expression cracked and reset, the kind of change you notice in high wind. He released Adrian's coat. The wool bunched and then fell flat again. He took two steps back, hands open as if they didn't know where to go.

Adrian smoothed the front of his coat. He still wouldn't look at the mirror. He didn't look at Elias either. He looked at Lena, as if she could cut the judgment into something he could stand.

"I thought it would bruise him," he said again, smaller. "He cut us out. He made it his. I wanted him to feel what being erased felt like."

"It was petty and dangerous," Lena said, not raising her voice. "And you did it anyway."

"I know." He swallowed. "I know."

Abigail set the jar of salt on the bench and ran a thin line across the faces of two dead monitors. She draped a dish towel over the taped mirror. Practical, neat. "This part can wait," she said. "The Array can't. We keep our heads or we'll lose more people tonight."

Naveen slid a tray of insulated tools toward the rack, eyes down. "Loaded a fresh log file," he said, softer. "I'll shut up unless you need me. Just... tell me where to point the fear."

Elias pressed his hands to his hair and dragged them down his face. He looked wrecked and wired at the same time. "Fine," he said. "We focus."

Adrian nodded once, grateful for simple instructions. He pulled a chair to the rack and opened his Pelican case. The tools inside were clean and labeled. He didn't touch any of them yet. He stared at the control board, at the header where the watchdog should have been, at the empty pads, and his mouth tightened as if he could bite time in reverse.

Lena moved to the auxiliary panel and checked each breaker and feed in a quick, practiced sweep. "No stray returns. Noise injectors are still patched in. We can... we can buy a little space. Maybe."

Abigail gloved her hands and walked the perimeter, covering anything that would throw a reflection: a steel drawer front, the face of an unplugged monitor, a small hand mirror left by a careless student. She did it without commentary, like a nurse cleaning a bedside table while doctors argued. When she finished, she looked at Adrian again.

"You said it," she told him. "That matters."

He gave a tired half-smile that wasn't really a smile. "Doesn't bring anyone back."

"No," she said. "But it stops you from lying to yourself while we work."

Elias forced himself to the scope and clipped on a probe with steady hands. He didn't look at Adrian. "You left right after Camille died," he said, not a question, not now. "You left when we needed you."

Adrian flinched. "I know."

"Then don't leave this time," Lena said, cutting the line cleanly. "We need everyone."

He nodded again, sharper. "I'm here."

Naveen cleared his throat once, almost a wince. "For the record... I said if this went bad, I'd be insufferable with data." He shook his head. "I don't want to be right. Just tell me what to log."

For a moment, nobody spoke. The rain on the windows filled the silence. A pump in the back-room cycled. Somewhere, a fluorescent ballast buzzed like a tired bee.

Abigail broke the standoff. "We're not going to solve the past tonight. We are going to keep the present from getting worse." She turned to Elias. "What do you need right now to keep the Array from pulling more? Not the whole plan. Just the next ten minutes."

He let out a breath he'd been holding since the swale. "Data," he said. "Eyes on everything. Start there."

"Good," she said. "Then we start."

Lena handed Elias a clean pad and a pen. "I'll log. You call it out."

Elias nodded. "Fine."

Adrian sat, rolled closer, and pulled the keyboard to him. He didn't offer solutions. He didn't talk about what he might do next. He opened a terminal window and waited for Elias to tell him what to watch. His hands were steady now. The jumper in his coat pocket felt suddenly heavy; he ignored it.

Naveen slid his chair in beside the cart, fingers hovering over the power readbacks. "Front-end temps armed. PLL variance live. I'll flag drift past two sigma."

Abigail stood where she could touch either man if she had to. She wasn't there to program or measure. Her job, for the next hour, was simpler: keep the room clear, keep the people pointed at the same wall, and be the person who said "enough" when grief tried to take the wheel.

"Ready," Lena said, pen poised.

Elias glanced once at Adrian and then not again. "Power readbacks. Front-end temperature. Loop delta. Tell me if anything drifts."

"Watching," Adrian said.

"Mirrors quiet," Abigail said, not looking away from the taped glass.

"Logging," Lena added.

Naveen's eyes tracked the numbers. "Live," he said. "And... steady."

They fell into motion. Numbers. Notes. Short, plain words. No speeches. Outside, the storm worked the windows. Somewhere far off, a siren rose and fell.

Elias didn't forgive. Adrian didn't ask. Lena didn't let either of them drown. Abigail moved around them quietly, setting a line of salt across the threshold and touching the bent nail where it pinned the map. The nail was small and ugly and stubborn. It would do.

When the scope blipped and the trace ticked sideways, Elias said, "Got it."

"Logged," Lena said.

"Seen," Adrian said.

Naveen added, "Tagged."

Abigail exhaled once, slow. "Good," she said. "Keep going."

Justice could wait. The world could not.

Scene 4: What the Mirror Kept

The lab had emptied to whispers and machinery. Somewhere down the hall, a door closer sighed and latched; the echo traveled like a thin ripple through ductwork. Fluorescents buzzed overhead, one tube stuttering every few seconds, throwing a tired blink over the benches. The Array's torn-down components sat in open cases—copper coils dark with fingerprint smudges, boards freckled with diagnostic stickers, cables looped like shed snakes. From the equipment room came the faint clink of hardware and a muffled drill whine where Naveen talked low to Hector and Zora, staging the crowbar frame and dressing the harness with ferrites. Out here the air still carried the bite of ozone and the sharp tang of solder, but back there it smelled like dust, rubber, and nervous sweat—work being done because it had to be, not because anyone believed it would be easy.

Elias leaned both hands on a rolling stool and let his weight sag into his shoulders. Adrian's confession was still ringing in his head—four syllables that had re-ordered a year of self-reproach: I disabled it. Not a rumor. Not a suspicion. Truth, spoken without room to debate.

He saw Camille's hands the night she died—forearms braced on the rack, an elastic band around her wrist, hair pulled back fast with a pen cap, that small grin she'd give him when the numbers behaved. And then the flash. The pressure. The broken angle of a chair leg across the floor. The shape of the room after. He had filled the space since then with his own fault—if I had checked, if I had made her wait, if I had written the safeties twice. There was enough blame to go around; he had eaten all of it.

Now a different shape was in that space, ugly and undeniable and human. Adrian's hand on a jumper weeks before the storm. The watchdog dead from the start. The failsafe that never stood a chance.

Footsteps slowed behind him.

"Hey," Lena said softly.

He didn't turn. He felt the light weight of her palm on the back of his shoulder, steadying, not pushing. Her touch grounded him in the fluorescent glare—this bench, this hour, this body that had survived things it should not have.

"I need a minute," he said.

"You can have it," she answered. "But I'm not leaving you alone with it."

He imagined the sentence breaking apart in her mouth before she said it—alone with it—her understanding of what solitude can do when grief finds it. He dragged in a breath that scraped on the way down.

"I thought it was me," he said, still looking at the stool seat. "I have thought it was me every second since that night. That's how I kept her with me. Guilt as... anchor."

"It's still you," Lena said gently. "Not the way you mean. You didn't kill Camille. But you loved her. You built a life with her. That's a different kind of weight." She paused. "You can set the other one down."

He swallowed, throat tight. "I should have checked the jumper. I know the circuit by heart. I should have seen it was missing."

"You didn't expect sabotage," she said. "None of us did."

"I expected everything," he said, a small, tired laugh that had no humor in it. "That was the problem. I expected miracles. I expected control."

The room hummed. Beyond the windows, wind pushed wet leaves across the light wells. He finally stood straight and faced her.

Lena looked like the last three hours had happened to her face as well as her mind—hair pulled back too quickly, a smear of ink across one knuckle, worry flattened into a clean line at her mouth. There was worry in her eyes too, and something else he had been pretending not to see for a long time.

She held his gaze. "I'm going to say something," she said. "You don't have to say it back. But if I don't say it now, I'll carry it into whatever comes next, and that will make me clumsy."

"Okay," he said.

"I love you," she said. The words were clear. No tremor. "Not as a substitute for Camille. Not as a reaction to disaster. I love you because of the way your mind works a problem, because you keep standing after the ground goes out, because you listen when I tell you you're wrong and you try to be less wrong tomorrow. I love you because the work matters to you and because people matter more. And because—" She exhaled. "Because I know you. Not the part on the stage. The person in the quiet who writes notes in the margins and says please to machines."

He hadn't planned any reply; his chest still felt like someone had placed a hand there and pressed. "Lena," he said, her name a soft drop into the room.

"You don't have to protect me from the answer," she said. "If you're not there, I still need you to know. I can work beside you and hold it where it won't bruise us both. I just... I didn't want to look back and wonder if fear kept me from telling the truth."

He took a step closer. Then another. He was aware of small details—the frayed hem of her sleeve, a tiny burn scar near her wrist from a solder splash last winter. "I'm not protecting you from an answer," he said. "I've been protecting myself from one."

She waited.

"I have loved you for a while," he said, and when the words were out he knew how long he'd been holding them—long enough to lose their edges. "I kept telling myself it wasn't fair to say so. To you. To

Camille. To the work. I kept thinking that love was a fixed thing and I had used mine up. Or that if I reached for anything new it would tear what I was still holding."

Lena's shoulders softened. Not relief. Recognition.

He let out a breath. "And it felt like cheating. Even when you were just... there, brilliant and infuriating and right more often than anyone should be. You'd smile at a graph and it would feel like sunlight after a week of rain. And I would say, Don't. Don't do that. You don't get to have that again. You had it already."

"We don't have rations," she said, a small smile briefly, then gone. "Not for love."

He shook his head, eyes burning now for the first time tonight. "Adrian's confession— It took a weight off and put another on. It means I've been grieving the wrong shape of the truth. It also means... I can stop punishing myself by refusing anything good."

She stepped in and rested her forehead lightly against his. He closed his eyes. The lab blinked once, that stubborn fluorescent, then held steady. For a few breaths there were only simple things: warmth, air, tired hearts finding a shared rhythm.

When they pulled back a fraction, he kept his hands at her elbows, gentle, as if too much pressure might break the moment.

"I'm afraid," he admitted. "Not of this. Of what we still have to do. Of calling Adrian back into the room he poisoned. Of facing Avery. Of the world outside this building. But when I look at it with you, it stops feeling impossible. It just feels... big."

"Big we can do," she said. "Impossible is for people who think they're alone."

He half-laughed—again without humor, but lighter now. "Stay close," he said. "When I start to drift back into that person who thinks control is salvation, pull me by the sleeve."

"I plan on it," she said.

A minute stretched. The quiet around them had changed in flavor—less like a vacuum, more like a pause before the next necessary motion. Down the hallway, a printer "licked awake and printed a single sheet no one had asked for. The lab sometimes did that at night, as if dream-checking inventory.

Elias glanced at the dismantled coils. "When we shut it down," he said, "for real, forever—there won't be any glory. No papers. No press. Just... quiet. Maybe blame. Maybe lawsuits. Probably both."

"Then we aim for quiet," Lena said. "Let Avery chase cameras. We'll chase a closed gate."

He nodded. "We'll break our own machine. The right way. Not with a bar." He gave her a look. "Though for the record, I was two seconds from swinging with you."

She smiled, wider this time. "I know."

He sobered again. "Adrian's going to be in the room. We need him. I hate that we need him. But I'm not going to pretend I can do this without him. Not now."

"Needing someone and forgiving them aren't the same thing," Lena said. "One can happen before the other."

"Will you remind me of that when I forget," he asked.

"I will," she said.

They moved to the whiteboard. Its surface was a ghost of old calculations—half-erased phase plots, safety margins circled and starred, a list of test sites in green marker. Lena slid a fresh marker from the tray and clicked the cap off. Elias smelled the faint chemical bite.

"We need a plan to pause the Array long enough to force a shutdown," she said. "Even without the watchdog, there has to be a way to interrupt latch. Not brute force—parameter choke, timing choke, something the system won't see as attack."

Elias nodded slowly. The part of his mind that had always loved hard problems began to gather itself, but without the old hunger to conquer. "We buy seconds," he said. "Hold it in drift. Then we close the gate electronically from the inside out."

"Which means we need eyes on the gate while it's happening," Lena said. "Abigail, maybe Jacob."

"We'll ask," he said. "And when Adrian arrives, we decide what we risk. Not just the machine—us."

He capped the marker and set it down. Then he looked at her, really looked at her—no lab coats, no titles, no roles to buffer feeling. "Thank you," he said.

"For what?"

"For saying it," he said. "For being here. For being the person I should have seen sooner."

"You saw me," she said. "You just couldn't admit it yet."

He reached for her hand. She gave it. Their fingers fit in the ordinary way hands do, and the ordinary felt exactly right.

"We still have to survive tonight," he said, practical again. "We still have to call Adrian."

"We will," she said. "But not this second." She squeezed his hand once and let go. "Breathe with me."

They stood side by side, looking at the machine they would dismantle and the whiteboard they would fill. She counted them through five slow breaths, then five more. The room held. The lights steadied. Outside, rain ticked softly against the window glass, a sound like a clock that belonged to them again.

Elias lifted his phone, glanced at the screen, and set it facedown without dialing. "In five minutes," he said. "We start."

"In five," Lena agreed.

He turned back to her. "Lena?"

"Yeah?"

"I love you," he said, plain.

Her smile was quiet and complete. "I know."

Resolve settled between them like something they could lean against. When the five minutes were done, they would call. When the call was done, they would work. For now, they stood in the narrow slice of calm they'd made and let it hold.

16

The Flood

Scene 1: A Veilborne Crosses

I smell the breach before I see it—cold metal in snow, a clean, biting edge that always means an opening. We drift toward it through the In Between, past corridors of dark glass and sagging arches, until the thin skin of a puddle near the wetlands turns hard and bright. A machine is working there. Its song pulls on everything: on us, on the walls, on the Keeper himself.

I press my palm to the surface. Water becomes a pane. I push through.

The living world is wet and noisy. Sirens crisscross the hill below the college. People shout; someone drops a box of nails; dogs bark at nothing. The sky hangs low and gray. A pale smear runs across the clouds like a crack in ice—that is the machine's line, bright and wrong. It drinks from the Keeper, and the Keeper bends.

Around me, more of my kind rise from road puddles and metal signs, from dark phone screens and the backs of car mirrors. We spread into the thin places where crossing takes the least effort. Fear thickens the air and makes the living brighter; bright light is easier to take.

Near the swale a man and a woman stand over a frame of three glowing rings. Cables snake from a rack. Gauges climb and refuse to fall. The woman slams a red stop button again and again. The man throws breakers and yanks a lever that should kill the field. Nothing answers. The machine is listening to something that is not them.

Far above and far away, the Keeper lifts his shape. You do not see him the way you see a tower; you feel him the way you feel thunder inside your ribs. He is dimmer than I have known. When he speaks, the word is soft and heavy at once: "Stop."

We used to stop. Not today. Strength matters more than law, and his strength is thinning. Hunger decides.

We begin to feed.

It is simple. Any clean surface will do: a mirror, a kettle, a turned-off screen. Slide your hand through the thin layer and take hold of the bright strand inside a person. Pinch; pull. The filament quivers, gives, and a portion of light comes free. Eat. The person dulls. You steady. Repeat. In the old order we hid while we did this. Today the order is broken. Patrols do not come. The Keeper's rebuke no longer burns. Only scattered pockets of resistance remain—an old priest with a stubborn lantern, a few sheltered alcoves where the lost can hide for an hour.

I see that priest near the reeds, guiding dim shapes to a crack in shadow. His lamp lays a narrow band of gold across the ground. It stings when I draw too near, so I mark his path and leave him for later, when his arm shakes.

The city changes quickly. In apartments and shops people tape paper over bathroom mirrors and drape sheets over televisions. Elevators stop. A woman in a stairwell lifts a compact to peer around a corner, habit stronger than fear; my hand slips through before she understands what she offered. Someone yanks her away and slams the door. Down the block, workers in a hospital turn shiny cabinet fronts toward walls and throw cloth over the rest. They move with steady hands. They will last.

Beneath it all I feel a current moving through us. For years we took what leaked—bedtime fear, hallway grief, a last breath in an empty room. We were scavengers at seams. Today we are hunters in day-light. The Deceiver walked the high beams of the In Between and told us this hour would come: The Keeper is failing. Cross openly. Feed without restraint. No chains remain. We listened. We believed. We act.

I look up. The machine's line brightens. The Keeper's outline frays like smoke pulled thin by wind. He speaks again, smaller: "Cease." We do not. We cannot. A leader among us lifts his head and begins to direct the packs, sending them to the richest panes—storefronts, bus shelters, the glass skin of high-rise towers. Laughter answers him: not human laughter, but the short, pleased sound our bodies make when the hunt runs easy.

But ease carries a shadow. If the Keeper falls, the In Between will warp. The Deceiver says he will rule what remains. He says there will be rank for those who are useful. I want that rank. Many do. Want is different from trust.

By dusk the city is a field of doors. A shaded lamp throws our faces onto a wall; the dark in a phone screen holds our hands like ink holds letters. People learn new rules as they go. Cover glass. Break it if you must. Do not look when a surface breathes. Carry tape. Walk the stairs. Pray if you remember how. They forget other rules. A quiet pool of rain is still a mirror. The chrome strip on a microwave is still a mirror. The black eye of a camera is still a mirror.

We move through it all. My pack passes a church where men hang plain cloth over high windows. The place smells of wax and old wood, and their eyes do not break when they look at us. I am not eager to test that look. We keep going.

On the hill, the man at the rack is gray with fatigue. The woman braces her shoulder against his, shouting for others to run. They rip pieces off their own machine, and it hums on, now self-fed. The pud-dles nearby are all doors; we pass through them like fish through aligned nets, in and out, in and out, pulling light with each pass.

Where we meet the priest's lamp we veer—pain teaches quickly—but we have miles of glass that do not burn.

News cameras catch our shapes and send them everywhere. In a studio a man speaks faster than his heartbeat, trying to hold his voice steady. He is not my meal. Not now. We have larger currents to ride.

The biggest change is inside us. We can feel the Keeper falter. We can feel the Deceiver smile. This is the beginning, his thought-voice says, smooth as a hand on polished stone. Take what you want. The Father is far. The Keeper is tired. Eat. It sounds like permission. It feels like heat in cold bones.

We obey.

Later, when the sirens soften and the first waves of panic fade to an uneven quiet, I slip back toward the wetlands. The machine still sings. The man and woman are arguing now. She lifts a metal bar to smash the frame. He stops her. They don't know if breaking the hardware will shut the door or lock it open. Their fear tastes different from the rest—cleaner, sharper. It smells like choice.

I glance once more toward the college. A boy stands beside the priest and looks straight at the place where the Keeper should be. He does not flinch. I do not go near him. Some lights are not worth touching.

I press my hand to the thin skin of a shallow pool and slide home. Behind me, sirens return and screens glow. Ahead, the In Between waits, restless as a held breath. The Keeper is still upright, but every hour costs him. The Deceiver is pleased. Our packs are full, and our steps are light.

Today was easy. That is the truth under all the noise. We do not trust ease, but we will take it as long as the doors stay open.

Scene 2: After the Sirens

The newsroom had turned into a command center. Maps of Pierce and King Counties glowed on the wall screens, dotted with pins that moved in real time. Live feeds stacked along a monitor bank showed boarded storefronts, police tape fluttering in the rain, firefighters taping plastic over ambulance windows, and a city crew prying a mirror off a bus shelter with crowbars. Phones rang without pause. A printer chattered and spat out scripts that were obsolete by the time they cooled.

Reese Mathers stood in the middle of it like a post in a rushing tide. He'd been live four times already that day. His voice still had grit in it from the last hit near the wetlands. Now he was back at his desk, trimming a package while the station clock counted down to the top of the hour. Producer Erin brushed past and swapped his cold coffee for a fresh one without breaking stride.

"You're a machine," she said, already moving.

"Don't jinx it," Reese said, eyes on waveforms. He tightened a sound bite—sirens cutting across his live shot, a neighbor shouting, "Cover the mirrors!"—then smoothed his own tag. It felt strange to hear respect in the room when he spoke. Strange and overdue.

A hand tapped the frame of his cubicle. "Mathers. Office."

He glanced up. Denise Kincaid—news director, gray blazer, sharp eyes. The glass-walled office at the back of the pit looked out over the screens like a watchtower. He saved, stood, and followed her across the maze of desks.

Inside, Denise swung the door shut and dropped her voice. "Sit."

He did. She stayed standing, one palm flat on a stack of rundowns, studying him as if she were trying to reconcile two photos. One of the reporter she'd called sensational six months ago. One of the man the city was quoting today.

"I owe you an apology," she said finally.

Reese blinked. The words landed like a soft thud.

"I told you to stop chasing 'mirror hysteria,'" Denise continued, mouth tight at the memory. "I told you to cut the ghost language and stick to budget hearings and bread-and-butter crime. I was wrong. You were right. You did the work. You were early. And you kept going when it made you look crazy." She exhaled. "That took spine."

Reese let the silence hold for a beat. The noise of the pit leaked through the glass—someone calling for a photog, a producer counting down to a live shot in Federal Way. He thought of the nights he'd eaten vending machine pretzels at this desk because the only people who would talk to him were the ones everyone else ignored. He thought of the dashcam file sitting on the encrypted drive in his bag—and of the face on it.

"Thank you," he said. His voice wanted to add more. He didn't let it.

Denise planted both hands on the desk. "I want you to head our Veilborne coverage. You'll get a dedicated photog, two associate producers, and first slot whenever you've got something. Longer pieces for the magazine show. We'll build a digital vertical around your reporting. Resources. Time."

The offer should have lifted him. It did, for half a second, like the sensation of stepping onto an escalator. Then the escalator turned into a drop. His father's body doubling over the hood. The black sedan filling the frame. The gloved hand smashing the dashcam lens. No loose ends.

Reese wet his lips. "If I take it, I need something else."

Denise waited.

"I need clearance to pursue a related investigation. Quietly. Not in the daybook. Legal backup when it breaks." He held her gaze. "You know I've been looking into the death of my father."

Her eyes softened, then sharpened again. "I do."

"I have new evidence," he said carefully. "When it's time, it will be explosive. Until then, I need space to build it right."

She watched him for several seconds, long enough for the hum of the lights to become a sound. "If you're asking me to trust your judgment," she said, "you've earned it. Loop me in when you can. And when you can't, make sure you can defend every line you put on air." Her mouth twitched. "I'm done calling you a sensationalist."

A laugh escaped him—short, thin, genuine. "I'll put that on a plaque."

"Don't push it." Her expression softened. "Go. You're live in nine. And, Reese—" She hesitated. "I am sorry."

He nodded once and left before the apology made him unsteady.

Back at his desk, he slipped on his earpiece. Erin pressed a palm-sized IFB into his hand. "We're throwing to you out of the governor. He just expanded the emergency to Snohomish. Drive-time hit in ten, then a package for the six. You good?"

"I'm good," he said, and most of it was true.

His phone buzzed. A text from Natalie Chen: Keeping our powder dry. I've started a chain of custody log for the file. I'll brief you later.

He typed back: Understood.

Another buzz, this one from an unknown number: a tip about "a mirror that breathes in a bakery bathroom." He forwarded it to the assignment desk. Then he opened a photo on his screen and stared at it long enough to make his chest ache. His father at a picnic table, laughing at something out of frame. A magnolia leaf stuck to his shoulder. A plastic fork in his hand.

"Mathers?" Erin's voice in his ear. "You're up in five. Step into the studio."

He stood, tugged his jacket straight, and threaded through the cables to the small stand-up alcove where a camera waited. The studio lights made a bright island in the gray afternoon. A PA clipped a mic to his lapel, then smoothed it without a word. On the prompter, the anchor's script rolled: and joining us now from our newsroom is investigative correspondent Reese Mathers, who has been tracking these incidents for months—

He heard the toss and spoke into the lens. The words came clean, not because he was calm, but because the work was muscle memory now. He laid out the new abduction numbers, the governor's order, the latest guidance from Tacoma Fire on covering reflective surfaces. He nodded as the anchor asked about the ArcLine elevators shutting citywide. He tossed to his package and watched, off camera, as the images filled the studio monitors: a hospital staffer slapping tape over a medication cabinet; a teenager tearing down a mirror in a school locker room while a teacher counted and steadied; a frame of the wetlands where the Array had sung the air thin. His own voice tracked over it. His father's face flashed unbidden across the glass like a double exposure, then was gone.

When they came back, the anchor asked, "Reese, what are you hearing from officials?"

"The same thing I'm hearing from families," he said. "People are scared. They want clarity. And they're starting to understand there may be an engine behind what's happening." He let the sentence hang for the fraction of a second their lawyers would allow. "We're pressing for answers."

"Reese Mathers," the anchor said, "thank you."

The tally light on the camera went dark. Reese exhaled and stepped backward into the hallway's dimmer light. Erin gave him a quick thumbs-up and peeled away. He unclipped his mic, set it down, and leaned against the wall. For a few seconds he let the room be quiet.

"Hey."

Denise stood at his shoulder, softer now that the on-air push had passed. "That was solid. You're leading the city through this." She looked at him a moment longer. "Go take a breath. Then come back and do it again."

He nodded and drifted down to the stairwell. The concrete was cool under his palm. He sat on the second step and put his face in his hands. The building vibrated faintly with HVAC and the hum of the floors below. In the corner of the landing, someone had taped brown paper over the narrow wired-glass window in the door. There was a gap at the top. He stood and smoothed the paper down until it sealed. The motion eased something tight in him.

His phone buzzed again—another text from Natalie. One more thing: I traced a redaction in the file's metadata. Someone tried to bury it years ago. It survived because the auto-backup jumped servers mid-transfer. A crack of luck. Or something else.

He typed, then we make sure luck doesn't have to do the lifting next time.

He was still looking at the screen when a memory arrived so sharply he had to sit again. He was eight, crouched under the dining table with his father's tape recorder in his hands, aiming it at a nest of dust bunnies because he was convinced he could hear them talk. His father had ducked down, touched the microphone, and said, You want truth? Point this at the place that doesn't want it.

Reese stood and went back to his desk. He pulled a legal pad toward him and drew two columns. On the left: Veil Crisis. On the right: Avery. Under the first he wrote hospitals, schools, transit, fire guidance, priest with lantern. Under the second he wrote dashcam chain, alley camera, burner call, witness at service corridor, Natalie link. The fear that had been a smear in his chest began to take on edges.

Erin slid a note onto his keyboard. Governor at six. Want you live with reaction from families—can we pull the shelter group you interviewed last week?

He wrote back, Yes. Call Mrs. Peña first.

He shouldered his bag and paused long enough to slide the encrypted drive into the inner pocket. He'd kept it there for days now, close to his heart not because it was dramatic but because it made him less likely to leave it on a desk where a curious hand could find it. He thought of Avery's voice on the audio, smooth in rain: No loose ends. He thought of how men with power like that wrote their own weather systems and expected the rest of the world to carry umbrellas for them.

Not this time.

Reese took another breath and let it out slow. Credibility was a door, and today it had swung open. He could feel the air moving through it. The city finally believed him about the Veilborne. Now he would make them believe him about a different kind of predator.

He headed for the edit bay to polish the next piece. On the way, he stopped at a supply cabinet and grabbed two rolls of brown paper and a duct tape—one for Erin, one for the janitor whose hands were already raw from sealing glass. He tucked them under his arm and kept walking.

At his desk, he set the tape down and opened a new document. Headline: A Pattern of Silence. Subhead: What officials knew—and when. He wrote the first sentence, then deleted it, then wrote another. The words came easier the second time.

When the clock hit five-thirty, he stood again. Live at six. Then another package at nine. Then calls to a retired security guard, a hospital intake nurse, and the owner of the building off Commerce where the alley camera might still have a ghost of a feed. He texted Natalie: After my nine, can you talk? Her reply was instant: Yes.

Reese slid the photo of his father back behind the monitor's edge so it watched without accusing. He smoothed the brown paper covering the small safety mirror on the column near his desk. He checked his earpiece. He glanced at the legal pad, at the two columns that would soon become one story.

"Mathers!" Erin called. "You're up."

"I'm coming," he said, and this time the words felt like the start of something he'd been walking toward for years.

Scene 3: Two Lines of Fire

They took the smallest conference room in the back of the station, the one with a scarred oval table and a single window they'd already covered in brown paper. Someone had taped kraft over the chrome strip along the whiteboard frame and draped gaffer's tape across the blinking glass of the speakerphone. A roll of duct tape sat next to a box of stale doughnuts like a new office supply.

Natalie set her laptop down and slid an encrypted drive from her pocket, the same one she'd used when she found the dashcam clip. Reese dropped a legal pad, two pens, and a manila folder stuffed with printed emails. Night pressed against the papered window; the newsroom hum came through the door, a soft, steady current.

"Phones off," she said.

He nodded, powered his down, and set it face-down on the table. She did the same. They knew better than to leave themselves exposed allowing the blank screens to reflect back at them.

"Okay," Natalie said, drawing a line down Reese's legal pad and titling the columns with neat block letters. "Track A: Proof Avery forced dangerous deployments. Track B: Proof he killed your father and buried it."

Reese exhaled through his nose. "Two lines of fire."

"Two lines of protection," she said, meeting his eyes. "If he swats at one, the other keeps moving."

He nodded and wrote the headers again in his messy hand, as if copying them into himself. She plugged in the drive and opened a timeline she'd been building. Color bars scrolled down the screen: blue for Array deployments, red for spikes in abductions, gray for media pushes, green for Avery's travel and calls.

"Start with A." Natalie enlarged three dates, each with a pin. "Clover Park, Foxtrot Marsh, the utility swale behind the wetlands. We match the Array's setups to Avery's communications. See these?" She tapped three calendar invites from Avery's DOE account—"check-ins" that coincided with nights the Array went live. "He labels them 'program status' and 'stakeholder prep.' Looks routine. But the call logs show five-minute calls right before each switch-on." She clicked a tab; a simple list appeared: timestamps, cell IDs, durations.

Reese leaned in. "To Elias?"

"To a set of rotating numbers that never repeat," she said. "Burners. But the tower hits put him a mile from the sites, engine idling, the way he likes to be close without being on the record."

Reese felt his jaw tighten. "He wanted to watch."

"He wanted control," she said. "We need more than inference, though. Paper that shows pressure." Natalie pulled a thin stack from her bag—internal memos and draft talking points. Avery's notes bled through in tight handwriting: increase throughput; steer narrative; optics over objections. "These aren't smoking guns," she said. "But they're fingertips on the trigger."

Reese flipped a page. One margin note read, Voss too cautious. Stress national security frame. He looked up. "How do we make this stand up? A jury won't convict on adjectives."

"We don't try to convict yet," Natalie said. "We build a wall. On this side, what he knew and when. On the other, what he demanded and when. Then we drop sworn statements in between." She held up fingers as she counted. "Lena, if she'll do it. An intern or two. Abigail, if she'll sign something about the timing—when she told Elias the machine was weakening the Echo, when Avery still pushed."

Reese wrote names down the margin. "And Elias."

Natalie paused. "If we can get him to tell the truth on the record, yes."

"That's a lot of 'ifs.'"

"We make them smaller." She pointed to the board. "Evidence wish list: gate logs at the wetland access road; hotel key swipes; parking passes; the station that fueled Avery's sedan; purchase records for

SIMs that pinged those towers. We FOIA the benign stuff. For the rest, we use sources."

"Do you have sources for DOE internal?" he asked.

She tilted her head. "A few who still believe public means public. I'll ask for documents by category so no one sees the whole ask." She took a breath. "If he gets wind of it, he'll move fast. We have to move faster."

"Track B," Reese said, voice lower.

Natalie closed Track A and opened a still from the dashcam: the alley, the rain, the black sedan angling. She let it play five seconds; his father's face swung into view as he stepped toward his car. The impact. Body doubling over the hood. The blunt, unbelieving shock on his features—the last clear thing before the lens went to static.

Reese stared but did not reach for it. He had learned, these last weeks, to watch without breaking on every frame.

"We have the file and metadata," Natalie said gently. "It shows someone tried to bury it. We need to wrap it in steel: chain of custody, secondary corroboration, context."

"Who else was there?" Reese asked. "The alley camera?"

"I'm working it," she said. "A city contractor serviced that camera two days after the incident. The maintenance ticket says 'water incursion.' I want the raw pull from the server, not the edited copy." She ticked another item. "We need the building's loading dock logs. A security guard remembers a black government car parked in the service bay that night. He retired last year. I'll find him." A third finger. "Emergency room intake that received your father. We don't need medical details, just timestamps. The lag between impact and any official call."

Reese nodded, writing. "Body shop records for front-end work on a government sedan. Gas station CCTV on Avery's route. Cell tower pings for his phone and the burner. Highway cameras if he left the city."

"And the voice," she said. On the screen, a transcript of the dash-cam's audio flashed: *…taken care of. No loose ends.* "We get a voice print analysis. Not for court yet—for us. If it's as clean as I think, we hold it until we can't be ignored."

Reese didn't realize he'd braced his hands on the table until his palms hurt. He sat back and made himself breathe.

"How do we not get killed doing this?" he said, half a joke, not a joke at all.

"By being boring and relentless," Natalie answered. "We meet here, in rooms with taped glass. We use drives like this," she tapped the encrypted stick, "not cloud shares. We send nothing on work email. We print hard copies and store them offsite with timestamps in a neutral safe—your lawyer's, my friend's firm in Bellevue. We tell Denise the outlines, not the pieces. And we build a dead man's switch."

He raised an eyebrow.

"A simple script," she said. "If we miss a daily check-in, it releases a package: the dashcam file, the metadata, a letter to the state AG and three national outlets. It buys us protection because he can't risk silencing us if silence detonates the story."

Reese almost smiled. "You've done this before."

"I've worked around men like him," she said. "They count on people being sloppy or scared. We'll be neither."

He looked at her, really looked—at the threadbare cuff of her blazer, at the careful checkboxes she'd already drawn in the margin. "Why are you doing this?" he asked. "You owe me nothing. He's your boss."

"Because I can read what men like him think of families like mine," she said without heat. "Because my parents left Taiwan with two suitcases and a phrase book and believed if they were good and kept their heads down, those above them would at least follow the rules. Because some don't. And when they don't, someone has to make them."

Reese nodded once, throat tight. "Then let's make him."

They worked the list down to details. For Track A, Reese would reach out to Lena and the interns for sworn statements—off camera for now, notarized, time-stamped. He'd request gate logs and parking records through public records. Natalie would pull Avery's calendar invites into a clean timeline and cross-match tower hits from the burners she'd already flagged. She'd also contact a friendly staffer in Facilities for keycard entries at the secure DOE annex, the nights Avery left the building and how long he was gone.

For Track B, Reese would drive to the building off Commerce that night and try to charm a copy of any archived alley footage from the bored overnight manager. He would visit the body shop on 54th that handled municipal accounts and ask for old invoices. He would call the retired guard Natalie had located in Spanaway and show up with coffee and a recorder. Natalie would deliver the dashcam to a voice analyst she trusted and put a call into a small law firm that had handled whistleblower cases without grandstanding. If they liked her facts, they'd keep the envelope.

"And Denise?" Reese asked. "How much do we tell her?"

"The plan, not the pieces," Natalie said. "She can't protect what she doesn't know exists."

They both stood at the same time, as if the plan had given their legs permission. Natalie unplugged the drive, slid it back into her pocket, and gathered the memos into a stack she wrapped with a rubber band.

Reese tore the legal-page column down the perforation and tucked it into his folder. He glanced at the covered window. The brown paper had bubbled slightly with the building's heat, a puffed seam like a held breath.

"Tomorrow," he said. "I start with Lena. If she's willing to sign a sworn statement about Avery's pressure, it changes the math."

"She's brave," Natalie said. "She'll do it if she thinks it saves lives."

He nodded. "And I'll go to the body shop after the six o'clock hit. Then Spanaway." He paused. "Natalie—if he comes at you hard—"

"I've been poor and invisible," she said. "I can do it again." Then she softened. "But I'd rather win."

A quick rap came on the door; Erin poked her head in. "Reese, live from the shelter in twenty. They have a family willing to talk if we bring blankets."

"I'll swing by supply," he said. Erin vanished.

They packed without fuss. Natalie taped a small envelope under the table—a thumb drive labeled with a number and nothing else. Reese watched her do it and felt a knot in his chest loosen one notch.

"Dead man's switch goes live tonight," she said. "We check in at midnight. If one of us misses it, the package moves."

"Midnight," he echoed.

They paused at the door. Somewhere in the building, a TV carried the governor's voice into a hallway and turned it thin. Sirens passed outside and then faded. The paper over the window rustled as the heater kicked on.

"We'll do it carefully," Natalie said. "And we'll do it right."

Reese opened the door and held it for her. "Two lines of fire," he said.

"Two lines of protection," she corrected, and stepped into the newsroom glow.

Scene 4: A Commander in the Dark

The In Between steadied, as if the whole realm took one long breath. Shapes collected along the ribs of a ruined nave and the lips of black canals, eyes bright, claws tucked. Waiting. Listening.

Abaddon stepped out of the murk and did not hurry.

He was not the vastness that bent the horizon (that one was bowed and straining), and he was not the polished smile that slipped between chambers (that one never dirtied his hands). Abaddon was a hunter shaped into intent: taller than most, shoulders set, a pale seam running from jaw to collar where older power had once burned him and failed to kill. He moved like a blade found in a river—dark, honed by current, edges quiet.

He lifted one hand. The packs stilled.

They were the Hollowed—Veilborne who had shed almost everything that once made them specific. No names, no memories, just appetite and reflex. Other spirits haunted, watched, or lingered; the Hollowed hunted. They traveled in ranks, answered to strength, and learned fast. Hollowed because nothing human echoed inside them anymore. Hollowed because they had carved out the center and filled it with hunger.

"Line," Abaddon said, the word traveling without echo. It was a command more than a sound.

They arranged themselves as he preferred: three ranks, each packleader forward, lesser hunters tucked behind, all eyes on him. Hunger chattered low in their throats, a thousand knives tapping their sheaths. Abaddon raised his other hand. Silence tightened.

"Stop drifting," he told them. "Stop snatching. We hunt as one."

Impatience quivered along the line. He let it. Desire sharpened obedience.

With a hooked claw he drew a curve in the air that mirrored the arc around the hill above Clover Park. "You know this line," he said. "The skin is thinnest here. It has widened. Tonight we press, not in scratches, but in cuts."

Behind him, a free-standing sheet of glass sagged like a curtain—no frame, no room to reflect. The surface fumed, then cleared. On the other side lay a loading dock's high windows, a firehouse's bay doors, the lobby of an apartment tower paneled floor-to-ceiling in mirrors. The Hollow leaned forward, necks cupped by hunger.

Abaddon tapped the glass once. "Lures. Make the doors call. Make the screens brighten. Draw those who still look." He tapped twice. "Hold until all are in place." Three taps. "Surge."

Heat shimmered to their right. The Deceiver came on a wind that wasn't wind, handsome as a promise. Even the Hollowed pulled back a fraction out of instinct. He smiled, and the room remembered when smiles were always safe.

"Show me," the Deceiver said, voice laid with silk.

Abaddon bowed his head—deference without submission. "You asked for a field. I give you one."

He gestured. The glass became a map of moves.

In the firehouse bay, engine windows clouded from the inside. Frost wrote letters across tempered glass, then smeared them away. The lieutenant hit the opener; the rolling doors rose and stuck halfway. In that mechanical stutter four Hollowed slid out of side mirrors and chrome bumpers, bodies tightening around bone as they found air. They did not feed yet. They raked claws along polished steel in three even strokes and waited.

Across town, a shelter's bathroom mirror went black. A small boy turned his head to listen; someone called him away; he stepped back just as a hand pressed the other side, smearing a print that wasn't a hand. Two more Hollowed nested in the paper towel dispenser's steel, patient as ticks.

In an ICU, night nurses taped butcher paper across a window. The tape wrinkled as if breathing. A heart monitor's bezel threw back a perfect green reflection; three thin figures curled beneath it like shadows in a desk lamp's shade, waiting for the hall to clear.

Abaddon watched without hurry. Scattered abductions had been wasteful—noise without gain. Coordinated strikes would thin everything at once. He traced routes on the glass with a slow claw: here, then here, then here. He didn't say the places' names. He spoke their properties—bright, unguarded, soft. The Hollowed understood and shivered with approval.

The Deceiver's smile deepened. "At last," he murmured, "a spine in this hunger."

Abaddon kept his eyes on the work. "The keeper sags," he said. "Balance sleeps. We do not."

"And you lead," the Deceiver said. "As I asked."

A thin warmth traced Abaddon's old seam. He did not look down. Praise should land on the map. "We strike in crescents," he said. "Arcs that overlap. When men run from one mirror to another, they find us both."

He lifted his head. The Hollowed leaned toward him as if a scent had arrived.

"First wave."

In the firehouse, the doors stuck open like half-formed mouths. Alarms barked without purpose. The four Hollowed that had waited in the chrome came out thin and fast, drew a man by his reflection on the command console, and began to pull. Another team spread across the bay doors and pressed faces to the glass, making fog that did not disappear.

Second wave.

An apartment tower blinked in sequence as microwave doors popped under a hundred wet fingers. An elevator panel reflected a woman's face and bent it until her mouth was a dark door; when she leaned close, hands cupped her cheeks from the other side and drew her gently forward. In a church vestibule, a baptismal font trembled and showed a ceiling that wasn't there. The priest steadied it, saw a lantern burning far away, then nothing, as the room tilted.

Third wave.

Along the arc of Clover Park's hill, sheets people had taped over mirrors bubbled under pressure and let go. Windows flexed. Cellphone screens brightened at once and showed rooms no one remembered standing in. A bus mirror fogged; the driver wiped it with his sleeve and saw, in the oval, the back of his own head, the line of his neck a road.

The Hollowed did not howl. Abaddon did not allow it. This was not sport. It was clean work. They fed with mouths closed, bodies low, no waste. Those who captured one of the lost passed the next forward without pause. Those who thinned a room slipped one chamber over before resistance could gather. Those who saw a lantern glow in any shard flared out and away rather than lose two to the sting of memory.

"Good," the Deceiver said, watching like a man who already knew the ending he paid for. "Better than your first flurry at the wetland. You learn."

"We were drunk then," Abaddon said. "Now we are thirsty."

He showed how he had placed cutters to go after help—how two Hollowed slid through a dispatch center's wall monitor and turned the operator's screen into a trap; how three more pressed into the chrome lip of a patrol car's spotlight and waited for a hand to steady it; how one lay flat beneath a bridge puddle that looked like only rain, feeling for the vibration of boots. He outlined timing that would force public fear into private rooms: a cluster at the dome, a whisper through the clinic, a wink in the hardware aisle where people came to buy paint to cover mirrors and learned how many mirrors they had never noticed.

The Deceiver touched Abaddon's shoulder, fingers cool. "Field commander," he said, tasting the phrase. "Wear it."

Something like heat settled in Abaddon's seam—acknowledgment, not blessing. He bowed a fraction. "I wear the work," he said. "Keep the title if it pleases you."

Approval rippled through the Hollowed—soft, quick, like coins warmed in a palm. He lifted a wrist and cut it off before it became noise.

"Do not crowd the lantern-bearer," he warned. "He costs more than he feeds. If you see the boy, do not touch. Not yet."

A hiss traveled the line at the mention of the boy. Some raised their heads in dislike. Others lowered theirs in wary respect.

"Why spare them?" the Deceiver asked, mild curiosity over old malice.

"Because the keeper loves them," Abaddon said. "And because to pull too soon is to wake strength we do not need to test tonight."

The Deceiver's eyes brightened, black fire stirred by a draft. "Caution. From you."

"Strategy," Abaddon said. He raised his hand. "Fourth wave."

It moved like tide: ambulances jerking to a halt with windshields gone opaque; a bail-bond lobby flowering white from the center outward; a drive-thru screen flashing *ORDER READY* until the words became a door if stared at too long. People ran. Some were pulled. Some fought and won seconds. Some prayed, and sometimes that mattered.

Abaddon watched for the turn—the moment gluttony becomes sloppiness. When it came (a pack laughing with their shoulders, too pleased with the shine on their claws), he stepped to the glass and let his seam flare. The nearest Hollowed recoiled, chastened. Two fingers lifted. Focus returned.

"Hold the arc for an hour," he said. "Then we slip. We do not invite armies. We invite panic."

The packs shifted with pleasure. Orders felt good. Orders felt like a wall to push off from.

The Deceiver turned away, satisfied, and slid into a corridor that led where Abaddon could not see. The glass rippled and lay flat.

Abaddon stood among his ranks and listened to the other side answer: sirens in some shards, prayers in others, and in many only the ragged breathing of rooms where every mirror had been covered and people were learning how much glass a life contains. He raised his hand once more. The strikes tightened.

For the first time since the veil went thin, the Hollowed did not feel like scavengers chasing crumbs. They felt like a knife laid neatly across a throat.

17

The Keeper's Whisper

Scene 1: The Message and the Crossing

The news had stopped pretending to be calm.

On the television, a quilt of live shots filled the screen—sirens, plywood slapped over storefronts, families taping garbage bags across bathroom mirrors. The crawl at the bottom never ended: *GOVERNOR EXPANDS EMERGENCY ORDER; COVER ALL REFLECTIVE SURFACES; AVOID ELEVATORS.* The anchor's voice hopped from Tacoma to Lakewood to Kitsap, the map coloring outward like a bruise.

Abigail leaned forward on the couch, elbows on her knees. Samuel stood behind her with the remote in a tight fist, flipping channels as if a different angle might soften the edges. Every feed looked the same: glass fogging from the inside, a smear of smoke, a scream, then static.

Footsteps sounded on the stairs. Jacob came down two at a time, hair rumpled, a spiral notebook tucked under his arm. He paused by the television long enough to understand that today was worse than yesterday.

"Turn it down," he said gently.

Samuel clicked the volume lower. "Everything okay?" His voice had the gravel of a man who hadn't slept much and wasn't planning to.

328

Jacob nodded once, then looked to Abigail. "Father Allen sent a message," he said. "Through Russell. He came by earlier."

Abigail turned, alert. "Russell Langston?"

Jacob swallowed. "He told me to tell you right away. The Echo is faltering. Something else is taking charge in the In Between. A... new will. The Deceiver."

The room seemed to contract. On the television, a field reporter spoke beside a bus shelter as firefighters taped butcher paper across the glass. Behind her, the pane turned milky, as if it was frosting from the inside.

Abigail stood. "Say that again."

"Father Allen heard it," Jacob said. "The Echo is weak. And there's a Veilborne that isn't like the scavengers. He's stepping up to lead. They call him Abaddon. He answers to the Deceiver."

Samuel's jaw worked. He looked from Jacob to Abigail, the way a man checks both lanes before stepping into the street. "What does that even mean for us?"

"It means the rules are changing," Abigail said. "If the veil breaks, the one behind Abaddon won't just send hunters. He will come himself."

Jacob met her eyes. Fear showed, but it was disciplined. "We need to go to the In Between."

Samuel moved around the couch to face them. He was Abigail's equal in height, heavier at the shoulders, a man built more for stubbornness than speed. "Absolutely not." He pointed the remote at the screen like it could make a case for him. A split window showed Tacoma General boarding its atrium windows, a church draping its sanctuary mirrors, a traffic cam catching a driver abandoning a car in the middle of the road when the rearview went dark. "You want to step into that?"

Abigail didn't flinch. "We won't wander. We'll go to Allen."

Samuel looked at her for a long breath, then at his grandson. Love and fear pulled at his mouth in opposite directions. He lowered the remote. "Then don't waste time," he said, and the permission cost him.

Abigail led Jacob down the hall to the small bathroom. The mirror over the sink was already taped in an X from an earlier precaution. She peeled it back and set the tape aside. Her hands were steady, though Jacob heard the thin tremor in her breath.

"Same as before," she told him. "Don't run. Don't bargain. If you see 'exits' that look easier than the path I choose, they aren't for us. Stay with my light."

"Will Father Allen be there?" Jacob asked.

"If Russell reached you, Allen's still holding a line."

Abigail took the old silver hand mirror from its linen pouch. The glass was clouded from age. She breathed across its face and frost bloomed in branching veins. Under her breath she spoke the few words she always used—half prayer, half command. The frost widened; the bathroom's light seemed to lean toward it.

"Ready?" she asked.

Jacob nodded. "Ready."

They pressed their fingertips to the silver and stepped forward. The hand mirror took them, and the house fell away.

The In Between received them with its practiced hush. Not silence—an attentive quiet, like a building holding its breath. Corridors of black glass stretched in thoughtful angles. Some panels shone like oil; others were dull and porous, like cooled ash. A wind without source carried a faint mineral smell, rain on stone. Far overhead, a ceiling that wasn't a ceiling reflected a drift of wrong stars.

Abigail let the hand mirror fall against its cord at her wrist. Its dull glow painted a small coin of light on the floor. "This way," she said, choosing a corridor with a shallow curve. Her steps made no sound. Jacob followed close, staying in the draft of her light.

Here and there, the glass flashed with borrowed scenes from the living world—an empty bus aisle, an office at midnight, a school hallway after hours. Each image seemed thinner than last week, as if stretched tight to keep from tearing.

They took a narrow passage with faint whorls pressed into the surface like fingerprints in tar. Abigail had learned to trust the grain: not a perfect map, but most lines tugged toward will and company. Today, every line drew toward the same gravity.

Lantern light appeared ahead—a steady circle of warm gold. Father Allen stepped from a cleft, iron cage in both hands. He looked a little older here, as he always did. The lines at his mouth were deeper; the light made his eyes look tired and steady.

"Thank God," he said. "You came quickly."

"We heard from Russell," Abigail said.

"Good." Allen listened to the corridor past them, as if waiting for footsteps that hadn't decided whether to be heard. "Then I won't soften this. The Echo is spent. Not gone—don't say that—but spent. What strength remains, it's rationing. And where there is absence, something fills it."

"Abaddon," Jacob said.

Allen nodded to him. "A Veilborne teaching others to move like packs instead of scavengers. He's patient. He's learning command the way winter learns a town—one pipe at a time. And he answers when called."

Abigail's voice tightened. "By whom."

"The Deceiver," Allen said. He lifted the lantern a little; the light narrowed, bracing. "A will that refuses limits. I think you've felt its edge before—how wrong ease can feel when it's an invitation."

Jacob looked at the walls. Far down the corridor a smudge of movement passed behind a pane, like breath across glass. "If the Echo fails—"

"If it fails," Allen said, "what we called law here gets rewritten. The veil won't be a skin; it'll be a door left open. The living won't be hunted one at a time. They'll be processed."

Samuel's face flashed through Abigail's mind. Reese on television. Elias bent over a console. Avery's practiced smile. She pushed the thoughts aside. "What can we do right now?"

Allen looked to Jacob when he answered. "Say no when you're asked to consent."

"That's it?" Jacob asked, somewhere between frustrated and relieved.

"For now," Allen said. "Many small refusals make a wall. And warn those who can stand near the seams without being taken. Your scientist. The reporter. The ones who chose to see. Make sure they understand they're not tugging on a harmless fabric. They're touching a body."

"We're trying," Abigail said. "The Array—"

"I felt where it bit deepest today," Allen said quietly.

A tremor rolled under their feet, like an elevator starting a few floors away. Allen lifted the lantern; the nearest wall offered a vague reflection—three faces and a light, wavered by distance. Beyond that, shapes paused, then moved on when the lantern held.

"Abaddon is recruiting rogues and hungry ones," Allen said. "He's teaching them to wait near sameness—elevators, mirror banks, places where people see themselves without thinking."

Jacob absorbed this. "You sent Russell to me."

"I did," Allen said. "He can run the short crossings without the lantern. He complains the whole way, but he runs." A brief smile—gone as quickly as it arrived. "I cannot spare him forever."

"We'll carry messages when we can," Abigail said.

"Good." Allen studied both of them like a medic checking pupils. Satisfied, he turned toward a darker branch. "Stay close until we reach a safer cleft. Abaddon has lieutenants now. They watch the corridors I used to trust."

They moved together. The lantern pushed back a small circle of dark. On the left, a run of panels crowded with scenes from the living side: a locker room's mirror wall, a darkened office window, a classroom filled with thirty phones face-up on desks, each one a slim mirror. Abigail fought the useless urge to smash every surface in reach.

"Do you hear that?" Jacob whispered.

A low sound rolled and thinned, like distant voices trying to agree. It wasn't speech, exactly. It was the sound of many throats preparing. Abigail's skin prickled.

"Gathering," Allen said. "Don't give it fear. Give it caution."

At a bend, the corridor split. Allen angled toward the tighter passage. "This way—"

Abigail turned to draw Jacob closer, a hand already rising to his sleeve the way she always did when the path narrowed.

He wasn't there.

"Jacob?" She pivoted, quick, lifting the hand mirror to throw more light. The main corridor behind her lay empty for thirty yards—only black glass and the thin echo of their own steps fading. She listened hard for a scuff or a breath.

"Jacob!" The name went too far and came back thin.

Allen swung the lantern to sweep both branches, then the way they had come. A crease set in his brow, but his voice stayed even. "He was right behind you."

"I turned for a second," Abigail said, angry at herself for the waste of it. "Only a second."

"Then he's close," Allen said. "They take the ones who run. He did not run."

Abigail pulled her breath into order. Panic was bait here—she'd taught that to others; now she obeyed it. She took three steady breaths. "Jacob," she called again, quieter, like the name itself might mark a path.

Somewhere down the main passage, a light tap answered—two knuckles on glass. Once. Twice.

Abigail lifted the mirror and the light with it. "Hold," she told Allen, and took a step toward the sound.

The tap did not repeat. The corridor offered nothing back but their own small reflections and the weight of dark beyond.

"Jacob," she said, softer than a whisper.

Nothing.

She looked to Allen. In his eyes she saw worry edged with confidence—the steady look he used to hold lines when everything wanted to give.

"He's close," Allen said again, more for her spine than her ears. "We will find him."

Abigail nodded once, set her jaw, and turned toward the empty corridor where, a heartbeat ago, Samuel's grandson had been.

When she looked back to orient herself, there was no need.

Jacob was gone.

Scene 2: The Long Walk

Jacob stood still until the last trace of Abigail's light faded from the corner where she'd turned. He could have called out; the impulse rose and passed. The In Between did not reward shouting. It rewarded attention.

He took a breath the way Father Allen had taught him—slow, through the nose, all the way down—then another, and opened his eyes wider to the dark. The corridor around him held the careful quiet of a museum after hours: black glass panels cut at deliberate angles, seams like inked joints, a floor that reflected without quite giving anything back. Far above, a ceiling that was not a ceiling loomed with a disorder of dim shards, a broken constellation. The place felt thinner than the last time, as if the air itself had been stretched.

He chose the left-hand path, not from panic, not at random, but because a soft pull there tugged at his ribs. It wasn't exactly a direction; it was a tone in his bones, a note that said here.

As he walked, scenes from the living side drifted in the panels—an elevator bay like a line of black mouths; a kitchen window at night with a hallway light on behind it; a bar's bottle wall turned into a low-grade mirror. People moved at the other side of the glass, faces tight, hands covering reflections as if modesty could stop a hand from coming through. He watched long enough to place himself in the map of fear, then kept going. He had been sent for a reason, he told himself. Find Father Allen's line. Find the will at the center of this.

The first group of souls found him at a bend. They were gathered on a wide, shallow step where the floor sloped down toward darker corridors. A woman in her fifties held a boy of eight to her side; a tall man stared at his own translucent palms like instructions he couldn't follow. Their edges fuzzed and sharpened in cycles, as if a breeze he couldn't feel moved through them.

When they saw Jacob, they rose. The boy whispered something without sound. The man straightened and asked with his eyes.

"This way," Jacob said quietly, pointing back the way he'd come. "You'll see a warm light, like a small sun. A priest carrying a lantern. Stay in that glow. He'll lead you to a recess with walls."

They didn't move.

"It's safe," Jacob added, and laid his hand over his heart. "He's my friend."

Recognition lit the woman's face. "The Chosen," she mouthed. The word moved like a ripple through the group. The boy repeated it, awed, and reached for Jacob's sleeve; his fingers passed just through the fabric and left a prickling chill.

Jacob fought the reflex to shake his head. He had heard that name before—from Mara, from a Veilborne who'd recoiled, from the Echo itself in a voice like stone rolling. He didn't want the title; he wanted the job done.

"Go," he said gently. "Help each other. Keep your eyes on the light, not the glass." He pointed again. That simple gesture seemed to carry weight here. The tall man nodded, gathered the rest with a shepherd's motion, and they moved, drifting up the slope like fog that had decided to climb.

Noise rose from the right—metal dragged across tile, then layered whispers like a crowd agreeing to be cruel. Jacob turned the corner and found a basin where three corridors emptied into one wide space. A pack of Hollowed—the rogues—had cornered a clutch of phantoms and were feeding in a practiced spiral. The Hollowed were all bone and smoke, not much meat, their eyes bright with the wrong kind of life. Talons plunged into chests and drew out thin threads of light that hummed with static and grief; the threads snapped a little as they were pulled tight, then went slack as they were devoured.

Jacob did not announce himself. He walked in until the nearest Hollowed felt him and looked up. The first reaction was the one he expected: bristle, a hitch of the shoulders, claws angling to strike. They started in a lunge that said habit more than thought. Then they stopped, each in the same two-beat freeze, like a line of dogs reined short. Their jaws closed. Their heads dipped, not all the way, not yet, but enough to read as respect.

He raised his hand In acknowledgment—palm out, fingers open, neither threat nor blessing. "You know me," he said.

The nearest Hollowed tilted its head. Smoke curled from its joints like breath on a winter morning. The light in its eyes flickered, a little less feral.

"Do not be deceived by the handsome one," Jacob said, and the way the words sat in the air told him they belonged here. "Obedience to Abaddon is treachery to your keeper. If you can still remember the Echo's law, remember it now. Balance or nothing."

The pack leader's shoulders shivered with an unreadable motion. Around the basin, two more Hollowed had stalked closer. They slowed when they met Jacob's gaze. One made a sound like coins falling down a metal chute—derision or amusement, he couldn't tell. Then the leader stepped back. The others followed, not fleeing, but scattering along the room's edges, like a crowd making space when someone official walks through.

Jacob turned slightly toward the huddled phantoms. "Follow the warm light," he told them gently. "A priest's lantern. Go. Now." One by one they broke and drifted toward the upper corridor, clinging to each other's elbows and shoulders like people crossing ice.

He didn't wait to see the Hollowed change their minds. He kept moving, choosing paths that felt pulled taut toward a center. The sense of being drawn grew stronger—under his tongue, behind his sternum, the way a bass note sits in the chest. He passed more groups of the lost, always the same instructions: Find the lantern. Stay in its circle. Don't look back.

"The Chosen," two elderly men mouthed in unison as he pointed them on. A teenager with half a haircut looked at him as though he'd stepped out of a story someone had told her when she was seven. A mother holding a light-smudged infant pressed her cheek to the child's head and mouthed thank you. He nodded, never lingering. The pull was stronger now, a hand at his collarbone.

The corridors widened. The ceiling lowered and lifted in slow breaths. On his left, a run of black panes showed a hospital corridor, a grocery freezer door, a gym's mirrored wall—so many surfaces that could become doors. He kept walking and did not look into them long; you could lose time staring back at yourself.

A new pack of Hollowed swept out from a side passage with a speed that spoke of confidence. They came low, like wolves, tendons standing out in their forearms, jaws unhinged to show knives. Jacob did not step aside. He planted his feet on the line where the corridor floor changed from glossy to dull, lifted his chin, and raised his hand again, palm forward.

The lead Hollowed crashed to a halt so suddenly the ones behind it jostled. Claws scraped glass. The lead creature's gaze met Jacob's and held. Something like calculation passed over its face. It glanced once over its shoulder—as if to make sure no superior watched—then angled its body to give him space. The others mirrored it, stepping back, bowing their heads enough to admit that they recognized something in him, or at least could not deny it.

"Do not throw away what you are," Jacob said quietly. "The Echo kept you out of chaos. Help it, or this place will eat you too."

They did not answer. One hissed softly, not at him, at its pack mates, a warning not to test whatever line they'd just discovered. Jacob inclined his head in acknowledgment, then walked through the lane they gave him. He did not hurry. He did not gloat. When he passed the last of them, he heard their claws tick again as they moved off to hunt elsewhere.

The pull under his ribs became a cord. He followed it through a cleft that opened into a long terrace of black glass. From here the In Between fell away in layered planes—naves, basins, corridors—like a city built without regard for gravity. The place trembled faintly, the way a bridge trembles when heavy trucks cross.

He stepped to the terrace edge and looked out.

The Echo stood far off, so large it broke the mind's habit of counting. It was not a giant person; it was shape and force, a silhouette made of layered shadow and the ghost of radiance, as if someone had draped the memory of light across a mountain. It was bowed—not kneeling, not kneeling to anyone, but bowed like a tree in hard weather. Around it, the plain changed the way grass changes under wind: leaning, then lifting again. No voice reached Jacob; no proclamation. Only a weight, a pressure of attention that arrived without sound.

He felt it notice him. Not a look—the Echo did not have a face the way men did—but an awareness that touched him and did not pass. He closed his eyes and let that awareness settle. It was tired. It was watchful. It was still itself.

Below, packs of Hollowed poured toward one another's calls, their movements more coordinated than before. Here and there among them, larger shapes moved with purpose—Abaddon's influence, he guessed, drawing lines where there had been only hunger. The mirror-sky above flickered with borrowed scenes from the living world—offices, buses, bathrooms—more of them than an hour ago. The boundary was loosening.

Jacob opened his eyes. The cord in his chest eased—not gone, just less urgent, like a singer who had found the right note and held it. He stood with his hand on the terrace rail that wasn't a rail and weighed his options. He could go to the Echo. Part of him wanted to. But the thought came with a warning he could not name. Not yet. He was meant to see, to be seen, to carry this back.

He lifted his hand to the far silhouette and made a simple sign—not a salute, not a bow. A promise. He would return with whatever strength the other side could spare.

Behind him, a soft scuff sounded on the terrace stones. A small figure—a soul—had followed his light and now waited, eyes wide, for instruction.

"Back to the lantern," Jacob told it gently, pointing. "Find the priest. Tell him the keeper is bowed, not broken."

The figure nodded and drifted away.

Jacob looked once more across the dark plain. The Echo held its ground against a storm that had learned to grin. He turned from the terrace and began the walk back, the corridors making way for him as if they, too, remembered what balance felt like and wanted it again.

Scene 3: The Search

Abigail moved fast, one hand out, the other tight around the strap of her satchel. Father Allen's lantern threw an amber circle that crawled over black glass and broken arches, and every time the light slipped off a seam she fought the urge to run. The In Between would punish a sprint. It rewarded care.

"Jacob!" she called, not loud enough to carry far, just enough to test the air. Sound died quickly here, as if the place were tired of echoes that weren't its own.

"He was two turns behind us," she said, more to keep fear from filling the space than because Allen needed the reminder. "I told him to keep a hand on the wall."

"He heard you," Allen said, steady. "He also hears other things. We will find him."

They took a left under a low lintel and entered a corridor like a throat: ridged walls, a shallow slope, the floor polished to a dark sheen that held their reflections like thin shadows. In the panes to their right flickered slices of the living world—an airport bathroom, a liquor store window at midnight, a child's nightlight reflected in a bedroom mirror. Faces appeared and vanished, chalk-white with panic. Abigail kept her eyes on the floor, counting steps the way you count rosary beads when words are out of reach.

"Jacob!" she called again, softer. "Answer me if you can."

A soft draft moved past them, cool and chemical, like a hospital hallway after visiting hours. The lantern flinched and steadied. From the basin beyond the bend came a layered noise—whispers, claws on glass, a single thin scream. Allen angled the lantern and they turned into a wide room where three corridors met. The floor fell away into a shallow bowl and, along its rim, pale shapes drifted in small groups, huddled and unsure.

"Have you seen a boy?" Abigail asked them gently, scanning each blurred face for the sharp jaw and serious eyes she knew. "Brown hair. Quiet. He would have told you to look for a lantern."

Several turned toward the light, drawn like moths. A woman in a nurse's smock mouthed a word—priest—and pointed back the way they'd come. Another—older, coat collar clutched high—shook her head, then hesitated, and lifted a trembling hand toward the far ramp.

"The upper path," Allen translated quietly. "And the way they look when they say it tells me he has passed."

"How?" Abigail asked.

Allen tipped the lantern to widen their circle. "The way relief looks on a tired face is the same in every world."

They climbed the ramp. The ceiling lowered, a net of mirrored shards that held no stars, only reflections of reflections. Twice, Hollowed crossed their path, lean and quick, eyes burning. Twice, the creatures slowed when the lantern found them, not cowed—never cowed—but wary. They skirted the light's edge and moved on, shoulders flicking with impatience, as if something else were calling louder now than the easy meal in front of them.

"Do you feel it?" Abigail asked.

"Fever in a crowd," Allen said. "Someone has told them they are allowed to be wolves at noon."

A new sound cut across the corridor—a shoe scuff, fast, a man's muttered apology to a wall. A shape loomed from a side passage and nearly collided with them.

Russell threw both hands up, then sagged with relief. "Finally, faces I recognize," he said, breath visible in the cold. "And not the kind with knives for teeth."

"Russell," Abigail said, grabbing his forearm. "Have you seen Jacob? He's here. He wandered off."

"He's not lost," Russell said, tone firm for once. He pointed over his shoulder with his thumb. "I already found him. Gave him Father Allen's message—the one about the Echo faltering and the handsome devil with the new lieutenant. That's why he came this way. I tried to loop back fast to you and got turned around in the lower vaults. They… shifted on me."

Abigail's grip tightened. "Where did you leave him?"

"Guiding souls," Russell said. "He's been walking like he owns a map no one else can see. I watched him pull a cluster of the lost out of a feeding ring with five words and a look—'Follow the lantern; do not look back.' The Hollowed started to rush and then stalled when they saw him. Heads down. Gave him space."

Abigail frowned. "They attacked?"

"They wanted to," Russell said. "Then they saw him. Backed off, like someone yanked a leash. After, he sent the souls toward you, Father." He nodded to Allen. "Told them to find your light. They called him 'the Chosen.' Not as flattery—like naming gravity."

A breath she didn't know she was holding slid out of Abigail. "And then?"

"Up," Russell said, voice lowering with respect. "He took the terrace path that looks out over the plain. Toward the silhouette. Toward the keeper. Last I saw, he wasn't hurrying. He walked like the corridors were moving out of his way."

"The Echo," Allen said.

"Bowed, not broken," Russell added, repeating the phrase he'd heard traded like a password. "That's what they're saying."

A tremor ran through the floor, a long shiver that traveled up Abigail's legs and settled in her teeth. Far off, something fed and fed; closer, a thin cheer like coins down a chute suggested a pack's approval of itself. The lantern flickered, then steadied again under Allen's hand.

"How long ago?" Abigail asked.

"Minutes," Russell said. "Time here stretches. But he can't be far."

Abigail looked past him to a split in the wall—a notch where the corridor narrowed then opened like a keyhole. "That way?"

"That way," Russell said. "It climbs to the terrace. You'll see the plain. He'll be somewhere along the edge, near the rail that isn't a rail."

Allen studied Russell a heartbeat longer. "You were delayed only by the halls, not by harm?"

"I tripped twice, argued with a wall, and told two souls the wrong turn before I fixed it," Russell said, dry. "But I'm in one piece. And—" he tilted his head, listening—"I think some of the rogues are being pulled into lines. I heard a name: Abaddon. He's organizing. Your boy is safer than we are. That's the strange truth."

Abigail swallowed and pushed fear down where it couldn't reach her feet. "We go after Jacob."

"Carefully," Allen said. He lifted the lantern, brightening its edge so the dark made a narrow lane. "Take the notch. I will follow with the light."

Russell stepped back to make room, then glanced down the side passage he'd emerged from. Faint glows moved there like fireflies—souls catching on scraps of safety. "I'll sweep the lower vaults and keep sending them your way," he said. "If Jacob doubles back, I'll steer him to you."

"Some of them are turning back," Russell said, squinting down the passage. "Like a tide just changed."

"The Array starved the keeper," Allen answered. "When the starving ends, the road remembers which way is home."

Abigail nodded. "Be careful."

"For once," he said, managing half a smile.

She turned toward the notch. Allen raised the lantern, and the black gave them a path no wider than a doorframe. Russell took one steadying breath, then peeled off the other way to shepherd the dim lights he'd found, boots ticking into the deeper halls as Abigail and the priest climbed toward the terrace where the Echo, bowed but awake, waited somewhere beyond the next bend—and where a boy who was not lost at all had already gone ahead.

Scene 4: The Charge

They found Jacob where the terrace narrowed to a ledge and the world fell away into the plain. Far off, the Echo's silhouette loomed dim, bowed, a mountain that moved with breath. Jacob stood at the edge with his hands at his sides, calm in a place that tried to devour calm.

"Jacob," Abigail called—not loud, but the name carried. He turned at once and came toward them under the net of shattered panes overhead. Those shards showed restless scenes from the living world—bathroom mirrors fogging, storefront glass filmed with rain, elevator doors breathing chrome—and in more than a few of them, shadows pressed close.

Father Allen lifted the lantern. "Are you hurt?"

Jacob shook his head. "He spoke to me," he said. "Not with words. I understood."

Abigail's relief and dread arrived in the same heartbeat. "What did the Echo say?"

"Stop the Array," Jacob answered. "It's draining him. If we close it—if we stop the draw—he'll have the strength to stand. To face the one who whispers and the one who commands."

"The Deceiver," Allen murmured.

"And Abaddon," Jacob said. He didn't spit their names or shrink from them. He set them on the ground like facts. "He's gathering the Hollowed into ranks. Not all of them. Enough."

"How much time?" Abigail asked.

Jacob looked toward the plain. The distant silhouette shifted; the ledge under their feet gave a faint, answering shiver. "Not enough. He wanted me to be plain with you. No riddles. Stop the Array. Fast."

Allen's lantern steadied. "Listen," he said softly. "What the Hollowed take is not flesh—it is order. Some of that order still clings like dew; when the keeper breathes again, those droplets can be called back. Some is bitten through and scattered; that cannot be rebuilt quickly, and sometimes not at all. But most"—he glanced toward the hunched silhouette—"most are strands braided wrong by hunger. When the pump stops, the braids loosen. With light and a name, they can be guided home."

Footsteps rattled up from the lower ramp. Russell jogged into view, hair damp, jacket unzipped. "Told you he wasn't lost," he said, catching his breath. He took in Jacob, the ledge, the far horizon. "So it's as bad as it feels."

"Worse if we wait," Jacob said.

Russell nodded, swallowed, then lifted a hand. "Stupid question?" He didn't wait for permission. "Will the Father step in and help fight the Deceiver? I mean—if this is the endgame, doesn't He... intervene?"

Father Allen's face softened. He anchored the lantern against his chest so its light held steady. "The Father appointed the Echo to keep this realm," he said. "As long as the Echo still stands—however bowed—He honors that appointment. He understands that men helped weaken the keeper, but He gave men freedom, too. The fate of your side rests in your hands. He will not step in and overrule that. Not now."

"So it's on us," Russell said, voice smaller than he meant it to be.

"It always has been," Allen replied, not unkindly.

Abigail turned back to Jacob. "You said he spoke without words. How sure are you?"

"As sure as I am that you'll go," Jacob said. "And as sure as I am he asked me to tell the Veilborne they can choose."

"Choose?" Russell echoed, incredulous. "After what we saw in that clearing?"

"Some came at me," Jacob said. "They slowed when they recognized what stands with me. Others bowed and stepped aside. I told them: obedience to Abaddon betrays the keeper. If the balance breaks, all is lost—including them. Help the Echo. Guard the lost." He spread his hands. "Some listened. Not enough. The Deceiver's promise is easy."

Abigail squeezed his shoulder, a steadying pressure in a place with very little steady. "We'll do our part. We'll stop the Array." She looked to Allen. "Can you hold the lines here?"

"I'll hold what I can," the priest said. The lantern's light steadied, as if the words had weight to burn. "If you close what drains him, I believe the Echo will rise to meet what comes."

A ripple of movement ran across the plain—packs crossing a ridge in formation now, not in scavenger drift. Abaddon's order was taking root. From far below came a thin cry and the dry clatter of claws like falling coins. Abigail kept her eyes on the work ahead.

"We have to go," she said. "Now."

Russell straightened. "You sure you don't want a charming liability along?" He tried for a grin; it showed more nerves than charm.

"Find Father Allen's flock and bring them to him," Abigail said. "You're better at talking than you think. Use it."

A surprised smile flickered. "On it."

Allen stepped to Jacob. "When you stood before the Echo—did he ask you to remain?"

"No," Jacob said. "He asked me to move. To carry this to her. To them." He lifted his chin to the veil of reflections above, where a row of windowpanes showed the same stretch of wet floor from different angles. "To close the mouth that's eating him."

Abigail looked up. In one shard she saw the new portable frame of the Array being hustled into a familiar van, doors slamming in panic. In another, her own face earlier that night—set and pale—caught and thrown back at her. The shard's honesty tightened her throat. "We'll need Elias," she said. "And Lena. And Adrian if he'll come."

"He will," Jacob said. No boasting, no drama—just a steady certainty that made space for action.

A low tremor rolled through the ledge. The lantern dipped and recovered. The sound of the feast swelled and thinned like surf. Abigail pushed past the useless images of what might happen if they failed and fixed on steps.

"What's the nearest thin place?" she asked. "Fastest way to cross back."

"Past the notch, down the shelves," Allen said, tilting the lantern to paint a path. "Maintenance hall under the Clover Park gym. They taped the windows this morning. Cloth and tape slow; they don't seal. The place remembers you. It will let you out."

"Then that's where we go," Abigail said.

The priest widened the lantern's throw until it skinned the ledge in pale gold and made a lane where there hadn't been one. "Walk where I shine," he said. "Don't look up when the shards try to show you what you fear. Hold one another's sleeves."

He went first. Abigail and Jacob followed, fingers catching fabric because hands needed work that wasn't shaking. Russell fell in beside them for a dozen steps, then peeled off at Allen's nod to round up a knot of dim souls blinking in confusion.

They took the notch. The corridor pinched to a shoulder's width. Glass dust sifted down, peppering their hair. The lantern's heartbeat matched Allen's breath. He kept his voice low and even, giving them rails to hold.

"When you reach the floor," he said, "you'll smell bleach and old rubber. There's a red exit sign that flickers. Stand beneath it. Don't speak your names. Think them. The glass will thin. Step through together."

"Why not say our names?" Jacob asked.

"Because this place likes to keep what it can name," Allen said. "And you need your names where you're going."

They reached the shelves and went down heel-to-toe. Far out on the plain the sound gathered again—faint, sharp, the way knives sound when they're being honed. The shards above stilled. At the bottom, a narrow runnel of black water shone like oiled cord. The lantern turned it into a strip of mirror long enough to show three faces and a light that said no one here was alone.

"Call Elias from the lot," Abigail said. "If he balks, we'll drag him."

"He'll try," Jacob said. "He loves the machine. He doesn't love it more than us."

The last turn opened into the maintenance hall exactly where Allen had promised. On their side, the corridor was black glass and breath. On the other, through a long rank of taped windows, lay a concrete hallway with a rolling bin of mop heads and a vending machine humming to itself. A red exit sign flickered.

Allen raised the lantern until the panes shone like old ice. "Now."

Abigail, Jacob, and Allen stood shoulder to shoulder beneath the sign's echo and thought their names—not shouted, not begged, just set in their minds like anchors. The taped glass breathed cold. The black under their palms thinned.

"Step," Allen said.

They stepped, and the In Between let them go.

The maintenance hall's light was dim and too bright at once—buzzing fluorescents, waxed floor, air that smelled like chemicals and sweat. Abigail braced a hand on cinderblock until the crossing-sick eased. Jacob's jaw clenched, then settled.

Allen stayed on the other side. He passed the lantern to Abigail through the glass—on this side a battered flashlight with a tired beam—and laid his palm against the pane in benediction. "I'll hold what I can," he said. "Hurry."

"We will," Abigail answered.

She grabbed Jacob's hand and they ran—down the hall, up the service stair, out into rain. Sirens wound through the night. Somewhere nearby, someone shouted for a child to get away from the window. In the lot, a security light flickered and held.

Abigail pulled out her phone as they sprinted. Elias's number went to voicemail. She left three words he could not mistake: "Stop the Array." Lena answered on the first ring.

"We're coming," Abigail said. "With a message. From the Echo."

"Tell me," Lena said.

"Stop the drain," Abigail answered. "Or he falls."

No wasted breath on the other end. "I'll get Elias ready," Lena said. "Drive safe."

They piled into the car. The engine caught; the wipers beat time. Jacob strapped in without being told. Abigail checked the mirrors—every reflecting surface a possible mouth—and pulled out.

"Will he stand if we make it in time?" she asked, eyes on the wet lane.

"He said he will," Jacob said, looking out at the glass doors and puddled asphalt. "But we have to give him back his breath."

"Then we will," Abigail said, and pressed the accelerator.

They drove toward the lab and the thing they had built and now had to unbuild, carrying a boy's certainty, a priest's charge, and a keeper's word like a fuse already burning.

18

Terms of Mercy

Scene 1: Mountain View

The cemetery sloped gently toward the south, rows of stones step-ping down the lawn like pages turned in careful hands. Beyond the far fence, the neighborhoods thinned into alder and fir, and beyond that—on a clear day—Rainier shouldered the sky. It was clear enough today. The mountain stood white and solemn, a shape the eye couldn't quite hold all at once, as if the world had raised its own cathedral and set it there to keep people honest.

Elias stopped at the curb and stood for a moment with his palms on the steering wheel, listening to the soft click of the cooling engine. The air outside was the kind of cold that carried the smell of wet stone and cut grass. Crows worked the headstones in hop-steps, tilting their heads to see what he would do.

He brought no flowers. He had brought them a dozen times before and never once felt they matched her. Today he brought a small brush, a clean rag, and the chain he had taken off years ago, the one with his wedding ring on it. He held the chain a while, letting it warm in his fist, then slipped it back into his coat pocket and left the car.

Camille's marker was where he knew it would be—third row from the maple, the one that turned almost black in the rain, facing the mountain because that's what she wanted. "If I have to lie still," she'd

350

said once, months before the Array, "let me at least look at something that isn't finished yet." The stone had her name, the dates, a single line beneath: the work and the wonder. He had argued, briefly, for something more lyrical. She had laughed it off. "No," she'd said. "That's me."

Moss had gathered at the base. He knelt and brushed it away with the soft brush, careful of the lettering. The stone gave back a chill that got into his knees. When the moss was gone he wiped the face with the cloth until the granite darkened and the letters shone like wet ink.

"Hi," he said. The word seemed small out loud but it fit. "You got your view."

A slow breeze rounded the hill, tugged the rag against his fingers, set the maple leaves talking. He didn't read into it. He didn't come for signs. He rested his palms on the top of the stone and looked past it to the mountain, then back down to the dates. It was still a shock, sometimes, that numbers could be so final.

"I thought it was my fault," he said. No preamble. No dress rehearsal. If this was a reckoning, it needed clean lines. "I told myself a dozen different versions to make it survivable, but underneath all of it was that simple shape: I built the thing that killed you."

He let the shape sit between them in the quiet. It didn't crush him the way it used to. It didn't let him off the hook either.

"Abigail forced the truth into the light," he went on. "You and Adrian questioned the Array early. I pushed. He… sabotaged." The word still scraped leaving his mouth. "He cut out the watchdog. He thought he was humiliating me. He made sure the machine couldn't fall quiet when it should have. I've carried that as my sin for so long I didn't believe it could be anything else. It turns out there are a lot of ways to be guilty."

He looked at his hands on the stone. He had forgotten to bring gloves; his knuckles were raw from the cold. He flexed them. "I'm guilty of pride. Of rushing. Of wanting the door to open so badly I stopped asking what was on the other side. I'm guilty of not hearing you, Camille, when you said the hum felt wrong. I didn't put the jumper in my pocket and I didn't strike the match—but I built the room. I invited the weather. And now the weather's here."

Down the slope, a maintenance cart hummed past, cheerful and ordinary, and then it was quiet again. He could hear a woodpecker in the trees at the fence. Tap. Tap. Tap. A pause. Tap. The sound came and went like someone thinking.

He stood the brush upright in the grass and took the ring from his pocket. He had worn it on the chain against his chest since the day after the funeral, unable to keep it on his hand and unable to put it away. He rolled it once slowly between thumb and forefinger. It caught what light there was and made a small, true circle.

"I don't know what the right gesture is," he said, and felt a wry smile at the corner of his mouth. "I spent so much time learning precision for machines, and I still don't know the measurements for grief." He set the ring on the top edge of the stone and left his fingers there a moment, steadying it as if a wind might take it. "I needed to tell you: Adrian said it out loud. He told me. He told Lena. He told Abigail. And something moved in me I didn't know could move. I've been breathing like a man under a weight. Today I can stand up."

The admission wasn't triumphant. It was simple. He drew a breath that filled his ribs instead of skimming them. The mountain stayed. The grass moved. The crows worked their methodical, smart circles.

He lifted the ring again, leaned forward, and pressed his forehead to the cool top of the stone. He didn't pray in words. He did what he had done at the Array when he finally understood what it was doing—he made a promise and let it cut. "I'm going to stop it," he said, clear into the granite. "The thing I made. I'm going to break it if I have to. We opened a door we didn't understand, and the Echo is on its knees because of us. Because of me. I won't let it stay that way."

He lowered into a sit, back against the base of the stone, knees drawn up. He let the mountain fill the top half of his vision and the carved letters in the bottom. The balance felt right. Between the two, a life could fit.

"I'm with people now," he said after a while. "It isn't just me and a machine. Lena is… Lena is something I didn't let myself see. Not fully. I kept telling myself I'd be cheating—on you, on your memory—if I let anything else live in the same room. But that wasn't love, was it. That was fear pretending to be devotion."

A steady warmth spread through the cold in his hands, as if the words themselves did the unfreezing.

"She told me she loved me," he said. Saying it out loud made his voice go rough for a moment. "I wanted to say it back. I did say it back. And it felt like opening a window I'd nailed shut. Does that offend you?" He shook his head at himself. "I know. That isn't how you were made. You didn't hoard love. You gave it like air."

He took the ring in both hands and threaded the chain through it again, then slipped it over his head. The metal picked up his skin's heat fast, like it remembered where to live. He tucked the ring under his shirt, against his sternum, where he could feel it when he moved.

"I'm not leaving you here," he said. "I'm not taking you either. I'm going to carry you the right way this time—near the heart, not in front of it." He let out a breath that shook once and leveled. "And I'm choosing the living. I think you'd approve of that sentence."

A thin veil of cloud drew over the sun and folded the mountain into softer edges. He realized, suddenly, that he was hungry. He didn't think he'd said that word out loud in a graveyard since the funeral. The normalcy of it felt like a small, foolish blessing.

"I still hate him," he admitted, because honesty mattered here if it mattered anywhere. "Adrian. When I close my eyes I see my hands on him and I want more." He stared down at the grass. "But that isn't the work now. The work is mercy with teeth—mercy that ends harm, not mercy that excuses it. If he can help, I have to let him. If there's time later to judge, I'll decide then whether I have the right."

He pushed up from the base of the stone and stood. His knees cracked in protest. He brushed grass from his coat and didn't look away from the name again until he'd said what he came to say.

"Goodbye," he said quietly. "Not to you. To the weight that kept you from being a blessing and turned you into a sentence. Goodbye to the shape of guilt that says love must freeze to be pure." He touched his fingertips to the carved letters. "Thank you. For the work. For the wonder."

As he stepped back, movement at the edge of the path caught his eye. A young couple stood a few rows away, the woman with a hand on her belly, the man reading a name out loud in a voice that was trying to be steady. The way they leaned into each other made something in Elias unclench. The living, he thought again. Choose the living.

His phone buzzed in his pocket. He didn't answer. He let it buzz a second time and go quiet. He took one last look at Rainier, at the snow catching a weak sun, and at the stone with its plain words. He felt—for the first time since the lab went white and Camille went still—that stepping away wasn't betrayal.

As he turned toward the car, he pictured Lena in the lab's brutal light, hair swept up, hands steady even when her mouth trembled. He pictured Abigail's face when she said the Echo would fall if they didn't close the drain. He pictured Jacob's calm, the way the boy spoke about a realm older than churches as if it were a hallway he'd learned to cross.

The phone buzzed again. He answered this time. "Elias," Lena said, no hello. There was wind in her voice line, and behind her the faint, clean hum he did not want to hear anymore. "Abigail's on her way. Adrian too."

"I'm coming," he said. The words surprised him with how sure they sounded.

He looked once more over his shoulder. The crows had moved on. The maple leaves shifted like slow applause in the breeze. He lifted a hand—not a flourish, just a brief, ordinary wave—and walked back toward the car with his ring warm under his shirt and a decision set hard in his chest.

He would break what needed breaking. He would mend what could be mended. He would love the living. And when the time came to measure the cost, he would meet it upright, without bargaining.

The mountain watched and said nothing. That felt like approval. Or at least like being seen.

Scene 2: War Room

The lab had been turned into a war room because there wasn't anywhere else to go. Someone—Lena—had dragged two folding tables together under the whiteboards and covered them with printouts and notebooks: resonance maps, fault logs, oscilloscope screenshots, a hand-drawn diagram of the Array with thick circles around the coils and the mast. Cables lay coiled like sleeping ropes. A rolling cart held coffee, bottled water, and a battered first aid kit that suddenly felt relevant.

Abigail had taped kraft paper over every pane of glass—interior windows, a cabinet door, the framed poster of Faraday that had a glass front. The sink mirror wore masking tape in an X and a layer of duct tape on top of that. She'd laid thin lines of salt across the thresholds and across the floor in front of the rack, not trusting the light to hold alone. An iron nail and a jar of dried rosemary sat by her elbow. None of it looked theatrical. It looked like seatbelts.

Adrian stood at the end of the tables, hands flat on the paper. He had cleared a square of space and filled it with pencil sketches: a block diagram of the Array's signal path, the coil fields drawn as blunt loops, the mast's plasma chamber a box with teeth at the edges. In the margin he had written a list in small, neat capitals: PAUSE / BLOCK / RELEASE. He kept the paper turned slightly toward himself, a childish habit he hated and couldn't shake.

In the background, Hector crouched by the equipment cabinet, snapping ferrite chokes around a harness one by one, labeling each with blue tape. Zora worked at a rolling cart, measuring and cutting copper strap for a crowbar frame, the metal giving off a dull, clean smell where she deburred the edges. At the doorway to the equipment room, Naveen hovered with a tablet, watching a live feed from the loop sensors—quiet, jaw tight, making himself small and useful and saying nothing.

He hadn't told them his idea. Not yet. It needed all of them in the room, and he didn't trust himself not to flinch if he said it twice.

Lena crossed from the equipment rack to the tables. She had grease on her wrist and a smear of soot across the side of her hand where she'd brushed against a heat mark on the coil housing. Her hair was gathered up in a clip that kept losing the battle. She set a tablet down and looked at Adrian's drawings without reaching to turn them.

"How bad?" she asked.

Adrian didn't pretend not to understand. "We built something that won't accept 'no' from the usual places," he said. "It latched to a source we didn't respect. Telling it to ease off is like asking a riptide for manners."

Lena let out a breath through her nose. Close by, the Array's compact, field-tested frame looked almost modest—three rings, a mast, cables bundled and labeled. It was the quiet that bothered her. Even unplugged, the machine seemed to hold a note at the edge of hearing, the way a struck cymbal keeps singing after the room stops noticing.

She rubbed her thumb over the soot on her hand and didn't quite get it off. "Elias is on his way," she said, then added, more to herself than to him, "he needed to stop somewhere."

Abigail glanced up at that and softened without prying. She was moving efficiently, a small ritual loop: check the paper on the glass, set the nail in reach, mark a fresh salt line with the edge of a hotel spoon. Her eyes were tired, but when she looked at the Array there was nothing theatrical in her attention, only a steady reading of risk.

"It felt worse when you had it powered at the wetlands," she said. "Like standing at the lip of a drain. Here, it feels… contained. For now."

"Does he—" Adrian started, then stopped, not sure how to ask if the Echo watched. It felt stupid, saying it. It didn't feel stupid when Abigail said it.

"He hears all he can," Abigail said, as if answering a different question entirely. "He is not strong enough to shout."

Adrian didn't press. He had been the loudest man in too many rooms. Today quiet seemed the only currency that bought anything.

Lena pushed a legal pad toward him. "Walk me through the failure we saw yesterday, minus the part where everything went white."

"We designed the watchdog to trip at a threshold," he said, pointing at the diagram with the eraser. "If the Q spikes too fast or the phase drifts into the red, it throws the bus to dump and breaks the latch. But your trip didn't trip because the latch moved." He tapped the mast box. "The loop grabbed to the other side and treated the dump as a nuisance. It's not just over-coupled. It's self-feeding."

"Like a feedback howl," Lena said.

"Exactly," Adrian said. "Take the mic, stand in front of the speaker, and you're not amplifying a voice anymore, you're amplifying the amp. Only our 'amp' is the seam between worlds."

From the doorway, Naveen cleared his throat, not quite entering the circle. "I've got PLL variance streaming. It… still wants to drift toward Theta when we breathe near it." He tried for a joke and ended with a fact. "We're holding it with tape and glaring."

Abigail capped the rosemary. "You have a plan," she said, not quite a question.

Adrian's mouth twitched. "I do. I'm not ready to sell it until he's here." He jerked his chin toward the door. "There are parts of it that… I don't want to pretend the cost doesn't matter."

"Cost to who?" Lena asked.

"To us," he said, then looked away. "To someone."

They stood in the hum of fluorescent fixtures. Down the hall, a night custodian's cart squeaked, then rolled on. The world—this side of it—kept trying to be ordinary.

Lena moved to the rack and began checking connections she could recite in her sleep. She tightened a BNC fitting that didn't need it and reseated a fiber jumper that did. Her mind ran two tracks at once: the checklist of the machine, and a second list she didn't want to look at straight on. Elias at the cemetery. The way his voice had broken when he said he couldn't shut it down. Abigail in the field, palms up, light brightening around her fingers while the wind turned cold. The smell of sulfur in clean air.

She realized she was staring at her own reflection in a glossy panel and stepped sideways so she saw painted metal instead. "When it goes wrong again," she said to the room, "I want fewer moving parts between my hands and the off switch."

"We could wire in a hardware crowbar across the bus," Adrian said. "But if the latch is on the other side, all we'd do is make sparks and trip our own breakers while the loop thanks us for the diversion." He caught himself, jaw tightening. "I'm not saying don't try. I'm saying don't trust it."

"Crowbar frame's cut," Zora said softly without looking up, measuring another length of copper. "Lugs are crimped. Still waiting on your go for tie-in."

"And the ferrites are on every line that'll take one," Hector added, clicking a choke shut. "Harness looks like a bead shop. In a good way."

Abigail leaned against the table edge, palms flat. She had bandaged two small cuts on her fingers; a thin trace of salt dust clung to the adhesive. "Father Allen told Russell he would keep hiding those he could," she said softly. "He sent Russell back to warn Jacob. Jacob went anyway." The faintest smile touched her mouth. "He was right to. The Echo isn't dead. He isn't gone. He's waiting on us to stop cutting him."

Adrian swallowed against a sudden, ridiculous tightness in his throat. "He's a boy," he said, and hated that the words sounded like a complaint.

"He's chosen," Abigail said, without heat. "I didn't choose him. Neither did you. The Echo did. We can choose how we meet that fact."

The door clicked open. Cold air rolled in with Elias. He stood for a breath on the threshold, the half grin people wear when they're late and sorry, then stepped inside and let the door close behind him. He was bare-headed in the chill, hair wind-tossed, coat unbuttoned. He looked older than last week and lighter than yesterday.

Lena crossed to him. She didn't say anything. She put her hands on his arms and checked him the way you check a person who's just come in from a storm: here, present, whole. He nodded once, grateful, and for a second laid his forehead against hers.

"I went to see Camille," he said, for the room as much as for her. "I told her the truth and it didn't break me. I told her I was choosing the living." He looked at Abigail, then at Adrian. "And that starts here."

Something in Adrian's face eased and hardened at the same time. He didn't want the moment and he needed it. "I'm not asking you to forgive me," he said. "Not today."

"Today is about ending harm," Elias said. "After that, we'll find the right verbs."

On the periphery, Naveen shifted his weight and, to Hector and Zora, murmured, "Heads up—this is the part where we don't breathe wrong." They nodded and kept working.

Abigail's shoulders dropped a fraction, the kind of release you get when a tight knot finally accepts the first tug. She slid the iron nail closer to the edge of the table and checked the nearest salt line with the side of her shoe. "Then let's make a plan you can say out loud without lying to yourself."

Elias moved to the tables and looked down at Adrian's sketches. He didn't reach to turn them. He handed Adrian the pen instead. "Show me," he said.

Adrian didn't. Not yet. He looked from Elias to Lena to Abigail, and in each face he saw a separate reason to be careful. He set the pen down, pulled in a breath, and spoke instead to the room, as if naming the pieces would keep them honest.

"We tried 'off,'" he said. "It won't listen. We tried to smother peak with injected noise. It corrected. We can cut mains, we can starve fuel, we can rip cables. None of that touches a latch that's built itself on the other side." He tapped the mast square with the eraser. "We have to change the shape of the field from here and make it drop the bite. That buys time. Not a lot. Enough."

"How?" Elias asked.

Adrian's eyes flicked once toward the mast and back. He had his answer. He had decided not to say it until they were all standing upright and looking at him. He could feel the shape of the admission in his chest, heavy and exactly the right size.

He looked at Abigail and she knew, of course she did. Her gaze didn't waver, but the set of her mouth did. She gave the smallest nod a person can give and still mean it.

Adrian exhaled. "All right," he said. "Here's the part no one wants."

He reached for the pen. The others leaned in. In the background, Zora set the last copper strap on the cart; Hector clicked a choke closed; Naveen quelled a jitter in his knee and stilled the live graph with a fingertip.

And the scene broke there—the air holding the last fraction of a breath; the pen tip just above the paper; the coffee going cold; the Array waiting, quiet as a muzzle before a bite.

Scene 3: The Plan and the Price

They gathered around the workbench as if it were a battlefield map: a scuffed tabletop, a stack of graph paper, a marker that bled a little, the mast and coils of the Array sketched in quick blocks. Fluorescents hummed. Somewhere in the ductwork a rattle clicked every few seconds, the lab's tired metronome. Hector hovered by the door with a bin of ferrites hugged to his chest; Zora stood near the coffee cart, a coil of copper strap looped over one shoulder like a bandolier, both of them listening harder than they breathed. Naveen edged in at the corner of the table, tablet tucked under his arm, eyes flicking between the drawing and Adrian's face.

Adrian drew a small X at the mouth of the mast and put the marker down. "Three stages," he said. "First, I write a pause-loop—firmware that forces the Array to wobble its phase on purpose. It won't break the self-latch, but it'll stall the efficiency long enough to squeeze in a window."

He tapped the X. "Second, during that window, we block the intake. We deny the machine whatever it's sucking from the In Between."

He traced the coils. "Third, we open the gate for a heartbeat and dump the stacked energy into the rings. They'll take too much, too fast, and cook themselves. That's the kill shot."

The room went very still. Abigail's gaze stayed on the X. Lena folded her arms tight, as if that could hold the fear down where it belonged. Elias's eyes had settled into the old habit of measuring, then drifted to the mast itself—the real thing, not the drawing—standing ten feet away under a shroud of canvas like a guilty monument. Hector shifted his grip on the bin and stared at the floor. Zora's coil creaked against her shoulder.

"How long is that window?" Lena asked.

"Best case, forty-five seconds," Adrian said. "Worst case, five."

"And what blocks the intake?" she pressed. "A plate? A cage? We've tried metal. The flux ignores it."

"Not metal," Adrian said quietly. He rested his finger on the X again, then looked up. "Organic. Living."

"Organic… like living?" Naveen said, eyes narrowing. "Like a living what?"

"A person," Adrian answered.

The word cut the room in half. The fluorescent hum suddenly sounded too loud; the duct rattle missed a beat. Hector's arms tightened on the ferrite bin until the plastic creaked. Zora's coil slipped an inch on her shoulder and she caught it with a small, sharp inhale. Abigail's fingers flattened against the edge of the table, knuckles paling. Elias's jaw set, a muscle ticking once as if to keep speech from falling out. Naveen's breath hitched—half a syllable of "no" escaped before he strangled it down.

Lena's gaze flicked from the X to Adrian's face and back again. She hesitated—one beat, then two—swallowing whatever instinct rose first. When she spoke, her voice was steady by force. "Why a living person," she asked. "Why is that the only thing that works?"

Adrian didn't hedge. "Because the mouth of the Array is tuned to something that looks like us—layered, coherent, constantly changing. We built it that way, whether we admitted it to ourselves or not. Steel's a shadow; the field treats it like air. A body is pattern the intake recognizes. For a few seconds, a living presence in that throat confuses the draw. It stalls like a pump that hits a solid plug."

Abigail's attention returned to Adrian and settled there, cool and unmistakably human. "This isn't theater," she said. "What you're really saying is it needs a soul—something living the Array recognizes." "You don't stand in that mouth to win back dignity. You stand there because a world needs the seconds your body buys."

"And the cost?" she added, voice low.

"Fatal," Adrian said. "You don't stand in there and walk away. You take the field's load like radiation. It cooks you from the inside, even if I nail the timing."

Naveen's tablet clicked against the table as his hand tensed. "No. Absolutely not." He took a step toward the sketch and jabbed a finger at the X. "We're not turning a teammate into a fuse. Write a better plan."

No one jumped in to comfort the facts. They sat in the middle of the table and looked back at each of them.

Elias felt his old reflex unfold—automatic, tidy. I'll go. There had been months when he would have welcomed it. After Camille, he had carried the idea that if the world demanded a body for the balance sheet, it should be his. That instinct rose now, and for a heartbeat he almost spoke.

He didn't. Two truths blocked the words. First: he had stood at Camille's grave and told her good-bye without lies, and part of the weight he'd lived under for years had truly lifted. Second: Lena's hands trembling against his last night, and the simple fact that he wanted the living, not the ledger.

Abigail broke the silence. "If we do this, I'll ring the room. Iron, salt, prayer—whatever holds. They'll come when the machine stutters. I can buy seconds, not minutes."

Lena nodded, eyes never leaving Adrian. "And who takes the mouth?"

"I do," Adrian said, as if he'd been waiting for the question since the moment he'd drawn the X. His voice didn't wobble. "I pulled the watchdog weeks ago to humiliate you, Elias. I wanted the run to fail in front of funders. I didn't know Camille would die for it, but what I did made it possible. The machine runs without a brake because I removed it. The bill is due. I'll pay it."

"Hard pass," Naveen snapped, face gone pale and hot at once. "You don't get to solo-sacrifice your way out of guilt. If you die, we lose the person who understands the pause-loop best. We lose hands we need. And—newsflash—we still have to live with your code."

Adrian met his eyes. "I'm not asking for absolution. I'm telling you what will work."

"And I'm telling you no," Naveen shot back. "We don't vote people into the grinder."

Elias stepped in, voice even but edged. "Naveen." He waited until the younger man met his eyes. "It's not our choice to make about his body. Not yours. Not mine. If this is the only way—and I pray it isn't—it will be Adrian's choice." He held the line a beat longer. "We'll do everything to find another route. But you will respect that."

Naveen's jaw worked; the retort came up and hit the brakes behind his teeth. He looked at the X, then at Adrian, then away. "Fine," he muttered, the word dragging gravel. "But if there's any other way, we take it. And if you try to rush this, I'm chaining myself to the mast." He grumbled something inaudible and stepped back, shoulders still tight. Hector's grip eased a fraction on the ferrite bin; Zora exhaled, a quiet, shaky sound.

Lena slid between the points of heat with a small shake of her head, the trafficker of sanity. "We can debate philosophy when the world isn't cracking," she said. "Right now I need to know the choreography. How does it go, second by second?"

Adrian kept it simple. "I'll push the pause-loop. When the hum wobbles, that's our window. Someone—me—steps into the intake and chokes the draw. The energy spikes on the other side. Elias times the surge and calls the release. We pop the coils and the Array dies."

Abigail looked at Elias. "Can you time it?"

"If anyone can," Lena said before he could answer. She glanced at the mast. "But I want to hear it from you."

"I can," Elias said. He could already see the graphs in his head, the feel of the hum, the way the numbers would crest and break when they were perfect for the dump. "If the pause-loop buys anything more than a heartbeat, I can."

Lena turned back to Adrian. "There's no other plug." Not a plea—final confirmation.

He shook his head. "A cow carcass won't do it. A sack of meat won't do it. The intake is tuned to a living field."

Abigail's gaze didn't waver. "Then we do this with eyes open."

"I know what I'm saying," Adrian answered. His hands were steady on the table. For once, no sarcasm, no performance.

Naveen swallowed, anger cooling into something raw. "Then promise me this isn't a suicide note dressed up as a test plan. You write the loop. You don't step near that mast unless every single one of us signs off." He tried to smirk and couldn't find it. "I'm very annoying when I veto."

Lena's eyes flashed. "It shouldn't be you." Then, because she wouldn't lie, "But it makes sense that it is."

Elias exhaled. "All right," he said. The word felt like picking up a load he didn't want and was the only one strong enough to carry. "Here's what we agree to, and then we rest for two hours, because tired hands make mistakes and we don't get a second chance. Adrian writes the pause-loop. We test it cold—no power. We walk the steps until everyone could do them in their sleep." He looked hard at Adrian. "You do not go near that mast until I say the timing is perfect."

"Understood," Adrian said.

Abigail nodded once, satisfied with the shape of the plan, not the cost. "When you're ready, call me. I'll be here with iron and the words that make hungry things hesitate."

"Thank you," Adrian said, and meant it.

They stood there a moment as if the lab itself had asked them to be quiet. The fluorescents hummed. The clock over the sink ticked. Outside, somewhere on campus, a siren lifted and fell. Hector shifted the bin to the other arm; Zora unlooped the copper strap and laid it gently on the cart like a promise.

Elias looked down at the sketch again—the coils, the mast, the X where a person would stand—and then up at the faces around the table. One he had learned to forgive. One he had finally allowed himself to love. One who had been steady since the first day he'd met her.

"Adrian," he said, and the old arrogance didn't ride his voice. "When this is over—if there's an 'after' to argue in—I'll refile. We'll correct the patent. Names that should have been there from the start: yours, Camille's."

Adrian blinked, surprised into a grin that carried more life than Elias had seen in him for years. "Add my name to the patent for the machine that nearly destroyed the world?" He huffed a laugh. "No thanks."

Lena's mouth tugged upward despite everything. Abigail's eyes warmed. Elias let the corner of his own mouth lift.

"Fair," he said.

For the first time since the wetland tore open, the tension in the room thinned by a hair's breadth. Not because the plan was easy, or because anyone felt safe. Because they had named the price and, together, had stopped looking away. The laugh—brief, wry, real—hung in the cool lab air like a match struck in a dark room, small but honest.

"Tomorrow," Adrian said, tapping the X once with his fingertip. "We make this mark mean 'stop.'"

No one said goodnight. They didn't have that kind of night left. They stepped back from the table, each carrying their portion of the work, the humor still faintly echoing off metal and tile as they parted. Naveen lingered half a beat, looked at Adrian, and grumbled, "Don't make me chain myself to the mast." Then, lower, resigned but loyal: "Find the other way if it exists. We'll help you look."

Scene 4: The Weight, Shared

The lab had gone quiet in the way rooms do after a hard decision. Cables were coiled. Tools lay in neat rows. The canvas draped over the Array's mast rose and fell with the building's ventilation, a slow breath that made everyone glance up from time to time. No one spoke about alternatives anymore. They had done that an hour ago and run the math to the end. Now there was only the work ahead—and the cost named plainly.

Adrian stood apart at the far window, not looking into it. The glass showed the lab back to him—the benches, the taped floor lines, the shrouded machine—but not the night outside. He leaned his shoulders against the wall, thumbs hooked in his pockets as if he were worried his hands might shake if he let them hang free.

Elias watched him a moment from the center bench. The earlier heat—the flare of anger at the confession, the reflex to strike—had guttered down to something steadier and harder to name. He could feel Lena's quiet presence at his back, the soft clink of Abigail setting small tins of salt beside a lantern. No one said "don't" or "what if." That ground had been covered. This ground was different.

He crossed the room.

Up close, Adrian looked tired in a way coffee couldn't touch. Not wrecked. Not ruined. Just used up by the last few hours of honesty.

"Do you have a minute," Elias asked.

Adrian huffed a small breath that wasn't quite a laugh. "I have as many as I've got left."

They stood shoulder to shoulder, not facing each other. It was easier that way.

"I don't want to keep hating you," Elias said, and felt something uncoil in his chest just naming it. "Holding it has been... familiar. Simple. It gave shape to a lot of things I didn't want to look at."

"You had reason," Adrian said, voice even. "More than one."

"I know," Elias said. He looked down at the floor seam that ran straight toward the mast like a chalk line. "For a long time I also thought I had reason to hate myself. It was cleaner, in a way. I could blame the machine. The ambition. The blind spot. When you told me you'd pulled the watchdog and the failsafe never had a chance that night—" He stopped, swallowed. "The weight shifted. I wanted to put all of it on you. Camille. The nights since. The fear in these walls."

Adrian didn't move. "You could."

"I could," Elias agreed. "But if I keep it there, we don't get to the other side of this. We don't even get out of this room."

A silence stretched. Behind them, someone set a breaker map down on the bench and stepped away. The small, ordinary sound helped.

Adrian turned his head a fraction. "You're not excusing it."

"No," Elias said. "I'm forgiving you for it. Those aren't the same."

Adrian's mouth tightened; his eyes went glassy and cleared. "Thank you."

He let his head fall back gently against the wall. "You should know," he said after a beat, "what the last few years were. Not because it makes any of this better. Because you deserve the true story if we're going to do this together."

Elias didn't answer, but he stayed.

"I left angry," Adrian said. "I told myself I was taking a stand. I told anyone who would listen that you'd cut me out and I wouldn't feed your ego. The truth is I couldn't stand the lab after Camille died. I couldn't stand the way everything looked the same and nothing was. And I couldn't stand the mirror of it—how much I'd wanted your approval until I didn't get it exactly how I imagined. Pride is a drunk you can walk beside for years without noticing."

He glanced down at his hands. "Then I started drinking for real. The kind where you wake up on a floor and you don't know whose. The kind where your phone dies and you're relieved, because it means fewer people to ignore. I sold equipment I cared about to pay rent on a place I don't remember, and I told myself I was the righteous one while I crawled. It's not a noble decline. It's boring and mean."

He breathed out. "Two weeks ago, I hit a line that wouldn't move. I quit. No applause, no confetti. Just a decision. When you called today, I was still counting the days by hours and coffee cups. Hearing your voice… I won't pretend I was happy. But I was relieved. Finally, something to do that wasn't running from what I broke."

Elias stared at the canvas over the Array. "I called because I don't know how to fix what I built."

"And I answered because I broke the thing that was meant to stop it," Adrian said. "Feels honest, finally."

They stood in that truth. It wasn't comfortable, but it held.

"I'm sorry," Adrian added. "For the patents. For the sabotage. For lining up my anger and letting it pull a trigger I pretended wasn't aimed at anyone. Especially Camille."

Elias closed his eyes once, hard, then opened them. "You didn't intend to kill her."

"I intended to hurt you," Adrian said. "Camille is the person who had to carry the physics of that. That's on me."

Elias nodded slowly. "It is." He waited to see if the word burned as it left his mouth. It didn't. "And I forgive you."

Adrian's jaw worked. He looked at the floor, blinked twice. "I don't know what to do with that except try to deserve it, even if I can't."

"That's enough," Elias said.

Across the room, Abigail dimmed a set of lights and the lab shifted to a calmer tone. Lena brought over a small stack of folded blankets and dropped one by the bench near them, like a truce offering.

She didn't interrupt. She set a hand on Elias's shoulder and squeezed once, then crossed back to the console to check a cable list. The gesture landed like a reminder: you are not doing this alone.

Elias angled a look at Adrian. "I can't promise I won't feel angry again. But I can promise it won't lead me anymore."

"That promise counts," Adrian said.

They moved back toward the others. Abigail looked up; he met her eyes and she read, without asking, what had passed. Her shoulders eased a fraction. She set the old Iron nails in a small cloth pouch and tied it shut, her movements precise, ritual turning into readiness.

"Shift rest," she said. "Two hours on, two off. If the world lets us."

"I'll take first watch," Lena said.

"I'll take it with you," Elias said, then to Adrian, "get an hour if you can. You'll need it."

Adrian nodded and sat on the edge of a cart, elbows on his knees, head bowed—not in prayer exactly, but in something close. After a minute he looked up again.

"Elias."

"Mm?"

"If this goes the way we think… If I do what we agreed…" He hesitated, a man picking a careful step. "Thank you for calling me. You gave me a way to spend what I have left on purpose instead of spite."

Elias met his eyes. "You're welcome."

No speeches followed. No hands piled in the middle. The room shifted into practical gravity: lists checked, sockets taped, nails sorted, a lunch bag pushed toward whoever looked least likely to eat on their own.

Abigail crossed to Adrian and handed him a bottle of water. "Drink," she said, plain as a command. He did. She touched his shoulder lightly, a promise without words, then moved on.

When the room had settled, Elias drifted back to the window with Adrian one last time, and the two of them stood with the lab reflected around them and the dark pressing its face against the other side of the glass.

"I meant what I said," Elias told him. "About forgiveness. And about moving forward."

Adrian's mouth twitched. "I believe you."

They stayed there until Lena's voice cut through the hum: "We start again at five."

Elias turned from the glass. "Get some sleep," he said.

"You too," Adrian replied.

They separated—Adrian to a cleared patch of floor with a folded blanket as a pillow, Elias to the console where Lena had already lined up the tools they'd need at first light. Abigail dimmed another set of lights, and the lab settled into a half-dark that felt less like an ending than an agreement to continue.

No one talked about objections. They had already been spoken and set down. What remained was slimmer and heavier: a choice, a task, and a narrow path through.

Elias looked once at Adrian before he bent over the breaker map. He let go of the last thread of hatred like a wire he'd been gripping too long, fingers slow to uncurl. The release hurt. Then it didn't. He breathed, and the breath was cleaner.

"Morning," Lena said, not looking up from her list, "is coming whether we sleep or not."

"Then let's give it something to meet," Elias answered.

They worked quietly until the clocks disagreed about the hour and the first thin silver of dawn pressed at the edge of the blinds. Outside, the world was still. Inside, four people carried a weight together that none of them could carry alone.

19

Setting the Table

Scene 1: Live-Fire Plan

They met after hours in the smallest room at the Seattle Spectral—an old podcast booth with sound foam stapled to the walls and a single lamp throwing a cone of warm light over the table. Someone had taped black paper over the interior window so the bullpen couldn't look in. It felt like a place you could say a risky thing and have it stay put until you were ready to let it out.

Abigail set a leather folio on the table and looked from Natalie Chen to Reese Mathers. "No more soft launches," she said. "If you want Avery Shaw to fall, you do it where his armor is the thinnest—under his own spotlight."

Natalie's pen paused over a legal pad already crowded with arrows and times. "A live press conference," she said, nodding once as if the idea had been circling and finally landed. "He announces he's running for governor. He'll beg for cameras. I can get him there."

Reese leaned back, fingers drumming once, stopping. His Seattle Spectral badge hung from a lanyard, edge scuffed from a month of field reports. "And we spring the trap while the red lights are on."

"Not a trap," Abigail said. "A reveal. You ask the right questions; the screens answer for him."

Natalie slid a ruggedized thumb drive onto the table. A printed hash value was taped to its side. "Chain-of-custody on the dashcam is clean. Original cloud backup, recovered by a contractor, hashed on acquisition, mirrored to write-once media. Whoever scrubbed the metadata didn't know what they were doing—we can show the tampering."

Reese's jaw tightened. "It shows him hitting my father. Alley behind the bar. My dad walking toward his car, head turned by the back door slamming, then—" He stopped, let the sentence die. "You can see his face when he folds over the hood. No one gets to say 'unclear' anymore."

Abigail opened the folio. Inside: photos of the Array at field sites; emails with midnight timestamps and Avery's signature ordering "accelerated deployment at new frequency"; lab schedules aligning with the crescent of incidents around Clover Park. "You'll lead with public risk," she said. "Force him to lie about the science before he lies about the death."

Natalie flipped to a clean page. "Beat-by-beat. Let's board it."

Reese reached across, dragged a blank notepad close, and wrote a tidy ladder down the center:

T–7 days – Natalie courts Avery's ego. "Exploratory committee" becomes "launch."

T–48 hrs – Confirm venue A/V: main screen, overflow monitors, stage switch feed, and press pool splice.

T–12 hrs. – Spectral package (Array docs) preloaded to pool feed B with a private trigger; narrated by Reese.

T–0 – Avery steps up to announce.

Q1 – Spectral question: Array deployments, safety assurances, "new frequency."

Q2 – Spectral follow: "Did you order risky field runs against internal objections?"

Q3 – Spectral follow: "Did you kill my father, Robert Mathers?"

Cut – On his denial, Natalie signals A/V to roll Package A (emails/contracts) and then Package B (dashcam).

T+1 min – Spectral site pushes documents + hashes; mirrors publish simultaneously.

T+3 – AG and State Patrol receive prewritten complaints, time-stamped with published exhibits.

T+5 – Second Spectral push: eyewitness statements and DOE staff affidavits.

"Two packages," Natalie said, tapping the line. "The first is process: emails, memos, contracts. Establish that he forced dangerous deployments; keep the language clinical. The second is the alley: dashcam with narrated context and the hash burned into the corner of the frame. We don't give him a second to reset."

Reese glanced at Abigail. "You sure we aren't poking a hurricane?"

"You're calling a storm a storm," Abigail said. "He's already using it to drown people. This gives the crowd a rope."

Natalie's voice went cool and precise—the DOJ-trained part of her surfacing. "I'll handle venue access. If I'm on his 'advance' team for a gubernatorial rollout, I can place a tech with the contractor and get pool feed B registered as a 'remote graphic.' We won't have to touch the main switcher. We'll just… hand them something they think is his highlight reel."

Reese blew out a slow breath. "And when I ask the father question, he'll do what he always does. Smile, say he's sorry for my loss, claim a smear campaign—"

"And on the screens behind him," Natalie finished, "your voice will say, 'This is the raw dashcam recovered from a city maintenance archive. Here is the license plate. Here is the timestamp. Here is his face.'"

Abigail slid two printed stills across the table—one a freeze of Avery's sedan in the rain, the other a blurred frame of a man's body doubling over a hood, features clear enough to break you. "Do not ad-lib when it hits," she told Reese. "Let the pictures work. If you talk over them, you'll be accused of manipulating feeling."

He swallowed. "I can do that."

Natalie checked her watch, then her tone softened a notch. "Security. He'll be angry. He has friends in plainclothes. I've prepped a safe route from the ballroom to a side stairwell; Spectral's satellite office is two blocks away. Your producer will have two gophers to run data cards on foot if cell service collapses."

"Dead-man switch?" Reese asked.

"Already primed," Natalie said. "If either of you go dark, a BCC goes to fifty editors with links and files. Also—" she slid two gray flip phones across the table "—no apps, no tracking. We coordinate on these inside the venue."

Abigail watched them click forward—two people who had come up different ladders, meeting on a rung that mattered. "When the Array goes down," she said, "the room will feel it. Like someone lets breath out of a jar. That's your moment for the first package."

"And if it doesn't go down?" Reese asked.

"Then you take the moment anyway," Abigail said. "We can't wait for perfect timing from a world that's breaking."

Natalie jotted three names and underlined them—AG contact, State Patrol liaison, and a judge known for hating sealed filings. "We'll need an affidavit on the dashcam," she said, glancing at Reese. "Your narration will reference the hash on-screen and a sworn chain-of-custody posted to Spectral at the same minute. I'll get it notarized tonight."

Reese nodded. "I've got an editor who owes me. He'll sit on the publish button and push the docs the second the package rolls. We'll mirror to two international servers so the takedown letters arrive too late."

Abigail eased the folio closed, then reopened it to slide out a map ringed with pins around Clover Park. "When you ask your first question, use the phrase 'documented pattern of incidents.' Avoid saying 'Veilborne.' Talk like a watchdog, not a seer."

"'Documented pattern,'" Reese repeated, making the everyday language fit the nightmare. "Okay."

Natalie's pen stopped moving. For a moment, her face changed—anger and something simpler, older. "My parents left Guangzhou with two suitcases and a phrase: earn what you keep. He thinks he can keep anything without earning it. This is where that ends."

Reese met her eyes. "I want his mask off."

"It will come off," Abigail said. "And he will try to put on another. Don't chase the new mask until the first one is nailed to the wall."

They walked the flow again, tightening small screws. Natalie rehearsed the hand signal she'd give the A/V tech. Reese scripted two clean, neutral questions in his notebook and crossed out a handful of angrier formulations that would feel good and play badly. Abigail slid them a one-page sheet titled When the Room Tilts: step back from reflective surfaces, don't stare at a blank TV, listen for temperature shifts—simple ways to refuse invitations while the news did its work.

"Venue?" Reese asked.

"Hotel ballroom downtown," Natalie said. "He loves chandeliers. I'll stage a flag bank and two side screens. We'll make sure pool feed B routes to both. He'll feel ten feet tall until the pictures get taller."

"And if he tries to cut the feed?" Reese said.

"By the time he thinks to, thirty phones will have recorded the moment he lied and the screens told the truth," Natalie said. "Also, the packages will already be live on Spectral. The screens are theater. The site is the knife."

Abigail capped her pen. "When you say his name, say all of it. Not 'Avery,' not 'Shaw.' 'Avery William Shaw.' It slows people down. It makes them hear the man and not just the brand."

Reese wrote Avery William Shaw on the pad and boxed it. He looked up, chin set. "Say when."

Abigail stood, gathered her folio. "Soon. They're building the last pieces at the lab now. When I text light it, you go."

Natalie rose too, slid the drive back into a small Pelican case, latched it. "Tomorrow I sell him his own future," she said. "By the end of the week, we sell the public the truth."

They left the booth together. In the newsroom, screens showed tiled clips of smashed mirrors and boarded storefronts, a crawl muttering about a state emergency. Reese stopped in the doorway and touched the edge of the black paper covering the glass, then let it fall back. He had the look of a man who had held his breath too long and decided to breathe again even if the air hurt.

"Light it," he said under his breath, a promise to a minute that hadn't arrived yet.

Scene 2: The Crown He Wants (T-7 Days)

Natalie Chen found Avery Shaw at the window of his suite, sleeves rolled, tie loosened, city lights shining on the glass like a second skyline. Cable news ran on mute. He didn't turn when she entered.

"You're late," he said, watching his reflection more than the traffic below.

"I'm early for what you want," Natalie replied, setting a slim folio on the bar. "Governor."

He turned then. Not surprised—hungry. The word did to him what a starter's pistol does to a runner.

"Convince me," he said, but his smile already said yes.

"Seven days," Natalie said. "We announce at the Grand Fountain Ballroom. Prime time. You step into the panic and sell calm. 'I will steady this.' Short, repeatable lines. TV will eat it up."

Avery paced once, drink in hand, excitement loosening his stride. "What do I actually say?"

"Three promises," she answered. "Safer innovation. Transparency. Stability. Then you hit the refrain: We don't scare; we build. We measure; we lead."

He tried the words, nodding like he could feel the applause. "Press?"

"Seattle Spectral opens," she said. "Optics matter. You look fearless. We place friendly follow-ups behind them."

He smirked. "Give the doubters the first swing. Smart."

"Venue's on hold," she continued. "Two big screens. Flags. Good lighting. Their A/V will mirror your podium feed to the screens. I've added a secondary input—Pool Feed B—cleared on the switcher."

He waved the details away. "Just make it bright and full. I want that room packed."

"I'll pack it," Natalie said. She didn't push the rest. He never cared about the stitching—only the fit.

He came close enough that she could smell the expensive cologne. "I've been waiting for a moment like this," he said, low and quick. "People want a protector. They want a story that doesn't end with smashed mirrors and closed elevators. I give them that story, and then I give them me."

"And the donors," she said evenly.

"They'll follow the cameras," he said, pleased. He signed the venue and AV agreements without reading, the way he always did. "What about the weird questions? The ghost crowd. The conspiracy trolls."

"You acknowledge fear, demand facts, cite partners and weekly briefings," she said. "You are the briefing. Keep moving forward. Don't swat at flies."

He raised his glass, already half-elsewhere, picturing the dais, the step-and-repeat, the narrow corridor of cameras all aimed at him. "Seven days," he said again, savoring it. "Set the rehearsal. I want the walk, the lines, the pauses."

"Done," she said.

Natalie left and crossed to the Grand Fountain. The ballroom manager flipped work lights on: high ceiling, chandeliers, a stage that made power look easy.

"Podium center. Two confidence monitors on the floor. Flag bank here, screens left and right," she said, marking positions with a straight hand. "Register Pool Feed B on your switcher. My operator will cue it."

"Press risers?" the manager asked.

"Back wall, straight sightline. Clear aisle for camera left. Separate check-in. And I want a clean exit corridor behind the stage."

He jotted notes. The A/V chief joined them; Natalie ran the cues once, then again, fast and simple. "No drops, no stutter. He reads as inevitable."

"We can do inevitable," the chief said, half-grinning.

Outside, the air smelled like rain. Natalie texted Reese:

NATALIE: T–7 Grand Fountain locked. Spectral gets first question. AV: Pool Feed B ready. Prep your packages and clean VO. Wait for my cue.

REESE: Copy. I'll bring the hammer when you say swing.

At the Spectral's satellite office she taped a short timeline to a whiteboard:

T–7: venue locked, donors whispered
T–6: advisory drafted
T–5: set pieces & surrogates
T–3: press walkthrough
T–1: tech rehearsal
T–0: showtime

Below it, in small print: Screens tell the truth.

She checked her watch. Forty minutes to call lists. She'd seed the right anchors, line up the donor row, book the studio hits for the morning after. She wrote the advisory subject in one stroke—Avery Shaw to Make Major Announcement on Public Safety & Economic Stability—then closed the laptop. The plan was simple because it had to be. Complexity was how plans bled out.

Back in the suite, Avery stood again at the window, his reflection framed by the city. He could already feel the room on his skin: the heat of lights, the hush before applause, the first question landing like a ball he was born to catch.

"I want the side screens blazing," he'd told her. "I want people to see me and believe nothing can touch them while I'm in front of a microphone."

Natalie had nodded then and nodded now at the empty whiteboard. She thinks briefly of Guangzhou and her parents' small apartment, her father's hands always moving, her mother's voice steady:

Earn what you keep. Avery would keep because someone else earned. Fine. You let a man climb his ladder. You keep the ladder sturdy. And when he reaches for the crown, you make sure the lights are perfect.

And the screens are ready.

She shut off the office lights and stepped into the wet street, cars throwing ribbons of glare along the pavement. Seven days. That's all Avery needed to believe he was inevitable.

It was all she needed to make sure he wasn't.

Scene 3: Clockwork

The lab at Pierce College smelled like warm solder and coffee that had sat too long on a burner. Half the Array's frame hung from a gantry, ring segments labeled in tape and Sharpie, the central mast laid open on sawhorses like a spine in a textbook. Tarps covered the floor where coils would go; bins of connectors lined a wall, each one tagged and color-coded from their panicked teardown two nights ago.

Hector hovered near the parts wall, quietly ferrying labeled harness bundles to a staging cart. Zora knelt by the gantry with a torque wrench and a checklist, tagging each ring lug with neon dots as she worked—green for verified, orange for revisit.

Abigail stood at the end of the mast, one hand resting lightly on the resin hull as if feeling for a pulse through the casing. Lena and Elias had wheeled in a whiteboard and filled it with boxes: *REASSEMBLY, CALIBRATION, PAUSE CODE, SHIELDING, EXFIL.* Arrows ran between them like stitching. Adrian sat on a rolling stool with a laptop balanced on his knees, a tangle of jumper leads coiled at his feet. He looked tired and keyed up, the way people look when their mind is moving faster than their body can keep pace. Naveen leaned against a console with a tablet, chewing the cap of a Sharpie he didn't remember uncapping, eyes flicking between the board and the mast.

"How long?" Abigail asked. No preamble. "To have it ready for the takedown."

Elias checked the board, then the mast out of habit, as if it might answer for him. "Mechanical reassembly? Two days if nothing fights us. Three if it does."

"Wiring and ring alignment," Lena added, tapping the ring sketch. "We stripped a lot in the field. We have to seat the loops, verify the phase harness, and re-balance the mast. We can do it. We just can't rush the part where rushing cracks something."

Abigail turned to Adrian. "And the code? The pause-loop."

He scrubbed both hands over his face, then pushed his glasses up. "Not done," he said, blunt. "I've got scaffolding. I can spoof the watchdog heartbeat and insert a timing shim without bricking the controller. But the loop that actually stalls resonance? Two, maybe three days of real work if I get clean time on the bench and don't hit a wall. It's not trivial. We're trying to interrupt a self-held state the device was never supposed to enter—"

"—because you disabled the thing meant to keep it out of that state," Elias said, a flat edge still on his voice.

Adrian didn't flinch. "Yes. Because I did that."

Naveen shifted, then lifted his tablet in a small truce. "I can build you a hardware-in-the-loop rig tonight—dummy front-end, recorded spectra, fast DAC noise injection. You code; I make the machine lie convincingly so your loop thinks it's wrestling the real thing. Saves us a day of 'oops' on live hardware."

Silence settled for a beat. Abigail let it pass through them and moved on.

"Good," she said. "Then we're on schedule."

Lena lifted her head. "On schedule for what? We've all been working, yes, but there's a difference between ideas on a board and picking the day the world changes."

"Seven days," Abigail said.

"Why seven?" Elias asked. "That's... oddly specific."

"Because in seven days," she said, "Avery Shaw will stand at a podium in the Grand Fountain Ballroom and announce he's running for governor. Prime time. Packed room. Live coverage. Natalie set it up. Reese will lead with a question about the Array and follow with a question about his father. When Avery lies into the microphone, the screens behind him will run the proof. The emails. The internal memos. The dashcam. The whole city will watch him realize that the story isn't his to tell anymore."

Lena blinked. "You're sure."

Abigail nodded. "It's locked. They needed the week to make it look official. That timeline gives us what we need. While he's in lights—convinced he's untouchable—we finish this. We pause your machine, block it, and destroy it."

Elias leaned his knuckles on the table. For the first time in days, something like relief moved across his face. "He can't blame us," he said, more to the room than to her. "If it's public—if there's documentation—he can't hang it around our necks and walk away."

"He'll try," Abigail said. "But the sequence matters. He demanded the deployments. He ignored what we brought to him. The record will show that. And when he starts pointing, there will be too many fingers pointing back."

Naveen snorted softly. "Great. We finally weaponize bureaucracy. I'll sleep like a baby." He glanced at Adrian. "You heard the lady: seven days. I'll shave your build time if you let me stub the peripherals and fake the comb. No cowboy commits on live silicon."

Lena let out a breath she'd been holding tight. "Good. He put us in this corner and lit the match. He should answer for it."

Adrian closed the laptop enough to meet Abigail's eyes. "And you want to do our part while the city watches him burn on TV."

"I want to do our part while he's occupied and his people are distracted," she said. "Less chance of interference. Less chance of him sending anyone to pull plugs at the last minute."

Elias straightened and tapped the whiteboard with the marker. "Then this is our week. Rebuild," he said, pointing to the coil diagram. "Code," to Adrian. "Shielding," to Abigail. "And test every kill path we have left. If one trips, I want to know it trips before we put anyone within arm's reach."

"We'll need more than just lines of salt and iron nails," Lena said, thinking ahead, eyes on the lab's reflective surfaces. "We should tarp every mirror and window again, cover the monitors in the control room, and mount the lanterns—"

"I'll bring Jacob," Abigail said, evenly.

Three heads turned toward her. Naveen's head snapped up too. "Uh, define 'bring.' As in… into this lab?"

"No," Elias said at once. "He's a child."

"He's not," Abigail said. "Not in the way you mean. You've seen me work. You trust it. Trust me on this: Jacob is stronger than I am. The Veilborne feel it from across a room. They bend around him. He will hold space we cannot hold."

Lena bit the inside of her cheek. "He's a boy," she said, less certain than Elias but no less protective. "We can't put him between that thing and our mess because we don't like the alternative."

"The Echo has claimed him," Abigail said. "The Hollowed step back when he steps forward. He can walk between packs and they blink first. I don't like asking. I don't like any of this. But I won't pretend we aren't in a fight that's bigger than our feelings about what children should be protected from. We brought the fight here. We don't get to pretend we can keep the house quiet while the street burns."

Adrian watched her while she spoke, weighing the certainty against his own discomfort. "You're saying the kid is a shield."

"I'm saying he's a presence," Abigail said. "A boundary living in a body that listens when the Echo whispers. He can do it. He wants to do it. I'll keep him as far from the core as I can."

Elias held her gaze for a long count, jaw working. He'd seen Jacob once look straight into a screen gone black and say, calmly, "Not today." The temperature had lifted in the room. The mirrors had stayed mirrors.

"Fine," he said finally. "He comes. He stays back unless you say otherwise."

Naveen blew out a breath and scribbled a new line on his tablet: *"KID ZONE: NO SHINY / NO LINES OF SIGHT."* "Then we set hard boundaries," he said. "Tape on the floor, sightline blockers, no reflective surfaces inside fifteen feet. Hector, Zora—start pulling matte gaff tape and black cloth from the cage?"

Hector nodded and moved, Zora already unspooling tape as she went.

"Tell me the sequence," Lena said, back to business, marker in hand. "Day by day."

Abigail walked the room as she spoke, touching the things they would touch.

"Tonight," she said, "you two keep rebuilding. Sleep in shifts. Adrian, you lock yourself to that bench until your pause-loop works on a test rig. If you hit a wall, you call me. I can't code, but I can remove distractions."

Adrian smirked. "You've already removed the biggest one."

"I'll mirror your interface and write a harness," Naveen said, already tapping a diagram. "Recorder on the RF front end, canned combs, variable coherence dial. I'll even throw in a sarcastic progress bar so you feel judged."

"Tomorrow and the next day, I ward the building top to bottom," Abigail continued. "Basement to roof. Salt, iron, covered glass, borrowed church light if Father Allen can send any through. Jacob will help me reinforce the places where the walls are thin. He can feel where to push."

"Three days out," Elias said, catching the rhythm, "we assemble. Bench test. No field. No mirrors uncovered unless absolutely necessary."

"Two days out," Adrian added, warming to the cadence, "we run a live dry-run—pause and release—without the barrier. Make sure the code hooks and the machine actually... listens."

"Day-of," Abigail said, "we coordinate down to the minute. Natalie sends the advisory. The room fills. Avery steps up. We stand here with the doors locked and we end this."

Elias looked at the clock that never seemed to move in the lab and imagined it finally doing so. "Seven days," he said. "It feels like forever and no time at all."

"It's enough," Abigail said. "It has to be."

Lena capped the marker and set it on the board's tray. "What about Avery between now and then? If he sniffs that we're not falling in line, he'll push."

"He'll be busy," Abigail said. "Natalie will keep him busy. And if he calls, you tell him what you always do: tuning, safety, optimization. You don't lie. You don't volunteer."

Adrian slid off the stool and stood, joints popping. "And if the Hollowed decide to come early?"

"Then we practice before we perform," Abigail said, simple as that. "You write faster. I sew tighter. We hold."

Elias nodded once, firm. "All right."

They moved then, each to their corner of the work. Lena unrolled a fresh harness, the copper catching the overhead lights in a clean line. Elias knelt at the mast and began reseating a ring mount, hands steady now that the clock had a face. Adrian pulled the stool closer to the controller rack, opened the laptop, and dove back into the code, fingers finding a rhythm on the keys that sounded like intent. Abigail walked the perimeter with a small pouch, shaking salt into seams, tucking iron nails into sill corners, taping black cloth over the one monitor they'd left uncovered.

Naveen wheeled over a spare backplane and started bolting down a mock front-end. "Hector, dump me the RF captures from Wetlands-Zero and -One. Zora, I need the AM hash file and the mains harmonics sweep." He glanced up at Elias, a crooked half-grin showing despite everything. "I'll teach the simulator to be an uncooperative jerk so Adrian's code feels right at home."

After a few minutes, Elias looked up. "Abigail," he said, and when she turned he was smiling in a way that was new—tired but clear. "Thank you. Not only for this plan. For thinking about the other fight while we've been buried in ours."

She lifted a shoulder. "We're all in the same fight."

He glanced at the clock again, then at Adrian. "Seven days," he said.

Adrian didn't look up from the editor. "Then I better teach your stubborn machine to hold its breath," he said. "Because if it doesn't, we're going to make live television very interesting."

Lena snorted softly. "I'd like boring television for a change."

"Me too," Abigail said. "But I'll take a world that survives it."

At the door, she paused. "I'll bring Jacob tomorrow morning. We'll start upstairs and work down. If anything shifts, call me—no heroics. If you hear voices from the glass, you don't answer. You let them talk to themselves."

She started for the hallway. Elias stopped her with one more question. "Abigail—what if Avery moves the date?"

"He won't," she said. "He's waited his whole life to be seen. He won't give up a room full of cameras for anything."

She left them to the hum of work—the soft click of keys, the hiss of tape, a wrench on a bolt—and the lab felt, for the first time since the field, less like a place drowning and more like a place getting ready.

Seven days. Then the lights. Then the end of this machine. Then, if the Echo still stood, the rest of the work that always came after.

Scene 4: Lines to Hold

Rain had quieted to a drip by the time Abigail spread the Pierce lab plans across the kitchen table. Windows, screens, polished steel—every reflective surface was circled in red. Father Allen's lantern burned low beside the maps, steady as a heartbeat. Samuel stood at the window, curtain half-drawn, listening to water fall from the firs. Jacob sat with a pencil, drawing clean arrows through corridors.

"We'll funnel them," Abigail said, tapping the freight hallway on the west side. "Seal everything else. One mouth we choose."

Jacob nodded. "That hall already wants to open. I can feel the pull—like a draft under the tile."

Samuel glanced over. "You can feel that?"

"Like rivers," Jacob said, marking an X at the corridor's elbow. "The Echo showed me the lines. They run under the floor."

Abigail lifted her eyes. "Jacob, I want you in the lab when we break the Array."

Samuel turned from the window. "Abigail—"

She kept her voice even. "Veilborne will come. I can hold a front, but I need you at the seams—closing weak points before they flower. If we force everything toward that freight hall, we don't get flanked."

"I know," Jacob said. "When the Array stops drinking, they'll surge. The Echo pressed that into me. First minutes will be worst."

The lantern brightened, a small assent. Abigail felt Father Allen's calm through the glass.

"We'll need safe pockets," she added toward the light. "If souls spill, somewhere to put them."

The glow steadied. All three of them understood: the Hollowed would arrive in groups, test corners, vents, and high panes; when cornered, they'd whip from hunger to rage.

"Then we build the pen so it's ours," Abigail said, noting: skylights tarped; duct registers bracketed; top panes draped and taped. "Everything suffocated but the freight hall."

Samuel joined the table. "If it turns, he runs," he told Jacob. "You hear me?"

"If the line breaks, I'll follow Abigail out," Jacob said. "But it won't break if we point them where we want them."

Abigail took a breath. "There's something else?"

Jacob set the pencil down. "The Echo knows our plan. When I told it what we're doing, it said, 'This is according to my plan.'"

Samuel frowned. "Preordained?"

"Aligned," Abigail said. "We're choosing this. The keeper is choosing it, too."

Samuel's jaw eased a notch. "Then we choose it."

He looked at Jacob, fear and pride both plain. "You're sure you want that room?"

"I've been in that room since the day I drowned and didn't," Jacob said quietly.

Silence held for a beat. The lantern hummed. The house settled.

"We'll leave one door," Abigail summarized. "I'll take point with iron and lanterns. Jacob, you seal seams as you feel them open. Father Allen will steer strays away on the far side."

Jacob nodded. "I'll walk the building the day before and mark the weak spots."

Samuel asked, careful, "And if that handsome liar shows?"

Jacob's eyes cooled. "He knows me now. He won't come first. He'll send others and step in if we're winning. That's what he does."

Abigail covered Jacob's hand. "If he shows, you move with me. Promise."

"I promise."

The lantern brightened again—an endorsement and a warning. Expect the first strike from above: duct mouths, skylight seams, narrow transoms over doors. Expect hands where hands shouldn't be. Expect speed.

"We'll tarp the skylights," Abigail said, underlining it. "Bracket vents. Tape high glass. One corridor clean, the rest suffocated."

"I'll buy plywood at dawn," Samuel said. "Cloth for what we can't screw down."

"Thank you," Abigail said. "Make a place for yourself in that room."

"I'll take a corner and hold it," he answered simply.

Jacob gathered the plans into a neat stack. "I'll tell the Echo we're ready."

"You can tell it?" Abigail asked.

"It hears when I mean a thing," Jacob said. "It heard this."

She nodded, then hesitated. "When it said 'according to my plan'—did it sound certain?"

"It sounded like a promise it intends to keep," Jacob said, "if we do our part."

"Then we'll do ours." Abigail rose and packed her satchel: salt, iron nails, black cloth squares, gaffer tape, chalk, a small hammer; then a second bag with battery packs for the lantern mounts, a thermos, first aid, Father Allen's rosary thread.

"Jacob," she said, "in the lab, my voice over everything. If I say fall back, you fall back. If I say hold, you hold."

He nodded. "And if I say 'not today,' you don't argue."

She allowed herself a quick smile. "Deal."

Samuel stepped close and pulled both of them into a brief, tight hug. "We've got a week," he said, letting them go. "To turn a building into a funnel and teach a monster to die."

"A week," Abigail echoed. "And a keeper waiting for air."

The lantern brightened, then steadied. Through the glass came Father Allen's practical certainty: tar the skylights; block the ducts; darken the high panes; fix cloth to metal with magnets where screws won't hold; keep a dark room ready as shelter; expect lash-back the instant the drain stops.

"Noted," Abigail said, writing fast.

Jacob added one last mark on the plan. "The freight corridor bends just before the door," he said. "If we angle the last barrier there, we'll force them to show themselves before they're on us."

"Good," Abigail said. "We'll mount a lantern there, waist height, steady beam."

Samuel returned to the window and let the curtain fall. "I'll call a friend for the plywood," he said. "We'll have it staged by noon."

"Thank you," Abigail said again, and meant not only the wood.

The three of them walked the small house once—salt at thresholds, cloth on mirrors, latches checked—then came back to the table for a final look. The plan was simple on paper: starve every route but one, brace the one, and hold. It would be uglier in the room. But now each of them had a place to stand.

Abigail slung the satchel over her shoulder. "Tomorrow the site walk," she said. "Then we start cutting cloth."

Jacob stood, already memorizing. "The Echo will rise if it's refed," he said. "It told me that much."

"And the Hollowed will throw everything at us when they feel it," Samuel said.

"Then we stand," Abigail answered.

The lantern gave one last small nod of light—as if a hand pressed their backs—then settled. Outside, water ticked from the eaves. Inside, resolve did what machines could not: it held.

They blew out the candle and left the lantern on watch. Across a distance without miles, the keeper listened.

20

The Maw and the Flame

Scene 1: The Pause

They were ready because there was no choice but to be.

The Pierce College lab didn't look like a lab anymore. Skylights were tarped and taped, their seams bristling with screws and magnets. The upper panes were blacked out with heavy cloth. Vents were bracketed shut. Plywood sheets leaned like shields along the east wall. The only open path was the freight corridor—a long, straight throat they had cleared and marked, their funnel to the In Between.

The Array squatted at the room's center on shock feet, ring stacks rebuilt, power umbilicals tied down, monitors stacked on rolling carts. The mast's core threw a faint, unhealthy glow, a cold pulse that set teeth on edge. You could feel it in the bones more than hear it.

Abigail checked the lantern mounts one last time. Waist-high lamps had been bolted to steel plates along the corridor, every thirty feet—a steady run of warm circles leading to the freight door. Beside each lamp, a strip of iron chain hung ready. Buckets of salt, cloth squares, and a crate of old nails sat open by the wall.

Jacob walked the perimeter, palm out, eyes half-closed, feeling for seams. He would stop, press his hand to the plaster, and whisper. A faint tightening would come through the room, like a draft deciding

392

to go the other way. Father Allen's lantern—fixed to a stand at the corridor's mouth—stayed bright and clear, its little heart steady.

Elias and Lena stood at the console, sleeves rolled, faces drawn into focus. Naveen had claimed the secondary cart—headset on one ear, a laptop leashed to the control bus, a handheld EM meter clipped to his belt. He'd painted a hasty label on a utility switch with a Sharpie: *LANTERNS—ALL.* His knee bounced; his hands didn't. Hector and Zora moved quietly in the background, double-checking vent brackets, reseating sandbags against the base of the freight door, and staging spare tarps and duct tape along the corridor like fire extinguishers you hope you won't need.

Adrian had his laptop out on a steel stool, the cable to the Array's control bus looped over one wrist as if he didn't trust the wire to behave unless he felt it. He had labeled one toggle on a small auxiliary box *PAUSE* with a piece of masking tape. His thumb kept finding it and leaving it and finding it again.

Samuel paced between the plywood and the tools, checking what could be checked.

Abigail took a breath and pulled her phone from her pocket. "Last call," she said, and hit Natalie's number.

Natalie answered on the first buzz. The sound behind her was velvet and busy—ballroom acoustics, the smear of too many people in one place. "We're set," she said. "Press is in. Reese is in position. He's primed for the questions on the Array and his father. Control has his package ready to roll. You say when."

"Does he suspect?" Abigail asked.

"Not a bit," Natalie said, a dry smile in her voice. "He's been practicing the word 'governor' in front of a mirror for three days. Ego narrows the field of view."

"Then begin," Abigail said. "We'll do our part."

"Do yours fast," Natalie replied, then softened. "Be careful." The line clicked off.

Abigail slid the phone away. "They're starting," she told the room. "We're live."

Elias nodded without looking up from the screen. The diagnostics were ugly: resonance latching harder than it had any right to, harmonic energy stacked like plates, small flickers in the lab's dark glass even with the tarps and cloth.

Adrian lifted his head. "On your call," he said. He was steady, but sweat had worked a damp V through his shirt.

"Pause holds for three minutes at best," Lena reminded, eyes on the numbers. "Maybe less. When the draw stops, they'll hit us."

"That's why the corridor is ours," Abigail said. She checked the strap on her wrist where a loop of iron chain rested and settled the weight of Father Allen's rosary-thread coil in her pocket. "We hold the front. Jacob, you seal seams as you feel them. Samuel, you stay on that wall. Elias, Lena—eyes on load. If it slips, we shift to containment."

"Copy on seams," Jacob said.

Naveen lifted a hand without looking away from his cart. "Copy on everything terrifying. Batteries hot. Lantern bus ready." He flicked his gaze to Elias, then to the door. "When physics gets emotional, yell."

Jacob's gaze flicked toward the freight hall. "They're already pushing along the vents," he said. "It's like they're sniffing the cloth."

"Let them sniff," Abigail said. To Adrian: "Now."

He breathed once, a small, private thing—eyes closed, mouth thinning, the short prayer of a man who had run out of anything clever—and flipped the PAUSE toggle down.

The Array's hum didn't stop; it lunged. The room felt it—the way you feel the shift when an elevator car grips cable. Then the sound flattened to a tight, high thread. The mast's glow went dull. On the monitors, the resonance curve stuttered and held. A red banner lit across the diagnostics—*LOOP HOLD: ENGAGED*. Another—*INPUT FLOW: SUSPENDED*.

Every scrap of glass in the building answered at once.

Even tarped and taped, the skylights breathed cold. The sealed panes behind cloth gave a single, crisp knock, like knuckles on a door. The freight corridor darkened as if a shadow had poured down it—not absence of light, but a presence that ate what it touched.

"Lanterns!" Abigail snapped.

Naveen toggled his labeled switch. The waist-high lamps along the corridor came up together, warm circles biting into the dark. "Runway's lit," he muttered, then louder: "We're bright to the back wall." The shadows did not flee; they pressed against the edges of the light as if testing fabric. From the far end of the hall, a sound rose—metal dragged slow over stone. The hair on the back of Samuel's neck stood up. He set both palms on the plywood stack and pushed it tighter to the wall. Hector mirrored him, planting a boot and shoving shoulder-first, Zora bracing the opposite edge so the stack didn't skate.

"Front," Elias said, voice gone thin. "They're at the door."

The door didn't open so much as think about it. Bolts shivered in their housings; a thin frost feathered out along the seam and stopped, listening. Something on the other side exhaled—slow, deliberate—the breath of a cold room that knows your name. The metal answered with a faint, embarrassed ping, then another, like knuckles testing manners on a church door.

The seam darkened. Not shadow—weight. It pooled in the crack and thickened until the gasket creaked. A knuckle tapped once against the latch. Then twice. Then stilled, as if counting.

Only after a long, mean silence did the Hollowed show itself.

First a suggestion of finger lengths moving behind the slit, jointed wrong, tasting the gap. Then the latch bowed a fraction and a hand eased through—long and lean as a spider's leg, claws dragging bright, surgical lines across the steel. The air around it went thin and sharp, like breathing iron filings.

"Everyone sees that, right?" Naveen whispered, dry throat making the words sandpapery. He squinted at the EM meter and didn't like the number. "Copy. Hate it."

The instant the wrist touched the lantern's spill, the light bit. Smoke licked up from nothing. The Hollowed hissed—steam through a keyhole—and snapped back into the crack, leaving the door trembling as if the building had decided to shiver.

The push came a heartbeat later. The door jumped on the track, bolts flexing. The seam tore an inch wider, then two. Cold opened into the room, a breath out of a freezer. The first of them came through sideways, clever—shoulder and head and then a spill of smoke wrapped tight. It took one step and hit the line of light. It flinched and reeled back, but behind it more bodies pressed, forcing it forward whether it wanted to come or not.

"Chain!" Abigail barked. Samuel tossed the loop and she caught it without looking, swung it low and hard. The iron cut through the air and met the Hollowed thing across its middle. It slid, hissed, clawed for purchase, and the way a foot finds only ice, it found light and faltered.

A second one came, faster. It darted for the edge of the light and went low, testing where the circle thinned. Abigail stepped into it and brought the chain down across its reaching arm. Bone was there—always there—and the strike landed. It snarled and withdrew.

"Left seam," Jacob called. "It's opening."

"On it," Naveen said, already hustling. He skidded to the wall beside Jacob with a strip of heavy tape and a cloth square, slapped fabric over a hairline gleam and sealed the edges with the heel of his hand. "No windows, no snacks," he told the wall, then jogged back, breathing too fast and forcing it slower.

Abigail didn't turn. "Seal it."

Jacob pressed, and Abigail saw the small shift the way you see pressure leave a room: the cloth on the high pane next to him sagged less; the dark lost its angle. The seam tried to open again. He pressed harder. It gave up and slid back into the corridor's mouth, annoyed.

More bodies crowded the door. They didn't pour; they pressed. They were no longer scavenging—they were coordinated. They kept one another in the channel, testing the light at shoulder, hip, head. Every time they touched the lantern's spill, something in them smoked. They hated it and learned from it.

And then the room changed a degree that wasn't temperature or sound. The push at the door took on rhythm. The dark at the corridor's end sharpened.

"Abaddon," Jacob said, quiet, as if naming a storm he could see cresting in the distance.

He stepped through the gap as if it were a curtain he owned. Taller than the others by a head. Shoulders cut from smoke around a core that felt like weight. Eyes bright in a way that wasn't light at all—attention that cut. The pack behind him fanned with a neat, hungry respect. Zora's breath hitched. Hector set his feet wider, jaw clenched white.

He took a step into the light and it didn't stop him. It slowed him. He smiled without a mouth and set one clawed hand against the air as if he were testing glass with his palm.

Abigail drew the chain tight and settled her stance. "You don't cross here," she said.

He tilted his head, birdlike, amused that she would try the old rules in a new season. He leaned into the light and the waist-high lamps flickered, then steadied, then flickered again.

"Jacob," Abigail said through her teeth.

"I'm here," he said, already moving to the next seam. "Keep talking."

Abaddon stepped again. The Father Allen lantern guttered once. The iron in Abigail's hands vibrated, a thin song in the chain she felt in her wrists. She raised it and brought it down at the place where his weight felt most real—the centerline, where smoke pretends to spine. The blow landed. He stopped. Not from pain—from surprise that anything could meet him.

He looked past her toward the Array, then at Elias and Lena, a quick inventory. He pushed. The lamps thundered inside their housings; glass thought about cracking. The freight door banged against its track.

"Lantern two's flickering," Naveen called, already sprinting to it with a spare battery pack. He slammed the pack into the mount, twisted, and the light steadied. "Stay up, stay up," he told it, then loped back to the cart.

Abigail took one step forward, into him, and put the whole of her voice into one word. "Hold."

The lantern's flame shivered and flared. The chain sang. He rocked back half a foot. The pack behind him hissed and pressed forward; he lifted a hand and they froze, disciplined.

At the console, alarms stack-lit. *PAUSE WINDOW: 00:51...00:50...*

"Adrian," Elias said, tight. "How long can you hold this?"

Adrian didn't look up. "As long as it takes," he said. Lie or prayer—it didn't matter anymore.

"Fifty flat," Naveen echoed from the secondary cart, voice clipped now, sarcasm buried under triage. "Voltage stable. If anything pops, it's going to be the humans."

Abaddon lowered his head and pushed again, all his weight against that one word she had laid across the threshold. The light blew sideways, then found itself. Abigail's arms shook. The chain cut her palms. Sweat ran down her temple. He was stronger than anything she had held alone. He knew it and she knew it.

"Echo," she said under her breath, not as a plea, as a report. "We're still standing."

Abaddon's attention slid from her face to the rosary-thread at her wrist and back. Disgust flickered across him. He dug in.

"Abigail!" Jacob called, somewhere to her right. "Above you."

She didn't look. She felt the shift and swung the chain high. Something that had crawled into the seam of cloth above the door spit and fell back into the press of bodies. The pack hissed. The lamps held.

On the screen, *PAUSE WINDOW: 00:37.*

"Thirty-seven," Naveen called, breath fogging. "Hector—left vent! Tape's peeling."

Hector was already there, palming the bracket hard against the frame while Zora tore a fresh strip of gaffer and sealed the corner. "Got it," Zora said, voice thin but steady.

"Stay with me," Abigail told the light, the iron, her own shaking muscles. "Hold."

Abaddon leaned. The corridor felt like a wind tunnel the wrong way, pulling toward him. He raised his other hand, slow and deliberate, as if he were about to push open an ordinary door.

Abigail took a half step to meet him, set the chain like a bar, and met his eyes. "Not today."

For a stretched second, everything went silent except the thin tick of the lamps. Then the lantern brightened—a hair, no more. It was enough. The pressure eased by the weight of a breath. Abaddon's forward claw drew a faint curl of smoke and he paused, calculating.

He would try again. He would keep trying until the window closed or her knees did. But for that moment, she held him at the cut line, and he had not crossed.

"Thirty seconds," Lena said softly.

"Twenty-nine," Naveen followed, eyes on the banner. "We're still green. Keep breathing."

Abigail set her jaw, felt the ache in her arms settle into a steady burn, and fixed all of herself on that narrow strip of floor. The lab thrummed. The pack seethed. Hector and Zora stood shoulder to shoulder at the plywood stack, ready to shove if the door blew. Naveen's fingers hovered over his switch, waiting to punch every lamp again if even one so much as blinked.

Abaddon smiled without lips and pushed. She pushed back. And the line—just barely—held.

Scene 2: The Deceiver Enters

The pause held.

On the central monitor a thin green band lay flat across the graph—*LOOP STATUS: STALLED*—while a red countdown chewed seconds in the corner. *01:38... 01:37...*

The Array's voice changed from hungry to caged, a strained hum that seemed to vibrate in bone more than air. Heat rolled out of the freight-door breach in dry waves, turning every lantern flame thin and blue. Abaddon still crowded the threshold, claws testing the line of iron and light Abigail kept tight across the opening. Behind him, ranks of Hollowed shifted like wolves waiting for a signal.

Naveen worked the secondary cart with a headset crooked over one ear, eyes flicking between a handheld EM meter and a repeater feed of Adrian's pause-loop status. He'd sharpied two big labels on his panel: *LANTERNS BUS* and *AUX FEED*. His thumb worried the first switch; his voice stayed steady. "Lantern rail is green. Any flicker and I punch it again," he reported. Then, quieter, to the room at large: "In case anyone's wondering, we are officially at the 'don't sneeze near the physics' stage."

Hector and Zora were shadows at the margins—Hector braced against the freight door's frame with a breaker bar ready to jam the track if the bolts skipped, Zora moving station to station to re-seat sandbags, tape down curling edges of tarp, and stage spare lantern batteries along the corridor like magazines before a siege.

The air shifted again. Heat gathered, focused, and stepped forward as a man.

He could have passed for a dignitary arriving late: sharp suit that drank the glow, easy smile, perfect posture. Only his eyes betrayed the temperature of him—they were very black and very calm.

"Industrious," the Deceiver said, taking in the consoles, the rings, the chain. His voice wasn't loud; it landed exactly where he set it. "You've found a way to make the sea hold its breath."

Abigail's grip tightened; the chain sang between her hands. "Jacob," she said without looking back, "behind me."

Jacob moved past her instead and took the center of the corridor—ten feet from the breach, small and steady. He didn't raise his hands. He didn't need to. He only stood.

The Deceiver's smile softened. "The boy," he said, as if greeting a favorite pupil.

At the console, Adrian held the pause switch with a white-knuckled thumb. The same red timer glared up at him as at everyone else. *01:12... 01:11...* The intake pressure bar climbed in steady ticks toward the right-hand wall.

Lena bent over diagnostics, counting under her breath. "Coils latched. Phase grid held. Aperture pressure ninety... ninety-one." The intake throat shimmered like heat above asphalt, trying to decide whether to inhale or exhale.

Elias watched two things at once: numbers and people. "Abigail?"

"Holding," she said. The chain bit grooves into her palms. She welcomed the hurt—proof she was still here.

The Deceiver didn't spare her a second look. His attention stayed on Jacob. "This is a pause," he said pleasantly, "not a wall. When it ends, they will cross." He nodded toward the Hollowed packed shoulder to shoulder behind Abaddon. The ranks flexed in a single ripple, eager, disciplined.

"You don't decide that," Jacob said.

One of the lanterns guttered and caught again. Heat swelled. The Deceiver stepped a pace closer—polite, unhurried. The temperature rose with him.

"Everything you love is made of mirrors," he said quietly. "Elevators, storefronts, night windows. When this clever halt stops being clever, every one of them becomes a door. I will lift my hand, and they will pour through. There won't be enough hammer blows in your city to make a difference."

"Sixty seconds," Lena said. "Ninety-four percent."

Abaddon pressed until smoke came off the places the light touched, more angry than hurt. Abigail dropped her weight, setting the chain low and hard. Samuel slid a wrapped strip under her palms to save her skin and leaned in, both hands over hers. "Ten breaths," he murmured. "Then ten more."

Adrian didn't look away from the clock. "If I have to re-arm the pause, I can try," he said, voice thin. "It won't hold as long. Pressure keeps climbing."

"Can you keep the loop from slipping?" Elias asked.

"If the whole thing doesn't inhale the room," Adrian said. He flexed his thumb once, blood returning. 00:59.

Naveen's eyes cut to the EM meter and back. "EM spike trending ugly. Lantern rail still green. Zora, battery handoffs staged?"

"Every other post," Zora answered, already sliding a spare pack onto the nearest mount.

Hector shifted, shoulder set like a jack against the frame. "Door's bowing—track's singing."

The Deceiver studied Jacob the way a surgeon studies a pulse. "Come," he said mildly. "Leave these frightened people to their tools. Stand beside me; I'll show you what a world looks like when no one lies to it about barriers."

"I see you," Jacob said. The words were simple. "You're scared."

For the first time the smile cooled by a degree. "Of what?"

"Of losing what you've taken," Jacob said. "Of being shut out again. Of the keeper standing up when we stop starving him."

A beat. The lanterns hissed. The Deceiver's eyes darkened, not with heat, but with attention. "Charming," he said softly. "But he isn't standing. He's bowing. I can smell it."

"Fifty," Lena called. "Ninety-six."

Adrian's lip twitched. Elias caught the look—the apology that had not been spoken, the choice already made. He wanted to drag the man away from the console and keep him alive with his own hands. He wanted to let him do what he was here to do. Both wants sat in his chest like stones.

"Listen for Lena," Elias said, low.

Adrian nodded without looking up. "Always did."

The Deceiver breathed in, pleased by the furnace breath rising behind Abaddon. "You built a mouth," he said, gesturing lazily at the mast and rings. "Now you congratulate yourselves for making it hesitate. When it opens, it will take this place in a single swallow."

Jacob didn't blink. "Not today."

A murmur went through the Hollowed ranks at the word—not fear, not yet; recognition. Abaddon's head cocked. He tested the chain again and hissed where iron met smoke.

"Forty," Lena said. "Ninety-seven."

Abigail set her feet deeper, drawing the chain into a clean angle. Sweat ran from her wrists and fell sizzling where it touched the threshold. Samuel tightened his grip, steady and quiet.

"Have you counted your doors?" the Deceiver asked, almost conversational. "Every pocket mirror. Every phone screen. Every night window. You carry a thousand gates in your hands and call it progress."

"We built hammers too," Samuel said. It surprised him, speaking to that face. His voice stayed steady.

The Deceiver's eyes flicked to him and away, dismissing him the way a host dismisses a waiter. "There aren't enough hammers."

"Thirty," Adrian said. He shifted his stance to keep his thumb locked, knees loose, shoulders tight. The intake throat thrummed. The room felt like a lung that refused to breathe.

"Lantern three flicker," Naveen snapped, already sprinting. He slapped a fresh pack into the mount, twisted hard, and smacked the housing. The flame thickened. "Stay bright, sweetheart." He jogged backward to his cart without taking his eyes off the corridor. "All rails green."

Abigail's arms shook with the effort and still she smiled, teeth bared. "You're talking too much," she told the Deceiver, not unkindly. "Men like you always do when you're worried."

His smile returned, polished to a sheen. "Men like me," he said. "So unoriginal."

"Twenty," Lena called. "Ninety-nine." She watched the shimmer at the throat change texture—the fine, deadly moment when a surface stops pushing and starts to pull. "Adrian—on my mark."

He swallowed. "Ready."

The Deceiver spread his hands, small benediction, as if welcoming a congregation. "When your neat little trick ends," he said, "I will not have to raise my voice. A finger will do." He twitched one finger, and Abaddon answered with a ripple through the packs—discipline tightening, hunger thrilled by promise.

Jacob took a step forward. Not much. Enough to make the air harden between him and the breach like a pane that refused a hand. "You don't get to cross because you want to," he said. "Not today."

"Ten," Adrian said. The digits on his screen fell one by one. Naveen echoed them under his breath at the secondary cart like a spotter calling a count. Zora pressed both palms to a tarped pane and whispered with him; Hector never looked away from the door.

Elias's hands were open, then fists, then open. He could feel every relay and screw he'd ever turned. He could feel Camille's laugh in the corner of this room and shoved it away with a breath.

"Nine," Adrian said.

"Eight."

The Deceiver watched everything at once: the child, the chain, the clock, the way the heat made the lantern light thin. His eyes were very calm. "When this ends," he said, almost kindly, "I want you to look in your windows and know you did it to yourselves."

"Seven."

"Six."

The intake throat twitched—there. Lena's breath left her in a single word that was not a prayer but carried the same weight.

"Five."

"Four."

She saw the field tip.

"Three."

"Two."

"NOW!" Lena shouted, already moving.

Scene 3: The Release

"Now!"

Lena's shout snapped across the lab. Adrian didn't hesitate. He left the pause switch and climbed the service ladder to the intake collar—a black iris of graphite blades around a fist-sized void. The Array's tone had flattened into a hard, steady note you felt in your teeth. Pressure bars were pegged red. The concrete shivered underfoot.

"Adrian—" Elias started.

Adrian jammed both forearms into the intake and locked his chest to the housing. The void met him like cold fire. Light ran up his skin in thin threads, brightening with each breath. His back arched; he made one low sound, more effort than pain.

"Input blocked," Lena said, eyes on the board. "Flow is zero. Upstream is stacking."

By the secondary cart, Naveen planted his feet, one hand on the lanterns bus, the other gripping a handheld meter. He shot a look at the breach and muttered, "Congratulations, everyone—we've invented the world's angriest clogged drain."

Heat rolled off the breach like a furnace door opening behind glass. The Deceiver stepped through to the threshold—tall, immaculate, heat tugging at the edge of a perfect suit that didn't burn. His smile was generous. His eyes were not.

"What is this?" he asked, voice smooth as glass. "What are you doing?"

"Recycling," Naveen said without looking up. "Curbside pickup is Wednesdays."

Just inside the threshold, Abaddon crouched with his lieutenants tight behind him. He felt it first: a pull not in the lab but in the corridor beyond, down in the In Between where his Hollowed were jammed shoulder-to-shoulder, waiting. Their bodies bunched as the pause held. Now, with Adrian blocking the intake, the jam tightened. Rows five, six, seven slid backward an inch in unison, like a rope being hauled somewhere none of them could see.

"I did not order retreat," Abaddon snarled, the sound dry as claws on slate.

Naveen glanced up, deadpan. "Cool story, Captain Cuticle. Love what you've done with the talons."

"Hold your line," the Deceiver snapped without looking back, eyes fixed on Adrian. A seam crossed his expression—annoyance, then calculation. He flicked a glance toward Naveen, almost bored. "I will not be distracted by the jester."

"Great," Naveen said lightly, thumb steady on his switch. "I'm union anyway."

Abigail braced in front, iron chain looped between both hands, lantern lifted. Each time Abaddon's claw slashed for the floor, the lantern flared and pushed him a step back. Samuel set his shoulder behind her, weight steady. Between breach and mast, Jacob stepped forward and stood very still, as if telling the air itself where to go.

Elias scanned readouts: intake, shell charge, coil heat, the pause loop. "Is it working?"

"It's working," Lena said. She swallowed. "Pressure's curling the throat lip. We're beyond safe. When we let go, it all comes at once."

Adrian's glow intensified until it erased grime on the mast and threw clean shadows. He found Lena through the shine. Tried a grin. Almost made it.

"Hey," he whispered.

"Hey," she answered, voice breaking.

Down the corridor on the far side of the threshold, the Hollowed—scouts, runners, strays pressed forward by Abaddon—compacted like traffic on a sudden hill. Those at the opening dug in. Those behind crushed up, claws in spines, faces lifted in confusion and anger. The passage itself seemed to tighten, a throat refusing a mouthful.

The Deceiver's head tilted, listening to forces no living ear could hear. For the first time, his poise thinned. "You're not starving it," he murmured. "You're—"

"Your time is limited now," Jacob said, cutting across him without raising his voice. It carried anyway. "Any last requests?"

The Deceiver's smile returned, smaller and meaner. His gaze slid to the status lights: *RESUME IMPOSSIBLE — INTAKE BLOCKED — ENERGY ACCUMULATING.*

"What have you done?" he asked, the smoothness gone.

"Exactly what you were warned," Elias said, relief and terror tangled. "We're catching what you've been driving at us."

Another tick of pull ran down the corridor. The jammed ranks went from packed to bound. Hollowed in the eighth row lost their footing and scraped backward a handspan. Panic touched the far end and ran forward like a cold hand.

"Adrian," Elias called over the keen. "How long?"

Adrian couldn't answer. His jaw locked. Light pulsed faster under his skin, each wave leaving him dimmer for a heartbeat before the next flooded through. The smell of hot metal and rain filled the lab. The skin around the iris blistered his wrists. He held.

"Enough," the Deceiver said, and the word shoved. His front ranks steadied out of habit. The corridor still tugged.

Lena watched three needles climb together: intake pressure, loop stress, shell charge. She waited for the half breath where all three kissed the top of their arcs. "Ready—"

The Deceiver moved, lancing for the mast to rip Adrian free.

Jacob stepped into him.

They met like two opposite charges. The floor snarled. Heat swelled and recoiled. The Deceiver's face hardened. Jacob didn't give an inch. "No," he said, simple and final. The room believed him.

Abaddon lunged to break the line. Abigail pivoted and met him. Iron struck smoke-wrapped bone; sparks that weren't sparks spat from the impact and died midair. Abaddon reeled, hissed, and drove again. The lantern flame lengthened; she shoved light into his face. He threw himself back, clawing at nothing, half-blind with fury.

From the cart, Naveen called out, "Hey, Smokey—eyes on the 'no trespassing' sign. It's right there in iron and incandescent." He tapped the lantern rail back to full. "Abby, you've got clean power."

"Now!" Lena shouted.

Samuel went up the ladder in one burst, locked his arms under Adrian's ribs, and tore him free. There was no gentle in it. Static snapped all the way up Samuel's forearms. Adrian's grip failed. They fell backward together. Abigail caught Adrian by the collar and hauled him clear. The intake flashed white.

For a heartbeat, nothing changed. The hum held. The pressure needle sat pegged. The breach hissed.

Then the river broke.

The intake didn't inhale; it snapped shut on the backlog. Down the corridor in the In Between, the bunched Hollowed lost their anchor. The jam unspooled all at once. The second and third ranks went weightless, slammed into the first, and then slid, not into the lab, but sideways—into the invisible channel the Array had cut between realms. They were dragged as a mass, howling without sound, torn into long, bright tatters and sheets of ash as the machine's mouth took them.

Abaddon grabbed two by the spines to hold them. They tore free like wet rope. Rows five through ten vanished in a ragged line, bodies folded backward and fed to a hunger they had been meant to serve. The corridor beyond the breach gaped where his force had been.

The Deceiver realized it as the first empty spaces opened in his ranks. "Stop," he snapped to nothing that could obey. Heat pulsed from him in hard waves that scorched the mast black. The intake didn't care. It ate what had been stacked against it, the very army Abaddon had herded to the gate.

"Down!" Elias shouted.

The Array's core took those bodies and the stored charge together. A capacitor rang like a struck bell. The second blew in a white flash that erased the room for a blink. The third split with a sharp report and peppered the shields with glittering shards.

Abigail dragged Samuel and Adrian behind the nearest barrier. Elias folded down with Lena under the console hood. Jacob stayed where he was, feet set, hands open, as if finishing something he had started at birth. Naveen slammed his forearm over his eyes and ducked, still planted between the lantern rail and the auxiliary feed, refusing to abandon his switches. "Still here," he coughed. "Would love fewer fireworks."

The rings went incandescent, then failed. Wires snapped in bright beads. Solder flashed and vanished. The mast screamed and split from base to crown. A cone of white drove into the ceiling and came back as smoke. The freight door buckled and rang.

Silence clamped down. Tick tick tick of cooling metal. The air tasted like tin and rain after lightning.

"Samuel?" Abigail coughed.

"I'm here." He had Adrian's weight against him. "He's breathing."

"Elias? Lena?"

"Here," Elias answered. "Both."

Naveen lowered his arm and blinked through the smoke. "Lantern bus is still live. Aux feed's—uh—charbroiled, but we're lit." He gave a small, hoarse whoop. "Ten out of ten for dramatic exits."

Elias risked a look. The rack was peeled open like a steel flower. The monitors were black glass. The hum was gone. The breach face had dulled to slate gray. No hands. No eyes. No rush.

Jacob stepped forward through the smoke, untouched. Soot rolled off his shoulders as if the air made room. He stopped at the line and faced the threshold.

Abaddon sagged just inside, burned along the jaw, one eye a dark pit. The corridor behind him was stripped bare where his force had been. Space tugged at his shoulders—not forward, but back—as if the In Between itself wanted its temper returned. He bared his not-teeth at nothing.

The Deceiver stood framed in the slack gray, suit unmarked, eyes boiling black. The practiced warmth was gone. Panels rattled with the heat coming off him.

"What have you done," he said, each word a blade.

Jacob didn't blink. "Fed the Hollowed you stacked in the corridor to the machine you thought you could use. You brought them to our door. They were waiting. Now they're gone."

The Deceiver took a step to the very edge of the threshold. The heat rippled hard enough to rattle the loose shields. He looked at Jacob like a general looking at a single archer who spoiled the field.

He screamed—pure anger, no pretense.

Naveen, still at the cart, raised a hand like a weary stagehand. "Great projection, sir. Acoustics give you a solid A-minus."

The Deceiver's gaze flicked to him, voice dropping to a lethal calm. "I told you. I will not be distracted."

"Wouldn't dream of it," Naveen said. "I'm just customer support. Your complaint has been recorded."

Jacob didn't flinch. "Are you ready for what comes next?" he asked.

The question hung between them, sharp as a hook.

Scene 4: The Keeper Rises

Silence settled in the wake of the blast: the soft tick of cooling metal, the slow leak of steam, ash drifting like gray snow. The Array lay in pieces—one ring propped against a scorched wall, the mast split clean down, cables curled and blackened on the floor. The breach across the lab had dulled to slate. No hands. No eyes. Just a tired, gray pane.

"Sound off," Abigail said, lowering her chain but keeping the lantern high.

"Here," Elias answered, voice rough.

"Present," Lena coughed, rolling to a knee.

"Alive and crispy," Naveen said from behind a toppled cart, wiping soot from his cheek with the back of his wrist. "Would not recommend the spa."

Samuel eased Adrian upright against a pillar. "He's breathing."

"Hector," came a small voice to the right—Zora, crouched behind a tipped oscilloscope tower, eyes huge. "Here."

"Here," Hector added, already scrambling out to shove a battered first-aid kit across the floor to Samuel. "Got it."

Jacob stood in the center of the ruined room, ash refusing to cling to him, gaze steady on the dim threshold.

Abigail pulled out her phone with a shaking hand and hit the speed dial. "Natalie? Proceed with the news conference." A breath on the other end, then a crisp "Understood." She ended the call.

Across the room, the Deceiver straightened at the breach—immaculate suit, heat rippling off him in thin waves. He lifted his hands as if to throttle Jacob from twenty feet away.

"Enough," he said, velvet gone to wire.

Jacob didn't move. "No."

The air quivered around the boy, pressure with no grip. Abigail stepped closer, lantern up; the flame drew tall and held. Naveen slid along the wall toward the auxiliary panel, fingers finding the lantern bus and coaxing its last clean power from a half-melted strip. "Lights are good," he called softly, more to Abigail than anyone. "Blue on two, steady on three." Zora, jaw tight, passed him a spare battery pack without being asked.

Then the walls began to tremble. Not masonry—something behind it. A deep, measured pounding rolled in, too slow to be machinery, too certain to be wind. Dust sifted from the ceiling. Shattered glass chimed faintly. The gray face of the breach stirred as if remembering how to breathe.

"Back," Samuel said, dragging Adrian farther into a corner. Elias and Lena joined them, hauling a dented shield into place. Hector knelt beside Samuel, ripping gauze with his teeth; Zora braced the shield with both hands, knuckles white, but she held.

It arrived.

The Echo did not squeeze through a doorway; the room made space because it had to. Edges clarified. Smoke flattened. Light settled. No flash. No spectacle. Presence—immense, exact, inarguable.

Abigail felt it in her sternum the way a low note lives in bone. Her head dipped without thought. Beside her, Samuel did the same. Elias's hands stilled over dead controls. Naveen's mouth opened on a reflexive quip, closed again; he bowed his head a fraction like a man remembering he was in church.

The voice filled the lab, low and resonant. "Deceiver."

The name landed like a gavel.

"You schemed to steal what is not yours. You pressed the hungry against a door you did not keep." A heartbeat. "Return."

The Deceiver smiled with all his teeth. Heat climbed the ruined mast until metal glowed. "I do not answer to a fading shadow," he said, stepping forward. Abaddon moved with him, burned along the jaw, one eye gone dark, beta pack crowding the threshold.

The Echo did not raise Its voice. "Return."

The Deceiver's smile thinned. "No."

The Echo acted.

Pressure gathered—not crushing, binding. The gray plane of the breach deepened; a corridor showed like a throat ready to swallow. Every dark corner in the lab peeled loose: straggler Hollowed answering their master's unspoken call. The Echo turned its attention and they froze mid-step, pinned as if set in resin. With a small, exact pull, the keeper tore them loose and flung them back across.

The reach didn't stop at the lab. It went everywhere a surface watched: elevator doors in downtown towers bucked and went black; the chrome edge of a diner pass-through flashed and emptied; bathroom mirrors in apartments from Tacoma to Shoreline clouded hard, then cleared to ordinary glass. Storefront windows on rain-slick streets blinked like eyes and shut. Phone screens and blank TV panels shrugged off fingerprints of light that weren't reflections and spit the hunters back. Ambulances caught in gridlock, their rear cabinets full of polished steel, rattled as shapes were yanked out of their shine and dragged away. In basements and bedrooms where families had taped sheets over mirrors, the sheets bellied once and stilled. Across the city a thousand small rescues happened at once, quiet as a door relatching.

And in the breath after that relatching, some panes gave back what they had taken. Faces flattened in glass like pressed flowers blinked and rounded; a handful of bodies slumped to tile floors and wet sidewalks, alive and sobbing, as if drowning victims had been hauled up at the last second. Others did not return—only silhouettes thinned and faded behind the glass, threads tugged but not freed, as if they'd been knotted deeper than a single pull could unbind. The Echo didn't look at the saved or the missing. It held the door and held the law.

The Deceiver snarled and shoved. Heat hammered the floor. The room stuttered bright-dark-bright; panels rattled; the freight door slammed on its track. He reached again for Jacob, intent a blade.

Jacob lifted his chin and held him there. "Not me," he said, calm as a fact.

Abaddon lunged out of reflex, reaching for Abigail. She met him with the lantern's face. Light punched through smoke and bone; he reeled to the threshold, pinned by a force his rage couldn't name. Hector flinched, then forced himself to keep pressure on the gauze at Adrian's wrist. Zora, shaking, fed Samuel tape with quick, efficient hands.

"You had a moment," the Echo said, nothing theatrical in it. "It is over."

The Deceiver tried one last trick—glamour pushed like a tide, charm turned to weapon. It slid off the room as if the world no longer granted it permission. He set his palms against nothing anyone else could see and braced.

The Echo reached.

Not hands—judgment. Weight. Law. It took hold of the Deceiver and Abaddon together and pulled. Their heels scraped slick concrete that could not possibly resist. The Deceiver's perfect face tore; he showed what lived under it for a heartbeat—hatred, fear, a depthless hunger—then masked it again.

"You cannot—" he began.

"Enough," the Echo said.

They went backward through the deepening pane, not vanishing but crossing—dragged, resisting, beautiful and ruined, kicking in a medium with no purchase. The threshold flexed around them. For a breath the lab filled with elsewhere: Father Allen's lantern far away like a patient star; corridors clearing as outlaw things were yanked from stolen paths; reflections blinking out in a thousand panes. Then the gray settled again to dull slate and the pressure in the room let go.

Silence returned in a rush. Metal ticked. Someone—Zora—sobbed once and clamped a hand over her mouth, embarrassed by survival. Naveen, breathing hard, slid down the side of the auxiliary panel and sat, elbows on knees. "Okay," he said softly to no one and everyone. "Let's never do that again."

Abigail lowered the lantern a fraction and bowed her head. "Keeper."

The Echo's presence eased without leaving. It felt like the deep of a lake after storm—calm with movement under it. The attention shifted to Jacob and held. No words, not for the rest of them. Jacob straightened as if taking on a weight he knew how to carry and nodded once.

Abigail's phone buzzed. A text from Natalie: LIVE in five.

She met Elias's and Lena's eyes over the wreckage. No speeches. The machine was dead; the door was held; now the other reckoning would begin.

"Balance isn't finished with us," Samuel murmured.

"No," Abigail said, slipping the phone away and keeping the lantern high while, across the city, microphones warmed and the next battle stepped into the light. Hector tightened the last wrap of bandage, Zora steadied Adrian's shoulder, and Naveen—hands still shaking—checked the lantern bus one more time, as if keeping that small line of glow alive could keep the world from tipping again.

21

After the Thunder

Scene 1: The Array Falls Silent

Ash drifted in slow flakes, turning the lab into a snow globe someone had shaken too hard. The Array was a carcass: rings split and jammed under tables, the mast cracked open like a bone, scorched cables curled into black vines. The breach across the far wall had dulled to a tired, matte gray. No hands pressed against it. No eyes peered back.

No one said anything for a long half minute. The building itself seemed to be catching its breath—ducts ticking, a loose panel giving a small, uneven rattle each time the wind tugged the freight door.

Adrian moved first.

He coughed, winced, and pushed himself up on one elbow against a toppled tool cart. Blisters ringed his forearms where the intake collar had branded him. His shirt was burned through in a circle at the chest, fabric melted and fused in places, but his eyes were clear.

"Still here," he managed, hoarse. "Against the odds."

Lena was on him in three quick steps, dropping to her knees and taking his face in both hands, laugh and sob tangled. "Idiot," she said, relief making the word soft. "Absolute idiot."

"Learned from the best," he rasped, and then looked past her to Elias.

Elias stood with one hand braced on the ruined chassis, as if the metal could steady him. He stared at Adrian, and what moved across his face was complicated—shock first, then the shape grief would have taken if it had been asked to. Instead, something else arrived: release.

"You should be dead," he said, not accusing, just saying it aloud to make himself believe the opposite.

Adrian nodded once. "Thought so too."

Naveen slid out from behind a scorched monitor cart, hair dusted gray with ash, one sleeve singed to a fashionable ruin. He gave a two-finger salute. "For the record, if anyone asks, I told the Very Handsome Space Heater in a Suit that his monologue was mid. Seemed to rattle him. You're welcome."

Jacob stepped forward from the scorched center of the floor, ash refusing to cling to his sneakers, lantern-light from Abigail's hand finding him like a habit. He looked at Adrian, then at Elias and Lena.

"The Echo says he was spared," Jacob said simply. "For what he gave."

Adrian blinked. "It… spoke to you?"

"He hears me," Jacob said, as if describing the weather. "He heard what you did."

Silence followed, but it wasn't the heavy kind. It spread and thinned, making room.

Abigail lowered her chain and let the lantern settle to its normal flame. She touched Samuel's sleeve and he squeezed her fingers once, quietly proud and raw-eyed.

Lena smoothed a dark streak off Adrian's cheek with her thumb. "Does 'spared' come with 'no nerve damage'?" she asked, trying to keep the moment light while her hands shook.

"We'll get him to urgent care," Elias said. He took a breath, crossed the gap, and held out his hand. "Thank you."

Adrian looked at the hand like it might vanish if he blinked. Then he clasped it. His palm was hot and trembled against Elias's. "You did the math. I just… stood where the math needed a body."

"You stood where none of the rest of us could," Elias said. He held for a second longer, then let go, throat working. "I won't forget."

Hector appeared with a dented water jug and a roll of gauze, kneeling to dribble water over Adrian's wrists. "Careful," he murmured, eyes big but steady. Zora hovered beside him with a cracked plastic bin, collecting razor-edged bits of solder splash and feeding Hector tape when he tapped for it.

A muffled vibration buzzed in Abigail's pocket. She checked the screen: a text from Natalie—LIVE. Minutes. She met Reese's name in the preview, then slid the phone away.

"Everything okay?" Samuel asked.

"It's beginning," Abigail said. "The other half."

Across the room, the other intern—pale and soot-streaked—leaned back against a cabinet and began to cry without sound. Zora looked over, squeezed his shoulder once, then got him moving—away from the glass, toward a stool, practical and kind.

Elias turned once in a slow circle, taking in the wreckage. He had imagined this machine as an idea that would outlive him. Seeing it in pieces, he felt no loss he cared to keep.

"We break down what's left," he said, voice steady. "Every board, every coil. We pull the schematics from every drive and air-gap what we can't burn. There won't be a second Array."

"And the other units?" Lena asked, already scanning the room for cases and crates.

"They never leave their crates," Elias answered. "We'll notify the DOE… and then notify them again in public."

Adrian snorted softly. "Public first. Lessons learned."

Elias glanced at him. "Public first," he agreed.

"Also," Naveen added, pushing his glasses up with the side of a knuckle, "public record should reflect that I called Mister Sulfur

Screen Saver a 'powerpoint in a suit' to his face. He did not appreciate the feedback." He grinned, then winced as a cough hit. "Worth it."

He tipped his chin toward Jacob. "Kid, A+ force field. If he gives you trouble again, I've got more material. 'Deceiver' rhymes with a lot of things."

"Naveen," Elias said, a warning that held a weary smile.

"Right, right. Healing silence." He zippered imaginary lips… then cracked them. "Just saying, best heckle of my career."

He shuffled over to the lantern bus, fingers checking the pitted terminals out of habit. "Lantern circuit is still clean," he reported, tone softening. "Blue on two, steady on three."

He glanced toward the gray pane and lowered his voice. "In case the handsome furnace wants a rematch."

He got a look from Abigail that was not unkind and very clear. Naveen nodded and let the line die.

He drifted back to Hector and Zora, helped slide a shield panel upright and wedge it against a trembling cabinet. "Nice hands," he told Hector. "You missed your calling as a field medic."

"Pass," Hector said, but he smiled.

Elias turned back to Jacob. "What about him?" He tipped his head toward the muted pane of the breach.

Jacob studied the gray. "He's awake. Strong. Not here."

Abigail followed his gaze. "Will he show himself?" she asked.

"No," Jacob said. "Not now. He's… cleaning."

They all understood. Out there—every elevator door, every chrome ribbon, every mirror someone hadn't yet covered—the keeper was dragging back what had slipped through and closing what had been pried open. The thought brought a hush none of them minded.

Adrian eased to sitting. "If I pass out, tell the Echo I appreciate the encore."

"You pass out and I'm stapling you to the gurney," Lena said, half laughing.

Elias crouched beside them. "When you can stand, we get you checked out. After that… we'll need statements. Press will come. You don't have to talk."

Adrian's mouth twitched. "I will, actually. Not like before. Just… straight lines. No angles."

Abigail looked at Jacob again—at the boy who had stepped into a room with the Deceiver and said no like it was a door he could shut with a word. "You held him," she said softly. "All of them."

Jacob didn't preen. He just nodded, as if confirming something she already knew. "He'll try again," Jacob added. "Not here. Not now. But he remembers the door."

"Then we'll remember the lock," Samuel said.

Lena stood and crossed to Elias, wiping at her face with the back of her wrist, streaking ash. She leaned into him, and he folded an arm around her shoulders. No big ceremony. The room watched and pretended it wasn't.

Abigail's phone buzzed again. Natalie this time: Ready? Abigail thumbed back a single word—Go.

She imagined the ballroom downtown, the lights, Avery's practiced smile, the bank of cameras. She pictured Reese waiting with his questions, the edit queued, the dashcam frame that would freeze a smug man's face forever at the moment it should have burned. The thought didn't feel like revenge; it felt like math, too—cause and consequence finding their place.

Jacob tilted his head, listening to something no one else could hear. "He says thank you," he told Abigail, and then, after a beat, to Elias and Lena as well. "For stopping it."

Elias blinked. "The Echo… thanks us?"

"He keeps the balance," Jacob said. "But it isn't his world. It's ours."

"Put that on a poster," Naveen muttered, then lifted both hands. "Kidding. Not kidding. Kidding."

The breach made a soft noise then, like wind pulling at a door that didn't want to open. Everyone turned. A ripple moved across the gray, then calmed. No silhouette. No voice. Just the sense of a large thing with work to do elsewhere.

Abigail raised the lantern in a small salute. "We'll keep the lights on," she said to the quiet pane. "Do your part. We'll do ours."

Elias straightened. "Let's clear the lab," he said. "Pack what isn't cursed, tag what is. Then showers, doctors, whatever passes for food."

"Coffee," Adrian said, squinting at his blistered hands as if trying to decide if he could still hold a cup. "And, uh... since we're putting things right—this doesn't fix everything I broke. I know that."

"It fixes today," Elias said. "Tomorrow we fix what we can reach."

Lena's hand found Elias's again, fingers lacing with a steadiness that felt like a promise. Samuel slid an arm around Abigail's waist, grounding her. Jacob took one last look at the breach, then turned his back on it without fear.

Naveen, already coaxing a battered shop vac to life with Zora's help, glanced up. "For the record," he said, voice light again, "if the Deceiver swings by for customer feedback, tell him the reviews are mixed. Two stars. Would not breach again."

"Pack the reels, Shakespeare," Elias said, but he was smiling.

The ash kept falling in light, harmless flakes. Outside, sirens wound toward quiet. Somewhere downtown, a microphone warmed and a red light blinked on. In here, among wreckage and exhausted people, the next road waited—work that would not be glamorous: inventories, statements, long nights of explaining and mending.

Grace sometimes looked like that. Not trumpets. Not a hand from the sky. Just breath returning to chests that had been held too tight. Just a boy listening to a keeper. Just a man forgiven and spared when he should not have been.

"Let's go," Abigail said.

They started moving—slow, deliberate, together.

Scene 2: The Returned and the Missing

The ballroom looked built for verdicts: chandeliers, flags on brass poles, a wall of screens looping glossy B-roll—Tacoma skyline, shipyards, a staged handshake with a lab coat. The podium wore a navy banner stamped with a new slogan in white: *FORWARD WASHINGTON*. Donors packed the front rows in suits that didn't wrinkle; cameras clustered in a pen at center; staffers lined the walls with clipboards and headsets, all of them humming with the smug certainty of a rollout going right.

Avery Shaw made them hum louder.

He strode out in a trim charcoal suit and a smile honed by a thousand green rooms. The applause hit like surf—long, eager, loud enough to swallow the first line of his speech. He didn't mind. He drank it in, hands raised in a gesture halfway between benediction and embrace.

"Friends," he began, voice filling the room without strain, "tonight we stop reacting and start leading."

More applause. Natalie Chen, at the A/V table in the far corner, marked each beat against a rundown she knew by heart. T-0.00: entrance. T-2.15: pivot to message. T-7.30: announcement. She gave the lighting op a small nod; the podium warmed a shade, Avery's jawline sharpened, the banner glowed richer blue. Everything looked composed, controlled. That was the point.

"Washington needs a plan for energy, for safety, for hope," Avery said. "I intend to deliver that plan. Tonight, with humility and resolve, I am announcing my candidacy for governor of this great state."

The room erupted. Balloons didn't fall—Natalie had killed the balloons—but the donors stood; the staffers clapped until their palms stung. On the screens, the word *GOVERNOR* pulsed above a slow pan of Mount Rainier. Avery basked, chin lifted just enough to look like destiny.

When the noise ebbed, he signaled to the press pen. "I'll take a few questions."

Hands shot up. Natalie had already spoken to the floor manager; she had already spoken to the moderator; she had arranged the order. The moderator pointed past three local anchors to the man in a gray sports coat with a small microphone cube that read *SEATTLE SPEC-TRAL.*

"Reese Mathers," the moderator said. "Seattle Spectral."

Reese rose. His cheeks were pale under the lights, but his voice didn't wobble. "Congratulations, Mr. Shaw," he said. "Three questions."

Avery's smile widened. "Go ahead."

"First: internal memos from the Department of Energy show you pressured a private contractor to operate an experimental array at unsafe levels after scientists warned of unexplained side effects. Why?"

Avery let out a soft, practiced laugh. "We encourage innovation in this state. Consultation is not coercion, Mr. Mathers. We pushed for results with appropriate oversight. Any suggestion otherwise is conspiracy theory."

A few chuckles from the donor seats. Avery's eyes cut to them and back, comfortable again.

"Second," Reese said, unfazed, "did you, at any time, instruct Elias Voss to deploy that array specifically at Clover Park Technical College because it produced the highest 'harvest' despite spreading incidents of mirror-related abductions in the surrounding neighborhoods?"

Avery shook his head and layered on patience. "I am not in the business of ordering private research schedules. And with respect, Mr. Mathers, tales of 'mirror abductions' belong on late-night radio, not in serious policy discussions."

A ripple of laughter. Avery's supporters were happy to be told what was beneath them.

"Third," Reese said, "on a rainy night six years ago, did you strike Douglas Mathers with your car in an alley behind the Park Royal office tower and then arrange to destroy or hide evidence?"

The room tightened. Cameras leaned in. The donors stilled.

Avery didn't blink. "I did not. I did not know Mr. Mathers. I was at home that night; records will show that. This line of questioning is beneath this moment and, frankly, beneath you."

"Thank you," Reese said.

He didn't argue. He didn't press. He simply turned to the A/V table.

Natalie lifted a finger.

"Roll," she said.

The screens behind Avery cut from mountain and harbor to a stark slate: white letters on black—*INTERNAL CORRESPONDENCE, DOE*—then the first memo filled the wall. Avery's name. A timestamp. Language no consultant had vetted: accelerate deployment at Site CP-03, secure deliverables this quarter, litigation exposure acceptable. The room murmured. A second slide dropped in—calendar invites, call logs, a bullet list from a deputy: talking points to counter 'superstition' complaints. Another murmur, uglier.

Avery turned, palm up, smiling as if at a wedding montage gone out of order. "Folks, anyone can make a slide—"

The dashcam image cut him off.

The alley bloomed across three screens: rain silvering the asphalt, a brick wall with a metal back door propped on a wood wedge. A man stepped out—coat collar up, face bare to the weather. He crossed toward a parked sedan. The angle caught him clean, washed in sodium light: Douglas Mathers. Reese's father.

Headlights swung in from the left. A black government sedan nosed into frame, too fast for the slick. It didn't swerve away. It didn't brake. It struck. Douglas's body folded across the hood, face to glass—one terrible, unmistakable second—then slid out of frame.

A collective breath left the room. Somewhere in the second row, a woman put her hand to her mouth.

The clip jumped. The driver's door opened. Avery's face, came into view in the alley light—cold, dry, focused. He looked directly into the camera mounted low on the dash. He reached into his coat, pulled a phone, spoke into it—no audio here—and then lifted a flashlight and smashed the lens.

The footage froze on his face a beat before the blow.

"Metadata," Reese's voice said over the ballroom speakers, calm and precise. "Autobackup to a city server, timestamped by a network clock. Chain-of-custody preserved through three independent verifications. Hash match certifying no alteration. Cross-angle confirmation from a municipal traffic cam. Mr. Shaw's phone pinged a tower one block away at the time of impact."

Natalie let the still frame hang. The silence had a sound to it—static and disbelief and a room recalibrating.

Avery forced a laugh that didn't make it past his teeth. "Deepfake," he said. "This is grotesque. It's illegal. My lawyers—"

"Mr. Shaw," Reese said, live again, "earlier you said you didn't know Douglas Mathers and you were at home. Would you like to correct your statement?"

Avery grasped the sides of the podium. His knuckles whitened. "This is a smear. I have served this state with honor. I will not be tried by... by tabloid tactics."

"Then one more," Reese said. He didn't need it, but he had it: an email on the screen, subject line: clean-up, from a private account Avery used for "scheduling," to a name that had appeared in a corruption probe three years earlier. The body text was short and damning: Done. No loose ends.

It was Natalie's favorite line. It had scraped something raw in her the first time she saw it. It did again.

Avery looked out over the donors as if they might rescue him. Some wouldn't meet his eyes.

A uniformed officer who'd been posted at the back for "security optics" stirred. He'd seen enough. He stepped forward, hand on radio, head tilted as if listening. Two plainclothes detectives flanked him, badges out. Natalie—who had done her homework with a patient ADA—watched them thread through the aisles with the quiet inevitability of weather.

"Mr. Shaw," the officer said at the foot of the riser, voice steady through the mic feed, "based on presented evidence and a judge's signed warrant, you are under arrest for vehicular homicide, leaving the scene of an accident, and obstruction of justice. Please step down."

Avery didn't move. "Do you know who I am?" he asked, finally dropping the smile. It came out smaller than he meant.

"Yes, sir," the officer said. "Turn around, please."

For a heartbeat, Avery looked like he might bolt sideways into the staff lane. He glanced at Natalie—only a flick, a curl of contempt, of blame—and found nothing helpful there. He glanced at Reese, and Reese held his gaze without heat.

Avery turned. The cuffs clicked. The donors' row rustled with expensive discomfort. A few phones rose despite staff gestures to keep them down. The screens still held his face—caught mid-denial, time finally refusing to bend.

"Governor Shaw," Reese said, last question, voice even, "do you still intend to run?"

Avery half turned, wrists pinned, and started to speak—something about conspiracies, about enemies, about the price of leadership. The detectives guided him off the riser. The mic left his range. His words dissolved into the carpet and the soft whirr of cameras recording the end of a story he thought he controlled.

Natalie exhaled, long and quiet. She gave the A/V op a two-finger cut and the screens went black. The room didn't applaud. It didn't boo. It sat in the sudden absence of spin and watched a man who thought he was untouchable walk past a flag and a fallen slogan and into a side door.

In the pen, Reese lowered his mic. The hand that wasn't holding it shook. He steadied it against his thigh and looked up into the lights. For a moment, the noise of the ballroom fell away and he saw his father's face in alley light, the way the dashcam had caught it. He didn't smile. He didn't cry. He just stood there and remembered that justice sometimes arrived late and still mattered.

Across town, in a ruined lab that smelled of burned tin and rain, Abigail's phone buzzed with a single word from Natalie.

Done.

Scene 3: Terms of the Balance

Night laid a calm hand over the lake and the cottage finally felt like a house again, not a bunker. The lab smells were gone from their clothes; the grit of blown solder was washed from their hands. Samuel had fallen asleep on the couch with a quilt over his knees, a book face-down on his chest. The TV was off. Even the refrigerator seemed to hum softer.

Abigail set a coil of iron chain back in its drawer and checked the salt line along the baseboard out of habit more than fear. The hallway mirrors wore their cloth shrouds. For the first time in weeks, she didn't feel watched by anything but the ordinary room.

Jacob sat at the kitchen table with his sketch pad. He had drawn the mast broken in two, a ring tilted like a wheel against a wall, a small figure with hands held out—steady, not dramatic. When he caught Abigail watching, he gave a small, private smile and went back to the page.

It began with the glass.

The window over the sink didn't fog or frost; it deepened, as if the world behind it had been pulled closer. The reflection of the lamp and dish towel gathered weight. Pressure pricked at Abigail's ears—her sure sign. She touched Jacob's shoulder. He was already turning.

"Samuel," she said softly.

He woke fast, the way practice trains a person. He stood with one hand on the couch back, the other on the doorway frame. He saw the window and steadied himself.

The light in the room didn't change, but the space did. From the window's deepened pane, a shape assembled—the great, bowed silhouette they had seen in the lab when the world was still burning. It didn't step into the kitchen; it didn't need to. It filled the place behind the glass until their small night felt like a candle cupped in a hand.

The Echo.

Abigail's breath caught and settled. She dipped her head—not worship, simply due respect to a keeper who had kept them.

Jacob rose without scraping the chair. He stopped at the seam where house met window, lamp-light gilding his hair.

"Keeper," he said.

The answer came the way it should: not a blast, but a low resonance that lived just under the skin and made the bones agree.

"Abigail Jensen. Jacob."

No titles. The names held purpose inside them.

"Thank you," it said.

Abigail let out a small, relieved laugh. "We turned the right key," she said. "You did the rest."

The Echo's head—if that was what it was—tipped a degree. "I asked," it said. "You answered. Answering has weight."

Samuel stood two steps back, hands down, eyes bright. Awe mixed with the old worry and something like love. He gave Jacob a look he couldn't shape into words. Jacob didn't turn, but he reached back and squeezed Samuel's fingers once, quick.

"The breach is sealed," the Echo said. "The wide tears are closed. Those who fed in the open will be forced back into shadow, or taken.

The loudest mouths have been pulled across. Balance is work. I am working."

"Abaddon?" Abigail asked.

"Bound," the Echo said. "Clever still. He will test the fence. He remembers the taste of permission. He is watched."

"And the other one," Samuel said before he could stop himself. "The handsome one."

"The Deceiver is returned to my side," the Echo answered. "He knows your air now, so he will ache for it. He will press where surfaces pretend to be deep. He will be refused."

Abigail nodded. The cord in her chest loosened a notch. "What do you need from us now?" she asked.

The answer came plain.

"Abigail," the Echo said, "keep your house safe and teach others to keep theirs. Cover glass when you must. Do not answer knocks that are not hands. When you are called for help, do not go alone. Call on Father Allen when you cross. When the frightened come to you, test them and then be kind. Do not feed panic. Keep records—places, times, patterns—and share them quickly. Rest when the days are quiet; you will be needed when they are not."

Abigail took it in with a steady nod. Simple, clear, doable.

"Jacob," the Echo said, and the air leaned toward the boy. "You see. They know you see. Some will hate that. Some will want to follow you. Do not try to be their ruler. Point them to me and to the stewards I set. Listen before you speak. Learn from Allen and from Abigail. Do not provoke. If you are unsure, be still until you are sure. You are protected, but you are not made to stand alone for long. Ask for help."

Jacob's chin lifted a little—not defiance, attention. "I understand," he said.

The Echo's focus shifted, like a wind turning. "Father Allen will hold light where it is needed," it added. "Honor his work when you cross. Send those you can't carry to him."

Abigail glanced at Samuel. He exhaled, shoulders easing.

"You will be protected," the Echo said, and the words felt like an action, not a wish. Every reflective surface in the cottage trembled so lightly only trained nerves caught it—the sink window, the dark face of the TV, the framed photo, the thin mirrored strip inside the spice cabinet. Each filmed, for a heartbeat, with a rain-like sheen. It faded, but the room felt different after, as if a brace had been installed where the walls needed it.

"On both sides," the Echo added. "Here and in the In Between. Those who come to harm you will lose heart. Those who come to learn will be seen and not swallowed."

Samuel's throat worked. "Thank you," he said, and his voice held both the man and the grandfather in it.

The Echo's presence warmed around him. "You have carried fear without spreading it," it said. "Keep doing that."

"I will," he said.

Something like remembered light moved across the Echo's outline—a faint crown, a ripple in deep water. For a moment the kitchen felt like the edge of a wide field at night with a strong moon—small humans, big world, and belonging to it.

"There will be a stretch of quiet," it said. "Use it well. Build. Rest. Teach. The ones who broke law have been named. Your world will go back to its own arguments. Do not let the small ones distract you from the work you have taken."

Abigail glanced at Jacob. He had stopped drawing. His hands were empty and open.

"You spared Adrian," he said. "You told me you would."

"I did," the Echo replied. "He hurt you. He repented. You will decide what to do with both truths. Mercy is not blindness."

Abigail accepted that. Mercy always carried cost. She had paid it before and would again. "We understand."

The Echo seemed to settle, like a tide folding back on itself. "I remain," it said, and the room believed it.

"Keeper?" Jacob asked, quick, the way a child does before the last page turns.

"Yes."

"Will it happen again?"

"Not like this," the Echo said. "Never exactly like this. But you know the sound of the first wrong notes now. Hear them sooner next time."

The window cleared. The kitchen became only a kitchen again: lamp, towel, pencils on a pad. The pressure left their ears. The quiet didn't feel empty.

"Tea?" Abigail asked, because boiling water is a kind of prayer the house understood.

Samuel picked up the quilt and folded it, practical hands steady. "Please," he said.

He kept his voice low. "What about the ones who were taken? Do they come back now?"

Abigail stared at the black window, her reflection faint in the glass. "I don't know," she said. "Some… yes. Some, not yet."

Jacob turned from the pane. "He told me," the boy said, simple as weather. "When the pump stopped, the knots loosened. The ones taken at the edge feel the pull and slip free first. The ones bitten through have to be remade—slow, with help. And a few are gone—burned into the hunger that ate them. He knows their names. We can still carry light to the places that remember."

Samuel swallowed. "So it isn't over."

"No," Jacob said. "It's only quieter."

Jacob slid the drawing back and added one line—a firmer shadow under the small figure's feet, the weight of someone who knows where to stand.

The kettle began its low song. In the window, they saw only their own faces—ordinary, dear—and the faintest sheen that said the glass remembered being more than glass and was content with it. They were, too.

Scene 4: Charge to a Steward

The In Between had gone quiet in a way Father Allen had never heard—a deep, working quiet, like a city after snow when the plows have already passed and people are shoveling their own steps. The cathedral of broken glass still arched overhead, but the shards no longer crowded forward; they kept their distance, wary, as if remembering a boundary. The floor's black sheen breathed slower. Far off, the last of the Hollowed skittered back along corridors, tugged by a law stronger than appetite.

Allen stood in a shallow hollow he had used many times. Its low roof of tilted panes turned the lamplight into a bowl. Three freshly rescued souls huddled near the curve of wall—more present than before, their edges smoother, eyes less startled. Russell lingered at the mouth of the hollow, hands on his knees, catching his breath like a man who had run stairs he hadn't meant to climb.

"Okay," he panted. "Consensus: I am not built for parkour in haunted cathedrals."

"You did well," Allen said. The priest's lantern burned steady and taller than he had ever seen it, the flame inside no longer a nervous tongue but a column. Even Russell, who didn't have words for such things, could tell something in the air had shifted toward order.

The shift turned to presence.

It didn't arrive on wings or wind. It was just there, filling the space beyond the hollow and then, gently, the hollow itself. The pane at Allen's shoulder deepened. Reflections surrendered their little tricks and settled into a single silhouette, immense and composed. Pressure pricked at the corners of every aperture—window, shard edge, silvered puddle—as if the realm were holding its breath for a name.

"Keeper," Allen murmured, and bowed his head.

Russell straightened and swallowed hard. He had seen the Echo at the lab, seen its force, but here in its own house the thing felt even larger—not loud, not bright, simply undeniable.

"Father Allen," the Echo said. Its voice lived under the skin, the pitch that warms wood and makes old buildings sing. "You have kept watch. You have gathered the lost and refused panic. You have named the hungry as hungry and not as gods. You have done this without asking for rank."

Allen's knuckles tightened on the lantern handle. "I have tried to be faithful," he said.

"Then hear me plainly." The glass around them seemed to lean closer. "This realm needs stewards who remember the point of law. I give you charge."

The words landed like a mantle. Heat—not burning, more like a response—rose in the metal cage against Allen's palm. The lamp brightened without glare, and a second light, smaller, kindled in the air over his heart: a steady ember, seen and then sensed more than seen.

"What does that mean?" Russell asked, too honest to pretend he knew.

"It means this," the Echo said, and for once it spoke not in images but in tasks. "Allen, you may mark hollows safe with your word and the light you carry. Where you set a seal, Hollowed will not cross unless someone inside invites them. You may close a corridor for a time when a crossing must be protected. You may call my attention when you are pressed and I am far. You may kindle small lights in hands that have none—those who come to help in good order may carry a spark home and not be eaten for it. And when a rogue will not heed any lesser voice, you may bind it and send it to me."

Allen let out a breath he hadn't known he was keeping. They were not theatrics. They were tools. They were exactly what the work needed. "Thank you," he said, simple, because anything more would wobble.

The Echo's attention shifted to Russell. "You have stumbled," it said, "and still you followed. Your clumsy mercy saved more than you think. But you are not made to shepherd here."

Russell's laugh came out thin and real. "Strong agree."

Allen turned, a kindly reproach waiting on his tongue. Russell raised both hands. "I mean, look at my track record—nearly knocked over a sacred archway, almost tripped into a soul-lake, told a Veil-borne I was a 'big fan' mid-fight. I'm useful, but I'm also a hazard."

"Father," the Echo said.

Allen faced the silhouette again.

"Ask what you will for him."

Allen did not have to think. "Send him back," he said. "Whole and unharmed. He has work on the other side. He fumbles too much to shepherd here."

Russell blinked. "Hey—accurate, but ow."

"You will do more good where a microphone carries farther than a shout in these halls," Allen said gently. "And I would like you alive, if it's all the same."

The Echo considered a beat that felt like kindness itself. "Granted," it said. "He returns by a path that will not bite him. His memory of this place will blur at the edges when it must, but it will not be taken. He will carry what he can bear."

Relief, raw and immediate, broke across Russell's face. "Thank you," he said, and for once there was no joke caught under the words. He looked at Allen. "For pulling me out of dumb more than once."

Allen gripped his shoulder. "You came when it mattered. Now go where it matters next."

"Wait," Russell said, turning back to the Echo, sudden urgency tripping his tongue. "If you want me to say something, on the other side—what should it be? One sentence. I can do a sentence."

The Echo obliged him. "Tell them this," it said. "Panic fattens the dark. Help one another instead." It paused. "And listen to Abigail Jensen and to Jacob. When they say cover glass, cover it."

"I can sell that," Russell said, breathless. "No, not sell—carry. I can carry that."

The pane at the hollow's mouth cleared to a clean, round brightness, like the face of a lens wiped with a steady hand. In it, a room gathered itself: a studio's dim with a single work light on, a familiar mirror against a wall, a mug with cold coffee, the kind of silence that belongs to a place between shows.

"That's my side door," Russell said, wonder flattening his vowels. "I know that dent in the baseboard."

Allen squeezed once and let go. "Peace," he said.

Russell nodded too many times, then forced himself to stillness. "Keeper," he said to the silhouette, and surprised himself by bowing. "Thanks for the loaner time."

"Stand straight," the Echo said, not unkindly. "You are not owned."

"Right. Standing. Going."

He stepped forward. The bright circle met him like cool air at the mouth of a tunnel. For one second the glass showed him back to them—a man who was scared and trying anyway. Then he moved through, and the circle sealed with a soft, decisive sound, like a book closing.

Silence folded in behind him. The souls in the hollow watched the spot with the mild, patient attention of people waiting for their turn at a window. Allen felt an ache—loss braided with relief—and let it be what it was.

"Steward," the Echo said.

Allen looked up. The new name fit like a coat he'd been wearing in the dark and had only now seen.

"I will not do this perfectly," he said.

"You will do it," the Echo answered. "Perfection is a story pride tells. Order is work." A faint shimmer ran along the arch above them, like stress testing a beam. "Use your gifts. Ask when you are unsure. Teach others."

"I will," Allen said.

The Echo's presence thinned, not withdrawn so much as spread wider. Before it went fully to its other tasks, it added one last, practical instruction. "Where you set your seal," it said, "draw it with light and speak it: 'Rest is kept here.' The Hollowed will understand. The obedient will keep away. The stubborn will learn."

Allen nodded. He lifted the lantern and, with a motion that felt like writing and prayer together, traced a small circle on the hollow's entrance. The light hung in the air a moment and then settled, a mark plain as chalk.

"Rest is kept here," he said.

The mark held. Far down the corridor, something tested the air and decided it did not care to argue with that door. The hush of the place deepened by a shade.

The Echo was already elsewhere—Allen could feel it—walking the long grid of byways, checking what it had mended, listening for thin places that still needed brace and band. But its last word to him washed back along the glass, quiet enough that only a man who had learned to listen could hear it.

"Well done."

Allen stood a while with the lantern in his hand, not because the dark frightened him now, but because the light meant what it meant. Then he turned from the hollow to the corridor and went back to work, a steward in a realm that had nearly forgotten what stewardship felt like, grateful to remember.

The End

Epilogue

They found Russell sitting on the low stone wall outside the station, sleeves rolled, tie crooked, watching morning traffic ease past the glass doors of Northwest Point. The receptionist spotted him first and cried out; then came the flood—handshakes, quick hugs, backslaps that said more than words. He'd been gone long enough to become a rumor. Now he was back, thinner around the eyes, gentler at the edges. People kept saying, "You look good," and what they meant was, "You look different."

Outside the studio windows, the city wore tentative normalcy. Crews were unboarding shopfronts; a flatbed rumbled by stacked with sheets of new safety glass. Maintenance placards came off elevator doors. Street mirrors—rearview, bus, storefront—caught sky again without turning to frost. The emergency scrolls were gone from the bottom of local broadcasts. A few homes still kept tape crosses on the bathroom mirror, superstition no one felt like mocking yet. But the tide had gone out. The snatching had stopped.

Russell held the lobby door for Abigail when she arrived, cameras slung along her shoulder by habit. He bowed a little—old-school manners, newly earned humility.

"Thanks for doing this," he said.

"You asked kindly," she replied, and his smile said he understood that mattered now.

They threaded the hallway to Studio B. The room hummed with pre-show routine: a floor manager calling timing, a makeup artist dabbing down shine, a graphics tech swapping slates. The set was all warm wood and soft blues, the kind of palette meant to say: you can breathe here. A polished panel behind the interview desk threw back a clean reflection of the lights.

"Thirty seconds," someone called.

Russell took his seat opposite Abigail. Up close, his change was clearer: the quick quip that used to sit behind every sentence had been replaced by care. He glanced at his notes, then set them aside.

"Ten."

A red light woke on the main camera. The hush settled.

"Good evening," Russell began, voice steady, human. "Tonight we're joined by Abigail Jensen—investigator, witness, and, many would say, the reason so many of us made it through these last weeks. Abigail... thank you."

"Thank you for having me," she said, folding her hands. The lantern and iron she trusted were miles away; in their place she kept a small iron nail in her jacket pocket. Just in case. Old habits weren't dying today.

Russell didn't read the next question. He let the silence open a door. "What happened—truly? For the record we'll remember."

Abigail chose her words like stepping stones. "A machine was built that shouldn't have been. It found a seam and fed on it. It took from a place that already carries the weight for the living. When it starved that place, the Veil thinned. Things on the other side reached through—not all monsters, but none of them belonged here. We shut the machine down. We paid a price. Many did."

"Is it over?" His tone wasn't a challenge; it was the question every person at home was holding in their chest.

"It's stopped," she said. "The doors are shut. What tried to claim us has been pushed back where it cannot harm. But 'over' is a story we'll write every day we choose not to forget how this started."

Russell nodded, eyes flicking to the lens for the folks at home. "There was talk of a... keeper. A presence that stands between." He wet his lips. "Is that... real?"

Abigail let out a small breath. "There is a balance. Call it the Echo, the Keeper, the order that holds the middle space. It was weakened when we took what wasn't ours. It's stronger again. It... made that clear." She didn't say the name of the other one. She didn't need to.

He swallowed and changed lanes. "For families who lost someone... or got them back." His voice softened. "What do you say?"

"That grief isn't a headline," she said. "That love holds across a line glass can't break. And that we owe you better—truth, vigilance, and each other."

They moved through the rest with care. He asked about the crews replacing mirrors, the state's plan for elevators, the quiet heroism of the nurses who painted over reflective panels with flat primer so a frightened patient could sleep. She gave names when she could. She let some lie. It wasn't the night for secrets, but neither was it the night to turn mystery into content.

"Last question," Russell said, glancing once more at his abandoned notes. "What kept you going?"

Abigail looked across at him and, for a moment, saw the shivering man who had wandered the In Between and found his way back by grace and stubbornness. "People," she said. "People always do."

The tally light blinked off. Applause rose from the control room—soft, real. The floor manager cut across with a grin. "We're clear. That was... good TV."

Russell stood and offered his hand. "Not TV," he said, almost to himself. "Thank you for not letting me be who I was."

She squeezed his fingers once and watched him be swallowed by crew offering thanks and cups of coffee and relief. When they drifted away, the studio quieted to the tick of cooling lights. Someone dimmed the rigs to half. The set regained its shape without all the brightness.

Abigail stayed a moment longer, alone with the after-silence. The polished panel behind the desk showed her reflection: tired eyes, hair pulled back, a woman whose hands remembered the weight of iron.

She reached the edge of the set and rested two fingers against the panel, a habit she'd picked up from a dozen old ritualists—know the door you stand beside.

At first it was only a change in the air—the tiniest shift in temperature, the sensation of someone stepping into the next room. Then a curl of smoke bloomed inside the glass, as if exhaled from behind it. Not the soft fog of a winter window; this was darker, ash-shot. The smooth surface buckled a hair's breadth under her touch.

A face pressed up from the other side.

Abaddon's features were wrong in a way that had nothing to do with anatomy and everything to do with hunger. Anger rolled off him like heat from blacktop. The glass held, and that made him more furious. He raked at the inside surface with claws that left no mark, only a faint sound like nails across a wet plate. His eyes found Abigail and widened, not with surprise but with a promise.

"Not here," she said, voice level. She didn't step back.

The panel cooled by degrees beneath her fingertips. Behind her reflection—behind Abaddon's muffled rage—something vast moved like a shadow across deep water. No thunder, no trumpet. Just a weight that settled, a presence that restored the geometry of the room. The smoke clenched and thinned. For a heartbeat the Echo's silhouette loomed, unadorned, undeniable. Abaddon's face faltered, the way a wild animal flinches at a handler's whistle.

Across the city—across many cities—mirrors darkened for an instant and cleared. Commuters blinked at elevator doors that no longer frosted. A boy in a barbershop found only his own nervous grin staring back. Somewhere a grieving mother touched the surface of a bathroom mirror and felt only glass.

The studio panel eased to simple reflection again: a woman touching a rectangle of glass, a camera asleep on a tripod, the soft glow of a sign that read *ON AIR*, dark now.

Abigail let her hand fall. She met her own eyes in the panel—the filament of fear still there, the thread of resolve brighter.

"Not over," she whispered.

Behind the glass, for the smallest fraction, the shadow answered without sound. Then it was just her again in the quiet set, the city breathing outside, and the faint echo of applause lingering in the rafters like a promise.

Scott J. Clauss

Scott J. Clauss is a technical writer, ghost hunter, and horror novelist with a lifelong fascination for the thin places between worlds. Drawing from real-life investigations, personal experiences with the unexplained, and a background in science and technology, he crafts stories that explore the line between logic and fear.

Originally from upstate New York, Scott has lived and written across the country—from the rain-soaked streets of Washington to the wide skies of Texas. He is the author of *Echoes in the Glass*, the first book in the Echo Series, and continues to expand the world of the Echo through his blend of eerie atmosphere, layered characters, and grounded speculative horror.

When he's not writing or researching the paranormal, Scott enjoys collecting haunted artifacts, walking the ruins of forgotten places, and connecting with readers through his website, scottjclauss.com.

He currently lives with his wife, who shares his love of ghost hunting and once helped retrieve a haunted clock across the country—because some stories are too real to ignore.